Elizabeth Heiter likes her suspense to feature strong heroines, chilling villains, psychological twists and a little romance. Her research has taken her into the minds of serial killers, through murder investigations and onto the FBI Academy's shooting range. Elizabeth graduated from the University of Michigan with a degree in English Literature. She's a member of International Thriller Writers and Romance Writers of America. Visit Elizabeth at www.elizabethheiter.com

Rachel Lee was hooked on writing by the age of twelve and practiced her craft as she moved from place to place all over the United States. This *New York Times* best-selling author now resides in Florida and has the joy of writing full-time.

SECRET INVESTIGATION

ELIZABETH HEITER

CONARD COUNTY JUSTICE

RACHEL LEE

MILLS & BOON

First Published in Great Britain 2020
by Mills & Boon, an imprint of HarperCollins*Publishers*
1 London Bridge Street, London, SE1 9GF

Secret Investigation © 2020 Harlequin Books S.A.
Conard County Justice © 2020 Susan Civil Brown

Special thanks and acknowledgement are given to Elizabeth Heiter for her contribution to the *Tactical Crime Division* series.

ISBN: 978-0-263-28029-6

0520

MIX
Paper from
responsible sources
FSC™ C007454

Printed and bound in Spain
by CPI, Barcelona

SECRET INVESTIGATION

ELIZABETH HEITER

For my mom, who gets to be surprised by this book
(even though there are no aliens).

Thanks to Denise Zaza, for inviting me to be a part of
the Tactical Crime Division team's story! Thanks to my
sister, Caroline, for beta-reading this book for me.
To my writer pals Tyler Anne Snell and Heather Novak
for keeping me on track. And to my new husband,
for all of the brainstorming.

Prologue

The sandstorm came first. Then came the bullets.

Training had been going well. The locals wanted to take the lead in the fight on their land, and US Army captain Jessica Carpenter was more than willing to let them. Leave behind the ninety-degree heat—and that was before she loaded herself up with fifty pounds of gear, which made it feel a million degrees hotter. Leave behind the sand that swept up out of nowhere, got into your eyes and nose and mouth until everything was gritty. Leave behind trudging for miles up mountainsides, where one wrong step sent you on a downward slide over nothing but sharp shale and deadly rocks.

Go home to her kids. Her oldest was starting middle school this year. He was getting into gaming and skateboarding, and losing interest in talking to his mom over satellite phones when his friends were down the street waiting. The youngest was about to start kindergarten. Her baby, who'd never met her dad and cried every time her mom left for another tour. Ironic that Jessica, who ran headfirst into firefights, was still here and her unassuming engineer husband had been taken from them with a simple wrong turn in a thunderstorm and a head-on collision with a telephone pole.

"What was that?" The young soldier at her side jerked,

his weapon coming up fast, sweeping the space in front of him even though there was no way he could see anything.

Jessica slapped her hand over the top of the weapon, forcing it toward the ground. "Don't fire unless you can see what you're shooting."

It was going to be nearly impossible. She tried to ignore the hard *thump-thump* of her heart warning her something was wrong. Sandstorms came hard and fast here, with the ability to shred away the top layer of skin. They reduced visibility to almost nothing, and the sound—like high-velocity wind—meant she could barely hear the soldier screaming beside her.

She put her hand on his shoulder, hoping to calm him, as she strained to hear over the wind. Had she imagined the gunshots? Maybe it was a local, startled by the ferocity of the sandstorm. More likely it was one of the newer members of her team, still not used to the violence of it.

The sand whipped up from her feet, stinging every inch of exposed skin like a thousand tiny needles. Times like these, she was grateful for the uniform that stuck to her skin in the heat and the full body armor she and her team had donned. Yes, it was a training op, but they'd chosen to take the locals into a dangerous pass, practice tactical approaches. Out here, you could never discount an ambush.

Yanking her goggles down over her eyes, Jessica blinked and blinked, trying to get the grit out. No matter how much her eyes watered, the sand wouldn't clear. Her vision was still compromised. She hunched her shoulders upward, trying to protect the exposed skin on her face, but it didn't matter. If this kept up, it would be raw in minutes.

Time to bug out. She lifted her radio—her best bet of them hearing through the storm—to tell the team to get back to the vehicles when another shot rang out.

Instinctively she ducked low, forcing the soldier beside

her down, too. Her MP4 carbine assault rifle was up without conscious thought, but she couldn't see a thing. Was there a real threat? Or was someone panicking in the storm?

"Report!" Jessica yelled, but her voice whipped away on the wind.

Even though it would make her a target, Jessica flipped the light on her helmet, trying to illuminate the space in front of her. Her hand brushed the camera strapped to her head, reminding her she'd been taping the training session. Little good it would do them now, even if the camera wasn't ruined.

She didn't expect the light to make a bit of difference, but it actually helped. Or at least that's what she thought until she realized it was just the storm dying down as fast as it had come. She had a moment's relief until movement caught her eye. An insurgent, darting from an outcropping in the mountain above, the muzzle on his rifle flashing.

"Take cover," Jessica screamed as she took aim.

The insurgent ducked into a mountain crevice, but as the howling wind abated, the heavy *boom-boom-boom* of automatic fire took its place. He wasn't alone.

Toggling her radio, Jessica told base, "We're taking fire. Sandstorm moving out. Insurgents…" She paused, glancing around and trying to gauge numbers. Dread sunk low in her chest, bottoming out as she saw her soldiers racing for cover. "At least twenty, maybe more. Send—"

The radio flew out of her hand before she could finish and Jessica swung her weapon up, ignoring the way her other hand burned. She didn't dare look to see how bad it was. First she had to assess her team. At least she'd made them wear their body armor. Brand-new and the best the army had, it was lightweight but ultrastrong. It could stop a bullet from anything short of a .50 caliber. And her soldiers were wearing full-body plating today.

It wouldn't save them from a shot to the face or a lucky hit that found its way underneath the plates, but she had faith in their training and their gear.

Then the soldier next to her—the new recruit who'd been on her team for less than a week—let out a wail that made her stomach clench. He hit the ground hard, head thrown back at an impossible angle.

Still, Jessica dropped next to him, reaching for a pulse beneath his neck guard. That's when she saw the bullet holes. Straight through the chest, five of them in an arced line. She slammed a hand down over them, furious at him for not wearing his vest, and pain ricocheted up her arm. Not just from the bullet that had nicked the fleshy part of her thumb, but from the hard plating that should have protected him.

Her dread intensified, a new panic like she'd never felt in the almost ten years she'd dodged bullets for the army. Her head whipped up, surveying the scene. The locals, diving for cover or already down and not moving. Her soldiers, taking hits that should have knocked them down but not taken them out, crumpling under the fire of the insurgents.

Too many of them.

The panic worsened, tensing all her muscles and dimming her vision even more, a tunnel within the specks of sand. She didn't want to die seven thousand miles from home. Didn't want to fail her team. Didn't want to leave behind the kids who meant everything to her. The kids she'd taken this job to support, back when her husband was still studying for his degree. The job she'd discovered she loved enough to keep even after he was gone.

But she didn't want to die for it.

Fire seared through Jessica's arm and the force of the bullet made her stagger backward. She'd been hit. She shifted her MP4 to the other hand, blood from her thumb smearing across the trigger guard as she returned fire. The next shot knocked her back. She slammed into the ground, gasping for breath.

Bullets hitting your body armor always did that. Ripped the air from your lungs and left a nasty bruise.

But this time the pressure wasn't lessening. It was getting worse. Jessica gasped for air, trying to raise her MP4 as she saw another insurgent taking aim at her. She couldn't lift it, so she went for her pistol instead, strapped to her side and much lighter than the assault rifle.

Her fingers closed around it even as her vision began to blur. Then the whole world went dark.

Chapter One

"I assume everyone's seen the news coverage." Jill Pembrook, director of the FBI's Tactical Crime Division, didn't bother to wait until her team was settled in the conference room. She stood at the front of the long table, arms crossed over her tailored navy blue skirt suit. On a large screen behind her, a video was paused, frozen on the terrified face of a soldier.

Pembrook was petite enough that even standing while most of the team was sitting didn't give her much clearance over those assembled. But she didn't need it. Pembrook had been with the Bureau for almost forty years, meaning they'd opted to keep her on past the regular mandatory retirement age. With her pale, lined skin and well-coiffed gray hair, she might look like someone's sweet yet chic grandma, until you locked eyes with her. Then you knew exactly why the FBI had handpicked her to lead TCD—a rapid response team that could activate quickly and take on almost any threat.

Davis Rogers was still amazed he'd made the cut to join the team. He looked around the room at the other agents, with backgrounds ranging from the military like him to hostage negotiation and profiling to missing persons and computer hacking. He'd only been here for a few months. But they'd welcomed him into the fold fast, with the kind of camaraderie he'd only felt with his family—in and out of the military.

Normally he'd sit back and take the assignment the director gave him. He'd be willing to bide his time and prove himself, without any of the hotshot antics that had motivated many an army ranger. But not today. Not with this case.

He gritted his teeth as Hendrick Maynard stepped up beside Pembrook. Hendrick was their resident computer genius. With his tall, lanky frame and a face that was still battling acne, he looked young enough to be in high school, but that facade hid a genius mind and mature outlook.

Hendrick seemed more serious than usual as he pressed the handheld remote and started playing the video on the screen behind the director. The clip he played was one Davis had seen last night on the news and again this morning in slightly more detail on the YouTube version.

It started suddenly, in the middle of a firefight, with gunshots blasting in the background and sand whipping everywhere, the sound intense even over video. The soldier who'd been frozen on screen finished his fall and didn't get up again. The camera made a quick scan of soldiers and Afghan locals going down, all of it hard to see through the sand that shot up from the ground like a tornado. Then everything suddenly cleared as the camera dived in for a close-up of a young soldier, eyes and mouth open with the shock of death. The camera panned down, a hand slapping against his chest as the bullet holes became visible.

The average American probably wouldn't have realized from the brief footage that the soldier had been wearing full body armor. But somehow the news station had known. They'd also known who'd been running the camera: decorated US Army captain Jessica Carpenter. Widow,

mother of three, and as of 6:52 a.m. Tennessee time, a confirmed casualty.

Davis pictured her the way she'd looked a decade ago,
the day he'd met her. Only a few inches shorter than his
own six feet, with gorgeous dark skin and hair she'd had
twisted up and away from her face in braids, she'd worn
that army uniform with a confidence he'd envied. She'd
been five years older, and with two months more military
experience, it had seemed like much more. If she hadn't
been happily married, with a toddler and a new baby at
home, he might have taken his shot with her.

Instead, they'd become friends. She'd even trained him
early on, back before she'd become a captain and he'd
headed for Special Operations. If he wasn't sitting in this
conference room right now, waiting for the chance to go
after the people responsible for her death, he'd be flying to
Mississippi to attend her funeral this weekend.

Davis squeezed the underside of the table to keep himself from slamming a fist on top of it. As he refocused,
he realized Hendrick had turned off the video screen and
taken a seat. Around him, agents were nodding thought-
fully, professionally. Only fellow agent Jace Cantrell—JC
to the team—showed a hint of anger on his face. But JC
had been military too. And once a soldier, always a soldier.

As in the Bureau, dying in the field was a possibility you
accepted. You did whatever you could to prevent it, but if it
happened, you knew you'd be going out doing something
you believed in. But not like this. Not the way Jessica had
died, trusting the military, trusting her training, trusting
her equipment.

"I want to take the lead on this case," Davis blurted.

Gazes darted to him: from profiler Dr. Melinda Larsen,
silently assessing, suspicion in her eyes, as if she somehow
knew he had a history with one of the victims. Always but-

toned-up Laura Smith was quiet and unreadable, but her Ivy League brain was probably processing every nuance of his words. JC, staring at him with understanding, even though he didn't realize Davis knew Jessica personally. No one on the team did.

"Is your personal investment in this case going to be a hindrance or a help?" Pembrook asked, voice and gaze steady.

Davis's spine stiffened even more. She was talking about his army background. She had to be. But if she thought he was going to fidget, she underestimated the hell he'd gone through training to be a ranger for the army. "A help. I'm familiar with how the army works. And I'm familiar with the product. I've worn Petrov Armor vests."

Petrov Armor had supplied the body armor Jessica and her team had been wearing during the ambush. That armor—supposedly the newest and best technology—had failed spectacularly, resulting in the deaths of all but three of the soldiers and one of the locals. In his mind it wasn't the insurgents who had killed Jessica and her team. It was Petrov Armor.

He didn't mention the rest. He'd more than just worn the vests. He'd had a chance to be an early tester of their body armor, back when he was an elite ranger and Petrov Armor was better known for the pistols they made than their armor. He'd given the thumbs-up, raving about the vest's bullet-stopping power and comfort in his report. He'd given the army an enthusiastic endorsement to start using Petrov Armor's products more broadly. And they had.

"I'm not talking about the armor," Pembrook replied, her gaze still laser-locked on his, even as agent-at-large Kane Bradshaw slipped into the meeting late and leaned against the doorway. "I'm talking about Jessica Carpenter." Her voice softened. "I'm sorry for your loss."

The gazes on him seemed to intensify, but Davis didn't shift his from Pembrook's. "Thank you. And no, it won't affect my judgment in the case."

Pembrook nodded, but he wasn't sure if she believed him as she looked back at the rest of the group and continued her briefing. "Petrov Armor won a big contract with the military five years ago. The armor this team was wearing is their latest and greatest. It's not worn widely yet, but their earlier version armor is commonly used. The military is doing a full round of testing across all their branches. They've never had a problem with Petrov Armor before, and they don't intend to have another.

"Meanwhile, they've asked us to investigate at home. We got lucky with the news coverage. We're still not sure how it was leaked, but not all of it got out. Or if it did, the news station only played a small part. And somehow they don't have the name of the body armor supplier. *Not yet*," she said emphatically. "Rowan, we don't have to worry about PD this time. I'm putting you on the media. Hendrick can lend computer support if you need it."

Rowan Cooper nodded, looking a little paler than usual, but sitting straighter.

Since the TCD team traveled all over the country and abroad, they regularly had to work with police departments. Sometimes their assistance was requested and cooperation was easy. Other times the local PD didn't want federal help at all, and it became Rowan's job to smooth everything over. Davis had never envied her that job. But he envied her dealing with the media even less.

"What's our initial read on the situation?" JC asked. "Did Petrov Armor just start sending inferior products or are we talking about some kind of sabotage?"

"At this point, we don't know. The army hasn't had a

chance to begin evaluating the vests yet. They're still dealing with death notifications and shipping home remains."

The clamp that had seemed to lock around Davis's chest the moment he'd heard the news ratcheted tighter. Jessica had lost her husband a few years earlier. Davis had met him once, when he and Jessica happened to rotate back home at the same time. He'd never met her kids in person, but he'd gotten to talk with them once over a ridiculously clear video chat from seven thousand miles away. They'd been funny and cute, jostling for the best position in front of the camera and all trying to talk at once. They were orphans now.

Davis took a deep breath and tried to focus as Pembrook continued. "Petrov Armor has recently gone through some big changes. About a year ago, founder and CEO Neal Petrov retired. He passed the torch to his daughter, Leila Petrov, formerly in charge of the company's client services division. One of the biggest changes she's made has been to shut down the weapons side of their business and focus entirely on the armor. But you can bet Neal Petrov was the one to convince the board of directors to agree to that decision. He had controlling stock share and a lot of influence. He stayed involved in the business until three weeks ago, when he got caught up in a mugging gone bad and was killed."

"You think the new CEO is cutting corners with dad out of the picture?" Kane asked, not moving from where he'd planted himself near the doorway.

That strategic position was probably in case he wanted to make a quick getaway. The agent-at-large had known the director for a long time, but he was one of the few members of the team Davis couldn't quite get a read on. He seemed to flit in and out of the office at random, more often away on some secret assignment than working with the team.

"Maybe," Pembrook replied. She looked at JC. "I want you to bring her in. Take Smitty with you."

Laura Smith nodded, tucking a stray blond hair behind her ear as Davis opened his mouth to argue.

Before he could, Melinda jumped in, sounding every bit the profiler as she suggested, "Make it a spectacle. Do it in front of her people. We don't have enough for a formal arrest at this point, but Leila Petrov is only thirty, pretty young for a CEO. Technically, she's been in charge for a year, but we have to assume her father has been holding her hand until recently. Almost certainly he convinced the board of directors to let her take the helm when he retired. If we shake her up from the start, get her off balance and scared, she's more likely to cooperate before contacting a lawyer. And she's more likely to slip up."

Pembrook nodded and glanced at her watch. "Do it in an hour. That should give her employees plenty of time to get settled in before you march her out of there."

Davis squeezed his hands together tighter under the table. He could feel the veins in his arms starting to throb from the pressure, but he couldn't stop himself any more than he could prevent blurting angrily, "Director—"

That was all he got out before she spoke over him. "Davis, I think your military background will come in handy, too. I'm going to let you run lead on this."

Shock kept him silent, but his hands loosened and the pain in his chest eased up. "Thank—"

"You're dismissed, everyone. Let's jump on this." Pembrook turned toward him. "Follow me, Davis. Let's have a chat." Before he could reply, she was out the door.

Davis was slower getting to his feet. As he passed Kane in the doorway, the other agent offered him a raised eyebrow and a sardonic grin, but Davis didn't care. Not about Kane's opinion and not about whatever warnings Pembrook was about to level at him.

He was on the case. Whether it was new CEO Leila

Petrov to blame or someone else, he wasn't stopping until he brought that person down.

He glanced skyward as he stepped through the threshold of the director's office, saying a silent goodbye to his old friend. Promising to avenge her death.

"THE SOLDIER YOU see died at the scene. Army captain Jessica Carpenter, who took the video, also died when she was shot through her bulletproof vest. The army is looking into the circumstances. Keep watching for updates on this story and more. Next up—"

Eric Ross turned off the TV and Leila Petrov had to force herself to swivel toward him. She tried to wipe the horror and disbelief she was feeling off her face, but Eric had known her since she was a lonely thirteen-year-old. He'd been her first kiss two years later. Three years after that, he'd broken her heart.

He read her now just as easily as he always had. "Maybe it's not our armor."

"Maybe it is." Petrov Armor had supplied the military with millions of dollars' worth of guns and armor in the past thirty years. Their accounts had started out slow, with her father barely showing a profit in those early years. Now, the military not only kept them in business with their big armor purchases, but those sales also allowed her to employ almost two hundred people. It was her father's legacy. But it was now her responsibility.

The numbers said there was a good chance those soldiers had been wearing some version of Petrov Armor. But logic said they couldn't be. Petrov Armor was serious about its testing. Any tweak, no matter how minor, was checked against every bullet and blade in its testing facility. Every single piece of armor that left its building was inspected for quality. If the armor was damaged, it went in the trash. The company could afford the waste; it couldn't afford to screw up.

Leila breathed in and out through her nose, praying she wasn't going to throw up. Not that she had much in her system to throw up anyway. She'd barely been eating since her dad had stood up to that mugger instead of just handing over his wallet. In a single, stupid instant, she'd lost one of the only two close family members she had left. Tears welled up and she blinked them back, not wanting Eric to see.

Maybe once he'd been her first confidant, her closest friend, and her lover, but now he was her employee. The last thing she needed was for anyone to doubt her strength as a leader.

It had been an uphill battle for a year, getting her employees to take her seriously as CEO. She thought it was working until her dad died. Then she realized just how much resentment remained that she'd succeeded him. She'd come in every day since, not taking any time off to mourn, in part because she'd known her father would have wanted her to focus on work. And in part because work was the only thing that could take her mind off her crushing loss. But it was mostly to prove to the staff that she'd earned her position. She couldn't afford to lose her cool now, not when so much was at stake.

Leila took a deep breath and tipped her chin back. She spotted the slight smile that disappeared as quickly as it slid onto Eric's lips, and knew it was because he recognized her battle face. Ignoring it, she said, "We need to get ahead of this. Start making phone calls. Anyone you've made a sale to in the army in the past year. Find out if it's ours, so we can figure out what happened. And we'd better see if we can track down the actual shipment. If there are any other problems, I want to find them first."

"Leila—"

"I need you to start right now, Eric. We don't have time to waste."

"Maybe you should call your uncle."

Joel Petrov, her dad's younger brother and the company's COO, hadn't come in yet. If somehow he'd managed to miss the news reports, she wanted to keep him in the dark as long as possible. He'd handled so much for her family, keeping the business afloat all those years ago when her mom died and her dad had been so lost in his grief he'd forgotten everything, including her. Her uncle had picked up the slack there, too, making sure she was fed and made it to school on time. Making sure she still felt loved.

Right now, she could use a break. Hopefully they'd find out those devastating deaths weren't due to their armor. She'd worked hard to transition the company from producing both weapons and armor to solely armor. She wanted Petrov Armor to be known as a life-saving company, not a life-ending one. This incident put that at risk.

Maybe the panic Leila was feeling over the whole situation would be a thing of the past before her uncle climbed out of whatever woman's bed he'd found himself in last night and she'd be able to tell him calmly that she'd handled it.

"We're looking for Leila Petrov."

The unfamiliar voice was booming, echoing through Petrov Armor's open-concept layout, breaching the closed door of her office. Even before that door burst open and a man and woman in suits followed, looking serious as they held up FBI badges, she knew.

Petrov Armor was in serious trouble.

She stepped forward, trying not to let them see all the emotions battling inside her—the fear, the guilt, the panic. Her voice was strong and steady as she replied, "I'm Leila Petrov."

"FBI," the woman announced, and the steel in her voice put Leila's to shame. "Agents Smith and Cantrell. We have some questions for you. We'd like you to come with us—"

Eric pushed his way up beside her, taking a step slightly forward. "You can't possibly have warrants. What kind of scare-tactic BS—"

"Stop," Leila hissed at him.

The other agent spoke over them both, his voice raised to carry to the employees behind him, their heads all peering over their cubicle walls. "We can talk here if you prefer."

Leila grabbed her purse and shook her head. "I'll come with you."

"And I'll contact our lawyer," Eric said, his too-loud voice a stark contrast to her too-soft one.

She kept her head up, met the gazes of her employees with confident, "don't worry" nods as she followed Agents Smith and Cantrell out of Petrov Armor.

She prayed that slow, humiliating walk wouldn't be the beginning of the end of everything her father had worked for, of the legacy she'd promised herself she'd keep safe for him.

Chapter Two

Despite its location in a nondescript building on the outskirts of Old City, Tennessee, the Tactical Crime Division had an interview room that would be the envy of most FBI field offices. Maybe it was a result of working with a profiler who believed in setting the stage for each individual interview. That meant sometimes the room looked like a plush hotel lobby and other times it was as stark as a prison cell. It all depended what Melinda thought would work best to get the subject talking.

Today it leaned closer to prison cell, with uncomfortable, hard-backed chairs pulled up to a drab gray table. But what Davis was most cognizant of was the video camera up in the corner, ready to broadcast in real time to the rest of the team everything he was doing.

Don't lose your cool, he reminded himself as the door opened. He could hear Smitty telling the CEO of Petrov Armor to go ahead in.

He'd read Leila Petrov's bio. Even with her undergraduate degree in business with minors in communications and marketing followed by an MBA, thirty years old was awfully young to be the CEO of a billion-dollar company. Then again, nepotism had a way of opening doors that little else could.

He'd seen her picture, too. She was undeniably gorgeous,

with shiny, dark hair and big brown eyes. But she looked more like a college student getting ready for her first job interview than a CEO. Still, he wasn't about to underestimate her. He'd seen what that could do on too many missions overseas, when soldiers thought just because someone was a young female meant they couldn't be strapped with a bomb.

But as she came through the door, he was unprepared for the little kick his heart gave, sending extra blood pumping to places it had no business going. Maybe it was her determined stride, the nothing-fazes-me tilt of her chin in a room that made hardened criminals buckle. He felt her reciprocal jolt of attraction as much as he saw it in the sudden sweep her gaze made over his body, the slight flush on her cheeks.

She recovered faster than he did, scowling at the setup. "If you're trying to intimidate me, it's not going to work. I'm here voluntarily. I want to help, but I don't appreciate being bullied."

He debated rethinking the whole interview plan, but decided to trust Melinda. He'd never worked with a profiler before coming to TCD, but in the short time he'd been here, he'd become a believer. "If you think this is being bullied, you have no business working with the military. Take a seat."

Instead of following the directive, she narrowed her eyes and crossed her arms over her chest. Her stance shifted, as if she was considering walking right out.

Silently Davis cursed, because the truth was, she could leave whenever she wanted. But he'd picked a course and he refused to back down now. So, he crossed his own arms, lifted his eyebrows and waited.

A brief, hard smile tilted her lips up, and then she pulled one of the chairs away from the table and perched on the edge of it. Rather than looking poised to run, with her perfect posture and well-tailored black suit, she managed to look like she was in charge.

Never underestimate someone who'd made CEO by thirty, no matter the circumstances, he told himself. Then he pulled his own chair around the table and positioned it across from her. Settling into the seat, he leaned forward, reducing the space between them to almost nothing.

If he couldn't intimidate her with this room and his job title, maybe sheer size would work. She was tall for a woman—probably five foot ten without the low heels she wore—but he still had a few inches on her. And a lot of breadth with muscles he'd earned the hard way in the rangers.

Her eyes locked on his without hesitation. They were the shade of a perfect cup of coffee, with just a hint of cream added. This close to him, he could see how smooth and clear her skin was, with deeper undertones than he'd first realized. The flush on her cheeks was still there, but now it was darker, tinged from anger. And damn it all, she smelled like citrus, probably some expensive perfume to go with the designer clothes.

Clothes that hung just a little looser than they should suggested she'd been skipping meals. Despite her appeal, he didn't miss the heavy application of makeup underneath her eyes that couldn't quite hide the dark circles. He didn't miss the redness in those eyes either, as if she'd been up late crying. Most likely still grieving the father she'd lost unexpectedly three weeks ago.

"I'm Special Agent Davis Rogers. I'm sure Agents Smith and Cantrell told you what this was about—assuming you didn't watch the news this morning." Davis knew Smitty and JC wouldn't have given her much in the way of details. They wanted to keep her off balance by having different agents bring her in than the one questioning her. But so far, nothing seemed to faze her much.

He didn't want to respect that, but it was a trait that was crucial in Special Operations. He couldn't help admiring it in a civilian CEO facing a massive investigation of her company and possible jail time.

"The soldiers who were killed in an ambush," Leila replied. "Reporters say they were wearing armor. I'm guessing, since I'm here, that the army thinks they were wearing Petrov Armor?"

He could see the hope in her eyes, the wish that he'd correct her, say it was all a mistake or she'd just been brought in for her expertise. He actually felt bad for a nanosecond, then he remembered hearing the news about Jessica—over the television as her family had since the video had leaked before notifications could be made. "They don't *think* it. They've confirmed it."

She sighed heavily, then nodded. Her gaze stayed serious, no trace of panic, just sadness lurking beneath determination. "I want to see the plates."

"Excuse me?" Was she joking? "They're evidence in an open investigation."

His words should have made her blanch, but instead the hardness in her gaze just intensified. "They're not ours."

He couldn't stop the snort of disbelief that escaped. *This* was her spin?

She rushed on before he could figure out how to respond to that ridiculousness. "We have a lot of checks and balances in place. My dad joined the military when he was eighteen. He stayed in four years and watched three fellow soldiers die in a training accident. It stuck with him, made him want to do something to prevent it. He decided to dedicate himself to making better gear and weapons. The army paid for his tuition, helped him get the knowledge and skills to start Petrov Armor. It mattered to him—and it matters to me—that what we make saves lives. From the beginning, most of our gun and armor sales were to the military."

The words out of her mouth were passionate, but Davis had been an FBI agent in white collar crime for four years before getting recruited to TCD. He'd learned quickly that one of the most valued qualities in CEOs of crooked companies was being a good liar. He'd also learned that when things got dicey, those same CEOs would throw others under the bus as fast as they could. So, he leaned back and waited for it.

Leila leaned forward, closing the gap between them again.

He hid his surprise at her boldness, trying not to breathe her subtle citrusy perfume.

"Nothing leaves our facility without being inspected. Furthermore, we don't make changes without testing them with every kind of weapon we promise to protect against. There's no way our products were breached by the kind of weapons the news reported were being used. So, either the bullets the insurgents were using changed or those soldiers weren't wearing Petrov Armor."

Since she was sticking with her story and he had no idea how long she'd hang around, Davis decided to help her out. "What about the person in charge of inspections? Or the people in charge of testing? Isn't there a possibility that corners were cut without you realizing it?"

If she had any brains, she'd agree with him, give herself a little distance in case the whole thing blew up in her face—which he was pretty sure it was going to do.

Instead, the fury in her gaze deepened. "You really think I'm going to sell out one of my employees? No. That's not possible. Anyone in a key role like that has been at Petrov Armor a long time. We don't concentrate power without unannounced checks by other members of the team. It was my father's rule long before he took the company public and the board of directors and I stand by that to this day."

Davis felt himself frown and tried to smooth out his features. She was either a better liar than she seemed or she actually believed what she was saying.

The problem was, he believed the army. Jessica had been wearing Petrov Armor when she died. Which meant someone else was lying.

He had a bad feeling it might have been Leila Petrov's father, longtime CEO of Petrov Armor and as of three weeks ago, dead. If Davis was right, then he'd already missed his chance to throw the bastard in jail. If he was right, there'd be no way left to truly avenge his friend's death.

MELINDA LARSEN HAD seen some of the best liars in the country during her twelve years with the FBI. Before that, while doing her graduate thesis in psychology, she'd talked to incarcerated serial killers. They'd woven the most convincing tales she'd ever heard about their innocence with almost no body language tells that contradicted what they were saying. They'd also scared the hell out of her, with so much evil lurking beneath calm or even neighborly exteriors.

It had all been practice for her role at TCD, where she didn't have the luxury of months-or years-long investigations, but had to make assessments almost on the spot. It was a near impossible task, but Melinda had discovered she thrived on the challenge.

It was also the best distraction she'd found in the past decade to keep her from thinking about the losses in her own life. Because no matter how much she'd thrown herself into her cases before TCD, there was always one unsolved case at the forefront of her mind. But here, that case was starting to fade into the background. She was starting to finally accept that she might never know the truth about the most important case she'd never been able to officially investigate. At TCD, she was finally starting to move on with her life.

Leila Petrov hadn't presented much of a challenge. But Melinda still gave her standard disclaimer as she stared at Davis and Pembrook. Because no matter how good she was—and she knew she was one of the best—she wasn't immune from mistakes. "One interview isn't enough time to form a complete assessment."

Jill Pembrook gave a slight smile as she nodded, half amusement and half encouragement. It was a look Melinda had come to expect in the year she'd worked for Pembrook. Davis just crossed his arms over his chest, looking pissed off in what Melinda thought of as his civvies—well-worn jeans and a dark T-shirt that emphasized the strength in his arms and chest. But she knew Davis's anger wasn't directed at her. It was for the high-priced lawyer who'd shown up in the middle of his interview with Leila Petrov and pulled her out of there.

"I think she's telling the truth. She doesn't know anything about it."

At Melinda's proclamation, Davis seemed to deflate. "I agree," he said. "And let's be honest, Petrov Armor isn't small, but it's not exactly a huge company. Unless it was pure sloppiness—which I doubt, given their history supplying the military—there's something unusual going on here."

"Cutting corners," Melinda suggested. "Maybe these checks she thinks are in place aren't being followed. Or she's too distracted grieving her father to notice they messed up a big shipment. Or we could be talking about sabotage."

Davis looked intrigued. "Cutting corners could suggest

her father knew about it and was just trying to make more money from substandard, cheaper materials, and maybe less vigorous testing, too. Sloppiness would suggest one or more of her employees are taking advantage of her grief to be lazy. Or maybe they're all grieving and distracted, too. But sabotage? Are you thinking someone inside the company or out?"

"Given what I've read about their process, sabotage from someone who doesn't work there seems unlikely. So, I'd say inside. If that's the case, it could be someone with a grudge against the military."

"That's unlikely too, considering what Leila said about the people in charge of anything important being there for years," Davis cut in. "If this had been happening a long time, what are the chances the military wouldn't have already found out?"

"I agree," Melinda said. "So, if it's sabotage, it's probably someone who wanted to discredit Neal Petrov himself. But honestly, I think the most likely motive is the most obvious."

"Greed." Davis nodded. "They produced inferior products to save money, get a bigger profit. Well, it sure backfired. But if that's the case, we're back to Neal Petrov. As CEO and biggest shareholder, he'd be in the most likely position to profit. With him dead…"

"JC has been on the phone with the army while you were interviewing Ms. Petrov," Pembrook said. "He's confirmed that the shipment of armor the soldiers who were killed were wearing went out after Neal Petrov was killed. It's possible he set it up before he died, but I think there could be an accomplice."

"It makes sense," Melinda agreed. "If there are really as many checks and balances as Leila Petrov claimed, it might be hard for one person to pull this off, even if he was the CEO. Two, on the other hand..."

Davis nodded, anticipation back on his face that told Melinda how badly he wanted to put someone behind bars for his friend's death. The case was probably too personal for him. It could lead to mistakes. But it could also be exactly the dogged determination they needed.

"Melinda and I have been talking about sending someone inside," Pembrook said, staring at Davis.

"Undercover?" He sounded frustrated as he said, "Well, Leila Petrov knows me, JC and Smitty, so we're all out. Who were you thinking about sending in?"

"I think you should do it," Melinda said, before Pembrook could respond. They hadn't had a chance to talk about who might go undercover before Davis had come into the room.

Before the interview, Davis would have been the last person she'd have suggested. But the more she'd watched him and Leila, seen the sparks practically flying between them from both anger and attraction, the more the idea had grown.

Davis stared at her like she'd gotten into the head of one too many criminals and finally cracked. "What would I do undercover that—"

"This." Melinda cut him off, holding up her cell phone. She'd found an advertisement for a job as an office assistant to Leila Petrov. "We lucked out."

"How?" Davis demanded, glancing from her to Pembrook as if their boss would set her straight—or suggest Melinda get her own head checked. "Leila Petrov is never going to go along with this."

"I think she will," Melinda contradicted as Pembrook just watched them, her mind probably running through a million scenarios at the speed of a computer.

"And why's that?" Davis demanded, even though he had to be dying to be the one to go in.

"Attraction," Melinda said simply.

As she spoke, Kane Bradshaw walked past the open doorway. He didn't pause, just lifted an eyebrow at her, looking amused.

Forcing herself to ignore him, Melinda told Davis, "There was an immediate physical attraction between you two."

When Davis frowned, she added quickly, "It's my job to catch these things. I'm not saying you were unprofessional. But you can play on that attraction to gain her trust."

"She's in charge of the company," Davis argued. "There's no way she's going to go along with this."

"I think she will."

"Because she thinks I'm cute? Come on. This isn't high school, Melinda."

She couldn't help a wry smile in return. The six-foot tall, broad-shouldered African-American agent *was* cute. That would probably influence Leila Petrov, whether she wanted it to or not. But it wouldn't get Davis into the company; it would merely stop the door from being slammed in his face before he could make his case to her. "No, but we both agree she's probably innocent. I think she wants to find the truth. You can help her get it."

That quieted him down, but only for a minute, before he frowned and shook his head again. "Believe me, I want to be the one to find whoever's responsible. But this seems like a crazy risk. It's not worth it."

"How sure are you about this?" Pembrook asked Melinda.

Her heart beat harder at the possibility she was suggesting the wrong course of action and it could blow up an important investigation. But as she mentally reviewed Davis's interview with Leila, her gut insisted this would work. "Davis needs to convince her the only way to save the company her father founded is to get ahead of this. Which means she needs to think they're on the same side. If that happens, I'm very sure."

Pembrook turned her steely gaze on Davis, who stood at attention like he was undergoing military inspection. Finally she gave a curt, final nod. "You're going in."

Chapter Three

"There's been a mistake. The FBI is investigating, and they'll track down who's really responsible soon enough. In the meantime, we need to focus on getting our next shipments ready."

Those were the words Leila had used to rally her employees when she'd finally returned to the office. They'd all nodded and smiled back at her. Tight, worried smiles that led to whispers as soon as she went into her office.

Hopefully, there'd still be next shipments to deliver. Eighty percent of their business was with the military. The rest was domestic law enforcement and private companies, usually civilian security firms. They'd already absorbed a significant revenue loss by closing the weapon side of the business. Now that armor was their only product, the military's business and their reputation were crucial. But it would all dry up if the tragedy overseas came back to them.

Leila shut the door to her office because she was tired of pretending not to hear the whispers. Then she let out the heavy sigh she'd been holding in since first thing that morning, when FBI agents had taken her to their oddly nondescript office to be questioned.

When Eric had sent the company lawyer to haul her out of there, she'd been half relieved and half annoyed. Relieved because as hard as she tried not to let it get to her, that stark office and that muscle-bound federal agent with the too-intense stare had started to raise her anxiety. Annoyed because the more she thought about it, the more certain she was there'd been a mistake. No way had their armor failed.

She'd bet her reputation on it. Sinking into the plush chair behind her desk, she opened her laptop, ready to get to work. Because it was more than her reputation that would be destroyed if she didn't figure out what had really happened—and fast.

The question was, how? With the FBI unwilling to let her see the armor the soldiers had been wearing, how could she prove it wasn't theirs?

She should have started working on that question as soon as the lawyer had gotten her out of the FBI office, but she'd been too unnerved to come directly back to work. So, she'd gone to her father's gravesite first, spent a long while talking to him the way she used to. Only this time, the conversation was one-sided.

It was the first time she'd been there since she'd had to dump a shovelful of dirt over his coffin, watch it slowly disappear from view. She hadn't been ready to see his name on that sleek granite headstone. But after too long sitting there battling her grief, she'd started to feel his presence. Started to feel his love. It had helped her focus on what she needed to do.

The knock on her office door startled her, and Leila called out a distracted "Come in" as she pulled up the latest military invoices. She'd already charged Eric—the company's head of sales—with reaching out to his contacts, but maybe she should be doing the same. Between the people she knew and her father's connections, maybe someone would be able to get her more details about the armor the soldiers had been wearing.

"Leila, I know today has been a little crazy, but I've got some good news."

Leila glanced up at their head of HR. Ben Jameson was young and new, but anxious to prove himself. So far, he'd been efficient and always full of energy. "I could use some good news."

"I found you an assistant."

"Oh."

He frowned at her lack of excitement, but with everything else going on, the last thing she wanted to deal with was a new employee who needed training. Glancing back at her laptop screen, she debated how she could put him off for a while. Just until she could deal with the disaster with the FBI.

"We got his résumé a few hours ago," Ben continued quickly. "Normally, I'd do more of a formal process, but he was available for an immediate interview and he's exactly what we've been looking for. I called his references right away and figured we should scoop him up before someone else does. He said he could start today, so I thought, why not let him get the lay of the land?"

When she didn't reply, he added, "I mean, I thought if the FBI stuff has blown over…"

Finally she looked up and nodded, hoping her CEO face hadn't slipped. "Great. I could use the help."

Ben's face lit up. "Perfect! Let me introduce you." He turned back toward the door and called, "Davis!"

No way. Two men named Davis in one day?

Leila got to her feet, anxiety already tensing the back of her neck before Davis Rogers entered her office.

This morning, he'd looked more like the brawny owner of a night club in jeans, and a T-shirt that clung to a muscled chest and arms. He'd even had a layer of scruff on his chin. Definitely not what she'd expected for an FBI agent.

Now, he was clean-shaven in dark dress pants and a blazer. He should have looked less appealing in clothes that hid his physique. Instead, it made her focus more on his face. On hypnotizing dark brown eyes made even more intense beneath heavy brows. On unlined brown skin she wanted to run her hands over, feel for the last traces of this morning's scruff. On generous lips she wanted to kiss.

The thought startled her. She wasn't the type to lust over men she barely knew. Putting it down to too many emotions near the surface—stress, grief and anxiety mixing together and messing with her head—Leila straightened her blazer, trying to focus. "What do you think you're—"

"It's nice to meet you," Davis spoke over her. "I'm so excited to join Petrov Armor. I can provide any assistance you need," he added, only a hint of sarcasm there, probably so small Ben wouldn't notice.

But Leila sure had. She felt her face scrunch up with disbelief as Ben looked back and forth between them. But before she could toss Davis out of her office, one side of those lush lips lifted in a slow grin. It was a smile half full of amusement and half full of confidence, like he knew exactly what she was thinking.

What kind of game was he playing? Did he honestly think she was going to let him screw with her company, with her employees?

She smiled too, but infused hers with enough warning that he should have taken a step back. It was a trick she'd learned long before rising to CEO, back in university when walking home from the library at night meant passing drunk guys who thought it was acceptable to follow. It never failed to drop the smirks off people's faces.

But Davis stepped closer, held out his hand. "I think we can work well together to do what needs to be done."

Nervy. She should have expected it from an FBI agent.

And he should have expected her to immediately call his bluff. But as she looked past that cocky grin into his steady gaze, she saw something she hadn't expected, something that looked like honesty.

"Thank you, Ben." She flicked her gaze to her young head of HR, who opened and closed his mouth like he was trying to figure out what to say. Then he nodded, stepped backward out of her office and shut the door behind him. Leaving her alone with Davis.

"I'm letting you stay out of pure curiosity," she told him, crossing her arms over her chest. "But you've got about two minutes to explain why I'd let you run this charade. Then, I'm tossing you out and my lawyer will be back down at your office, asking questions about the FBI's ethics."

Instead of looking worried, Davis stepped closer, his gaze locked on hers in a way that made the hairs on the backs of her arms stand up and each breath come faster. Then, he was holding a folder up between them, almost in her face.

She frowned and stepped back, taking the folder. One glance and she understood the cocky grin he'd given her. It was a close-up of a piece of body armor. It had been pierced by three bullet holes. And there, stamped on the edges in their trademark, was the Petrov Armor logo and a rating that should have stopped the kind of bullet that had made those holes.

Her gaze returned to his, as dread rose from her gut and seemed to lodge in her throat.

"We've tracked this to a recent batch of armor. I don't believe you know anything about this or I wouldn't be telling you. So, right now you have two choices—keep my cover and let me figure out how this defective armor got out, or blow it and bring the rest of my team down here to tear apart this place until we find the truth. We're getting warrants right now."

Leila looked at the photo again. It could have been faked. Or the bullets could have been some new form of armor-piercing technology that their armor didn't protect against. But deep down, she knew something was very wrong in her company.

A recent batch probably meant it had happened on her watch. The way the company was set up, this wasn't a sloppy error. It was intentional, someone trying to destroy what her father had spent so much of his life building.

She lifted her gaze back to Davis's, suddenly understanding that he—and the FBI—might be her best bet to find the person responsible. That letting a stranger try to tear apart her company could very well be the only way to save it. A secret investigation might find a single person responsible, might allow her a chance to save Petrov Armor. A public one—no matter the outcome—would destroy them.

"I want you to keep me updated on everything you do here. If I agree to this, you let me be involved in the investigation." She held out her own hand, the way he'd done before. "Agreed?"

That smile returned, smaller and more serious this time, as he put his big hand in hers and shook. "Agreed."

With that single touch, Leila hoped she hadn't just doomed her company.

ULTIMATELY, IT DIDN'T matter if Leila Petrov was unaware that defective products were being delivered to the military. As the CEO, she was responsible for what happened here.

Ultimately, she was responsible for every piece of armor that had been sent overseas with the promise to save lives that had betrayed the soldiers who'd worn it. That made her responsible for every single death. Including Jessica's.

That truth would be easier to accept if Davis wasn't more impressed with her with each passing minute. The woman was tough. So far, as she'd walked him around the office and introduced him to her employees, he could see that she was respected. Sometimes grudgingly, but most of them seemed to genuinely like her as a boss.

Then again, most of them seemed to have truly liked her father. They kept touching her elbow or bowing their heads, sadness in their eyes as they spoke his name. Still, if Leila hadn't known about the defective products, what were the chances her father hadn't either? The more he saw of their process and security as he walked around, the lower those chances appeared. Because even though the recent shipment had been sent out after her father died, it had probably been made while he was alive.

It had become immediately obvious that Petrov Armor took its security seriously. No way were these systems ignored until the news report yesterday. They were too ingrained, too second nature as he watched employees without hesitation card in and out of not just the building, but also any sensitive areas. He'd noticed the security cameras around the outside of the building, but they were inside, too. Whoever was behind the defective products knew how to get around all of it. Either that or the company's own security would be what ultimately brought them down.

Making a mental note to ask to see some of the camera footage from when the defective armor had been made, Davis pasted on a smile as he was introduced to yet another employee.

"Davis, this is Theresa Quinn, head of research and development at Petrov Armor. Theresa, this is my new assistant, Davis Rogers."

Leila's voice hadn't wavered through any of the introductions and none of her employees seemed to have picked up on anything strange, but he could feel her discomfort. She didn't like lying to them. He hoped she wouldn't break down and tell anyone who he really was.

He'd have to stick close to her. He already needed to pretend to work with her if he wanted to keep his access to Petrov Armor. But a CEO with a conscience was both good and bad. Good because if he was right and she really wasn't involved, then Melinda was right, too. Leila would want the truth, even if she didn't want it to get out. Bad because lying obviously didn't come easily for her.

"What happened with those FBI agents?" Theresa demanded, with the tone of someone who'd been around a long time and held a position of power. It was also a tone that held a bit of irreverence, as though she was Leila's equal instead of her employee.

Davis looked Theresa over more closely. Wearing jeans and a blouse with the sleeves rolled up past her elbows and reddish-brown hair knotted up in a messy bun, Theresa's attire made her seem younger than the crinkles around her eyes suggested. Davis pegged her at close to fifty. He wondered if the aura of confidence and authority she radiated was just age and position, or if she had more sway at Petrov Armor than the average head of R and D.

Leila visibly stiffened at Theresa's question, and Davis made a mental note that the two women didn't like each other.

"Like I said earlier, everything is fine," Leila answered.

Theresa's eyes narrowed. "Just like that?"

"Just like that. It wasn't our armor."

"Do we know whose it was?" There was still suspicion in Theresa's voice, but it was overridden by curiosity. "Because that's going to take out some of the competition."

Davis tensed at her callous comment, but he kept his body language calm and eager, like he imagined a new assistant would act.

"The FBI isn't going to share that kind of thing," Leila replied. She turned toward Davis. "Let me introduce you to our head of sales." Then she called across the open concept main office area. "Eric!"

The man who turned toward them looked about his and Leila's age. With blond hair gelled into perfect place and dark blue eyes almost the exact shade as his suit, he looked like a head of sales. But as he walked toward them, his gaze landing briefly on Davis before focusing entirely on Leila, all Davis could see was a man with a crush.

Probably betraying her company wasn't the way to win the woman over. Unless Leila hadn't returned his affection and Eric wanted revenge.

As Eric reached their side, his attention still entirely focused on Leila as if no one else was there, Davis stuck his hand in the man's path. "Davis Rogers, Leila's new assistant."

Eric's eyes narrowed slightly with his assessing gaze, but he offered a slightly less than genuine smile and held out his hand. "Eric Ross. Head of sales." His hand closed a little too tightly around Davis's as he added, "I'm glad Leila finally got an assistant. She works too much. You make sure she takes it easy."

Before Davis could reply—or even figure out how to reply to that—Eric had dropped his hand and turned his attention back to Leila. His voice lowered slightly as he added, "Your dad was just like a father to me, too, Leila. You know you can talk to me." He put his hand on Leila's upper arm, comforting but a little too familiar. "No one is going to think less of you if you take time off to grieve."

Leila shrugged free with a stiff nod and a slight flush.

She cleared her throat, ducking her head momentarily. Her voice wavered just slightly as she answered, "I know he was, Eric. Thank you."

Davis glanced between them, wondering at their history, as Theresa interjected with less emotion, "We all miss your father. He was a great CEO and a great guy." Then she walked away, leaving Davis to wonder if her comment had been meant as sympathy or a subtle dig at Leila's leadership.

Based on the way Eric scowled after Theresa, he thought it was a dig. Davis studied him a little closer. His history with Leila and her family obviously went back a long time. If Neal Petrov was like a father to Eric, maybe the man had let him in on his secrets. Or had him help make a little more money off the books.

Before Davis could ponder that, a man came hurrying across the office, making a beeline for Leila. Probably mid-fifties, with dark brown hair and light blue eyes, he looked like a younger, more handsome version of the man Davis had studied in pictures just that morning. It had to be Neal Petrov's younger brother, Joel.

As soon as he reached them, the man gripped Leila by her upper arms, staring intently at her face. "Are you okay? I heard the FBI pulled you in for questioning about this military disaster."

Leila's gaze darted to Davis, then back to the man who had to be her uncle. She didn't quite look him in the eyes as she replied, "I'm fine. It was a mistake. Don't worry."

"Don't worry? You know I always worry. With your dad gone…" He sighed, gave Leila a sad smile, then let go of her arms. "I'm sorry," he said more softly. "We should have talked in private. But I wish you'd called me right away. Eric said—"

"Everything is okay," Leila said, cutting him off. "Uncle,

this is my new assistant, Davis Rogers. Davis, this is Joel Petrov, our COO."

Joel's attention shifted to him, and the intensity of the man's scrutiny was like a father inspecting his teenage daughter's first date. Fleetingly Davis wondered why Neal Petrov hadn't convinced the board of directors to make his brother CEO instead of his daughter.

Then Joel's hand closed around his. "Davis. Nice to meet you. I'm sure you'll like it here." Just as quickly, Joel let go, dismissing him as effectively as if he'd left the room.

"I'm glad it was all a mistake," he told Leila. "But if anything else comes up, let me help you handle it. You've got enough to deal with right now." He squeezed her hand, then headed off into a private office on the edges of the open space and closed the door.

"Let's finish our tour," Leila told him, all business as she strode past her uncle's office and toward the testing area.

Davis hurried after her, his mind spinning. Neal Petrov's brother was COO of the company and yet, when Neal had stepped back, he'd talked the board into putting his twenty-nine-year-old daughter in charge instead. And even after leaving his CEO role, from what his employees had said, Neal Petrov was still in the office all the time. As founder and biggest shareholder, he still profited. Maybe stepping back protected him from liability if things went sideways. Maybe he hadn't pushed to have his young daughter in charge because of nepotism, but because he thought she was too inexperienced to realize what was happening under her nose.

He frowned, remembering the sadness in her eyes when Eric had talked about her father. If Davis's suspicion was true, her father hadn't really cared about her. Because by using her inexperience and trust against her, he was also putting her in the position to be the first one law enforcement came after if it all unraveled. He was making her his scapegoat.

Davis was a long way from proving any of it, but if he was right, he wished more than ever that Neal Petrov was still here, so he could truly make the man pay.

"Let me show you the area where we do testing," Leila said, her tone strong and confident, as if showing him their process would prove there was no way for someone to have sabotaged the armor. "We used to have a separate section of the building for gun testing, but that closed last year and we're in the process of converting it into another R and D area for our armor." She used her security card to key through a new doorway, holding it open for him.

As he followed, his phone dinged and Davis glanced at it. A message from Hendrick lit up on his screen.

This case is much bigger than we thought. Turns out Petrov Armor's name has come up in Bureau cases before—a LOT of them over more than a decade. But nothing panned out.

Frowning, Davis texted back a quick question: Military cases? Defects?

The response came back fast and made Davis swear under his breath.

No. Supplying guns to known criminals.

Chapter Four

Kane Bradshaw hated being stuck inside an FBI office, digging through old case files. He especially hated doing it with Dr. Melinda Larsen.

He snuck a glance at her, head bent over her laptop, wearing her default serious expression. She looked more like an academic than an FBI agent, with her small frame and that dark hair she always wore loose around her shoulders. Her Asian heritage had given her skin warm undertones and along with how perfectly unlined her face was despite her job, she looked a decade younger than the early forties he knew her to be. But one glance into those deep brown eyes and he could see every year, every tough case.

She was one of the Bureau's foremost experts on body language and a damn good profiler. He'd worked with her peripherally over the years, but had hoped to avoid being teamed up with her at TCD.

He'd seen her around the office, quick to offer her opinions on cases and silently studying anyone else who spoke. Profiling them, he was sure. She'd done it to him, too. If her reputation was deserved, she'd seen way too far into his mind, into his soul. He had no intention of letting her see any more.

He'd prefer to keep his secrets.

If anyone else had asked him to work with Melinda, he

would have refused. But he owed Jill Pembrook more than he could ever repay her. So, if she wanted him to partner with the too-serious profiler to look into Petrov Armor's connection to criminals, he'd keep his mouth shut and do it.

"I've got another one," Melinda said, angling her laptop so he could see the most recent case she'd pulled up.

They'd been at it since yesterday, when Hendrick had found Petrov Armor listed in a number of Bureau cases. Their computer expert had flagged all the files, but Pembrook had assigned him and Melinda to go through each one, since Petrov Armor had never been officially charged.

So far, most of the mentions were offhand and too small to be useful. Like a single Petrov Armor pistol found at the scene of a mass killing. Although the man had been a convicted felon before that incident, he hadn't bought the gun himself. A friend without a criminal history had purchased it and lent it to him, so Petrov Armor hadn't done anything wrong.

He and Melinda had read and eliminated more than a dozen cases like that. Small numbers of guns, purchases traced back to someone with no criminal record, even if they ultimately handed it off to a criminal. But no indication that Petrov Armor had facilitated an illegal sale.

But every so often, a case would pop up with more guns—boxes of them rather than a single piece. They'd be sitting in the attic of a known gang member's house. Or on the scene of a large, coordinated armed robbery. Although the guns were Petrov Armor's, the serial numbers had been filed off, so investigators hadn't been able to trace any back to a sale. It was why Petrov Armor had been investigated, but never charged.

It was legal for them to sell guns to civilians; they just couldn't sell to convicted felons. Since that was a crime the ATF investigated, most of the cases Hendrick had tagged for them were joint FBI-ATF files. Which meant there could be more.

"What have you got?" Kane asked, leaning closer.

Like she did every time he got too close to her, Melinda twitched slightly, then stilled. She probably didn't want to work with him, either. Although the director never talked about it, the role Kane had played in the death of Pembrook's daughter was common knowledge.

Kane gritted his teeth and tried not to let Melinda's reaction bother him. It was part of the reason he liked to work alone. But Pembrook had insisted she wanted both Melinda's ability to read people's intentions—even from a case file—and Kane's extensive experience in the field, undercover with criminals, on this case review. So far, he had to admit, they made a good team. When she wasn't flinching at his nearness, anyway.

"Convicted murderer, released on early parole. About a month after he got out, he strapped on some Petrov Armor body armor, took out a Petrov Armor pistol and killed five people in his old workplace, including the guy who turned him in. He bought the armor directly from Petrov Armor, which isn't illegal. But the gun is a different matter. ATF could never figure out where he got the pistol, but his friend, who was also a convicted felon, told FBI agents that buying the gun was even easier than buying the armor. Then he shut up and wouldn't give us anything else. But it sure seems like he could have gotten them at the same time, one on the books and one off."

Kane leaned back in his chair, letting it tilt so he was staring up at the ceiling as he stacked his hands behind his head. "Maybe he just means it's easy to get a friend to buy a firearm for you legally and then lend it. Happens all the time."

Even though he could see her only from his peripheral

vision, the way her lips twisted in disbelief wasn't hard to picture. "Come on. Why does the average person need body armor and a gun? If this was your friend and you knew he was a violent criminal who'd just bought body armor, would you lend him a gun?"

Kane shrugged. Melinda could see through people better than anyone he'd ever met. But she'd never spent time undercover. Kane had spent so much of his career pretending to be someone else that his own identity sometimes felt nebulous. Which wasn't such a bad thing, as far as he was concerned.

It had taught him just how much people wanted to believe those they loved, even when all the evidence warned them they were making a big mistake. Lending a criminal a gun and lying to yourself that they were just afraid—maybe of a system you'd also convinced yourself had railroaded that person—didn't seem like much of a stretch.

"Well, maybe this one is less convincing than some of the other cases where we've got big boxes of guns. But add all these cases up and there's something here."

"I don't know," Kane argued. "There's a huge black market for guns. It doesn't mean Petrov Armor is involved in the sales."

Melinda sat up straighter, folding her hands in front of her on the table, in a move Kane recognized. She was ready to make an argument.

He hid his smile as he gave her all his attention.

"Selling guns off the books means a huge markup. Criminals will pay more because they need to go through back channels. But a year ago, Leila Petrov shut down that part of the business."

Kane let his chair tip him forward again as he wished he'd realized the connection sooner. "So, now whoever was making those backdoor deals—if that was happening—

could be sending out inferior armor at the same prices as the good armor, pocketing the money left over from using cheaper materials."

"Yes," Melinda agreed, finally smiling at him.

It was probably the first real smile she'd given him since they'd been working together at TCD, or even in all the years before when he'd cross paths briefly with her. The hair on the back of his neck stood up as he noticed how much it changed her face. Not that she wasn't always pretty, but academic and too insightful had never been his type. But a smiling, proud Melinda was someone he needed to avoid even more.

"We need to find a way to get a look at Petrov Armor's finances," Melinda said.

"They've probably got double books," Kane argued, putting his brief, ridiculous burst of attraction aside. "But maybe we need to try and set up a sale. Pretend to be a criminal and buy from them. An undercover op like this is a piece of cake. I've done a million of them."

If he was trying to buy guns from someone at Petrov Armor, he wouldn't be stuck in a tiny office with Melinda Larsen, pretending not to care that she could read anyone with a single glance. Pretending not to care if she did it to him.

"No," Melinda insisted. "We've got to do more legwork first or we could blow the whole case and make whoever is doing this suspicious of Davis."

Kane clamped his mouth shut over the argument he wanted to make. He was dying to get back in the field, put on a new persona like a new pair of clothes. Get away from Melinda's scrutiny. But he knew she was right.

He'd have to wait to jump into the action and the danger he craved, the chance to go out in a hail of bullets like his old partner—Pembrook's only daughter—had done.

The chance to die doing something worthwhile. The way he should have done years ago, beside her.

DAVIS HAD BEEN undercover at Leila's company for a day and a half. To Leila, it felt like he'd been there for a week.

She was overanxious, having to watch every word around him, resist sending him suspicious glances that her employees might notice. Most of them would likely just attribute it to her overprotectiveness of the company and everyone and everything inside it. But Uncle Neal or Eric would have probably known something was off. She was amazed they hadn't realized it already.

Then again, she never lied to either of them.

She and Eric had once shared a bond she thought would never break. He'd been the friend who'd pulled her out of a deep depression three years after she lost her mom. The first boyfriend she'd ever had a year after that. Once their relationship had ended, they'd eventually returned to friendship. It would never be the same as when they were kids, but Leila couldn't forget what he'd done for her or how much he'd meant to her family.

She and her uncle were close. They didn't do much together outside of the office, but mostly that was because they were both so busy with work—and in her uncle's case, with the women he seemed to attract with a single smile. It was a skill she'd never mastered with the opposite sex and, after the way Eric had broken things off with her, had never really wanted to.

The thought made her glance sideways at Davis as he walked alongside her out to her car. Eric was on her other side, making too-fast small talk about his latest sale that told her one thing he *had* noticed: her attraction to Davis.

Eric knew her too well. He'd probably spotted that she glanced at Davis a little too much. Eric wouldn't know only part of that was attraction and the rest was worry because of why Davis was here. All he'd see was that Davis intrigued her.

Eric was jealous. Frustration nipped at her, and with it, a little bit of anger. He'd given up his right to be jealous a long time ago, when he'd broken her heart.

"Oh, you've *got* to be kidding me." Leila sighed as they reached her car in the lot. The front right tire was completely flat. "Damn construction. That was my spare tire."

Davis leaned closer to the wheel, frowning. "I don't suppose you have another? If you do, I can change this for you, no problem."

"Yeah," Leila said. "So could I, but I don't have a second spare. I probably ran over another nail."

She ignored the little voice in the back of her head suggesting one of her employees had done it. She knew quite a few of them weren't happy she'd assumed the role of CEO when her father retired. But they had to be expecting it. Since the day she'd started at the company five years ago, she'd put in more hours than anyone besides her dad. This had started out as a family business, and the board of directors had seen the benefits of keeping it that way. No one could begrudge her that. Especially not with something this juvenile.

"I'll drive you home," Eric said, putting a hand on her arm.

"Not a problem. I can do it." The curiosity on Davis's face told her he hadn't missed Eric's jealousy either.

Before Leila could tell them she'd just call for a car, Davis added, "I am her assistant, after all. Might be a good time for us to talk about how I can help Petrov Armor."

"It's your job to support Leila on the job," Eric said. "Not—"

"That's a good idea," Leila cut him off. "Thank you."

She told Eric a quick good-night, then pivoted to follow Davis to his vehicle.

She swore she could feel Eric's unhappy gaze on her as she climbed into Davis's black SUV, but she didn't look back. Instead, she sank into the surprisingly comfortable bucket seat of what she assumed was his FBI vehicle and closed her eyes. The past two days had been stressful, the past three weeks some of the worst of her life.

No matter how hard she threw herself into work, how much she tried not to think about her dad, he was all around her. Not only had he built the business up from nothing, but he'd also been involved in every decision when they'd moved into their building. He'd picked the furniture and artwork in the lobby, designated the office right next to his for her. When he'd retired, they'd changed the label on his door from CEO to Founder, but he'd kept the office since he was there so often, consulting. She hadn't been able to bring herself to go inside since his death.

Thinking about that terrible moment when she'd gotten the call, the back of Leila's throat stung and she knew tears weren't far behind. Swallowing the pain, she opened her eyes and blinked back the moisture. Realizing Davis had already left the parking lot and was navigating the streets of Old City, she forced her attention back to the one thing she could still control: her father's legacy. "So, what have you found?"

Her heart pounded faster as she waited for his answer, both hoping for and dreading the news. True, she didn't personally know every one of her nearly two hundred employees. But she did know the ones in key positions, roles that would give them the kind of access required to pull this off. And every one of *those* employees, she trusted. Maybe even more telling, her dad had trusted them. He'd had thirty-four years of experience either owning Petrov

Armor or—once he'd taken it public—being the largest shareholder. For all but the last five, he'd run it. Even after he'd turned it over to her, he'd been there to guide her every step of the way.

"Your security is solid," Davis responded, not taking his eyes off the road. "But tomorrow, I want to take a look at your security video for the days connected to the armor being built and shipped out. I want to look at your security card access logs, too. See who went in and out of sensitive areas who shouldn't have been there or who was there at odd hours."

"Sure." Her mind rebelled at the idea of letting an outsider sift through their security footage, but better Davis find the truth than some big, public FBI investigation. Assuming she really could trust him to keep her in the loop and let her manage the betrayal without a huge media fallout.

She wasn't naive enough to think the press wouldn't eventually get the story. But better it came from Petrov Armor than in the form of an FBI statement.

"What about suspects? Who do you think did this? Is it possible it was a switch that happened after the armor left our facilities?" As she said it, the idea gained traction in her mind and gave her hope that she hadn't massively misjudged someone crucial inside her company.

A switch along the delivery route still meant a Petrov Armor employee was probably involved. But it wouldn't be someone she'd known well for years. It wouldn't be the same level of betrayal to the company or to her father's memory.

"I've been inside for a day and a half," Davis answered, still not looking at her. "Right now, everyone is a suspect."

"You want me to work with you, Davis? I need you to work with me, too. I can't give you insight into anyone if I don't know who you need to check out."

His head moved just slightly toward her, his gaze sweeping over her face like he was looking for something. Then he focused on the road again, probably training drilled into him at the FBI. Never take your eyes off the task ahead.

"Tell me about Eric Ross."

She choked on nothing, on air, on the ridiculousness of that statement. Eric, a traitor? "I've known him since I was thirteen. He was almost as close to my dad as I was. Trust me. He had nothing to do with this."

"Are you sure you can be impartial? The man obviously has a crush on you."

"He doesn't…" She let out a heavy sigh. "That's ridiculous. Look, I get it. I misjudged someone at the company. But it's not Eric."

She shifted in her seat so she could see him better and got distracted by the way he looked in dress pants and a blazer. The bulge at his hip under his seat belt caught her attention, and she realized what it was. "You're wearing a gun."

He gave her another one of those quick, searching gazes, then replied, "Always. Even if the FBI didn't require it, I was an army ranger before I joined the Bureau. I like being prepared."

A ranger. Leila let that image fill her mind—Davis in an army uniform, wearing that revered tan beret that identified him as a member of the elite Special Forces unit. It was easy to imagine him parachuting out of a plane, steering a small boat full of soldiers through a jungle river, or rappelling down the side of a mountain. Something about the quiet confidence in his gaze, the outright cockiness of his grin and the muscles that his blazer seemed barely able to contain.

Forcing the image out of her head, she joked, "So, if

you're always prepared, what's in the back? An inflatable boat and a parachute?"

He gave her that quick look again, but this time there was laughter in his eyes and that sexy, amused tilt to his lips.

He'd probably already put her in a box in his mind: serious CEO determined to live up to her father's example. Not a real, rounded person who went home to a too-quiet house, couldn't sleep without background noise and liked to dance by herself in the living room.

Leila instantly regretted letting him see her ridiculous sense of humor. She shifted her left leg back to the floor, no longer facing him as she tried to focus. But it was hard not to think about that smile, those lips. It made her belly tighten with awareness, and she wondered if this was part of his arsenal.

How often did he use sex appeal undercover in order to get what he wanted?

And what exactly did he want? He'd implied that he suspected Eric, made the absurd suggestion that Eric had a crush on her. But surely he'd looked into her past before coming into her company. Did he know she and Eric had dated for four years? Did he know how badly Eric had broken her heart? Or how hard it had been to come into a company where Eric already worked, to try to treat him like any other colleague?

As Davis pulled up in front of her house and Leila realized she'd never given him the address, dread sank to the bottom of her stomach, replacing any twinges of lust.

Of course he knew all of those things. Probably a lot more, too. Even worse, he hadn't told her a single real thing about his investigation.

She didn't know if he'd done it on purpose. Or if he planned to let her in only when he needed her.

But one thing was certain: she couldn't trust Davis either.

Chapter Five

"You do realize I could blow your cover whenever I want, right?"

Leila Petrov stared at him with narrowed eyes. Her lips pursed tight, and the muscles in her forearms and biceps twitched as she crossed them over her chest. She'd pivoted in her seat again, this time snapping off her seat belt. But she'd made no move to get out of his vehicle and disappear into her house.

As furious as she looked, Davis knew none of his own worry showed. He'd spent too many years running or parachuting into enemy territory with only as much gear as he could carry and no backup that could reach him and his team for days. He was well practiced in faking confidence in moments of doubt. If his fellow soldiers couldn't see through it, neither would the young CEO heir of Petrov Armor.

"Well?" she demanded when he was silent too long.

A smile threatened and Davis fought to hide it. She was nothing like he'd expected when he'd first opened her file. Whether or not she'd gotten her role as CEO because she was the founder's daughter, she knew the company inside out. She wasn't afraid to call him on things, no matter the FBI's involvement. He definitely hadn't expected her dry sense of humor.

A laugh bubbled up thinking about her comment about the inflatable boat he probably kept in his SUV. If she only knew how often an inflatable boat had come in handy in his previous job.

"Are you *laughing* at me?" Leila demanded. "Because if those vests are truly ours, I plan to figure out who was behind it. I'm going to do it with or without your—"

"I'm not laughing at you," Davis cut her off. He leaned closer, saw her chest rise and fall faster in response. "Why would you want to blow my cover?"

"You're not holding up your end of the deal. I don't appreciate you trying to manipulate me with flirtation, with… this." She gestured in front of her, indicating their nearness.

This time, Davis knew his surprise showed. He leaned away from her, trying to regroup.

Leila pivoted even more in her seat, getting into his personal space the same way she had in that interview room. Going on the offensive when most people would do the opposite. "Is this your thing when you go undercover? Try to seduce your contacts?"

"I'm not…" Davis blew out a breath that ended on a laugh. "This is my first time undercover."

He wasn't at all comfortable with it. Sneaking into enemy territory as a ranger or doing dangerous raids as an FBI agent was far more his speed than pretending to be someone he wasn't. Manipulating people into giving him information or access felt foreign and vaguely wrong, even if those people had criminal intentions.

"You've never gone undercover before? Oh." She sat back fast, facing the windshield and giving him a chance to study her profile.

She looked nothing like Jessica Carpenter. Leila's file said she was Russian and Pakistani, while Jessica was African American. Leila had a delicate, almost dainty profile, while Jessica had the bearing of a soldier. But there was something similar underneath the surface, something about the balance between a serious exterior and a softer, goofier side they both tried to hide.

Except Leila was still here, protecting a company that had killed Jessica.

The fact that she hadn't known about it didn't matter. The fact that he liked her more with every moment he spent in her company didn't matter. All that mattered was using whatever means necessary to keep her trust and find the person responsible.

So, he forced a slow, knowing smile and added, "I can't help finding you attractive."

Her lips parted like she was going to say something, but he didn't give her a chance. Instead, he continued. "I *am* keeping up my end of the deal. I told you I wanted more information on Eric Ross."

Her head swung toward him, a frown already in place that told him he'd guessed correctly: she and Eric had a history that went way beyond the company. His plan had worked, to distract her from the real issue—whether he was telling her everything. Because of course he wasn't. And he never would.

The jolt of jealousy at her reaction surprised him, but he ignored it and pressed on. "Unless that's what this is really about? You don't want me digging up dirt on your ex?"

She sputtered for a second, then frowned harder. "Just how involved is your file on me? You know who I dated when I was a teenager?"

Davis hadn't known anything about it, but sensing that her anger might lead to answers, he shrugged, gave a vague answer. "We're the FBI. We try to learn everything we can about suspects in active cases."

"Suspects?" Leila said. "I thought we were past that."

"We are," Davis said, drawing his answers out, long and slow, the opposite of her fast-paced words. "But we had to start at the top, Leila. We know a lot about you."

A flush rose high on her cheeks. "Does that mean you know how Eric befriended me after I pushed everyone else away after my mom died? How he got me help before I really hurt myself? How he dropped out of my life with no explanation when I graduated from high school? Or how he's been calling me every night since my dad died just to make sure I don't fall back into that same depression?"

The jealousy shifted, turned into appreciation that Eric had been there when Leila needed him, despite their history. Davis had seen her strong mask crack, seen how much she missed her father, how she was quietly grieving him. But he couldn't imagine Leila depressed or self-destructive. The thought actually made his stomach hurt.

Leila's voice wobbled just a little, then anger came through again. "Why does the FBI need to know about the hardest things in my life? Is it so you can use it all against me?"

Instantly regretting his tactics, Davis resisted reaching out for her hand. "We don't have any of that in a file, Leila."

Not really, anyway. The file had told him her mother died twenty years ago, but he hadn't known anything about Eric. "I just guessed that you'd dated Eric from the way he talks to you, the way he looks at you."

"Oh." She stared down at her lap, then back at him. There was confusion on her face, but something else, too, something that looked too much like hope.

His gut clenched in response, a mix of guilt and nerves. It was one thing to take on an enemy who was an obvious threat, someone aiming a weapon back at him. It was totally different to try to earn someone's trust when he knew he might have to betray that trust in the end.

But this was the job. His colleague Kane did it all the time. The agent seemed to thrive on it. If it meant getting justice for Jessica, it was what Davis had to do too.

Trying to hold the guilt at bay, Davis unhooked his seat belt and shifted so he was facing her more fully. "How are you holding up since your dad died?"

Her forehead furrowed, like she was trying to gauge his sincerity. Then she sighed and said, "My dad and I are—were—like best friends. In some ways it was just the two of us. My mom died when I was ten. I've never met her family except for a few cousins over video chat. They're all back in Pakistan. My mom moved here for my dad and mostly lost touch when she did. They never really forgave her for leaving. His family is…not so great. Except for my uncle. My uncle is wonderful. He helped get me through losing my mom back then, and he's helping me get through losing my dad now."

She heaved out another sigh and leaned back against the seat. "I can't believe he's gone."

"I'm sorry."

"Of course he had to stand up to that mugger." She let out a bitter laugh. "That's my dad. Never give in to anyone."

Davis's chest constricted at the pain in her voice. He understood Neal Petrov's response. The police report said Neal had been armed, carrying a small Petrov Armor pistol hidden at the small of his back. Apparently, it wasn't unusual, and he had a concealed carry license. He'd probably thought the mugger was no real threat. Probably figured he could pull the gun, warn the guy off. Instead, he'd gotten shot. "He sounds tough."

"Yeah, I guess so. Not with me. He was…" She shrugged. "A softie."

"You were his only daughter."

Still not looking at him, she nodded. "When my mom

died, he lost it. Just withdrew from everything and everyone—including me."

Davis frowned. No wonder she'd sunk into depression. At ten she'd lost her mom, and her dad hadn't been there for her. "I'm glad you met Eric then."

She looked over at him, surprise on her features. "I didn't meet Eric for another three years. But my uncle stepped up. Before that, Uncle Joel was…" A wistful, amused smile tilted one side of her mouth, then dropped off. "Flighty, I guess. He was always off chasing women and fun. Not that he ever stopped that. But when he saw how checked out Dad was, he stepped in. Practically raised me for a few years, practically ran the business too, until Dad got it together. That's when my dad and I really got close. Right before my dad got it together was when I met Eric."

"Your uncle ran the business for a while?"

"Yeah. He spent so much time dealing with Dad's job that he lost his own."

"What do you mean?"

"He didn't work for the company before that. He was a sales rep at a pharmaceutical company. But when my dad got himself together, he gave Uncle Joel a job."

Davis nodded, trying to sound casual when he asked, "After all that, why didn't your dad convince the board of directors to appoint your uncle as CEO when he stepped down?"

Leila frowned. "What makes you think my dad talked them into that decision?"

"Are you telling me he didn't? He was the largest shareholder, wasn't he, before he died?" Before those shares had been split up between Leila and Joel.

"Yes," Leila admitted. "But—"

"So why not push for your uncle to take on the role?" Was there any lingering resentment on the uncle's part?

Maybe enough to sabotage the business, even all these years later?

Leila laughed. "Uncle Joel, CEO? No way. I mean, obviously he was the de facto CEO for a few years when I was a kid. He can do it. He even grew the business. But he doesn't want to. Never has. He likes being COO. Gives him security and a say in the company's direction, but not all of the responsibility."

"How does he feel about reporting to you?"

She shrugged. "Fine. It's a little weird. He is my uncle, after all. But he's great about it. A lot better than some of the others."

"Like Theresa Quinn?" The head of Petrov Armor's R and D had struck him as less than thrilled about Leila's leadership.

"How'd you guess?" Leila sighed. "She's not the only one. But they all know me. They all know how much I care about the business, about my father's legacy." She gave him a hard look. "They know how hard I worked for this position. They'll come around eventually."

There was less confidence in her last words, so Davis said, "I'm sure they will."

Her expression turned pensive. But as she stared at him, the worry in her gaze slowly softened. Her lips parted and he could hear her swallow, and suddenly the vehicle felt way too hot.

Then she was leaning toward him, her eyes dropping closed.

He felt his body sway forward in response, and his hand reached up to cup her cheek as his own lips parted in anticipation of touching hers. But sanity returned before the distance between them disappeared.

Jerking away, Davis couldn't quite hold her gaze. "I

should probably get going. Call me if you need anything or if you have any thoughts about the case, okay?"

She blinked back at him, confusion and embarrassment in her stare. Then, she blinked again and it was gone, replaced with a hard professionalism. "Good night, Davis."

She stepped out of his vehicle, walked up the stone pathway to her house and let herself inside without a backward glance.

HE WAS AN IDIOT.

Leila Petrov had been inches from kissing him and he'd backed away. Now, not only had he missed out on the chance to taste her, he'd blown the tenuous trust they'd been building. But that was a professional line he couldn't cross.

Besides, she'd been vulnerable. And he'd been lying. Every moment he spent with her was a lie, because even though she knew he was there to find out the truth about the defective armor, she had no idea how badly he needed to see someone punished for it. She had no idea that regardless of whether she'd been involved, he would always hold her responsible, since she ran the company.

He liked her. Too much, probably. He didn't want to use her. Not even to help the investigation. Not even to avenge Jessica's death.

Davis slammed his fist on the top of the steering wheel as he drove away from Leila's house. His body was telling him to turn around, knock on her door and come clean with her. His mind was telling him he needed to do the same thing, for the sake of the case.

But he couldn't do it. She'd had too much loss and betrayal in her life already. He wasn't about to add to it.

His cell phone rang and Davis hit the Bluetooth button on the steering wheel, eyes still on the road. He glanced at the dashboard screen, an apology already on his lips. But he swallowed it as he realized the name on the display. Melinda Larsen was calling him. Not Leila.

The surge of disappointment he felt surprised him as Melinda asked, "Hello? Davis, are you there?"

"Yeah." His voice didn't sound quite right, so he cleared his throat. "Yeah, what's up?"

"Kane and I have been looking through Petrov Armor's potential illegal gun sales, as you know."

That was quite a partnership. Even though they sat in the same briefings all the time, Davis couldn't imagine quietly confident Melinda Larsen and now-you-see-me-now-you-don't Kane Bradshaw working a case together. "Did you find anything?"

"Maybe. We've got photos from a joint FBI-ATF gang case. Illegal arms sales were only a peripheral part of the case, but we were running anything we could find, no matter how small. One of those things was a partial plate on a Lexus that showed up in a photo. The driver isn't visible and we've only got part of the vehicle, but the partial matches up to Theresa Quinn, head of—"

"Research and development at Petrov Armor," Davis finished. "But a partial plate? How partial?"

"It's not a slam dunk, not even close. Hundreds of red Lexuses match this partial. But in Tennessee? On the edge of a gang meeting?"

"What do you mean by the *edge* of a meeting?" Davis asked as he changed lanes, heading toward the TCD office instead of home.

"It's possible it's not connected. But again, a Lexus in this part of town? Right near where a gang member was meeting up with someone for a gun sale?"

"Who made the sale?" Davis asked.

"We don't know. They never showed. ATF said they

think the guy got spooked. Or the gal, if this vehicle really does belong to Theresa Quinn."

"Anything else?" Davis asked hopefully. It did sound like a potential lead. Theresa definitely didn't seem to respect Leila, maybe a result of working with her father for years in illegal sales without the young CEO realizing it?

"I'm coming into the office," Davis told Melinda.

"Good. Kane and I are still wading through case files, but we'd love to hear how you're faring on the inside."

"Having a lot more fun, I'm sure." Kane's voice carried from the background.

"Not really," Davis muttered. Before Melinda could ask, he said, "I'll be there in two," and hung up.

He made it in one minute, and found Kane and Melinda sitting on opposite sides of the long conference table where the team had its morning briefings. Each had a laptop open, and Davis wondered how many hours they'd managed to work together without actually talking.

"There's a reason Petrov Armor has never been charged," Kane told him. "If they're selling guns on the side to criminals—which I think they are—they're savvy."

A hard ball of dread made Davis's stomach cramp. It should have been good news—not that Petrov Armor was talented at avoiding prosecution, but that there was another route to try to collect evidence. But all Davis could think of was the conviction in Leila's face when she'd told him it wasn't their armor. The hope in her eyes when she'd suggested maybe the armor had been switched after it had been shipped out of their facility.

She truly believed the core of her company was good. It looked like she was very, very wrong.

"Undercover work is tough, isn't it?" Melinda asked, making Davis realize she could probably read every one of his emotions.

Suddenly Kane's attention was fixed on him, too, and Davis forced a shrug. Tried to push Leila out of his mind. "It's a big company. But the number of people who could have pulled off both illegal gun sales *and* defective armor shipments is probably pretty low. Assuming we think it's the same person."

"Someone in power," Kane agreed. "Possibly more than one person, since we still think it's pretty likely Neal Petrov was involved when he was alive. Who's on your short list for his partner in crime?"

"Obviously Theresa Quinn is on our list," Melinda said, then looked at Davis. "What about Neal's brother, Joel?"

"Maybe," Davis hedged, not liking the idea that both Leila's father and her uncle might be criminals. But he tried to think objectively. "Neal and Joel could have been in it together all along. After Neal's wife died, Joel managed everything for a few years, so maybe he handled the criminal side for his brother, too. Maybe that's why Neal kept his brother on after he was ready to return to work."

Melinda's eyebrows rose. "That's promising. Although that red Lexus still seems awfully coincidental."

"Who else?" Kane asked. "What about the head of sales?"

"Eric Ross." Leila's ex. A man who'd broken her heart years ago, but had called her every night for the past three weeks to make sure she was okay after her father's death. "Also possible. He's got access to everything, and his job takes him out of the office a lot. It probably wouldn't raise eyebrows if he took samples with him, saying they were for sales calls demos. Maybe he used that as a way to get bigger quantities out. He was really close to Neal Petrov, so they could have definitely been partners."

"Even though the most obvious answer initially looked like Neal's daughter was working with him, Leila seemed genuinely shocked in that interview," Melinda said. "A year ago, she was the one who initiated the shutdown of the gun side of their business to focus on the armor. No way she'd do that if she was making tons of money from guns off-book."

"Leila's not involved." The words came out of his mouth before he could pull them back, but Davis knew they were true.

Kane lifted an eyebrow, but all he said was, "Have you considered that her dad put her in charge because she'd never suspect him of wrongdoing? That she'd be easier to fool? Seems like it backfired when she shut down the gun part of the business, but he still had a tidy fall girl."

Melinda frowned. "That's pretty heartless."

"Yeah, well, have you read the guy's file?" Kane shoved a manila folder across the table, and Davis snagged it.

"What is this?" Most of the FBI's files were computerized, unless they were so old they hadn't been transitioned over. But this looked like a PD file.

"Police file on Neal Petrov's mugging is in there somewhere. I just skimmed that. But there's also a really old file from a welfare check. A neighbor called it in twenty years ago, saying a ten-year-old girl—Leila—had been on her own for a week. Police checked it out, and even though the girl claimed everything was fine and her dad had just run out, the state of the house said otherwise. They were going to call Children's Services, but the girl's uncle showed up and smoothed things over."

"Neal's wife had just died," Davis said, his shoulders slumping as he read the details of a dirty, hungry Leila, alone and trying hard to be brave when police had arrived.

Knowing things had turned out okay and feeling like he was spying on a part of her life she hadn't given him permission to see, Davis turned to the report on the mugging.

It was brief, but this report had ended much worse. Davis started to close the file when a small detail caught his eye. He swore, sitting up straighter, and read it again.

"What is it?" Kane asked.

"I don't think this was a random mugging." Davis looked at Kane, then Melinda. "I think Neal Petrov was murdered."

Chapter Six

"Neal Petrov was murdered?" Kane asked. "That's not what the report said."

"The official story is that someone tried to mug Neal, he went for his gun and the mugger shot him. But they never caught the mugger," Davis said.

"So what?" Kane demanded. "He was in an area that had seen a rash of muggings. It was inevitable that it would get violent eventually. If he was trying to pull a gun, probably the mugger panicked and shot first."

"Neal Petrov holstered his gun at the small of his back." Davis skimmed the report once more to be sure he hadn't missed something, then swore under his breath. He was right. "According to this report, his right arm was positioned under his back, like he was reaching for the gun when he fell."

"All consistent with a mugging gone wrong," Kane said, but he was leaning forward now, his tone suggesting he was waiting for something inconsistent.

"Neal Petrov had no damage to that arm. No broken fingers from landing on them. No scraped-up arms when he hit the pavement. It's as if—"

"His arm was positioned that way after he fell," Melinda finished, looking pensive.

"Exactly."

"Well, this case just took an interesting turn," Kane said, settling back into his chair.

It *was* interesting. Because if it wasn't a random mugging and the scene had been staged, that suggested someone Neal knew. It seemed likely the murderer was connected to the faulty armor coming out of Petrov Armor. That potentially put a completely different spin on what was happening at Petrov Armor and who was involved.

But all Davis could think about was the sadness in Leila's voice when she'd talked about losing her mom, the grief in her eyes when her employees had talked about missing her dad. He didn't want her to face more hurt. He definitely didn't want to have to tell her that someone she knew might have murdered her dad.

"So, who might have wanted Neal Petrov dead?" Melinda asked.

Davis forced himself to focus, but he couldn't quite get Leila's sad eyes out of his head as he replied, "Potentially a lot of people if he was involved in illegal gun sales and defective body armor sales."

"Or even if he wasn't, and he found out what was happening at his company," Kane added. "Though I'm betting he was part of this, probably the instigator. My guess is that he was making a lot of money off the illegal gun sales, letting him retire at sixty. With a partner inside, that person still had the necessary access. So did Neal, since he was still at the office all the time as a consultant and member of the board. This way, Neal could focus on the illegal side of the business. I bet he put his daughter in charge because she'd never suspect him of this. Right?" Kane stared questioningly at Davis.

He nodded reluctantly. "Leila loved her dad. She'd never suspect him of anything illegal or immoral. But honestly, she still doesn't think it's anyone at the company. She's convinced a switch happened after the shipment left Petrov Armor."

"Well, that might have been plausible—if unlikely—when we were talking about one defective armor shipment. But she doesn't know how big this case has gotten, including all the illegal arms sales," Kane replied. "So, he helps get his daughter put in charge, thinking she'll be clueless. Then, she shuts down the gun business, so Neal switches to defective armor. As the biggest shareholder, he's still getting plenty of the company's profits. So, he's swapping out the materials for cheaper stuff and pocketing the balance. That would suggest he was working with Theresa."

"And then she had him killed?" Melinda interrupted. "Why?"

"Maybe she wanted more of the profits for herself," Davis suggested, able to imagine the determined head of R and D paying someone to kill Neal. Or even pulling the trigger herself. "She resented Leila being put in charge. Maybe she blamed Neil for putting her there and giving her a chance to shut down the gun side of the business."

"Or it wasn't Theresa who killed him at all," Melinda suggested. "Maybe it was someone who learned what he was doing and took their own revenge."

"But the faulty armor only caused deaths after Neal was already murdered," Davis said.

"At least as far as we know," Melinda contradicted. "But what if it was someone internal? Someone who learned about the gun sales and wanted them stopped? Maybe they sent the faulty armor to get him investigated and when that took too long, they had him killed instead."

"There are easier ways of dealing with that, though. Anonymous tip to police, for one. Sending out bad armor to trigger an investigation seems pretty drastic and complicated. Too many variables the perp can't control," Davis argued.

"Yeah, but what revenge murder do you know of that's not drastic?"

"Point taken. If it's revenge. But I don't think it is. It seems more likely he was killed by his partner in the illegal gun sales, doesn't it?" Davis glanced at Kane, wondering about his take. Melinda might be the profiler, but Kane had spent most of his career undercover. He'd worked with the CIA repeatedly. He understood the underhanded dealings of criminals better than most, because he'd seen them up close. Rumor had it that sometimes he'd even participated to keep his cover intact.

"Maybe," Kane said, but there was uncertainty in his tone. "It's the timing I'm interested in. What happened three weeks ago that got Neal Petrov killed? It's interesting that it's close to the timing of that faulty shipment. Then, there's the fact that the gun side of the business shut down last year. My gut says all those things are somehow connected."

"Leila has agreed to give me access to the security camera footage and logs from the time the latest batch of armor was made," Davis told them. "Hopefully that will give us some insight."

"In the meantime, you need to continue to act like you're just there about one shipment of defective armor," Melinda said. "Leila can't suspect her father was murdered or she might just blow open this whole investigation."

"I know," Davis answered, not quite meeting her gaze. He had no intention of telling Leila the truth, at least not until they had someone in custody. But lying to her even a little bit made him feel terrible. How was he going to keep something this huge from her?

IT WAS SEVENTY degrees and the sun was shining, but Kane Bradshaw was tucked into a dark corner beneath an underpass. Fifty feet away, a low-level drug deal was taking place. A hundred feet beyond that, a cluster of cardboard boxes and blankets housed more people than should have been able to fit in the tight space.

Kane ignored all of it. He kept his back to a pillar and swept the area with his gaze until he spotted his confidential informant. Dougie Zimmerman sauntered over with his typical cocky attitude, hiking up pants that never seemed to stay above his bony hips. With what little hair he had on his head shaved close and a goatee hiding some of his pockmarked face, Dougie looked like he was more arrogance than real threat.

The truth was somewhere in between.

Dougie had dropped out of high school and started driving trucks full of illegal goods when he was seventeen. By the time he was nineteen, he'd done two short stints in jail, but hadn't turned on anyone. It had earned him trust among the criminal element and more illegal jobs. A year after that, he'd been caught again, this time with enough drugs to send him away for a long time.

Instead of going to jail, Kane's then-partner at the FBI had made the arrest disappear and turned Dougie into a confidential informant. That had been eight years ago. Since then, Dougie had become one of Kane's best CIs. Kane had helped disappear multiple drug possession charges, an illegal gun charge and even an armed robbery charge to keep Dougie on the streets. Because he always delivered more than the damage he caused.

Still, Dougie had become a CI to stay out of jail and for the way the thrill of double-crossing boosted his ego. At the end of the day, Dougie was still a criminal. And Kane was still FBI.

Although he kept his hands loose at his sides, Kane was ready to react if Dougie showed any sign of a double-cross. Kane had one of the quickest draws at TCD. He'd never had a meeting with a CI go sideways, but he'd had plenty of undercover operations turn bad, so he was always prepared. Usually with multiple weapons hidden on his body.

Only once had his preparedness not been enough. Back then, his partner had paid the ultimate price. Which was why Kane was standing beneath the underpass alone and hadn't even let Melinda know where he was going. If Pembrook was going to force him to work with Melinda, she could handle the parts of the investigation that involved reading case files in an air-conditioned office. He'd manage the rest.

"What have you got for me?" he asked Dougie, giving him a quick scan. But Dougie's ill-fitting clothes didn't leave a lot of good places to hide a weapon. Kane doubted he had backup of his own. Although the man had made contacts with a ton of Tennessee's criminal elements, he rarely liked to work with anyone long-term. As far as Kane could tell, their relationship was the longest one Dougie had ever had.

Dougie's head swiveled slowly left and right, looking more like a slow-motion dance move than a scan of his surroundings. Then he gave Kane a quick nod. "Word is that if you want guns on the down low, you can get some Petrov Armor pistols around here. I asked as much as I could without making people suspicious, but no one seemed to know exactly who the contact was. Least not anyone I know."

Kane frowned. Dougie knew everyone. Then again, if someone had been illegally selling Petrov Armor guns to criminals for more than a decade, they were good at hiding both the activity itself and their identity.

"What about recent sales?" Officially, the gun side of the business was shut down, but that didn't mean Petrov Armor didn't have excess weapons or that someone wasn't still secretly making them and selling them at a huge markup to criminals.

"I don't know how recent these sales are, but…" Dougie glanced around once more, then leaned closer and dropped his voice to a whisper. "Supposedly BECA has been buying up a lot of guns lately. Word is they've got a whole room full of Petrov Armor pistols."

Dougie's words sent an electric current along Kane's skin, the rush of a new lead that his gut said was real. The Brotherhood of an Ethnically Clean America—BECA for short—was a nasty zealot group that specialized in equal-opportunity hate. The FBI had been watching them ever since they'd popped onto the radar four years earlier, but so far, none of the attacks by members had been connected strongly enough back to the group to make a large-scale arrest.

"How do you feel about making an introduction?" Kane asked.

Dougie shook his head. "No way, man. Those guys are all crazy. I don't want to work with them."

"You don't have to. Just tell them I want to."

Dougie's lips twisted upward, making him look even more unattractive. "I don't have connections there, but I know a guy who does. He's the one who told me about the guns. I can get you in with him, but I'm gonna need some cash."

Usually Kane played up the fact that Dougie wasn't in jail to keep the man from asking for too much cash for information. It helped keep Dougie honest, prevented him from making things up for money. But today, he just nodded. "How fast can you do it?"

"Maybe tomorrow?" Dougie glanced around once more, then started walking away. "I'll call you."

Kane waited another few minutes before he left in the

opposite direction. Protocol said he was supposed to let his partner—for this case, Melinda—know about the information. But Melinda would fight him on his plan to get close to BECA. She'd argue that it was too dangerous. She'd want to do more legwork first. Or worse yet, she'd want to go with him.

Kane shuddered at the very idea of Melinda Larsen in the field. The idea of working beside her undercover sent deeper fear through him.

But something had to be done. They couldn't wait for Davis to find the perpetrator. Not when he was getting more attached to Leila Petrov with every minute he spent undercover. The fact that his connection to her was more than just physical had been apparent last night at the office when he'd talked about her with admiration and empathy and an unwillingness to put her on the suspect list.

Davis was a nice guy. He was formidable in close-quarters battle or a firefight, and Kane would choose to have the guy next to him in most dangerous situations. But undercover? It wasn't his forte. He was too straitlaced military, too honest and straightforward. He didn't know how to inhabit a persona like a second skin.

And that was a mistake that could be fatal.

Chapter Seven

For what felt like the hundredth time today, Leila glanced at the closed door to her office. She'd barely spoken to Davis since he'd come in to work this morning. He'd offered to pick her up, but she'd risen early and taken a cab so she'd have an excuse to avoid him.

She couldn't believe she'd tried to kiss him yesterday. He hadn't said a word about it, but considering how fast he'd backed away, there was no need. Apparently, even though he'd been using flirtation and attraction to get information for his investigation, she'd crossed the line with him by acting on those feelings.

She should be glad he hadn't let it get that far. She'd been overemotional, looking for comfort in the wrong way. If he *had* let her kiss him, she probably would have been even more embarrassed today. Yet, a part of her wished she'd still been able to press herself against that broad chest and lose herself in his kisses. For even half an hour, to take a break from the reality that her dad was gone and her company—the biggest part of her dad she had left—was in serious trouble.

Closing her eyes against the rush of tears threatening, Leila focused on taking deep breaths in and out until she got control of her grief. When she opened them again, Davis was standing in the doorway, quietly closing the door behind him.

Just her luck that he'd seen her break down. She forced a smile, hoping to mask her sadness. "How did you do with the security card log and the videos?"

That morning, she'd given him access to the computer program that tracked who had been in and out of which areas at which times. She'd also handed over all their internal and external security video footage. The internal footage was automatically erased every week unless it was tagged for saving, but they held on to their external video for months. Letting Davis access all of it had been her attempt at getting their mutual goal back on track.

He frowned at her, the expression on his face telling her he was going to ask if she was okay.

"Well?" She was finished getting personal with him. From this point forward, she needed to remember that they were unwilling partners in an investigation to uncover the truth about what had happened to those soldiers. That was it.

Even if they were working together, even if she respected his intelligence and investigative experience, ultimately, they were going to end up on opposite sides. Yes, right now, they wanted the same thing. But once they found the perpetrator, he was unlikely to care whether Petrov Armor went down with the culprits. She couldn't let that happen. Not only because of her dad, but also because of all the employees who counted on the company for their paychecks.

"I found something."

Her heart seemed to plummet to her stomach. Leila clamped her hands on her desk for stability as she got to her feet. "What did you find?" Or rather, who? Who had been betraying her father, the company and their country?

Who at Petrov Armor didn't care if soldiers died thinking they were protected by body armor?

"Nothing on the external video. Not really, anyway."

Davis stepped around to the back of her desk. She could smell his morning-fresh scent and feel the brush of his arm as he shifted her laptop toward him.

He leaned past her, typing away as he said, "I don't know exactly when to look, so it's a little tough to sort through all that raw footage. But you do have some gaps. I don't know if it's a system error or someone erased footage. What I didn't find was anything obviously suspicious, like a truck being loaded with crates at night."

"Well, I still think someone could have swapped out that armor after it left our facility," Leila said, peering around him to see what he was doing on the laptop.

His fingers stalled and his whole body went unnaturally still. It couldn't have been more than a few seconds before he was straightening and shrugging, but Leila's mouth went dry. There was something he wasn't telling her.

Before she could figure out what, he spun the laptop toward her. "This is a bit more interesting."

Leila peered closer, recognizing their security card access logs. Every time someone used their security card to key into the building or any of the secure areas, the system logged it.

"Theresa Quinn was here late at night during the time you said that shipment of armor was being made."

Leila sighed. "That's not really a smoking gun, Davis. Theresa lives for the work. She's here on weekends sometimes."

"But these super-late-night visits don't seem to happen except during this time period."

Leaning in again, Leila scrolled through the dates in question, realizing he was right. "It still might not mean anything."

She and Theresa had never gotten along. Maybe it was because the head of Research and Development had been part of Petrov Armor since Leila was a kid. Although her father had never told her about it, Leila had overheard Theresa arguing with him about recommending the board put Leila in charge. Theresa hadn't seemed to want the CEO spot for herself, just thought Leila hadn't earned it and wasn't capable of running the company.

But Theresa was a professional. Once Leila had been given the job anyway, Leila had never heard a word about it from her head of R and D. They might not like each other personally, but it had never gotten in the way of work. Leila couldn't imagine Theresa betraying the company she'd spent the last twenty years helping to build. Not even if that company was handed over to someone she'd called "the person who's going to destroy Petrov Armor."

"You and Theresa don't get along," Davis said.

"You noticed," Leila said dryly. "Look, I've known Theresa since I was ten years old. My uncle brought her in while my dad wasn't functioning after losing my mom. But when he got back to work, Dad said finding Theresa was one of the best things his brother had done. She can be prickly, but she wouldn't betray this company. She helped make it what it is today."

"So, how did she feel about you shutting down the firearm side of the business?"

Thrown by the topic change, Leila sank into her chair, wheeling it away from her desk to put a little space between them. "She wasn't happy about it. Honestly, no one at the top was. But I'd been thinking about it for a long time. I didn't do it right away, but last year, the timing seemed right. The ultralight body armor the military had been testing was a big success, and they finally started ordering in massive quantities. It was time to stop splitting our focus, and armor seemed like the way to go."

"That's why you did it?" Davis pressed.

"Mostly, yeah. But on the weapon side, we just made pistols. Honestly, I've just always been more comfortable selling to the military. Protecting soldiers by providing them with solid armor seemed like the best way to spend our company's resources. Plus our armor was profitable. It seemed right, since it was where my dad started the business anyway."

"So that was it? What about the excess?"

Leila shrugged. "Most of the excess was destroyed. Yes, we lost money at first, but we got the board of directors to wait out the slump, so we could move our focus completely to armor." She stared up at him, captivated by the intensity that was always on his face, even when he was giving her one of his slow, cocky grins. "Why do you want to know about the shift in our business plan?"

"I'm just surprised, that's all. Your dad was really okay with it? He spent a long time building up weapons sales."

"Then he and the board entrusted the future of the business to me. It wasn't what he would have done. My dad and I didn't always agree, but he always supported me. He knew I was already in an uphill battle with the employees over being named CEO." She frowned down at her lap. "I think he knew if he didn't support me on this, my leadership would be in trouble."

"He was a good dad," Davis said, but Leila wasn't sure if it was a statement or a question.

"Yes," she stressed, standing up and facing him. "He was the best."

She could practically see his mind working, going over what she'd said about her uncle looking after her when her dad had checked out after her mom died. But it had been a long time ago. Her dad had grown up with parents who'd abused him. It had been just him and Uncle Joel for so long, only counting on each other. He'd once told her that when he'd met her mom overseas when he'd been there on business, a single glance from her had changed the entire trajectory of his life. Leila knew it was the fanciful memory of a man who'd loved his wife deeply and then lost her too young, but the idea always made her smile.

"Yeah, my dad took a while to get over losing his wife. That's pretty normal, I think. Especially when you have no one to lean on besides your brother—who's busy running your company and watching your ten-year-old daughter."

Davis didn't say anything, but she could tell he wanted to, probably about her own care in that time.

"Anyway, once he dealt with his grief, you couldn't ask for a more involved father." She smiled at the sudden memory of the first day she'd brought Eric home to meet her dad. When she'd met Eric, she'd been thirteen and just seen him as a friend, nothing more. But her dad had probably seen that Eric—two years older—had a deeper interest.

"What's so funny?" Davis asked.

"If my dad had met you, he wouldn't let you out of his sight for a second."

Davis frowned, maybe thinking she'd meant because her dad would have known Davis was undercover.

She used a lighthearted tone, intending to be playful, make a joke out of their mutual attraction and this impossible situation. "Not for the investigation, although he probably would have figured that out. But he would have watched you closely for another reason entirely." She raised her eyebrows, waiting for him to catch on.

Finally a smile stretched his lips, starting slow like it always did. With it came a gleam in his eyes. "Is that right?"

She swallowed, resisting the sudden urge to lick her lips. She'd meant it as a joke. She'd let her serious CEO persona slip with him yet again, and oddly, it didn't feel strange. She was actually more comfortable being herself around Davis than she'd been with anyone in a long time.

Spinning away from him, she tried to get her guard back up. It made no sense to feel this normal around Davis. Not so soon after her dad had died and not considering who Davis was, why he was here.

At the end of this investigation, he'd be leaving. And he might try to take down Petrov Armor when he did it.

No matter how he made her feel, she couldn't let him in. Couldn't let him destroy the one thing she had left.

"ANY NEWS?" DAVIS asked Melinda. He'd retreated to the privacy of his SUV in Petrov Armor's parking lot to talk to her without being overheard. He felt a little ridiculous sitting in his vehicle while the sun baked him through the windows. But he couldn't take his jacket off without the possibility of his gun showing. He didn't want Leila—or anyone else—to overhear his discussion with Melinda.

"Kane is off on some meeting." Impatience crackled in her words as Melinda added, "He's been gone for a while."

"How's that going, working with Kane Bradshaw?" Davis couldn't help asking. He'd liked Melinda from the minute he'd met her. She was smart and always willing to lend her psychological expertise on a case. She was also quiet and a bit of a loner, but Davis didn't mind that. She'd gone out with the team for drinks a time or two. Although she kept her personal life to herself, she'd been friendly.

Kane, on the other hand, managed to be both a charmer and antisocial. The fact that he'd once been partnered with Pembrook's daughter—had actually been undercover with her when she'd been killed—was common knowledge. But what exactly had happened, no one seemed to know. His MO was to avoid the team as much as possible while running his own operations. Davis still wasn't sure why Pembrook let him get away with it, although it was hard to argue that the guy got results.

"Fine."

Her short answer was obviously a lie, but she couldn't see his amusement, so Davis didn't bother hiding his grin. It served him right that Eric Ross chose that moment to stride through the lot, probably returning from a sales call. He gave Davis a quizzical look, then kept going, disappearing inside the building.

Davis felt a visceral dislike toward Eric, but he tried to quell it because Eric hadn't actually done anything to deserve it, besides once date Leila.

Focusing back on Melinda, Davis told her what he'd learned that put some questions in his mind about Neal Petrov. "So, according to Leila, her dad supported her when she wanted to stop the gun side of the business. She says his support allowed her to do it without massive pushback from her employees or a flat-out refusal from the board."

"Well, that's interesting," Melinda replied. "You think she's telling the truth?"

"Why would she lie?" Before Melinda could answer, he continued, "I realize that she wouldn't want to implicate her dad, whether or not he was involved, but she still thinks this is just about defective armor. I almost blew it just now when I was talking to her about what I found on her security logs, though."

Thank goodness he'd caught himself before he'd started talking about trying to track down anomalies throughout the years. She'd definitely caught on that he was holding something back, but he was pretty sure she didn't know what.

It was a rookie mistake. Although he was a rookie at un-

dercover work, he definitely wasn't when it came to "need
to know." Most of his missions with the rangers had been
highly classified. He'd had no problem keeping everything
about them secret. But something about Leila made him
speak without thinking.

"She probably wouldn't lie," Melinda agreed, bringing
him back on track. "But maybe her father figured he didn't
need to get into a fight with her over it if the rest of the
company would do it for him. Push back on dropping the
gun sales, that is. Or maybe he'd already planned to move
over to making money illegally off of the armor and didn't
need the gun sales."

"Really? I know we're talking about dealing with criminals, but in some ways selling guns illegally seems safer.
At least that way, he wasn't risking a major incident with
the military and a large-scale investigation. Not to mention the bad publicity."

"Well, we also don't know how many people are involved," Melinda said. "Maybe he planned to keep making guns and just hide it from Leila. Or they had enough
excess that he figured he could just sell those for a while."

"Leila said the excess was mostly destroyed."

"Maybe that's just what her dad told her and she believed him. For all we know, he just moved the excess and
continued to sell it."

Davis stared at the entrance to Petrov Armor. It was a
huge facility, representing almost three decades of work,
most of it with Neal Petrov at the helm. The FBI hadn't requested Neal's personal finances, but Davis was willing
to bet he'd made millions legally. In Davis's cases, he'd
seen plenty of greed that didn't make any sense to him,
people who had more money than they should ever need
who still wanted more. He'd come across plenty of people
who framed spouses, children or friends for their crimes.

Even though Kane had described Neal Petrov as heart-less, Leila spoke of him with such love. Could she just not see his faults because she adored him? Was he that good a liar? Or was the truth something more complex?

"What are you thinking, Davis?" Melinda asked, making him realize how long he'd gone silent.

He was thinking that he felt guilty for not telling Leila that he suspected her dad had been involved in killing the soldiers. That he felt worse for not telling her that her dad might have been murdered over it.

Instead of admitting to Melinda how complicated his feelings were becoming when it came to the woman he was supposed to be using to get information on the case, he sighed. "I'm wondering if her dad saw how much Leila wanted to stop selling guns and focus on the armor. I'm wondering if he supported her because he loved her."

"You think he loved her enough to sacrifice a more than ten-year-long criminal business that was probably netting him millions on top of his legal income? It doesn't seem likely, but no matter how much you break down people's motivations and the things that form them, they surprise me all the time. Love is a pretty powerful motive."

"What if he wanted to quit the illegal business altogether for her?" The idea gained traction in Davis's mind. If anyone was worth giving up millions of dollars and changing your way of life for, wouldn't it be someone like Leila Petrov? A strong, determined leader who refused to suspect anyone she trusted of wrongdoing? Who had a goofy side she tried to hide so people wouldn't stop taking her seriously? He'd laughed more than once at her silly jokes, had caught her humming popular tunes while working, and seen her bopping along to music as soon as she got into her car to head home at the end of the day.

Yet she was serious when it came to her responsibility

to the company and her employees. She held strong morals about investigating the business she ran—risking her own livelihood—to do what was right.

"So, he supported her in shutting down the gun side of the business," Melinda said. "Maybe that was his attempt at taking the company legal again. Maybe he wasn't setting her up to take a fall if things went south. Maybe he was trying to get rid of that threat for her."

"Then what happened with this armor?" Davis asked. "Could it have really been an accident?"

"I doubt it." Melinda echoed his thoughts. "What if it was Neal's partner, trying to undermine the armor side of the business? Bring the guns back?"

"It's possible," Davis said. "But that's quite a risk, purposely drawing all that attention to Petrov Armor."

"Or maybe Neal Petrov saw a new opportunity to make money off the books by using cheap armor material, and he couldn't help himself. Ten years is a long time to be involved with criminals and then just quit. It's not always just about money," Melinda reminded him. "It's also a thrill for some people."

That felt right to Davis. It even opened up a new motivation for Neal's death. "What if his partner was unhappy with the change?" Davis suggested. "Theresa—or whoever he was working with—thought he'd come around and start selling guns again. When he switched to armor, maybe she had a problem with it."

"That could be," Melinda agreed. "Selling guns to criminals is one thing. Purposely sending armor to soldiers that was defective is another. Maybe Neal's partner was afraid it was too risky. Or maybe she just drew a moral line in the sand."

"Hell of a moral line," Davis said. "I think maybe she killed him over it."

Chapter Eight

Had Theresa Quinn—or someone else at Petrov Armor—really murdered Neal Petrov?

Davis glanced at Leila from the spot where he'd taken up residence in the corner of her office. He'd managed to avoid her for the rest of the day yesterday, but when he'd come in today, he knew he couldn't do it any longer. He needed the kind of access only she could give him.

To her credit, when he'd asked to see the company's financial records, she'd frowned but given him access. He'd been reading through them ever since. The problem was, if Petrov Armor's finances had been doctored, whoever was responsible would try to make things look legitimate. Davis might have to bring in some forensic accountants to drill down to the truth.

According to Leila, Theresa Quinn didn't have access to these records. So, if Theresa was still trying to sell weapons to criminals or pass off faulty body armor to the military, maybe something wouldn't look right in the financial records in the weeks since Neal Petrov had been killed. Of course, that was assuming he'd still had access to the finances and she'd just dealt with the production and delivery end of things.

Even if nothing looked off in the past month, maybe Neal himself would have made an error along the way.

Presumably, he'd gotten away with making illegal weapons sales for so long, he was skilled at hiding all evidence. But sometimes people who got away with something for that long started making mistakes. If Theresa wasn't involved, maybe Neal had gotten sloppy and someone else had noticed a discrepancy. Maybe they'd tried to blackmail Neal and when he hadn't paid up, they'd killed him.

Right now, everything was conjecture. Davis sighed and stretched his legs underneath the desk Leila had set up for him on the far side of her office.

For what felt like the millionth time since he'd arrived that morning, Davis glanced up at Leila. Her office smelled faintly of citrus, the same scent he'd noticed when she'd been brought into the TCD office. The same scent he noticed every time he stood close to her. He was starting to have a real fondness for citrus.

Since he'd met her three days ago, he'd only seen her wearing pant suits in shades of gray, black and dark blue. Her makeup was always subtle, her hair constantly knotted up into a bun. It was as if she dressed as straitlaced as possible to try to hide her youth and beauty. But there was only so much she could disguise. Today was no different.

Still, ever since she'd made that ridiculous joke about an inflatable boat, he'd been imagining her differently. Wearing jeans and a button-down that was too big for her, with her hair long and loose around her shoulders. Instead of her standard too-serious expression, she'd be laughing.

Except right now, she had nothing to laugh about. If he was right about her father's murder, things were only going to get worse.

He didn't even know if it was true or just a far-fetched theory and yet, he felt guilty not telling her.

"What?" Leila asked, a half smile lifting the corners of lips that had been so close to his just the other day.

"I didn't say anything."

"You didn't have to. You keep staring." She came around from behind her desk, striding across the room and stopping in front of him. "What is it? What did you find?"

Davis glanced down at his laptop screen again, not wanting to look her in the eyes as he said, "I haven't found anything. I'm just looking for discrepancies."

"Because the armor used cheaper materials? You think there will be a double entry for supplies somewhere?"

"Maybe," he hedged. He'd worked in white collar crime long enough to know that someone who'd been cooking the books for a decade was unlikely to make such an amateur mistake. But TCD expected him to keep the fact that Petrov Armor might have been illegally selling weapons from Leila. He closed the lid of his laptop, not wanting her to see the dates he was reviewing.

"Stop lying to me."

He finally looked up at her, surprised by the vehemence in her voice. "I'm not lying. I don't know what I'm going to find. Probably nothing. But if there's anything that doesn't seem right, it's a place to start."

"You don't know what you might find, but you're looking for something specific, aren't you?" Her eyes narrowed. "Or is there something else you're not telling me? You suspect someone besides Theresa? Don't tell me this is about Eric again."

"No, it's not about Eric." He wasn't Davis's top suspect at the moment, but that didn't mean he'd been eliminated. And since Leila had brought him up… "You said Eric and your dad were close. Was that true even after you and Eric broke up?" Realizing the time line, he answered his own question. "I guess so if he hired Eric then, right?"

"He hired Eric back when the two of us were still dating. Eric is two years older than me, so when he graduated from high school, my dad brought him on. He went to school to get his bachelor's degree at night. I was still in high school then. I didn't join the company until I finished grad school. I've only been here full-time for five years—I started a couple of years before my dad took the company public. By the time I joined the company, Eric had already been working here for nine years. But yes, my dad and Eric stayed close. Eric was the son my dad never had."

Davis squinted at her, trying to see through the mask she'd put over her features. Did she resent Eric's place in her dad's life? Did Eric resent the fact that Leila had come in only a few years ago and sailed into the CEO role, when Eric had been toiling away at the company for over a decade?

Leila let out a heavy, exaggerated sigh obviously meant for him to hear, and slapped her hands on her hips. "My dad was the father Eric never had, too, since his dad was out of the picture more often than he was in it. Believe me, Eric would never have betrayed my father. Never."

"Would he have betrayed you?" Davis asked.

She scowled down at him. "You honestly believe Eric would send out a faulty shipment of armor to hurt *me*? What for? It's been twelve years since he broke up with me. And I think the key words there are that *he* broke up with *me*, not the other way around. We're friends now. He's got one of the top positions in the company. If he wanted to bring me down by destroying the company, he'd be taking himself down with me. He's not that stupid. Or that self-destructive."

Davis nodded slowly. Her logic all made sense, and yet he couldn't stop picturing the expression on Eric's face when Leila had agreed to let Davis drive her home two days ago. No matter what Leila thought, that wasn't a man who had no romantic feelings for her.

Since talking about Eric had already put her on the defensive, Davis figured he'd get the rest of his unpleasant questions out now. "What about your uncle?"

Her hands fell off her hips as she shook her head. "Are you kidding me? You want to talk about the only person besides me who's more invested in this place than Eric? That's Uncle Joel. He gave up another career to help Dad keep this business going. He's been here ever since."

"Maybe he resents it," Davis suggested.

"I doubt it. He makes more money than he ever did before, and he sets his own hours. Dad gave him a lot of freedom, said it was only fair after everything he did for the company, for our family, after Mom died. I still do the same thing with his hours and the board doesn't care, as long as he gets the job done. He's less than ten years out from retirement—although, honestly, he could retire now if he felt like it. I think he's still here for me."

"Okay, but—"

"Davis, I get it. You don't know these people. This is nothing but another case for you. But this is my *life.* This is my *family* you're investigating."

She took a visible breath as Davis wondered whether she considered Eric part of her family.

"You're right that it looks like we've got someone rotten in our company, and I understand why you're starting at the top. But the truth is that none of the people you're asking about order the raw materials. None of them ship out the armor. We've got good security and good checks. You said it yourself. Obviously someone has found a way around them. But it's not my uncle. And it's not my ex. And honestly, even with the time stamps you found for Theresa's security card, I don't think it's her, either."

"Leila—"

"I understand that you have a job to do. Believe me, I

want to figure out who's doing this, so they can be prosecuted. But I need to keep the rest of the company intact in the meantime. When we figure out who did this, you'll be leaving and the guilty person will be arrested—rightfully so. But the rest of us are going to have to band together and push forward. I'm not letting this destroy the company my dad spent his life building. I'm not letting *you* destroy it."

"I'm not destroying anything," Davis snapped. "I'm not the one running a company and not knowing *fatally* defective products were being sent out."

Leila's shoulders dropped, the anger on her face shifting to a mix of guilt and pain.

He sucked in a breath, as a ball of dread filled his gut. He believed that the head of a company was responsible for what was happening inside of it, even if they didn't know anything about it and had no legal liability. But over the past three days, he'd found that Leila was a good, caring person. Seeing how his words had wounded her, he regretted them.

He regretted them even more when she said softly, steadily, "If you think I'm to blame for this, I'm not sure how you can trust me to work with you to find the truth. I'm not sure you should be here at all, Davis."

Dougie had come through.

Kane smiled at the text message on his FBI-issued phone. Dougie had gotten in touch with the lowlife who'd been telling him about guns and said a friend was interested in joining BECA. Apparently Dougie had sweetened the pot by also telling the guy that Kane might have a weapons connection of his own. That part was less ideal, but Kane could work with it.

"What are you smiling about?" There was suspicion in Melinda's question.

Kane tucked his phone away as he looked up at Melinda. "I've got a date tonight."

She blinked rapidly, telling him he'd surprised her, but her eyes narrowed just as fast. "Wasn't that your work phone you were looking at?"

He shrugged carelessly, glad he had a reputation as a rule-breaker. "Yeah, well, it's another agent."

Melinda continued to stare at him with narrowed eyes.

He was a great liar. He had to be, with all the under-cover work he'd done, or he would have been killed on the job a long time ago. But apparently Melinda was an even better profiler, because she always seemed to know when he wasn't being straight with her.

Instead of trying to outstare her, he changed the subject. "I did also hear back from my CI. He's got a friend who knows someone at BECA. That person might be able to get us some more details about BECA and their connection to Petrov Armor. I want to look a little closer at BECA, see if we can find anything in our files about a possible link."

"I've already been doing that," Melinda said, her atten-tion returning to her laptop. "The reason we've never been able to make anything stick with BECA is because it's such a loose network. We refer to them as a group, but the re-ality is they're not that formally organized. On purpose, I'm sure, to give each member plausible deniability if any single one gets caught."

"Which has happened plenty," Kane agreed. The group was most known for having connections to individuals who had set bombs in minority-owned businesses and even places of worship. Maybe because it was such a loosely knit group, the specific biases were different from place to place. Still, more than once, a perpetrator had mentioned that they'd learned how to make bombs from a connection at BECA. A few times, the FBI had tracked down the connection and made an arrest. But then any other local members of the network seemed to scatter.

As far as the FBI had ever found, BECA didn't keep any official books or lists of membership. Instead of connecting online like a lot of criminal organizations, they'd gone old-school and networked through word of mouth. In theory, that should have made the organization easier to penetrate. But besides being fanatics, BECA members also tended to be extremely paranoid of outsiders.

"You're thinking about trying to set up a meet with your CI's contact, the one who knows someone at BECA, aren't you?" Melinda asked.

When he refocused, he realized she was staring at him again.

"I don't think so. But if someone at Petrov Armor really is selling to BECA members, that might be how we get them."

"I don't believe you that you're not trying to set up a meet."

Melinda's words were straightforward, with no anger or frustration in her tone. Strangely, the lack of emotion made Kane feel even more guilty about lying to her. But in the end, he was doing her a favor.

"Well, believe what you want," he answered, glancing at his phone as it beeped with the notification of a new text. "Be right back."

He didn't give her a chance to argue, just slipped into the hallway where she couldn't try to read over his shoulder.

The text was from Dougie again. You're on, man. My connection says he can get you a meeting with someone from BECA. Told them exactly what you said I should. That I know you from my time in Vegas. Said you left because you were getting heat after some fires you set at businesses run by Asians and Middle Easterners. Also told them you want to buy some guns, but you've got a record. Claimed I didn't know why, but that your connection here had fallen through.

Kane smiled to himself. The bit about the fires in Vegas was something he'd given Dougie. It had really happened; it just hadn't been him. The person who'd really done it was six feet under, a casualty of a revenge plot gone wrong. Kane had come in too late to save the idiot—and put him in jail. Instead of releasing the truth about the fires, Kane had kept it under wraps, knowing one day he'd be able to use it. It had turned out to be perfect for this case. BECA was known for fostering that kind of random hate.

The bit about the weapons connection was Dougie's own improvisation, but Kane had worked with worse.

Great job, he texted back. When's the meet?

Tomorrow.

Friday. Kane nodded to himself. A weekend meet would have been better, would have made it harder for Melinda to try to track him there. But he wasn't about to complain. Getting a meet with BECA wasn't easy.

Perfect. Thanks, man.

Sliding his phone back in his pocket, Kane spun around to return to the conference room and nearly slammed into Melinda. "What the hell?"

"You setting up another date?" There was mocking in her tone.

"What if I am?"

"When's the meet?"

"There's no meet, Melinda." He tried to walk around her, but she shifted, blocking his way.

He raised an eyebrow. Yeah, she'd gone through the FBI Academy just like him, but he had seven inches and probably a good fifty pounds on her. Did she really think she could stop him from going somewhere?

Holding in his annoyance, he turned and walked off in the other direction. A meet with a dangerous group of zealots could far too easily go sideways. One thing Melinda needed to learn about him was that when it came to undercover work, he liked to go alone. No backup. No net. It was better for everyone that way.

"We're supposed to be partners," she called after him, frustration in her tone, but less than he'd expected.

Kane gritted his teeth, keeping his response inside. Images of Pembrook's daughter's broken body when he'd finally reached her during that mission gone wrong filled his head, the way they did every night in his sleep.

He was never going to have a partner again, least of all Melinda Larsen.

Chapter Nine

Davis blamed her for everything that had happened. Blamed her for the deaths of all those soldiers.

The knowledge made her chest hurt, made each breath laborious. Because the truth was, she blamed herself, too.

How had she not seen that someone was willing to betray the company, and missed all the signs that bad armor was being produced? And for what? More profit? They were doing fine. Sales were increasing. They were looking at expanding their markets. Why would someone go to such lengths for higher numbers on their bottom line? No, someone had to be pocketing that extra cash for their own benefit, using her company to enhance their personal finances.

It shouldn't have been possible to get faulty armor out the door. Not with the security and checks in place. Her father had managed the company for twenty-nine years without a single incident. She'd been doing it without him for three weeks and there'd been a huge tragedy.

She hadn't changed anything, but had her lack of focus during her time of grief allowed this to happen? The armor wasn't made overnight. Someone had come up with this plan, introduced the cheaper materials, gotten them past testing and shipped the defective armor. At least some of that must have happened while her father was still here. But probably not all of it. Had she missed something she should have caught? Been so preoccupied trying to prove that she was worthy of being CEO even after her father's death that she'd missed what really mattered?

Leila stared at the loading area at the back of their facility where they packed boxes of armor into trucks that delivered them to military installations. It was empty now, with no new deliveries scheduled until next week.

Even those were unlikely to go out. Her employees didn't know it yet, but unless they found out who was responsible fast, she doubted the military would want this shipment—or any other. The fact was, even if they did resolve it, the incident could be the end of her company. The end of everything her dad had worked for.

Focus, Leila reminded herself, looking around. The loading area was hidden from the road, but visible from some of the windows at the back of the building, where they kept supplies. It was a quiet area. Not many people were there on any given day, but it didn't mean someone couldn't be. If someone had loaded defective products after hours to avoid detection, how would that work? Drivers wouldn't have a way to order cheaper materials to replace the good armor, and the people who loaded the trucks didn't have access to secure areas.

Theresa's research and development rooms were back here, too. There were no windows in Theresa's dedicated development space, but she was always wandering around; she claimed that pacing made her more creative. She often worked late. So, planning to have a truck come after hours on a certain day was dicey, too. Unless Theresa was involved.

Normally someone in a management position signed off on shipments. So, someone must have signed off on either the defective armor or good armor that had later been swapped. But if it had been swapped out, why? Was someone after the good armor rather than the money?

She pondered that for a few minutes. It didn't seem likely, but she couldn't rule it out. Maybe whoever had signed off on the defective armor was working with someone in shipping.

The potential lead gave her energy, lifted some of the anxiety pressing on her chest. She swiped her security card to go back inside and slipped into the empty testing room. Then she pulled up the shipment log from the computer there. The date was the first thing that surprised her. The armor hadn't gone out after her dad had died, when she was lost in her grief and had possibly made unforgiveable errors. It had happened before.

But it was the name in the log that made her sink back into the chair Theresa usually used.

Her father's name was beside the shipment.

Technically, as their primary consultant, he could still do that. But he rarely did, usually preferring to leave it to one of their management team.

Had he done a sloppy job of inspecting the armor? Or had the fakes been good enough to pass inspection? They'd certainly looked right in the photo Davis had shown her. Leila knew her company's products well enough to spot even small imperfections. Someone had done a good job of making them look legit.

Leila leaned close to the screen, scrutinizing the electronic copy of the signature. Could it have been faked? Her dad's signature was sloppy, probably easy to duplicate. It was impossible to know for sure.

"What's going on, honey?"

Leila spun in her chair at her uncle's voice. He was frowning at her with concern.

"You look upset. And we don't have any shipments going

out for a week." He glanced around, then added, "I know you're not back here to shoot the breeze with Theresa. So what's going on?"

Had Theresa really betrayed them? The idea left a sour taste in the back of her mouth, but it just felt wrong. Theresa was protective of the company, proud to the point of braggadocio of the armor she helped develop, rightfully so. The latest incarnation had been tested by army rangers in real battle conditions before the military had begun ordering them in bulk. They'd stood up to everything the Special Operations soldiers encountered, which was no small feat.

Theresa was unmarried, had no kids. She spoke occasionally of an older sister and a nephew, and every so often of a man she was seeing, something that had been on-again, off-again for years. But the latter always seemed more casual than a real relationship. Her life was the company. Even if Theresa was in the most likely position to betray it, Leila just couldn't imagine her doing so.

But if she had, why now? If it was anger over Leila being given the CEO position, Theresa had had a full year to take action. Or she could have quit and used her talents elsewhere. That would have been the easiest path if she was unhappy. Instead, she'd stayed, continued to innovate for Petrov Armor. Leila had continued to give her well-deserved raises.

"Leila?" her uncle Joel asked, stepping closer and putting his hand on her arm.

She blinked his face into focus and felt a bittersweet smile form. He looked so much like her dad.

She wasn't supposed to tell anyone what was really going on. It was part of her agreement with Davis. But it wasn't as if he was holding up his end of the bargain and keeping her in the loop. And her uncle was the last person who'd ever betray her father's legacy.

"Uncle Joel, there's something—"

"Leila."

Davis's voice, firm and laced with anger, startled her. She glanced toward the long hallway that led from the main part of the office and there he was, arms crossed over his chest and a scowl on his face.

When her uncle followed her gaze, Davis's expression shifted into something more neutral. "I found those numbers you wanted."

Her uncle looked back at her, and Leila tried not to let her smile falter. "Never mind, Uncle Joel. It's nothing."

His hand didn't leave her arm. "Are you sure?"

"Yeah." She turned and followed Davis back toward her office, fully aware that her uncle didn't believe her.

Even worse, Davis had clearly realized what she had been about to do. If he'd been lying to her before, what were the chances he'd give her any real information ever again?

LEILA PETROV HAD almost blown his entire investigation.

Davis tried to hold back his fury as Leila followed him into her office and shut the door behind her. As soon as it was closed, he whirled around to face her, ready to lecture her about all the reasons she should want to keep his secret. Not the least of which was keeping her out of jail.

Right before he blurted that out, he got control of his anger. Admonishing Leila wasn't going to help. He'd already lost his cool with her earlier, blaming her for what had happened. That was probably what had made her seek out her uncle in the first place. If he compounded it now, he was the one who was going to blow the investigation. Along with it, he'd blow his chance to prove himself at TCD, and his chance to get justice for Jessica.

He took a few deep, measured breaths the way he used

to do right before leaving on a ranger mission. His body recognized the cue and his heart rate slowed immediately.

"So, you found something in the ledger?" Leila asked.

Her chin was tipped up, her jaw tight, her gaze defying him to call her on what he'd overheard. On what he knew she'd been about to do.

"No. I said that to get you out of there. This is a *secret* investigation, Leila. The FBI could have sent anyone undercover here. Maybe they should have sent someone you wouldn't have recognized, someone who could dig into the company without sharing a thing with you."

Standing so close to her, he actually heard her nervous swallow, saw her blink rapidly a few times.

Good. She should be nervous.

"We didn't try to hide what we were doing from you. TCD chose to bring me in because we believed you were innocent. We believed you'd help us find the truth for those soldiers who were killed."

"You believed—" she started.

He cut her off before she could scoff at his statement about her innocence. He didn't want to get into the technicalities with her. He *did* believe she'd had nothing to do with the faulty armor and the illegal guns. But he also believed that was no excuse not to know what was happening in the company she ran.

"I understand that you trust your uncle, but then maybe he tells someone *he* trusts and that person does the same. Faster than you think, our chance to catch this person— and potentially save your company—is gone."

Leila blew out a loud breath. The proud, angry tilt to her chin was gone. So was the defiant look in her eyes, replaced by wariness and something else.

It took him longer than it should have to realize the other thing he saw was guilt.

He'd put that there. The thought made him hate himself and his job just a little. It was easy to believe that someone who ran a company should know everything that happened in it, take responsibility for all of it. It was another to see someone as honest and diligent as Leila suffer because she hadn't caught a criminal inside her organization.

Should she have really been able to do that? Or was that his job?

The unexpected thought deflated the last of his anger.

"Look, I'm sorry about what I said earlier. I was out of line." Davis wasn't entirely sure what he believed right now, but one thing he knew: Leila would never intentionally let anyone get hurt. "I knew one of the soldiers."

Leila's lips formed a small O and she blinked again, this time as moisture filled her eyes.

"She was a friend of mine," Davis continued, not sure why he was sharing this with Leila, but suddenly wanting her to know. "Jessica Carpenter. She was the one running that video footage, probably for training purposes. She was a single mom of three. Those little kids are all alone in the world now. Jessica was a great person. Strong, smart, willing to put up with all the crap that comes along with being a woman in a powerful role where too many men think it should only be for them."

He paused, realizing Leila fit that description, too.

Shaking the thought away, he continued. "I'm here right now for Jessica. Whatever it takes, I need to get the truth. No matter who you think you can trust with inside information about our investigation, if I think you're going to tell someone who I really am, that's it. I'm out and the FBI is coming in with warrants to take this place apart."

Leila stared back at him with a mixture of horror, sadness and anger, and he realized that just as he'd gotten her trust back, he'd ruined it again with a threat. Why couldn't he find the right balance with her? Why couldn't he be like Kane Bradshaw, step into whatever persona would get the job done, and to hell with real honesty? To hell with anyone's feelings?

"I don't—"

He wasn't sure what she was about to say, but he didn't let her finish the thought. There was only one way to remedy the mess he'd made of his connection with Leila. That was to be more honest with her, so she'd think she could trust him. So she wouldn't feel like she needed to go to someone else for advice.

"Your dad…" He'd planned to tell her that someone connected to the defective armor had killed her father, but what if he was wrong? What if it *was* just a botched mugging and he gave her extra grief over nothing?

"What?" Leila asked, anxiety in her voice that told him she'd recognized he was about to say something serious.

"What I was going to say is that the defective armor isn't the only problem right now. Even when your dad was CEO, there was something illegal happening."

"What?" Leila's voice dropped to a whisper. She shifted her feet, widening her stance like she was preparing for a physical blow.

"Someone at Petrov Armor has been selling guns to criminals for a long time."

Chapter Ten

The old construction site where Dougie's BECA connection had wanted to meet was the kind of place where you shot someone and left their body to be found weeks or months later.

Adding to the ominous vibe was the sun setting, casting eerie shadows everywhere. Kane leaned casually against a half-standing wall, not putting any real weight on it in case only gravity was keeping it upright. Dougie's connection was picking his way through the abandoned pieces of building, thinking he was being stealthy. Playing along as if he hadn't spotted the guy—or his armed backup—Kane made a show of checking his watch and frowning.

It was almost twenty minutes past the scheduled meet time. Kane had been watched from the moment he'd parked his car off the side of the road and picked his way by foot down to the construction site. It was a smart spot for a meet, deserted and easy to watch all possible access points. It was the kind of place a smart agent wouldn't come alone.

As his contact finally showed himself, Kane offered a cocky grin. He'd been in worse spots dozens of times. If he had to rely on his own ability to spin a good story or someone else to keep him safe and stay out of trouble themselves, he'd choose to go in alone every time. It was probably why he was still alive.

"Guess you're Kane Bullet, huh?" the guy asked, looking him over. "What kind of name is that?"

Kane kept his irreverent grin in place, didn't step forward to greet the guy. "The kind I gave myself."

The man laughed. He was blond and blue-eyed, wearing tattered jeans and a T-shirt that read Armed and Dangerous on the front. With his overmuscular build, the guy's loose clothes still didn't hide that at least the first part of that statement was true. The bulge of a holster was clearly visible at his hip.

"So, Dougie says you had some trouble in Vegas, wanted to start over in Tennessee?"

"Yeah." Kane shrugged, stepped slightly away from the half-standing wall. He kept his hands loose at his sides, not wanting to give the guy—or his backup—any reason to get twitchy.

"I looked up those fires. Nasty business."

Kane spewed the kind of offhand hate he knew the BECA member would eat up. "If they didn't want to get burned out, they should have left on their own."

The guy laughed again, a grating sound that would have made Kane grit his teeth hard if he weren't in character. Right now, he wasn't Kane Bradshaw. That person was buried deep, beneath a layer of filth he called Kane Bullet.

So, instead he let his grin shift into something nastier, filled with determination and fury. "There was more I wanted to do in Vegas, but you know, I can't be useful if I'm locked up. So, I skipped town before they got too close."

The guy's humor dried up. "Your friend said it was a close call." His eyes narrowed, as if he was trying to read from Kane's expression whether the cops were tracking him down as they spoke.

Kane rolled his eyes. "Yeah, right. The way those pigs like to brag, don't you think it would have been all over the papers if they had a real lead? Instead, nothing but 'we're still investigating' and 'we won't stop looking' BS. I knew it was time to get out, but I did it before they could get a lead on me. Don't worry, man. I wouldn't bring my heat on you. I'm looking to make friends, not enemies."

The man visibly relaxed. "Well, that's good, because we deal with betrayal real quick."

"Not a problem. What do I have to betray, anyway? All I'm looking for is a hookup. Maybe Dougie told you, but I'd gotten a gun connection out here and it dried up." He scowled again, then took a risk. "Had myself a potential in with Petrov Armor, but ever since that idiot CEO shut down the legal side of their gun business, apparently things have been a little dry on the not-so-legal side of it, too."

The guy stiffened fast, then seemed to forcibly pull his shoulders away from his ears. He cracked his neck in both directions, then gave a tight smile. "Really?"

The hairs on the back of Kane's neck popped up, telling him he'd made a mistake. But what? Had they been wrong and Leila was actually involved? Even though Davis's judgment was clearly trashed when it came to her, Kane didn't think he was wrong about this. Had the intel about the BECA connection been bad? If so, this was a waste of time. Maybe not for the FBI, for future information, but for him with this case.

The guy reached into his pocket and Kane tensed, but when he pulled his hand out, he was holding a phone. He typed something, then tucked it away again. "Who was that contact?"

Kane tried to backtrack without raising suspicion. "Look, maybe my contact was screwing with me from the start. But I'm no rat. I can't give up his name, you know? But it sounds like he was more talk than action. I just don't know people in Tennessee the way I did in Vegas. That's why I looked up Dougie."

The guy nodded, but his eyes were still narrowed, his tone slightly off. "Hard to trust people you don't know, right?"

Kane pretended not to catch the double meaning. "Guess not. But I've heard enough about BECA to know I can trust you. Hopefully, you've seen enough of my work to know we're on the same side."

Finally the guy seemed to relax again. "So what new work are you planning? Guns are a long way from fire-setting."

Kane made his tone hard and serious. "Same goal, different method. Plus cops got too good at connecting my fires in Vegas. I figured it was time to switch things up."

"I hear you. Gotta keep 'em on their toes, right?" The guy stared for a minute, and when Kane didn't break eye contact, he finally smiled. "I think we can help you out."

"Honey!"

The too-high-pitched, feminine voice made Kane's gut clench, filling him with fear he hadn't felt in a long time. When he turned around, already knowing who it was, his eyes felt like they were going to bug right out of his head.

Melinda was picking her way through the demolition mess in a pair of heels that were dangerously high, wearing a tiny dress so skintight that no one would ever consider she could be hiding a weapon.

A million swear words lodged in his brain as she reached his side and looped an arm through his.

"I got so worried about you," she whined, her expression more vapid than he would have ever imagined too-smart Melinda could have pulled off. Maybe it was the makeup she'd plastered all over her face, disguising her natural beauty.

She was playing a role the FBI had given its female agents for decades, that of clingy, jealous girlfriend. It worked especially well in Mob cases, where the targets didn't let females into their ranks, but commonly offered prostitutes to new recruits. Saying no meant losing trust. Unless you had a girlfriend by your side. The added bonus was that particular jealous woman would be an undercover federal agent trained in close-quarters combat.

But in this case, it was the exact wrong move.

Even before he turned back to face his contact, he knew the guy had pulled his gun.

Melinda let out a giggle. "Hey, chill. I'm just checking on my man. I track his phone." She stroked his arm, making his muscles jump with anxiety.

The contact gave Melinda a quick once-over, then settled his hard gaze on Kane. "You hate Asians so much, you burn them out of their businesses, but then you date one?"

He felt Melinda's fingers spasm on his arm as she realized what she'd done.

He'd purposely misled her, focused on how Dougie's connection only knew someone at BECA, not that he could get Kane a meeting with an actual member. She probably thought she was busting in on a meet that was solely about weapons, not truly connected to the racist hate spewed by BECA.

The guy lifted his gun and aimed it at Kane's forehead. "You know what? You try to fool me?" He smiled and shifted the weapon to point at Melinda. "You can watch her die before I kill you."

"SOMEONE AT PETROV ARMOR has been selling guns to criminals for a long time."

Davis's words haunted Leila as she strode away from the office as fast as she could. Her low heels made a satisfying *click* with every step, giving her something to focus on, to keep her from screaming in denial or frustration.

Who had they inadvertently let into their company who'd used it for their own gain? Who'd gone against the very reason her dad had formed the company in the first place? To protect soldiers. Not to aid killing.

The feeling of anger and betrayal built up until it felt like a ball of lead in her chest and she kept walking, trying to get control of her emotions. She veered away from the route that would take her toward town, toward people who might see her or even worse, try to talk to her.

It was already dusk, the time when Old City started shifting from window-shopping tourists to evening bar-hoppers. But the other direction was quiet, peaceful. Filled with old trees and a beautiful, fast-moving river. A good place to think about all the things she'd done wrong. All the things she could never undo.

She'd left Davis with a barely coherent excuse about needing to use the ladies' room. He probably thought she was still in there, trying to get herself together. But what she'd really needed was to get out. To get away from everyone and everything.

In the past three weeks, the only times she'd been alone was at night, at home after work. Time she spent hoping to sleep, but instead all she could do was try not to weep in grief or anger over her father's death. During the day, she'd surrounded herself with the business, with reassuring the people who worked for her, with trying to keep it all going, make everyone believe she was still capable.

And what for? The whole time, someone had been betraying her. It was far worse than a single batch of defective armor, a single tragedy. For all she knew, guns made at Petrov Armor and purposely put in the hands of criminals had caused hundreds or thousands of tragedies over the years.

She was responsible. Her father, too. Neither of them had seen it. Neither of them had even *suspected* something that terrible had been happening.

How had it happened?

Her pace slowed until she was standing still on the center of a walking bridge. She stared out over the murky water, stepping close to the edge. There was only a low railing that looked like it should have been replaced years ago. It would be easy to just step off and let that fast-moving water take away all her troubles.

Except she wasn't that person anymore. It was still her company, still her responsibility. She wasn't going to walk away from it, even if it destroyed her. Even if it destroyed her father's legacy.

She was going to help Davis find the person responsible. She was going to make sure they paid for it.

Davis hadn't told her how long the illegal gun sales had been going on exactly, but it was more than five years, if it had been happening during her dad's time as CEO, too. Gun manufacturing had always been a separate part of the business from body armor. Yes, there was a certain overlap, but very few lower-level employees would have had access to both sides of the business. And the number of employees who'd been there long enough would dwindle, too.

Leila sighed, realizing that what was terrible for her company—and her conscience—was probably good for the investigation. It narrowed the suspect pool a lot.

It was probably someone she trusted. Someone she'd known for a long time. Someone who'd been to her father's house over the years. Maybe even someone she'd cried with at her father's funeral.

The thought made her hands ball into fists. How could someone do this to her father? To her? To all the soldiers who'd been killed and whoever else had been hurt that Leila didn't even know about yet?

The creak of the walking bridge told her someone else was there. Leila straightened, realizing she'd been so caught up in her thoughts that the person was already upon her.

The sudden, fierce pounding of her heart intensified when his hand came up, the flash of silver telling her he had a gun.

Instinct—and the self-defense training her father had insisted she take before she left for college—took over. Leila's hand darted up, swatting the gun away as he fired. The shot boomed in her ears, making them ring, as the bullet disappeared somewhere over the water.

The man who'd fired it snarled, surprise in his eyes as he stepped back slightly. Details filled in as time seemed to slow. He was taller than her. White, with brown hair and gray eyes that looked like steel. She didn't know him.

Then his hand swung back toward her and time sped up again. Instead of turning to run—and surely getting a bullet in the back—she rushed closer, getting inside his range of fire. Twisting sideways, she gripped his gun hand with both of hers, trying to break his grip.

But he was strong. His free hand came up and fisted in her hair, yanking with enough force to send pain racing down her neck.

Her feet went out from under her, but she didn't let go. She slammed onto the bridge, taking him down with her.

The back of her head pounded and her vision wavered, but she still had his wrist gripped in both of her hands. She twisted in opposite directions and he yelped, but didn't drop the gun. Yanking her body away from him, she tried to rip it out of his grasp, but he twisted, too, shifting in a different direction.

Then the ground slipped away from her as they both crashed through the flimsy guardrail and dropped into the water below.

Chapter Eleven

Davis didn't recognize the sound that tore from his throat as Leila and her attacker rolled off the bridge and into the fast-moving water below.

He'd been too far away when the guy had appeared out of nowhere and lifted his gun. He'd been trying to keep his distance, let her come to grips with what was happening in her company without his interference. He'd let her get ahead of him, paused to text Kane and Melinda for an update. He'd spent too many minutes staring impatiently at his phone, waiting for them to reply, then checked his other messages. He'd gotten distracted, and it might have just cost Leila her life.

The thought filled his throat with an angry lump, made it hard to breathe as he ran faster, then dived into the water where Leila and the man had disappeared.

Davis was a strong swimmer. He'd had to learn when he'd become a ranger. But the current was unusually fast, probably because of the storm that had rolled through earlier in the day. It spun him under, then back up again, but he got control of himself quickly.

But someone who wasn't a good swimmer? It could disorient the person, make them swim down instead of up.

If that person was already frantic and panicked, trying

to escape an attacker? It could easily be the difference between living and dying.

"Leila!" he called, scanning the water for her as he let himself be swept forward. He didn't see her anywhere.

Taking a deep breath, he dived under, looking for any sign of movement. Silently he cursed Leila for the serious, dark clothing she always wore. Why couldn't she have been partial to red or bright yellow? Something that would have been easier to see in the dark water?

He swam with the current, hoping to spot her, until he ran out of air and popped back to the surface. Then he yelled her name again, his heart going way too fast to be as efficient as he needed it to be right now, to let him search underwater longer.

He sucked in a deep breath, almost took in river water as choppy waves rose again. But even his battle-tested method of self-calming that had gotten him through his most dangerous ranger missions wasn't working.

Where was she?

He couldn't be too late. He refused to believe it.

But he still couldn't see her. If she'd been underwater this long, it probably wasn't of her own choosing.

Panic threatened, but he refused to accept defeat. Then, the current swept him around a bend and there she was, fifty feet ahead of him, still grappling with the guy who'd attacked her.

Davis forced himself forward in a burst of speed, trying to get to them. Fury fueled him as his gaze locked on the man still trying to harm her. The man Davis was going to strangle if he succeeded.

It felt like an hour, but he knew it was less than a minute before he reached them. But just before he could tear the guy's hands away from Leila's throat, her fist came up, angled skyward, and smashed into the bottom of the guy's nose.

His head snapped back with a noise that made Davis cringe. Blood streamed from his nose, and he dropped below the surface of the water.

"Are you okay?" Davis demanded, reaching for Leila's arms, ready to swim her to shore.

She pulled free, sucking in unnatural-sounding breaths. "Yes," she rasped. "Get him. Don't want—" She stopped on a fit of coughing.

Davis reached to steady her again, and she slapped at his hand.

He nodded, trusting that if she was strong enough to take down her attacker while he was choking her, she could make it to shore.

Giving her one last glance, he dived underwater. Leila's attacker was sinking toward the bottom, but still being swept along by the current, too.

Davis adjusted his angle, picking up his speed so he could grab the guy before he ran out of air himself. He wrapped his arms underneath the guy's armpits, then kicked upward with all his strength, shooting them back toward the surface.

Then it was instinct taking over, the familiar feel of someone needing help in his arms as he swam for shore and dragged the man out of the water. He checked for a heartbeat and heard one, faint but there. But when he checked for breath, there was nothing.

He paused for a moment, took in Leila sitting on the ground, her knees hugged up to her chest, then returned his attention to her attacker. If he'd managed to kill Leila, Davis would have been hard-pressed not to wrap his hands around the guy's throat. But now he was no threat and he was in trouble.

Davis bent down and gave him mouth-to-mouth until the guy jerked and spit out a stream of water. Davis sat back as the guy coughed and gasped for air, not seeming to know where he was.

Finally he got control of himself and looked up. A shock ran through Davis's body. He knew this man, recognized him from files Melinda had shown him the other day.

He was connected to BECA.

ANOTHER PARTNER WAS going to die on a mission with him. Another woman he cared about, who had made a name for herself in the Bureau through so many other dangerous cases, got partnered up with him and that was the end.

At least this time, he'd go with her.

Kane tried to snap out of the fatalistic mood, return to his cocky, nothing-scares-me Kane Bullet persona. How many times had he had a gun to his head? And he'd always walked away.

But how to explain *this*?

He shoved Melinda backward, hard enough to make her stumble on those ridiculous heels and fall to the ground. He held his hand toward her, palm down, telling her to stay there as his contact's gun shifted up and down from him to Melinda and back again.

"You're screwing this up for me, man," he snapped at the guy, taking an aggressive step forward and praying he wasn't about to get a bullet in the head. Or if he was, that at least Melinda would be able to leap forward fast enough to disarm the guy after he was dead.

Of course, that wouldn't help her outrun the guy's backup, which was probably moving in closer right now.

The guy's gun shifted back to Kane, centered on his forehead. He brought his other hand up to brace it, holding it closer to his own body to make it less likely Kane could rush him. But his curiosity won out. "Screwing what up, exactly?"

"I've been using her for months to get close to her dad, get access to a big bank he owns downtown with massive security. Now, you've messed it all up for me."

The guy's eyes narrowed as he looked Melinda over speculatively.

For a few seconds, Kane thought he'd bought it. Then, the guy let out a humorless laugh. "How stupid do you think I am? You're a cop."

He was blown. Kane had been undercover enough times, in enough different situations, to know he wasn't winning back this guy's trust. But he'd agreed to this meet too fast, not set up enough precautions. If it had just been him, he probably could have rushed the guy and taken his gun. Then, Kane would have used him as a human shield, banking that the guy's backup wouldn't want to shoot their boss in order to kill Kane. But that was dicey with Melinda here, still on the ground in heels there was no way she could run in, and with the guy's backup closing in fast.

Kane could see them in his peripheral vision every few seconds, as they picked their way through the rubble.

It was time to gamble. "I wouldn't come any closer!" he called out.

His contact glanced behind him, fast enough that Kane knew it was instinct. But not so fast Kane couldn't have rushed him. He would have, too, if the backup wasn't close enough to shoot Melinda while he did it.

Kane was armed, but the gun was at his ankle. Not the most easily accessible spot right now, and there was no good way to tell Melinda where it was without alerting the contact. Even if he leaped on top of her and let himself get shot, there was no way to know what sort of bullets they were using. There was too high a chance the bullets would go through him and kill her anyway.

He cursed her in his mind as he told his contact calmly, "I'm not a cop. But you were right about the fires. That *was* nasty business. But it wasn't me. I just figured you'd like that story better than what I really want." He took another step closer, saw the guy's eyes widen with surprise and just a touch of fear.

It was exactly what he needed. Keep them guessing, make them wonder why you weren't afraid when you should be terrified. It had worked for him before. But this was the biggest gamble he'd ever taken. This time, it was more than just his own life at stake.

"I'm ex-military. Ex-ranger, actually," he added, using the first specialty that came to mind, the Special Operations unit Davis had worked with until he left the military. "My friends and I, we all got dishonorably discharged for a little…incident. We've all got rifles and pistols, things we owned before we went in, but now? After those court-martials?" He scowled, put as much anger as he could on his face, knowing it turned him from irreverent and easygoing to threatening. "Now, I can't legally buy guns. And for our plan to get even with the military? We need more guns."

The guy's gaze darted to Melinda again and he shook his head. "You really think we're going to help you now?"

Kane shrugged, tried to insert a bit of that cocky attitude back into his persona. But it felt flat this time, like he wasn't fully occupying his cover, like he was still partly Kane Bradshaw, FBI agent terrified of losing another partner. "No. But if your backup moves any closer—or you pull that trigger—my ranger brothers are going to put neat little holes in your forehead from about five hundred feet that way." He pointed behind him, in the direction where there was high cover.

His contact's gaze darted that way, and he took an instinctive step backward. Then, his lips twisted up in a snarl and Kane knew his bluff hadn't worked.

It was all over.

Knowing it was futile didn't stop Kane from spinning around and leaping on top of Melinda as the *boom* of a bullet rang out. He felt the air whoosh out of her lungs as he flattened her with his body.

Still, she was squirming under him, and as she partially shoved him off her, he realized she was holding a tiny pistol. Where she'd been hiding it, he had no idea.

He yanked the gun from his ankle holster even as he shifted, getting a look at the contact, who was lying dead on the ground. He looked beyond the guy, toward his backup, and saw they had their arms up, with agents advancing on them.

Kane looked from Melinda to the contact, then he realized the guy hadn't been shot with a small-caliber gun. He glanced back toward high cover, where he'd bluffed and said he had backup. Apparently it hadn't been a lie.

Rolling fully off Melinda, he lifted his arm in a half salute, half wave in the direction he knew Laura Smith must have been hiding with a rifle. She looked like someone who worked in some high-powered civilian firm, with her no-nonsense attitude and her affinity for suits. But she was the perfect proof that looks could be deceiving. He'd never seen anyone without military sniper training who could shoot a rifle like that.

Then, he stared back at his partner, who'd somehow figured out not only what he was up to but also where his meet was going down. Instead of talking it over with him, she'd taken it upon herself to just show up. Not only had she completely blown their chances of getting him inside BECA, but also she'd blown the CI he'd cultivated for years.

Now the FBI would have to help Dougie relocate, maybe even disappear.

The longer he stared at Melinda, the more his anger grew, until he wasn't even sure he could speak at all. When he could finally form words, he expected it to come out in a scream, so he was surprised when his voice was barely above a whisper.

"What have you done?"

Chapter Twelve

Leila had been sitting there, shivering in the sixty-degree weather, sopping wet and staring blankly at the river that had almost swept her under, for too long.

Davis had zip-tied her attacker's hands and feet together, so there was no way he could go anywhere fast, then called in the attack to TCD headquarters. In turn, they'd contacted local PD to take the perp in for now, because apparently Davis's team was out helping Kane and Melinda, who'd run into trouble in a meeting with a BECA contact.

It was no coincidence. Davis felt it in his gut, but couldn't worry about it at the moment.

He showed his credentials to the cops who were taking in Leila's attacker, and spoke in whispered tones to them for a few minutes about holding him until someone from his team could come in and get a statement. Then, he turned his back on them, focused on Leila.

She'd already been in shock over what he'd told her about the illegal gun sales coming out of Petrov Armor. Now, she looked completely lost.

It wasn't even remotely close to being over. He still hadn't told her the truth about her father.

He needed to get her out of here. The river water had been cold, not enough to send her body into shock, but enough that he was getting worried about how long she'd sat there immobile.

He knelt in front of her, waiting for her to make eye contact. She didn't for a long moment.

Then she blinked slowly, awareness returning as she shifted her gaze to him. The dazed look disappeared, replaced by wariness and fear.

"It's going to be okay," he promised her softly. "We're going to figure this out."

His words didn't ease the fear in her eyes, but the wariness shifted into anger. Not wanting to wait to find out if that anger was directed at him, he hooked his hands under her elbows and pulled her carefully to her feet.

"Let's get you home." She let him lead her out of the woods, then he had one of the responding officers give them a ride back to her house. He'd worry about their vehicles later.

Luckily, she had a keypad at her back door, so they could get in. She seemed to be moving on autopilot as he followed her inside, waved the cop off and locked the door behind them.

As the dead bolt slid into place with a *click* that echoed in her granite and tile kitchen, she turned toward him, looking perplexed. Her mouth opened, like she wanted to say something.

Before she could, he stepped forward. He gripped her elbows with his hands, the way he had in the woods. But this time, he wasn't doing it to help her up. This time, he felt like he needed to hold her to keep *him* from falling as it hit him all over again, the fear he'd felt when he couldn't see her in that river.

"Davis," she croaked.

He lifted his hand from her elbow to her cheek, discovering it was ice-cold. "Are you okay?"

She let out a choked laugh. "Are you kidding me? Of course not. But maybe this will help."

She leaned into him and he took a step back, dropping his hands to her elbows to keep her at arm's length. "I want to," he whispered, his voice deeper, gruffer than it should have been. "Believe me, I do. But—"

"What? The smell of river water and mud isn't an aphrodisiac?" she joked, then immediately averted her gaze and moved out of reach.

A smile trembled on his lips. She wasn't the too-serious, all-business CEO with him anymore. Even if he'd messed things up repeatedly, she was starting to let her guard down. Enough to let him see glimpses of who she really was. The more he saw, the more he liked her.

Still, he couldn't believe they'd almost kissed yet again. But he couldn't cross that line. He might know in his gut that she was innocent, but the FBI hadn't truly eliminated her as a suspect. She was connected somehow to the person who *was* guilty, the person he needed to find and arrest. To do that, he had to stay impartial.

But staring at her now, her clothes sagging with water, her hair a ragged mess and her makeup smeared down her face from being in the river, he wished things were different. It actually physically hurt how much he wished that he'd met her under different circumstances, that he was free to truly pursue her. That he could really forgive her for running a business that had sent out the armor that had killed Jessica.

When she met his gaze again, he knew she could see longing there from the way her eyes dilated. Then she was back to serious, but something had changed—something important. He could see it in her eyes, could feel it in the more relaxed way she was moving. "I'm going to get in a hot shower for five minutes and then change. I don't have anything here you'll fit, but there's a dryer in the mudroom we just came through. Then we can talk."

She left the room, not giving him a chance to disagree. Not that he would have, when she'd finally decided to trust him.

When she returned downstairs a few minutes later, he'd tossed his pants, button-down, and socks in her dryer and set his gun and badge on her coffee table. He'd wrapped himself in a throw blanket he'd spotted tossed over the couch in her living room next to a paperback romance novel.

Her gaze slid over him, seeming to burn a trail across any exposed skin even as her lips quirked upward with obvious amusement. "Nice look."

Then, she sank onto the other side of the couch, close enough to talk easily but not close enough to touch.

She'd changed into sweatpants and a T-shirt, scrubbed her face clean of any makeup and pulled her hair out of the remnants of its bun. Now it fell in loose wet tangles past her shoulders, and he longed to reach out and run his hands through it, follow the trail of water that dripped down her bare arms.

Instead, he hugged the blanket more tightly to himself and told her, "Eric stopped by to check on you. I told him you were overtired, so I drove you home."

She nodded, seeming uninterested, and he waited for her to ask him what was happening.

He expected her to want more details about the illegal gun sales. Or maybe to know whether he had any idea who her attacker was, why he'd come after her. When she finally did speak, her words were soft and surprising.

"Thanks for having my back, Davis. Thanks for making me feel like I have someone I can count on when everything in my world seems to be falling apart."

SHE WAS BACK at work like nothing had happened, like someone hadn't tried to kill her yesterday.

Leila shivered in the confines of her office, where no one could see how freaked out she was. She'd already turned the heat up several times, but it was never enough.

At least it was a Saturday. Far fewer employees here to notice her acting strangely, to wonder why. She and Davis had agreed that no one in the company should know what had happened to her yesterday evening. He'd told her the attack was from someone connected to a criminal enterprise, and that group might have been sold Petrov Armor pistols illegally. He still didn't know why that person would attack *her*. Apparently, so far, the guy wasn't talking. And somehow, Davis had managed to keep the police report out of the media.

Despite the fact that she'd probably been followed from the office yesterday, she felt safer here right now than she did at home by herself. It probably didn't hurt that she'd started carrying a small pistol in her handbag. She planned to keep it there until she was sure the threat was over.

Even the idea of it made her slightly uncomfortable. Despite having sold weapons for so many years, she'd never liked firing one. The regular classes her dad had made her take, to stay refreshed in proper shooting technique, hadn't changed that. But right now, she was glad for it. She touched the outline of the gun through her bag, then locked it in her desk drawer and tried to focus.

The plan had been to distract herself with work, but instead she was distracted by Davis. He'd come in to the office today, too, both because there would be fewer people to see him looking into things an assistant didn't need to access and to stick close to her. He'd stuck close to her all last night, too, sleeping on her couch in whatever he'd had on beneath her blanket. She'd been up most of the night wondering about it.

But she'd managed to stay away from him, spent the night tossing and turning in her own bed. From the first day, she couldn't help but have a physical attraction to Davis, which surely gave him an advantage as he dug for information. But yesterday had been different. Yesterday, he'd truly seemed shocked when he'd almost kissed her. The way he'd stared at her afterward... She was starting to believe he might actually be developing feelings for her.

The idea made her stomach flip-flop with nerves, made a smile tremble on her lips. But it could never come to anything. He was investigating her company. If she and Davis got together, it would put the integrity of the whole investigation in question, maybe even throw suspicion on her, even after they found the person responsible. Unlike a fling with a handsome FBI agent with an intriguing smile and admirable ethics, that suspicion could stick. It could destroy one of the few things in her life with any permanence. Her job.

"Leila."

Her head popped up. She'd been so focused on her thoughts she hadn't even noticed the door open, hadn't even heard the knock that had probably preceded it.

"Eric."

Her head of sales was shutting the door behind him, his eyebrows lowered with a concerned expression she recognized.

She held in a sigh, because he meant well. They both missed her father desperately. Eric had taken time off to grieve after the funeral, had called her every day, pushing her to do the same. But the idea of not coming into work, of trying to find some other way to fill her days to distract herself from the fact that her father was never coming back? Even now, it made her skin feel prickly with anxiety.

"What's going on?"

She shook her head, thrown by his question. "What do you mean?"

"Something happened yesterday after you left work. You left your purse in your office. You never came back for your car. I drove all the way to your house and your assistant answered the door—dripping wet for some reason..."

He paused, like he was waiting for an explanation, then continued. "He swore you were fine, that you'd gone for a walk and realized you were too tired to drive, so he took you home. I would have pushed him aside and come in to check, but I heard the shower going upstairs. Leila, I know it's not my business, but—"

"I'm not sleeping with my assistant, Eric," she cut him off, hoping he wouldn't notice the too-high-pitched tone to her voice. Or that if he did, he would accept it for what it mostly was—embarrassment.

"Good." Eric's eyebrows returned to a normal position on his face, but his tone was still troubled as he walked around to her side of her desk. Having him in her personal space felt odd, like they'd gone back in time to when they were more than just colleagues and friends.

"Leila, yesterday when I saw your car still here when I was ready to go home and then I came back inside and saw your purse, I panicked. I was really scared. I mean, after what happened to your dad..." He closed his eyes, blew out a breath that fanned across her face and finished, "It made me realize how much I miss you, Leila."

A sudden rush of nerves and uncertainty made her feel too hot. She tried to play it off like his words weren't a big deal. "You see me every day, Eric."

He put his hands on her arms, slid them down to take her hands in his.

His touch was familiar, but still strange. Eric's hands were bigger than she remembered, the skin rougher. But they were still warm, still comforting the way they'd been the very first time he'd held her hand when she was thirteen.

"I care about you, Leila." He met her gaze steadily, his voice solid and clear. "Way more than I should, considering how long it's been since we were together."

Her heart rate picked up, but she tried to ignore how close he was standing, tried to act like it was normal for him to be holding her hands in her office. "We've been friends for a long time, Eric. We have a lot of history together. Of course you were worried."

"Maybe we never should have broken up."

She blinked back at him, speechless, as a mix of emotions surged inside her. Happiness, confusion and uncertainty. She'd waited so many years to hear those words from him. He'd been her first love, the one that got away.

But because it had been so many years ago, things had changed. Were they even the same people they'd been when they were in love? And why now? Was it just fear of losing her, grief over losing her father making him say things he'd later regret?

He knew her well enough that she was sure he sensed her hesitation, even before she said quietly, "Our time is gone."

Saying the words out loud hurt, but it had been twelve long years since he'd broken her heart without a single word of explanation. Twelve years of them growing into the people they were now. Twelve years of working to forge a real friendship, without the baggage of their relationship.

"Don't say that." Eric shook his head, stepping even closer to her, so his feet touched hers and his lips were mere inches away. "Our time never should have ended, Leila."

She blew out a breath that made him blink as the expelled air hit him. "*You* ended it, Eric. It was—"

"I did it because your dad asked me to stop seeing you."

"What?" The shock of the words made her step backward. She pulled her hands free from his, suddenly colder than she'd been before he came into the office. The serious look in his eyes, one she knew so well, told her he wasn't lying. "Why?"

Eric sighed, ran a hand through his blond hair, tousling it the way she'd loved as a teenager. "I swore to myself I'd never tell you, because I didn't want you to be mad at him. He wanted you to have a clean break when you went to college. I fought with him over it, but he felt like it was important for you to find your own way, learn to be strong alone."

He lifted his shoulders, a helpless look in his eyes. "I thought one day, he'd change his mind. But then you started working here and…honestly, it was awkward. I didn't know how to be your colleague. I tried to be your friend. We both dated other people. Then you became my boss, and it was strange all over again. But there's never been anyone like you, Leila. Never."

She shook her head, totally at a loss for how to respond. Over the years, she'd dreamed so many times that Eric would change his mind, tell her he was a fool and wanted her back. In her dreams, she'd always leaped into his arms. She'd never imagined he'd tell her that her dad had instigated the breakup. She'd never thought she'd be unsure if she wanted *him* back.

"I get it," Eric said, when she stayed silent. "This is a lot. But just think it over, okay? We can figure the company part out. I mean, this was your dad's business, his dream. Maybe you and I can cash in our stock options and start over, partners in some new venture." He smiled, his eyes hopeful. Then, he lifted her hand to his lips and kissed it.

As she continued to stare mutely at him, his smile grew, then he turned and headed for the door. He glanced back at her once more as he opened it to leave, then almost walked into Davis, who was standing in the doorway, scowling.

"Davis," Eric said, giving the agent a nod as he maneuvered around him.

Then, Eric was gone and Davis shut the door and strode toward her like a man on a mission. She stared at him, still feeling stunned from Eric's revelations. But the closer Davis got, the more she realized that he'd been in the back of her mind as she'd told Eric their time was over. The closer he got, the more all the nerve endings on her skin seemed to fire to life, the more shallow each breath became.

It made no sense. She barely knew Davis. Eric, she'd known forever.

"He's not right for you," Davis told her as he strode around her desk the same way Eric had.

"What?" He'd been listening in on their conversation? How much had he heard?

Instead of answering, he slid his hands around her waist and yanked her to him. Her body crashed into his, the hard planes of his chest stealing her breath even as she instinctively pressed tighter.

Then, his head ducked toward hers, his lips hovering a few centimeters away, actually brushing against hers as he asked, "Leila?"

She responded by pushing up on her tiptoes, wrapping her arms tight around his neck and pressing her lips to his. The softness of his lips contrasted with the hardness of his kisses, then his tongue swept into her mouth. She felt it all the way down to her toes: no matter what happened in the future, this was exactly where she was supposed to be right now.

Chapter Thirteen

He'd kissed Leila Petrov. It hadn't been some brief passionate mistake that had burned out as fast as it happened. No, the more he'd kissed her, the more he'd wanted. If they hadn't been in her office…

His ability to look at this case impartially was blown. He needed to come clean with Pembrook, ask her to pull him out. The next logical step would be to get warrants and have the FBI go in full force, the way he'd told Leila.

No matter how quietly they tried to execute something like that, word would get out. Someone would take a video on their phone of FBI agents going into the office or talk to the press. No matter who turned out to be behind this, it would put a stain on Leila's company that might destroy it. He didn't want to do that to her.

"You're getting too close to her."

Kane's voice made Davis jerk and spin toward his colleague. He didn't need to ask who Kane meant, didn't bother to justify why he'd responded immediately when he'd felt his phone buzzing with an incoming text. Why he'd rushed right over when Kane's message said they wanted to give him a debrief on the BECA meet. He'd just pulled his lips slowly away from Leila's, skimming his hands along her skin as he extracted himself. Trying to memorize the feel of her lips and skin and hair, the dazed look in her gorgeous brown eyes. Knowing he couldn't let it happen again.

He needed to regain his professionalism. Because no matter what he *should* do, he wasn't asking Pembrook to pull him out of his cover. He was seeing this case through to the end.

Ignoring Kane's statement, he demanded, "What the hell happened out there?"

"Melinda happened." Kane pursed his lips, glanced around like he was afraid their fellow TCD agent would hear, then held open the door to the conference room.

Inside, Melinda was waiting, a laptop in front of her. She was dressed in one of her standard high-neck blouses, her hair loosely styled, with minimal makeup. There was no indication she'd overheard Kane in the hallway, but the tension on her face and the scrapes covering her arms suggested the meet had gone even worse than Davis had realized.

"We think we know what happened with Leila," Melinda said even before he and Kane were seated.

Kane scowled as she looked at him pointedly, but he spoke up. "My CI set up the meet for me. He told the BECA contact that I'd had someone here willing to sell me guns illegally, but it fell through. I probed a little, trying to see if I'd get a reaction. Said my contact was inside Petrov Armor, but it seemed like the illegal gun sales there dried up when the new CEO stopped the legal side of the gun distribution. He texted someone right after I said that." Kane cringed. "I'm sorry, man. Given the timing…"

The person Kane's BECA contact had texted was the man who'd followed Leila from her office and tried to kill her. That guy still wasn't talking, and Kane's contact was now dead.

Davis's hands fisted hard under the table and he could

feel his heart beat faster, rushing blood to those hands, ready to fight. But he pushed back the instinct, nodded tightly. It was a logical move on Kane's part. They knew someone inside Petrov Armor was selling guns off the books. Bringing it up was what any good investigator— one who wasn't blinded by a target in the investigation— would do.

"The good news is, that tells us something," Melinda said, her gaze darting from him to Kane and back again.

"The guy you were meeting with didn't know why the gun production was halted. Once he realized who was to blame, he wanted revenge," Davis stated, a million possible implications running through his mind. If BECA members really had been getting guns off the books from someone at Petrov Armor, they'd probably been feeling the pinch since Leila stopped gun production. The inside source couldn't get as many guns out without drawing attention. Typically, someone in that position would tell their customer about their pain. The fact that the seller *hadn't* told BECA the guns were drying up because of Leila probably meant that person was protecting her, didn't want BECA or any other buyers to know she'd been the one who'd shut things down.

"It seems more and more likely that Leila's dad was in charge of the illegal gun sales. And that his partner killed him because of what Leila did. Maybe he'd meant to just threaten him, try to get him to restart production, but the threat went wrong, and Neal ended up dead. It probably took about a year for their stock to run out to the point where the illegal sales would be noticed. Turning to cheap armor to bank the extra money isn't working out the way this person expected," Kane said.

"Leila said the excess guns were destroyed, but I assume that's just what she was told, and Neal or his partner simply moved the remainder to sell off books. But what if it wasn't Neal?" Davis thought of the picture Leila kept on the credenza behind her desk. An image of her and her father, sitting next to each other at some outdoor function, both of them with heads thrown back and laughing. "What if he was never involved at all?"

Kane's lips turned up in a "give me a break" expression. "Your objectivity is shot."

"Maybe," Davis admitted, because the truth was that he didn't want Leila's father to be involved. Not because of anything to do with the investigation. Simply because he didn't want Leila to feel that kind of betrayal from the father she'd loved so much and who she'd barely begun to grieve.

"But hear me out," Davis pressed when Kane looked like he was going to keep theorizing how the attack pointed even more to Leila's father being involved. "Her father has been dead for three weeks. If his partner killed him because he was angry that Neal supported Leila's decision to stop the gun side of the business, why didn't he tell his customers as soon as Neal was out of the way? If it was just Neal who was trying to hide Leila's involvement, why wouldn't his partner spill what had happened as soon as he killed Neal? Wouldn't he have bragged to BECA that he was going to turn things around, get the guns flowing again? Three weeks after Neal's death, why wouldn't they already know who was to blame, before Kane told them?"

Melinda nodded slowly and even Kane looked a little less skeptical now.

"Maybe Neal's partner is also trying to protect Leila," Melinda suggested. "It makes sense that Neal would run the illegal side of the business with someone he trusts, someone he's close to. It also makes sense that he'd want to keep his daughter out of it. But what about his brother? Or the guy he thought of like a son, but wasn't *really* his son?"

"Yeah," Davis agreed, even though he didn't like this

theory much better, because it still meant someone Leila cared about deeply was betraying her. "Both Joel and Eric would want to protect Leila. But would either of them really kill Neal? They're both taking his death hard."

"Or pretending to," Kane interjected. "You've been FBI long enough to know that the most successful criminals are two-faced. They've all got families they probably love. They're loved at the office. But deep down, it's all about number one. Anyone who's pulled this off for at least a decade—and honestly, I've got to believe it's a lot longer—is a pretty successful criminal."

"It makes Theresa less likely as a suspect," Melinda said. "She and Leila don't get along, right? She wouldn't protect Leila, try to keep her name out of it?"

"Probably not." Davis sighed. "But she was the one with the best access for swapping out the armor. Neither Joel nor Eric have a lot of contact with the raw materials."

"But they all have general access. They could go in after hours," Kane said. "Any luck with that?"

Davis shook his head, his mind still trying to unravel a scenario where Leila's father wasn't involved at all. But he'd founded the company; he was one of the few people who'd been there long enough to be behind the illegal gun sales. The only other probable scenario was if he *hadn't* known and he'd recently found out. "What if someone killed Neal because he discovered what they were doing? What if *that* person was behind both the illegal gun sales and the defective armor? What if they never had a partner?"

Both Kane and Melinda looked skeptical, but Melinda gave his theory the benefit of the doubt by saying, "Maybe. But that still means it's someone who wanted to protect Leila. To try and prevent what ended up happening when Kane inadvertently let them know she was responsible for the gun supply drying up."

"No matter how you look at this," Kane said, his gaze steady on Davis, broadcasting that he thought Davis was in way too deep, "someone Leila cares about is behind all of this. *And* they're the reason her father is dead."

"ARE WE GOING to talk about this?" Melinda demanded. She stood in the doorway of the conference room, one hand on each side of the frame, blocking Kane's exit.

Davis had left an hour earlier, not wanting Leila to leave the office alone. Melinda and Kane had dug through backgrounds on Joel Petrov and Eric Ross after he'd left, trying to find any indication one of them was making millions of dollars off-book. Then, Kane had looked up at her, the exhaustion in his eyes not doing a thing to hide the anger, and announced he was calling it quits until tomorrow.

"I'm not finding anything in either of their backgrounds," Kane said, and she knew he was purposely misunderstanding her question. "Our best chance to figure out who's behind this is the guy who needs a crash course in undercover work."

"Davis is in a tough spot." Melinda couldn't stop herself from arguing, even though she knew Kane had been egging her on, trying to get her to fight about something else. "He's got real feelings for Leila."

"It's one of the biggest dangers in undercover work," Kane told her, flicking away hair that had fallen down over his forehead. "If you're any good, you have to *inhabit* the skin of someone else. That means it's easy to become what you're pretending to be. It's easy to see the humans behind the criminals. No one is one hundred percent bad. But you cross those lines and it's hard to step back, watch them all get arrested and walk away."

"How do you keep doing it?" Melinda asked softly. It was something she'd always wondered about Kane. The profiler in her knew part of him craved the danger, craved the chance to disappear inside a persona and escape himself. Escape into the skin of others, over and over again, until maybe the things he was running from in his own life wouldn't be there anymore.

Melinda didn't know the details of what had happened with him and Pembrook's daughter. But she did know he'd never be able to run away from the guilt he felt over her death.

"Simple," Kane answered, taking her hand and pulling it away from the door frame. "I always go alone."

He slipped past her, his gaze holding hers for a brief moment before it flicked away. The man was the very definition of tall, dark and handsome. He was dangerous and mysterious in a way she would have swooned over as a foolish teenager.

But she was an adult now, with way too much education in psychology not to recognize exactly what he was doing. She turned around in the doorway, holding her ground. "You think I blew your cover."

He spun back toward her, the anger on his face so harsh she almost backed up. *Almost.*

"Yeah, I think you blew my cover. I also think you blew Dougie as my CI, as an FBI resource. I also think..." He sighed heavily, not finishing his sentence.

But he didn't have to. He thought she'd almost gotten them killed.

His judgment stung, even though she thought the same things herself. She'd had no idea that the very fact that she was Asian would be enough to bring his cover crashing down. But how could she? He'd hidden it all from her, hidden that there even *was* a meet. She'd had to follow him, sneak glances at his phone, to figure out the when and where, because she'd known from the minute he'd walked out of the room to take the call from his CI what he was doing.

"Don't you think that if you'd just been honest with me, we could have come up with a plan for the meet together? Then you would have had backup and I would have known not to go in that way."

"We didn't need to come up with a plan together," Kane snapped. "I came up with a plan myself. I work alone. I always have."

"Not always."

Melinda knew it was a risk referring to Pembrook's daughter, but she didn't expect the level of fury that lit in Kane's eyes. She had to brace her hands in the doorway again to keep herself from backing away.

"You have no idea what it's like to watch someone you care about die like that. So, don't give me your profiling BS about how I'm not a team player when *you're* the one who blew that meet."

Melinda saw the instant Kane realized he'd gone too far, the moment the raw fury in his gaze turned to regret. She also knew why.

He'd seen it on her face that she *did* know. "You're right that I've never lost a partner," Melinda agreed, stepping away from the doorway. Her hand twitched toward the ring she always wore on a necklace hidden beneath her shirts, but she resisted the urge to touch it. Her personal life was no one's business, least of all Kane Bradshaw's.

In Tennessee, only Pembrook knew she'd once had a husband, had a son, had a *life* outside of work. The chance to escape the pitying looks of colleagues who knew about her loss was why she'd accepted the job here in the first place.

An ironic smile spread across her lips as she realized in some ways, she and Kane were more alike than she'd ever expected. Both of them were running from their grief. The difference was, she'd buried herself in the intellectual puzzle of the job, whereas he'd run straight to the danger.

"Melinda, I'm—"

"You're right about something else, too, Kane. You and me? We're not partners. But right now, there's a zealot group buying up illegal guns. They think it's okay to put out a hit on the woman who dared to infringe on their ability to get those guns, intentionally or not. We're going to see this through and shut this source down. Then we can go back to the way things were before."

The muscle in his jaw pulsed, his eyes narrowed assessingly. But in the end, he just nodded. "Deal."

In the instant before he turned and walked away, she regretted all of it. She regretted giving him any hint of the loss she'd experienced when both her husband and son had been killed at the same time. She regretted showing him the way to piss her off and push her away. Maybe most of all, she regretted agreeing to keep working with him.

Chapter Fourteen

When the doorbell rang at close to midnight Sunday night, Davis frowned and tucked his gun into the waistband of his jeans before he checked the peephole. Then he swore and opened the door wide for Leila.

She stepped inside without waiting for an invitation and he peered past her, onto the street, looking for the patrol car he'd requested to be stationed outside her house until they solved this case. Until they knew for sure no other BECA members would come after her.

A black and white was idling in front of his house. Leila's protection.

"I told the cops I was coming here. They insisted on following me over," Leila said.

He closed and locked the front door as she glanced past his entryway into the living room, curiosity on her face.

When was the last time he'd had a woman he was dating in his home? It had been too long. Not that he didn't date. But his relationships never lasted long enough to get to the "why don't you come over?" stage. A few dates in and he'd know whether it was going anywhere. Rather than hurt the woman later, he broke it off sooner. It had happened for so many years, he'd figured that long-term just wasn't for him. It was disappointing—he'd always imagined settling down some day—but he'd prefer to be alone than pretend a relationship was going somewhere permanent when it wasn't.

But Leila looked good in his house. As she strode past him and settled onto his big, comfortable couch without an invitation, he hid a smile.

He hadn't called her. He'd kissed her like he needed her as much as he needed air yesterday morning, and then he'd left for the TCD office. When he'd returned, he'd avoided being alone with her, avoided an awkward conversation or another kiss. Because when it came to Leila, his willpower was shot. But he needed to solve this case first. Needed to figure out who was behind the illegal arms sales and the defective armor before he could even begin to think about whether a relationship with Leila Petrov was possible.

Leave it to her to force the issue. He should have known she wasn't going to wait for him to decide he was ready.

He followed her into the living room, settling on the edge of the chair across from her, not trusting himself to sit beside her and not reach for her.

Her eyes narrowed slightly at his seating choice, but then she leaned forward. "Tell me about the illegal gun sales."

"What?"

She smiled slightly, but then the expression was gone, replaced by her serious, CEO face. "You thought I was going to demand answers about that kiss in my office?" She lifted an eyebrow. "Don't worry. We'll get to that."

He couldn't help it. He laughed.

Kane was right that he'd lost all focus when it came to Leila, but was it any wonder he couldn't resist this woman? If he'd met her under other circumstances, he would have long since invited her into his house.

The thought made any amusement fade fast. He was going to do everything he could to shelter her from any fallout from whoever had been using her company as a source for illegal activity. But when it was all over, he had to walk away. Had to go back to his job and let her try to pick up the pieces. Because no matter how much he wanted everything to be okay for her, it was unlikely her company would come out of this unscathed. It was unlikely *she* would come out of this unscathed.

No matter how much he wanted to separate his growing feelings for Leila from the investigation, he couldn't really do it. When this was all over, she was sure to resent him. Regardless of how he felt about her, would he ever be able to separate that from what had happened to Jessica? Could he ever truly forgive her for running the company that had caused his friend's death?

"Don't get all closed up on me now," Leila said, misunderstanding whatever emotions she'd seen on his face. "I know it's an active investigation. But we agreed that we're in this together. You told me there have been illegal gun sales coming from my company for more than a decade. So, let me help you figure this out. How much longer has it been? How many guns?"

Davis studied her, her expression intense despite the skinny jeans and long, loose T-shirt she wore. Her hair was down again, her makeup nonexistent, and he realized how much he liked her non-CEO look. The real Leila, the one people in her office didn't get to see. But she'd let him in, let him see her vulnerable, trusted him with information about the business she'd worked so hard to help build and shape. Trusted him to help her find out who was sabotaging it, without destroying it in the process.

He swallowed hard, knowing he hadn't truly earned that trust. Then he tried to channel Kane and meet her gaze with what he hoped looked like honesty. He could tell her the truth about the details: the timeline and the volume of guns. But there would always be too much he'd have to hide.

"We're on the same side," she told him softly, making him realize that he'd never be able to truly hide from her.

Nodding, he pushed his conflicted feelings to the back of his mind and focused on business. "How much longer have the illegal gun sales been happening? We're not sure. It's been at least eleven years. Possibly as many as twenty."

"*Twenty?* Almost no one has been with the company that long," Leila said, looking shocked as she sank back against the pillows on his couch.

Just her uncle and Theresa, Davis knew. But even if they could definitively say the guns had been sold illegally for twenty years, that didn't necessarily narrow the suspect pool. Because there was a strong chance her father had started the illegal side of the business as well as the legal side. He might have only brought someone else in later. Someone like Eric.

He hadn't told Leila that the FBI had narrowed the suspect pool. Now, it wasn't just those employees with high-level access who'd worked there for a while, but also those who cared about Leila enough to protect her from the BECA scum even when it was costing them huge amounts of money. But she was no fool. She'd figured out that his prime suspects were people she knew well, even people she loved.

Yet, she was still helping him. Some emotion he couldn't quite identify swelled in his chest. Pride? Attachment?

"How many guns were sold illegally?" she asked, more tension in her voice.

"A lot," he told her. "Over a decade or more, at marked up prices of course, we're talking about millions of dollars' worth."

"Millions?" She stared up at his ceiling for a long moment, before meeting his gaze again, clearly trying to absorb the information. "Petrov Armor is never going to recover from this, is it?"

His whole body tensed, wanting to jump up and sit beside her, comfort her. He wanted to tell her that she was wrong, that if it was one criminal hiding in the company, taking advantage of it, that once that person was gone, Petrov Armor could regain its reputation. But would he be lying? She'd already shut down the weapons side of the business. Now, with the investigation clearly showing the defective armor was Petrov Armor's fault, no matter why it had happened, would the military ever work with them again? He knew they were the company's main client.

"I don't know," he admitted. Then, he told her the one thing that wasn't a lie. "But if anyone can make it happen, I believe it's you."

She gave him a shaky smile, then stood and closed the distance between them.

Just as he was ready to stand, maybe to back away, she knelt in front of his chair and put her hands on his knees. The muscles in his legs jumped in response and her smile returned, this time a little more steady. She lifted her hands from his legs to his cheeks, her fingers scraping over the stubble he'd ignored shaving this morning, making his face tingle.

His breath came faster in anticipation, and he had to grip the edges of his chair to keep himself from leaning down and fusing his lips to hers. When he didn't, the small smile on her lips shifted, making the skin around her eyes crinkle as she pushed herself upward.

Her lips were inches from his when panic made him say the thing he'd been keeping from her for too long, the other thing that he couldn't continue to hide from her if he ever wanted to be with her. "Your dad's death was no accident, Leila."

HER DAD'S DEATH wasn't a mugging gone wrong. It was intentional. A murder by not just someone her dad knew, but someone he trusted. Someone who had also been using his company to sell guns to criminals and inferior armor to soldiers. All for money. Someone had murdered her father for money.

Leila tried to blink back the tears, but they were coming too fast, rushing down her face in a waterfall she couldn't stop. More than just the horror of learning it was someone she knew—someone she worked with every day—who had probably killed her father, but also the pure grief of his death. Something she'd been pushing to the back of her mind as much as possible, focusing on work, on this investigation, so she could avoid facing it.

He was gone. The person closest to her in the world.

The sobs came harder, almost violently. Then Davis was kneeling in front of her on the floor, pulling her against him. She held on tight, weeping into his chest as he stroked her hair, until the sobs finally subsided.

He lifted the bottom of his T-shirt, offering it.

She managed a laugh, then did use it to mop up the remaining tears on her face. It was something she would have done as a teenager, with Eric's shirt, when she'd been grieving the loss of her mom. Now here she was, all these years later, and it was Davis she was leaning on for support. Davis she wanted beside her.

He made her feel safe. Made her feel like she could be herself, without fearing she'd look too weak or seem unfit for her role as CEO. The ironic thing was that she probably should have feared it in front of him—an FBI agent—most of all.

She was falling for him.

The realization hit hard and sudden, even though it should have been obvious long ago. Maybe even the first day she'd met him, she should have known he was more than just a danger to her hormones, but a real risk to her heart.

She blinked at him now, kneeling in front of her, her hands still fisted in his T-shirt. His soft hazel eyes were so serious, so worried. He cared about her, too. He hadn't admitted it, but she could see it all over his face.

But he was still an FBI agent. He was still a man investigating everyone in her company. The information he'd just shared made it more clear than ever that the person they were looking for was someone important in Petrov Armor. This was no swap-out in a truck, no one-time incident. This was someone who'd been undermining the company for a long, long time. It was someone she trusted. Someone her father had trusted.

"I shouldn't be here," Davis whispered.

His words made no sense and she shook her head. "You live here."

He laughed, the tension and worry on his face fading a little. "With you, Leila. I shouldn't be here with you." His hand cupped her face, and she couldn't stop herself from leaning into it. "But I can't stay away."

Instead of reminding him that she was the one who'd come to his place uninvited, she moved her hands from the front of his T-shirt to the center of his back. Just as he was taking the hint and leaning toward her, his phone buzzed, making both of them jump.

He scowled in the direction of his phone, and she could feel him debating silently before he finally swore and said, "I need to take this."

He stood, stepped away from her and answered in a serious, all-business tone, "Davis Rogers."

His gaze was still on hers, the look in his eyes still soft, almost a caress. Then, his gaze shifted away from her and his whole face hardened. "Hang on." He moved the phone away from his ear and told her, "I'll be back in a minute."

She stood slowly as he disappeared around the corner, then used her own T-shirt to dab at the edges of her eyes. Glancing around Davis's living room—which was a lot more colorful than she'd expected given his mostly dark blue and black wardrobe—she spotted a mirror over a console in the corner. Striding over to it, she looked into the mirror and grimaced.

Her eyes were red and puffy. Her nose, too. The rest of her skin was paler than usual, and Leila realized just how much the past few weeks without enough sleep had impacted her. She'd been avoiding a breakdown ever since hearing about her father's death. She'd been afraid that once she started, she might never stop. But her outburst of tears on Davis's chest had actually been freeing. It had lifted some of her ever-present tension, made her feel less like she was moving on autopilot.

Davis had helped her feel that way, too. Just having him around—despite the reason—had forced her to feel emotions, had pulled her partway out of the numbness she'd tried to bury herself in since her father's death. She was a long way from being finished grieving, but it was a start. Hopefully, when the investigation into her company was over—no matter how it turned out—Davis would still be here.

He'd said he shouldn't be here with her now, but he hadn't asked her to leave. He'd been the one leaning in to kiss her when his phone call had interrupted. They shouldn't date while he was undercover in her company. But maybe when it was all over...

Leila felt a smile burst on her face, huge and unexpected after how hard she'd just wept. Whatever was happening between her and Davis wasn't a byproduct of her needing someone during her grief. If that were true, she would have turned to Eric, the man she'd thought she was still half-way in love with until he'd told her he wanted her back. Until his words of being together had made her think of Davis, not him.

This was real. From the things Davis had been saying to her a few moments ago, he felt it, too.

They could make it work. Once the investigation was over, they could make it work. It wouldn't be easy, especially if she had to start over again professionally, after trials and interviews over the traitor inside Petrov Armor. But he was worth it.

She followed in the direction Davis had disappeared, listening for his voice to tell her where he was. Hopefully, he was finished with his phone call. Because she needed to tell him right now that she was willing to wait until the investigation was over, but no longer. That once they figured this all out—together—she wanted *him*.

"Yes, I know Leila is still officially a suspect."

Davis's words, spoken on a frustrated sigh, made Leila freeze and her smile instantly fade.

His voice quieted even more, to a whisper Leila had to strain to hear. "Yeah, I get that, Kane. But we both know it's not her. It's someone who wants her protected, even as they steal millions from her company right under her nose. Yeah, my bet's on the uncle or the ex." A pause, then, "Yes, Theresa's still in the mix, too, but she's at the bottom of my list now."

Leila's ears started to ring and she felt so off balance she actually reached out to the wall for support. Given what Davis had shared about the gun sales, she knew the person responsible was someone in a role of importance. She'd even known the people she loved were potential suspects.

But she'd thought Davis had believed her when she'd

explained why her uncle and Eric would never, ever betray her father. She'd thought he'd trusted her judgment when it came to Theresa, too.

She backed slowly down the hall, using the wall for support, stepping lightly so he wouldn't hear her. She needed to get out of here.

Davis had feelings for her. There was no way he was that good a liar. Yet, he would still use her to get what he needed for this investigation.

This was so much worse than the betrayal she'd felt from Eric. Davis had made her believe they were working together to stop the saboteur. All the while, he was hoping to yank another person she loved out of her life.

She pulled her hand from the wall, pressed it to her chest as she spun and walked a little faster, desperate for escape. The ringing in her ears slowed, and she could hear Davis's voice, farther away now, whispering, "I've got to go."

She turned the knob on the front door slowly, pulled the door open as quietly as possible, then bolted for her car. Putting the key in the ignition seemed to take forever, but then she was speeding away from his house as fast as she could.

It was time to make a clean break from all the people who were lying to her. It was time to stop relying on the FBI to get to the truth. If she was going to prove that the people she loved weren't responsible, she was going to have to do it herself.

It was time to investigate on her own.

Chapter Fifteen

The FBI still considered her a suspect. Not just for selling the military defective body armor, but also for illegally selling guns to criminals. Presumably even of killing her own father.

The fact that Davis didn't believe she was responsible didn't matter. He believed it was someone she loved. Despite all his promises to keep her informed, he was shutting her out.

On one hand, she understood. This was his job, and his top suspects were people close to her. But she'd given him access to everything, tried to help him find the person responsible, no matter who it was, no matter if it destroyed her career. Still, he didn't trust her with the truth.

That meant she couldn't trust him to keep her informed. She couldn't trust him to handle this in a way that would spare all the employees at her company who *weren't* guilty.

After she'd run from his house yesterday, he'd called her. She'd known if she ignored him, he would come over and check on her. So, she'd given herself a few minutes to calm down, for the ringing in her ears to fully subside, then she'd answered his call.

She'd been surprised how normal she'd sounded, how strangely calm she'd felt, as she told him that she'd needed to go home and process the news about her dad's murder. He'd expressed all the right words, even offered to come and sit with her. He'd sounded so genuine that she'd clutched the phone until her hand hurt. But still, her voice had come out even and suitably sad to convince him she just needed time alone.

This morning, she'd waited in her car until he pulled into the office, then cornered him outside when she knew they wouldn't have much time alone. She'd told him she wanted to focus on finding who was to blame for her father's murder, then figure out whatever was going on with them afterward. She'd even managed to say it with a straight face.

He'd nodded, slid his fingers along the edge of her hand and promised, "We're going to figure it out, Leila."

It had taken everything she had not to scream. She'd considered tossing him off the property, denying him access, but that wouldn't help anything. They still needed to find out who was destroying Petrov Armor, who was responsible for the deaths of all those soldiers. But she wasn't about to feed Davis details about the people she loved and let him use the information to destroy them.

He could look at the company finances and security logs all he wanted. Eventually—hopefully—those things would lead him to the truth. That someone else was responsible, someone other than Uncle Joel or Eric. Even though she wasn't Leila's favorite person, someone other than Theresa, too.

Meanwhile, Leila had started her own investigation. The first thing she'd done was put an additional alert on the security system, to notify her if anyone tried to manually override anything. If someone was trying to take armor outside the building without going through proper procedures, Leila wanted to be sure she spotted it.

Now it was time to call in backup, the person she'd

trusted with her deepest secrets since she was thirteen years old.

She hit an internal line on her phone and then asked, "Eric? Can you meet me at the loading dock? I want to discuss something with you."

She knew Eric was still on Davis's suspect list, but Eric had no motivation to wrong the company, to hurt her or her father. If he'd wanted to gain something—more money, a promotion—he could have done so easily without resorting to murder and sabotage.

She hung up before he could ask any questions, then slipped out through the front door. That morning, she'd set Davis up at a computer near where Theresa worked, giving him access to their gun database. She'd suggested he review it to see if he could figure out which gun identification numbers didn't match up to legitimate sales. Davis had told her the Petrov Armor pistols from FBI case files had their ID numbers filed off. So, it wouldn't be an easy match. But she'd suggested he look by date, see if he could come up with anything that seemed suspicious.

The truth was, she hoped he *did* find something, some evidence that would tie all of this to someone other than Joel, Eric or Theresa. The number of employees who'd been around long enough to be involved in the illegal sales for at least eleven years *and* had access to armor material wasn't large. But it was certainly larger than just her uncle, her ex and Theresa.

Thinking of Theresa made her frown. She was the only one on Davis's suspect list that Leila didn't know as well. The woman wasn't always friendly and could sometimes approach insubordinate. But she was paid well and seemed to love R and D. So why risk all of that?

No matter what, Leila knew it was a mystery that would take Davis some time. Which meant he'd be out of her way while she tried to investigate on her own. Or almost on her own.

When Eric rounded the corner of the back of their loading dock and caught sight of her, he grinned. She couldn't help but smile back. Eric had changed a lot since she'd first met him, from gawky teenager with acne to a man who looked like the head of a sales department. But his grin was exactly the same as when they'd first met. Their relationship was so different now, but she'd never forget how he'd been there for her when she'd desperately needed support.

Her uncle had done the exact same thing for her all those years ago, even moved in for a few years after her mom died. He'd made her lunches and driven her to school. Helped her with her homework and convinced her she was still loved, even if her father couldn't show it right then.

Neither of them would ever betray the company. Neither of them would ever deceive her. Most of all, neither of them would have killed her father, a man they both loved perhaps even more than they loved her.

When Eric reached her side, instead of stopping, he pulled her close, hugged her to him in a way that made her realize that unlike twelve years ago, he had no idea what she was thinking. He thought this was about the other day, about his suggestion that they give their relationship another try, maybe even leave the business and start something new together.

So much had happened since then. It was only now that she realized she hadn't actually told him a final *no*.

When she looked up to correct him, he was staring at her, his big smile shifting slowly into something more intimate.

But she couldn't. She pushed away slightly. "Eric, I have to tell you something."

"I know things have been awkward between us for years,

Leila, but I promise, it's going to change now. We can go back to how things used to be."

He dipped his head toward her and before he could reach her, Leila blurted, "Davis is an undercover FBI agent."

DAVIS HAD BARELY seen Leila since Monday. Now, three days later, he was settled in at the desk outside her office where she'd moved him, claiming he was a distraction. Initially, he'd liked the thought that his very presence could distract her from her work. But it was becoming obvious something was wrong.

She was avoiding him. Even worse, she was spending more and more time with Eric. One of his prime suspects. Of course, he couldn't tell her that. Especially since his other prime suspect was her uncle.

Joel Petrov didn't spend a lot of time at the office. As far as Davis could tell, he did his job with as much expediency as possible, then headed out with a charming smile and a wave. Living on all the overtime he'd banked twenty years ago when his brother had needed someone to handle his work and raise his daughter. He had access to everything, but based on both the offhand questions he'd asked other employees and Joel's access card records, he wasn't in restricted areas at unusual times. He was gone enough that he certainly could have been meeting contacts who needed illegal weapons, but he probably wasn't making those contacts through business channels.

Eric Ross was around a lot. To Davis's surprise, his access level was as high as Joel's and Theresa's. As high as Neal's had been before he died. Unlike Joel, he *did* have a lot of unusual activity on his access card, which Davis had somehow missed the first time he'd gone through the records. The legitimate sales calls he was often out on could have definitely also connected him to some less legitimate ones. Or they could have purely been cover for illegal meets. How simple would it be to claim he'd tried to make a sale that hadn't panned out, when actually he was connecting with criminals willing to buy the weapons at highly marked-up prices?

Was that the reason he was hanging around Leila more than usual lately, because he worried Leila knew about a traitor in the company? Or was it simply because he'd sensed the growing connection between her and Davis and he was jealous?

Then, there was Theresa. Even though he couldn't think of any reason she'd try to protect Leila from her contacts if she was the traitor, no one could have pulled off the armor switch with as much ease as the head of research and development.

Right now, he was paying Theresa a visit in her testing area at the back of the office. Other than Eric, Theresa's was the only card with particularly unusual time stamps. While Davis knew he had to tread lightly when it came to questioning Eric or Joel, because of their connections to Leila, the same wasn't true of Theresa.

When he opened the door to the area where Theresa always seemed to work, even when she wasn't testing anything, Davis realized how perfect a setup it was. No one could pass by without her noticing. Plenty of privacy to change records or swap out the material on armor.

She looked up as he entered, a mix of disdain and distrust on her face when she saw it was him. He frowned at the clipboard in his hands, pretending to read something on it, then told her, "We've got some discrepancies in the records. Leila wanted me to track down the reason."

Theresa sat a little straighter in her chair, frowned at him a little harder. But beneath the tough exterior…was that anxiety he saw?

"What kind of discrepancies?"

"Late night use of your access card," Davis said, watching her closely for a reaction.

He got one. But it wasn't quite what he expected. She looked taken aback.

"You mean weekend access? Everyone knows I sometimes work weekends," she added defensively.

"No," Davis replied, frowning. "I mean you returning to the office late at night, after you'd already left for the day."

Theresa shook her head. "That's wrong." Then she stood and crossed her arms over her chest. "I *work late* plenty. But I don't leave and come back. Sounds like a system error."

"You weren't here late at night, three weeks ago, on Friday night, about midnight?"

For a minute, he thought she wasn't going to answer him at all. But then, Theresa's eyes rolled upward and she shook her head. "No. Three weeks ago, on Friday night, I was at a concert. Here." She dug around in her purse, then pulled out her phone. She tapped something onto it, then held it toward him. "I don't know why I need to prove myself to Leila's *assistant*, but here's a picture from the concert. You see the date stamp?"

He studied it, then nodded and handed it back. She could have faked it, but how would she have known to have it ready? Unless she'd put some kind of electronic tag on the records, so she knew when the data was accessed? To give herself a heads-up if anyone ever suspected? "So, how was your card used that night then?"

"I don't know."

He stared hard at her, trying to read her, and she actually fidgeted.

"Look, I know Leila isn't my biggest fan. I'm not hers, either. Don't get me wrong—I think she's done a pretty good job as CEO. Believe me, I was skeptical. The truth is, she never would have had this job if her father didn't start the company. Everyone knows it."

"Word is that you told Leila's father not to recommend Leila her CEO," Davis said.

Theresa scowled, but nodded. "Yeah. She didn't have enough experience."

"Who did you think deserved the position? You?"

Theresa laughed, sat back down. "Maybe. If we're talking pure experience at the company. But all the boring administrative work of running a company?" She gave an exaggerated shudder. "That's not my idea of fun. I like to make things, and make them better. I'd never leave R and D."

"But at the end of the day, you don't get to make the final decisions on what gets made, right? That's Leila."

Theresa nodded slowly, studying him now as closely as he was watching her. "Like the guns? Yeah, that's true. I think it was a mistake, shutting down that side of the business. But so does everyone else here. Even her father. He just didn't say it publicly."

Davis frowned. That was what others at the company had told him, too. Which fit with the idea that Leila's father had been illegally selling guns, but willing to trade it in for the sake of his daughter's success. No matter what kind of man he'd been, he had loved her. The more time Davis spent here, the less he believed Neal Petrov had helped put his daughter in the role of CEO to be his scapegoat.

Maybe that was what had gotten him killed. Maybe he'd tried to go legitimate, to protect her, and his partner hadn't wanted it.

But was his partner Theresa? Maybe. Maybe she just hadn't had enough time to work things out with BECA if they were pressing for arms she couldn't yet deliver. According to everyone he'd talked to, it was Neal's support of Leila's plan to move solely to armor that had made it a reality. Maybe Theresa had hoped to use Neal's death to get gun production going again. That would make it easier for her to return to the illegal sales.

He frowned, not quite liking the logic or the timing. It still seemed like someone who was willing to kill to restart gun production would be willing to tell their contacts where to put the blame for it shutting down in the first place.

He must have stayed silent too long, because all of a sudden, Theresa blurted, "Look, I don't know what Leila thinks I did, or what's going on with my access card. We're not best friends, but when I told her dad that I thought she wasn't ready to be CEO, he made me promise to support her anyway. So, I'm not sure how you heard about what we discussed *in private*, but it's not common knowledge. Neal, Joel and I have known each other for a long time. Heck, I've known Leila since she was a kid. After Neal died, I committed to protecting Leila for him. And I have."

She stared at him with such intensity as she spoke, telling Davis that she'd done something she felt was big in order to protect Leila for Neal. Had she really killed Neal for letting their illegal business get screwed up and then thought she could make up for it by not selling out his daughter?

As Davis stared back at her, he realized it was a definite possibility.

Theresa Quinn had just shot to the top of his suspect list.

Chapter Sixteen

"What if it wasn't just a matter of cheaper materials getting swapped out so someone could pocket the extra cash?" Eric suggested.

"What do you mean?" Leila asked. It was strange, this secret investigation they were running. He'd helped her make an excuse for the armor shipments that weren't going out this week—claiming delays on the military's side. Her employees had seemed to buy it.

Instead of making her feel like they were in on something together, her time with Eric was just making her uncomfortable. She needed to repeat what she'd said earlier, that her feelings weren't the same as when they were younger. But she didn't want to dive into that discussion when there were so many more important things to figure out right now. The future of her company—not to mention justice for the soldiers who'd been killed—depended on her rooting out the traitor.

Pushing her worries about hurting Eric's feelings to the back of her mind, Leila tried to focus on what he'd said. What if it wasn't just a matter of cheaper materials being used for someone to pocket the extra money? "What do you mean?"

"What if *both* sets of armor were made?"

Leila shook her head, still not understanding.

"Leila, what if it's kind of like the guns?" Eric asked. "What if someone sent cheap armor to the military, but sold the good ones at a huge markup to criminals? I know convicted felons can buy body armor. But if these sales are as big as Davis seems to think they are, maybe the same criminals who are buying up boxes and boxes of illegal weapons are also buying armor now? Maybe they're willing to pay more money and keep it on the down-low to keep from attracting any attention from law enforcement."

The idea made a chill run through Leila strong enough to make her reach for the blazer she'd set aside an hour ago when she and Eric had started digging through purchase receipts, looking for anything unusual. Davis hadn't told her what kind of criminals were buying the illegal Petrov Armor pistols. But criminals who needed boxes of them *and* wanted armor to go with it? That sounded like a massacre in the making. She had to stop it.

She couldn't change the past. But she could help find the person responsible, prevent any more illegal sales. And hopefully when they found the traitor, that person would give up their sales list, help the FBI bring those people to justice, too.

"Even taking into account the cost of buying cheaper armor, it's a lot more profit," Eric continued, probably not realizing he didn't need to convince her that his theory made sense. "And I know you think Davis is crazy…" He paused and scowled a little. "Believe me, I don't like agreeing with the guy. But the person who's got the right security level at the company *and* the easiest access to the armor?"

"Theresa," Leila stated. She didn't even like the woman, not really. So, why couldn't she quite bring herself to believe that Theresa would betray Petrov Armor?

"It has to be her," Eric insisted, obviously reading

her reluctance to believe Theresa was the culprit. "It just makes sense."

He stared at her, eyebrows raised until she nodded slowly. Maybe he was right. Maybe he and Davis were both right.

"We don't need Davis here anymore," Eric said, sounding relieved that she'd agreed with his suggestion Theresa was involved. "Tell him what you suspect and stop letting him muck around in the company's private information. Send him on his way and let him deal with the investigation from the outside, where he belongs."

"Eric, I can't—"

"You need a break from all of this. It's been too much, with your father's death and now this. I know you care about the company, Leila. I know you feel like it's your father's legacy. But you're wrong."

She shook her head.

He smiled at her, this time a sadder, more serious smile. "Don't you get it, Leila? *You're* his real legacy. If everything you've told me is true, this company is finished. You need to cut your losses and let it go. Come with me. Let's start over. A new business, a fresh start together. It doesn't even need to be in Tennessee. Let's get away, take a break and go somewhere." He stared at her with those dark blue eyes she'd fallen for so long ago. "Maybe overseas, lie on a beach for a while. Then we can figure it all out."

She shook her head. No matter how much she wished she could pretend none of this had happened—not the faulty armor or the gun sales or her father's murder—she couldn't leave. Couldn't just run away and hope someone else fixed the threat inside Petrov Armor.

It was *her* business to run now. *Her* responsibility to find out the truth. She owed it to the soldiers who'd been killed, to the employees who'd done nothing wrong and to her father.

She saw the disappointment on Eric's face even before she spoke. "I have to see this through to the end. No matter what happens."

YESTERDAY, AT THE end of the day, Leila had slipped out of the office without Davis spotting her. She'd left him a text message telling him she'd gone home to rest and that she'd see him tomorrow. This morning, she'd been shut in her office nonstop. Davis was tired of waiting for her to emerge, tired of waiting for her to explain why she was avoiding him.

He strode to the door of her office, had his hand on the door handle when he heard Eric's voice from inside the office. Davis froze, withdrew his hand slowly as he realized how often he'd stopped by Leila's office to talk to her in private over the past few days and found her and Eric "talking business."

Initially, he'd been unconcerned. Eric was her head of sales. But last week, she'd answered his questions quickly and efficiently, rarely spent more than an hour or two in meetings with Eric. The last few days, it seemed as though Eric and Leila were constantly meeting.

A bad feeling settled in his stomach. Could she have confided in Eric about the investigation?

Like they had been all week, the blinds on the inside of Leila's window into the main part of the office were down. But there was a gap on one side where a few slats had stuck together. Davis glanced behind him to make sure other employees weren't paying him attention as he put his eye to it.

Inside the office, Leila was sitting at the chair behind her desk as usual. But instead of being at the chair on the other side, Eric had pulled his seat around next to Leila.

Eric was frowning, pointing at something on the computer while Leila looked serious and determined. As though they were investigating this case by themselves, the head of the company and one of his main suspects.

Davis stood straighter and backed away, and someone's hand clamped on his shoulder, preventing a collision. He felt himself heat with embarrassment at being caught spying as he turned and found Joel standing there.

Joel held out his hand. "Davis, right?"

When he nodded and shook hands, Joel said, "Why don't we go down the street and grab a drink, have a chat?" Not giving him a chance to say no, Joel added, "Come on," and headed for the door.

Giving Leila's closed office door one last look, Davis followed him to a pub a few blocks away. It had been hard to get to Joel to talk to him, so he wasn't about to let this opportunity go to waste. The man didn't keep regular hours, and hadn't returned Davis's few phone calls, on the pretense of doing business for Leila.

Joel was silent most of the walk, keeping up a good pace. It wasn't until they were seated in a booth and they'd both ordered club sodas that Joel finally spoke. "You're more than just an assistant, aren't you, Davis?"

Davis felt a flash of panic and surprise, then Joel continued. "I can tell you're ambitious. Assistant is a starting point for you."

He nodded at Davis's club soda as it arrived. "I respect a man who doesn't drink while he's on the job. Some people think it's social, but it can make you lose focus." He paused meaningfully, then added, "Women can make you lose focus, too."

Davis nodded, hanging his head a little. Trying to appear embarrassed wasn't a stretch. For an undercover agent, he hadn't done a very good job of hiding his interest in Leila.

At least Joel didn't suspect he was FBI. Leila's uncle reaching out to him like this was a perfect way to get information. Davis just needed to steer the conversation in the right direction.

"It's great working for Leila," he started, "but yeah, I took this job as a chance to see the inner workings of a big company. My degree is in business management," he added, sticking to the cover résumé TCD had made him. "I am wondering, though…" He trailed off, hoping Joel would prompt him.

"What? Spit it out. I'll give you one rule of business right now—you'll never get what you want if you're not willing to ask for it. Then you've got to be willing to follow through."

Davis nodded, wondering how much of her can-do attitude Leila got from her uncle, rather than her father. "I was actually wondering about Theresa. It seems like she's been here a lot longer than Leila. I was kind of surprised—"

"That Leila was made CEO?" Joel finished for him. "I know people see it as nepotism, and let's be honest, I'm a little biased. There was a period where I basically raised that girl. But if you underestimate what Leila is capable of, that's a mistake. She might have come into the role a little young, but she belongs there."

Davis felt pride swell in his chest at the words, even though the feeling was ridiculous. He had no reason to feel anything but impartial interest. But no matter how much Leila was pushing him away right now, he was never going to feel impartial toward her. Never.

The thought gave him pause, but he pushed it to the back of his mind. Something to pick apart later, when he wasn't undercover. When he didn't have a dead friend who deserved his full attention on finding out who had caused her death.

"Theresa's great," Joel continued. "She's driven and ridiculously intelligent when it comes to innovation. She can be too intense sometimes, but she's reliable. She's a workaholic, too, but believe me, that's because she loves the research, loves the process of creating a new product. Theresa has no interest in being CEO. Eric, on the other hand…"

Davis had been staring pensively into his club soda, and he couldn't stop his head from popping up at Joel's statement. Theresa was still the stronger suspect, but Eric's time stamp had shown unusual activity too. Davis wasn't sure how to approach him, especially if Leila might have confided in him.

"Look, I like Eric. I've known him since he was a kid. Even back then, he was always hanging around wherever Leila was." Joel fiddled with his glass, still mostly full. "So I'll just say this—Leila has a blind spot when it comes to Eric."

"How so?" Davis asked, wondering why Joel had reached out to him. Was it just to give him career advice? Or was this really about Eric? Did Joel suspect Eric of something and need a sounding board?

Joel sighed, sounding conflicted as he spoke. "Eric loved my brother like a father. His own old man was never around. Which is better than what Neal and I had, but that's a whole other story. Anyway, when Eric graduated from high school, my brother saw something in him. Knew he'd be a hard worker, could succeed with the right mentorship. Talked Eric into going to school at night and working here during the day."

Davis nodded, having heard as much from Leila.

"The thing is, Eric *wasn't* my brother's kid. Leila was. So, when it came time to suggest a name to the board for CEO…" Joel shrugged, took a long sip of his club soda.

"Eric's jealous that Leila took over?"

"Resentful, is more the way I see it." Joel set his glass down, looking troubled. "He still loves Leila, that I know. But I'm not sure that love is pure. It's too tied up in him wanting all the things he thinks should be his. That's not just Neal's daughter. It's also her job. I think he'd do almost anything to get it—or if he can't do that, to take it away from Leila."

Chapter Seventeen

Most days of the week, there were lots of employees in the office well into the evening. Leila's father had hired a dedicated group, people who cared about what they did. But on Fridays, many of them took off an hour early, got a jump-start on their weekend. A fair trade for the extra work they'd put in during the week, so both her father and Leila encouraged it.

Tonight, Leila wished she had a different policy. It was only six o'clock, but because it was Friday, the place was eerily empty. Normally she didn't mind being in the office alone. She should have been happy to have some time alone to think.

Right now, though, she wanted the background noise. She wanted the reminder that she wasn't all alone in the world, that she still had people she loved and who loved her, that she still had a company to run, to keep her going. When she was alone, it was too easy to fixate on what she'd lost. Her mother, so long ago. Her father, so recently. And soon, probably her father's company, too.

It was too easy to focus on Davis. Too easy to think about how much she already missed him, after a week of barely talking. Definitely too easy to worry about what else he might have uncovered in her company that he wasn't telling her.

By this point, he'd figured out that she was keeping something from him. But he hadn't pulled the plug on his undercover operation, so he didn't realize she'd told anyone about who he really was.

Guilt nagged her, an itch to come clean with him that she couldn't give in to. Half the reason she'd blurted the truth to Eric had been to stop him from kissing her. Right now, she wanted to talk to her uncle about what was going on. But even though Davis had betrayed her, she didn't want to do the same to him. She'd broken her promise by telling Eric, but Davis's words had rung in her head about the secrecy of the investigation. So, she'd made Eric promise repeatedly not to tell anyone else. And as bad as she wanted her uncle's insight right now, she'd resisted confiding in him.

She wondered if Davis had decided to do it himself. He and her uncle had disappeared in the afternoon. They'd returned after an hour, both looking serious. Her uncle had given Davis a pointed nod as they'd headed to their separate work spaces. It was a nod Leila recognized, one that said the men were on a shared mission.

It was a little surprising that Davis would spill FBI secrets voluntarily, but her uncle was persuasive. And he was insightful. If there was anyone who knew the ins and outs of the company as well as she did—or maybe even better—it was Uncle Joel.

Before Eric had taken off, Davis had popped his head into her office. He'd told her he was heading home in a subdued tone, given no hint that he still believed the lie she'd told him earlier in the week.

The desire to call him right back, demand that he come clean with her so they could figure out not just what was happening at Petrov Armor, but also what was happening between them, had almost been too strong to resist. But she had resisted, and now Davis was gone. A little voice in the back of her mind told her it was unlikely he'd be back on Monday morning. She wondered if a group of FBI agents holding up badges and making a scene would arrive instead.

Leila swore, rubbed the back of her neck and stood up. The darkness beyond her office was depressing, almost spooky, especially knowing that the person who'd attacked her had followed her from her office. But he was in jail, Leila reminded herself. After enough time had gone by without another incident, the police believed she was safe, so she no longer had cops following her. Davis seemed less convinced—or maybe he was just overprotective—but she needed to focus on things she could control.

Besides, what better time was there to get a jump on Davis's investigation? The question was, where could she look that she hadn't already checked?

The security access logs. It was one of the few things Davis had reviewed without her. She and Eric had talked about Theresa's easy access to the armor materials, and they'd looked through supply orders. Since Davis had already found Theresa's access card used at strange hours, Eric had suggested they not waste their time rechecking.

Still, Davis wasn't telling her everything. So maybe he'd found more than a single late-night access. Maybe he'd found a pattern. And as much as she didn't want to believe Theresa was involved, Eric was right. She was the most logical choice.

Besides being the one most familiar with the armor material, she was the one who'd have the easiest time swapping it out. Of all the employees who'd been here a long time and had sufficient security clearance to be able to pull this off, she was one of the few who hadn't been brought in by her father. Uncle Joel had found Theresa. When her father returned to work, he and Theresa seemed to have a mutual admiration, but maybe Leila had misread it.

She sank back into the chair behind her desk and pulled up the security card logs, scrolling back to the time when the defective armor had been shipped out. A single late-night access by Theresa, just as Davis had said.

Frowning, she leaned back in her chair and sighed. Then, she slid forward again and went back a few weeks. Before the shipment had been sent out, around the time the armor would have been made. Three late-night access logs that week. Her heart pounded faster, the excitement of finding something mixed with the anger of Theresa's betrayal.

Her breath stalled in her throat as she read the name on the log. Not Theresa, but Eric.

"No," Leila said out loud, leaning closer to the screen as if the proximity would suddenly change the name in front of her in black and white. "No way."

"No way what?" a familiar voice came from the doorway to her office.

Her heart seemed to freeze, then take off at an intensity that was almost painful as she lifted her gaze to find Eric leaning against the door frame, scowling.

DAVIS TOSSED HIS button-down on the floor and kicked out of his slacks, trading them for the jeans and T-shirt he preferred. He probably wouldn't be wearing the office attire again anytime soon. He doubted he'd go back to Petrov Armor on Monday morning. When he'd said goodbye to Leila in her office, it had felt final.

He was closing in on a suspect. As much as he'd hoped it would be Theresa, because it would be least devastating to Leila, it looked like Eric Ross was the traitor. After talking to Joel, he'd come back to the office and dug through the security records a little closer, going back much further than he had before. What he'd found was a pattern of unusual access. It wasn't a slam dunk, but it was enough.

The most logical next step was to send in a team with warrants in hand, and he expected that would happen before Monday morning. Joel had just thought he was helping Davis with a little career advice, then venting a bit about a guy he didn't think was good enough for his niece. But he'd given Davis the final pieces he'd needed to send his team in the right direction.

Joel had solidified the motivation for why the man who'd thought of Neal Petrov like a father would try to steal from him, then kill him. Jealousy and revenge. It was the thing Melinda, ever the profiler, would want to know when they asked for warrants. Why would Eric Ross do it? Well, he finally knew.

No way had Eric worked with someone else, least of all the man who'd forced him to break up with Leila. Eric had been in it alone.

It was time to get out. Davis still wasn't positive what had happened to make Leila suddenly stop trusting him, but as he'd thought back on the timing, he'd realized she'd started avoiding him after his phone call with Kane at his house. They'd mostly talked about the BECA side of the investigation, but Davis's progress at Petrov Armor had come up briefly. Still, once he'd remembered the few words he'd spoken about it, he'd known. That had to be what had changed. He'd been whispering, but Leila must have somehow overheard him say the people she cared about most were suspects in his investigation.

She hadn't denied him access, probably still believed the truth would come out and exonerate them. It physically hurt him that he was going to shatter that belief. But they couldn't go on like this. Especially not with Eric probably getting suspicious that Leila suspected something, which might explain why he'd suddenly sought her out at every opportunity. If she hadn't already, eventually, she'd let Davis's identity slip and Eric would start to cover his tracks. If that happened, he might do a good enough job that the FBI couldn't prove it, or he'd run off on a convenient "vacation" to a country without extradition.

The whole drive home, Davis had reached for his phone over and over, wanting to call Leila, wanting to explain that he'd never intended to hurt her, that he'd never intended to fall for her. But he couldn't tip her off that he was finished at Petrov Armor.

If she didn't hate him already, she was going to hate him soon.

Davis took a deep breath, trying to calm the urge to hit something, because he didn't have time to go to the gym and work out his aggression on a punching bag. He grabbed the attaché case he'd tossed on the floor and took it to his desk, dumping out the contents. Notes on relevant information about Eric. He needed to put it all together and present it to Pembrook so they could make the strongest case for the warrants. He wanted to serve them as soon as they could, get this over with, then move on with his life.

He was going to have to do it without Leila. Davis rubbed his temples, where a headache had suddenly formed. How had she gotten to him so quickly, so completely?

Focus, he reminded himself. He couldn't control what happened after those warrants were served. Couldn't control whether or not bringing down the person who'd swapped out the faulty armor dragged down the entire company with him. Couldn't control whether Leila's career and the legacy she'd tried so hard to preserve for her father crashed down around her.

All he could do was his job. He'd sworn an oath as an FBI agent to uphold the law. And he'd made a personal promise that he was going to find the person responsible for Jessica's death.

Gritting his teeth, Davis lined up his notes on Eric with the time line of possible illegal arms sales Kane and Melinda had put together. When his phone rang, he scowled at it, debating not answering. But it was a local number. Maybe Leila, calling from her office?

"Davis," he answered curtly, still in FBI mode. And trying to put as much of a barrier as possible between himself and Leila. Because if she asked him straight out, he wasn't sure he could lie to her and not hate himself.

But the voice that came over the line wasn't Leila. "Davis, it's Joel. Look, I'm sorry to call you after hours like this, but I've found something."

"What is it?" After Joel had shared that he thought Eric was out for Leila's job, Davis had acted like he was hesitant to say anything, but finally blurted that he'd felt something odd was going on at the company. He'd said he suspected it was preparation for a hostile takeover of Leila's CEO position, that maybe Eric had cut some corners in ways that would come back to her. Joel had promised to look into it.

When the end of the day had come and Joel had just headed out without a word, Davis figured the man had either been humoring him or hadn't found anything. But the intensity in Joel's voice now said otherwise.

"After we talked, I took a look at our purchase records. And you're right. Little things seem off, especially with recent armor purchases. All the odd purchases were logged in by Eric. There's nothing obvious enough to draw attention, but looking at it all together, it's not quite right."

"Not right, how?"

"Well, I know you thought Eric could be cutting corners and trying to make it seem like Leila's fault, but these purchases all seem just a bit too high. Like he was paying for more materials than he actually received."

Or he'd received plenty of materials, but he'd only

brought some of it into the office and kept the rest of it for illegal sales. "What if he wasn't paying for more than he got?"

"If we got all this material, I'm sure Theresa would have noticed. She's the one receiving it."

"What if she wasn't?"

"What do you mean?"

"Would Eric know how to build the armor? Theoretically?" Davis pressed. Could he have swapped out the faulty material himself?

"Sure," Joel replied simply. "He's been here a long time. He's seen Theresa and her team do it. But why would he want to build it himself? Anyway…"

"Something's not right," Davis stated, summing up. His pulse quickened at the thought of new, potentially more conclusive evidence to take to his boss. If he could get Joel to willingly hand it over, even better.

"Yeah," Joel agreed. "Normally I wouldn't talk about this at all with a brand-new employee, but I didn't even suspect anything until you brought it up. I'm going to have to tell Leila at some point, but she's been through so much lately. I don't want to bother her with this if there's some other explanation."

"I think that's a good idea," Davis agreed. For the investigation, he needed Leila to stay ignorant of this new development. But knowing that didn't stop guilt from flooding him. It didn't matter that they hadn't even known each other for two weeks. He owed her more than lies.

"I'm glad you agree," Joel said. "Even though I don't necessarily want to see my niece get back together with her ex, the truth is, Eric isn't the only one who still has feelings there. Leila never totally got over him, either. He broke up with her so out of the blue, but it wasn't his decision. I don't want to see my niece hurt, so if I'm wrong about this, I'd rather you help me figure it out before I break the news to Leila."

"What do you mean that breaking up with Leila wasn't Eric's decision?" Davis asked, a bad feeling forming.

"I'm sure my brother meant well, but asking Eric to break up with Leila all those years ago might have fueled some of this. I'm sure Eric figured one day Neal would change his mind, then hand over the company to him and offer his blessing on dating his daughter again, too. But it didn't happen that way."

"And his resentment has been building up ever since," Davis stated.

"Exactly. I think the other part of what's behind Eric's need to be CEO is to prove his worth to Leila. Doesn't make a whole lot of sense, since it would be at her expense, but it's a power thing." Joel sighed heavily. "At least, that's my suspicion. The fact is, I need an outside view. I've known Eric for so long, it's hard for me to be objective. Because there's something else I found."

"What is it?" Davis pressed when Joel took a breath.

"Something at our remote testing grounds. It could be connected to Eric too, but—"

"*Remote* testing grounds?" Davis knew about the second testing area in their office, a soundproofed area where the guns used to get tested. But Leila had never mentioned a remote facility. He resisted the urge to swear, held his silence while he waited for Joel to explain.

"Yeah, it's the other place we used to test the guns," Joel continued easily, probably not sensing Davis's anxiety.

But why would he? Joel thought he was uncovering a simple plot by Eric to undermine his niece, take over her position as CEO. He had no idea he was helping to unroot a long-running criminal enterprise.

"When Leila shut down the gun side of the business, we

didn't really need it anymore. We already had two testing areas inside the office, and those were much more convenient. So, this one was shut down. Or at least, it was supposed to be."

If it wasn't, it was the perfect place to test excess guns before selling them to criminals, instead of destroying them like Leila's plan dictated. It was probably also the perfect place to swap out the materials on armor, sell the good ones to criminals at a marked-up price and send the cheaper versions for contracts that had already been sold to the military. Make some cash and destroy the reputation of the woman he was trying to unseat at the same time.

Davis glanced down, realizing he'd fisted his hand so hard that he'd actually stopped blood flow to his fingertips. He forcibly loosened his fingers as he asked Joel, "Where is this place?"

"I'll text you the directions," Joel said. "Is it too much to ask you to meet me there tonight? I want to show you in person what I found before I tell Leila, get your thoughts on what the hell is going on here."

"Sure, I can do that," Davis said, fighting to keep his voice even and offhand.

Inside, he was screaming. This was it. He could feel it. This was the missing piece of the puzzle that would help him finally solve who was responsible for Jessica's death.

"Great," Joel said. "I just texted you the address. When can you meet me there?"

Davis glanced at the address. The remote testing facility *was* remote, at least in the sense that it was in a deserted area on the edge of Knoxville. The perfect place for Eric to conduct meetings with criminals, too.

"I can leave right now," Davis said.

"Great, I'll see you there."

Davis hung up, glanced at his phone to see if he had

any other messages. None, not a peep from Leila. Then, he grabbed his leather jacket and headed for his car. Right now, the rest of the TCD team was prepping for their own big arrest. They knew he was feeling close to finding answers at Petrov Armor. He'd contacted them after he checked out the initial lead from Leila's uncle, giving them the name of his suspect. But if this revealed what he thought it was going to, there'd be no delay in getting the warrants.

He'd be ready to make an arrest tonight.

Chapter Eighteen

"No way, what?" Eric repeated, striding into her office as if it was his.

Leila's fingers felt clumsy as she moved the mouse to exit the supply order information she'd been reviewing, the logs that listed Eric's name next to orders connected to the faulty armor. Her heart pounded way too fast as she finally got it closed, just before Eric rounded her desk to stare at her now-blank screen.

Eric's suspicious gaze traveled from the computer to her face, assessing with seventeen years of experience reading her. She scrambled to come up with an answer he'd believe, even as her mind struggled to accept that Eric could have been the person betraying the company for so many years. That he could have killed her father, and tried to have her killed.

She stood abruptly, her thighs bumping the chair awkwardly and sending it sliding backward into the wall. Her legs tensed, ready to run, and her hands fisted with the desire to take a swing at him so strong she was actually shaking. *Eric had killed her father.*

Seventeen years of memories flashed before her eyes as Eric put his hand on her arm, leaning close with wide, innocent eyes.

"Are you okay?"

Images of Eric at fifteen years old, lanky and shy, asking to sit next to her and not taking no for an answer. A few months later, meeting her father and seeming to bond with him almost immediately, their connection as strong as his feelings for her, just different. Supposedly, the father he'd never had. And all the years since, in the office, laughing with her father, celebrating new deals with him, breaking down and weeping at his funeral.

Were all those memories lies?

Had everything he'd done since been a lie? Pretending to help her with the investigation in order to keep her close, see what she knew? Pretending to have romantic feelings for her again, suggesting they go to some foreign country together, so she'd help him get away before the FBI closed in?

Leila pulled free without answering. She wanted to run, but she was breathing so fast it felt like she was going to hyperventilate. Eric had been a track star in high school. Was there really any chance she could outrun him?

Would he kill her himself? Make it look like another mugging gone wrong?

Her hands fisted again, her breathing evening out, becoming more measured, deeper, as anger replaced her panic and disbelief. If he'd killed her father, she wasn't running away, hoping to save herself. She was fighting. She was making sure there was no way it would look like anything but a deliberate murder if he killed her. If fury mattered as much as brute strength, she'd take him with her, the man she'd once loved so deeply.

That fact made his betrayal so much worse.

"Leila," Eric whispered. "What's happening right now?"

His tone was worried, but there was an undercurrent of something else, something she couldn't quite identify.

"Hey, Leila, I was wondering—oh!"

Leila spun toward the sound of Theresa's voice and found the head of R and D in the doorway of her office.

Theresa was looking back and forth between her and Eric with surprise and concern. She was also backing away, as if to give them privacy. "Sorry about that. I can come back la—"

"Theresa!" Leila's voice came out too high-pitched and she tried to breathe deeply, calm herself down. Even though it made her want to cringe, she clutched Eric's arm and gave him her best "follow my lead" look.

His forehead creased and his lips turned up, telling her he either didn't understand what she was doing or didn't believe it.

Pretend you still think it's Theresa, Leila told herself, as the way out came to her. *Pretend you'd been freaking out because you found something to suggest Theresa was the traitor.*

Could she pull it off? Avert Eric's suspicion long enough to tell Davis, to get him to check out Eric? Maybe even avert his suspicion long enough to save her life? Because if Eric was willing to kill her father over this, he was probably willing to do the same to her.

"It's come to my attention that you didn't ever want me to be CEO," Leila said, making her tone aggressive and taking a step toward Theresa. She mentally apologized to the woman, who'd never been particularly friendly with her, but as far as Leila knew, had never publicly questioned her leadership.

Theresa shook her head, but she seemed more baffled at the sudden outburst than denying the accusation.

"Worse than that, Theresa, I'm seeing signs that you've—"

"Is this about the security card discrepancies?" Theresa cut her off. She sighed heavily, meant to be heard. "Your assistant already grilled me about this. Didn't he tell you?" She frowned, glancing from Leila to Eric.

Leila followed her gaze. Eric wasn't looking at Theresa, but at her. There was still suspicion in his gaze, but it seemed more like confusion than malice.

"Look, you're right," Theresa blurted as Leila continued to stare at Eric, uncertainty hitting.

Had she misinterpreted the records? Could there be some other explanation? Hope filled her. Eric's friendship when they were kids had altered the trajectory of her life. And she knew Eric's assertion that her father was the dad he'd never had wasn't one-sided. Her father had loved Eric like a son. She desperately didn't want all of that to be tainted.

"I don't think you should have been made CEO," Theresa continued, as Leila only half listened. "But I've never said that publicly. Within the company, I always supported you. I did my best to protect you. I felt like I owed it to your dad. And your uncle, even though I shouldn't really owe him anything." She let out a nervous-sounding laugh that was unusual enough from always confident Theresa to get Leila's full attention.

"Why not?" Leila asked.

"Why not what?" Theresa squinted at her, her expression saying she wasn't sure if Leila had totally lost it or if she legitimately needed to defend herself and her loyalty.

"Why wouldn't you owe Uncle Joel anything?" He'd been the one to hire her after all, not Leila's dad.

"Well, I mean, he should feel pretty good about what he's gotten from me." She flushed a little, shrugged.

"You and Uncle Joel…"

"Yeah, for the last couple of months again," Theresa admitted, her gaze darting from Leila to Eric as her cheeks turned an even deeper red. "It's foolish, I know. We've been on-again, off-again for years. It's casual. Your uncle will never do serious."

"How casual?" Leila asked as a new, terrible possibility nudged at her. Davis had told his team that Theresa, Eric and Joel were his top suspects. If Uncle Joel had been dating Theresa, he could have easily swiped her card. Maybe even borrowed her car.

She tried to shrug off the idea. She loved her uncle. He loved her. He'd half raised her. And he loved her dad. The two brothers had grown up with abuse so bad that Leila had never met her grandparents. Uncle Joel and her dad had been incredibly close, until her dad had met her mom. Even afterward, they'd stuck together. Uncle Joel had taken over her dad's company at a time when it would have folded otherwise.

He'd saved her father's livelihood, ensured they still had the money to send Leila to the best schools. But that act had also given Uncle Joel a level of access to everything that he never would have had otherwise. It had given him contacts and opportunities. And he was often out of the office, something she'd never questioned because of all the years he'd put in holding the company together. What if he'd spent that time using the company for his own gain, the way he did women?

No way, Leila told herself, ashamed for even thinking it.

"…a charmer," Theresa was saying and Leila tried to focus, realizing the woman was talking about her relationship with Leila's uncle.

"It wouldn't have lasted anyway," Theresa said, still flushed a deep red. "I know you and your uncle are close, but there's a reason he's got a reputation with women as a love 'em and leave 'em kind of guy. He's…" She shook her head. "Never mind. Jeez. I don't know why I'm telling you this. And I don't know why there's suddenly all this scrutiny on my access card, but whatever you suspect me of, I didn't—"

"He's *what*?" Leila pressed, ignoring the rest of it.

Theresa shrugged, then said softly, "I don't know if he's really capable of loving anyone."

Theresa apologized, tried to backtrack, but Leila was only half paying attention. Words her father had spoken years ago, with embarrassment and a hint of shame popped into her mind. "He's just unreliable, honey. He's always in things for himself." It had been so long ago, before her mother had died, one of many times her uncle had promised to show up for something, but never appeared.

But he'd changed. Hadn't he? She couldn't possibly have misjudged him so thoroughly.

Leila clutched her stomach, which churned as she realized that if Uncle Joel had taken Theresa's access card to swap out the armor, if he'd been the one betraying the company for cash all these years, then it was so much worse than even thinking Eric had done it. It would mean Uncle Joel had killed his own brother.

"Leila."

Eric's tone, full of dark realization, snapped her out of her spiraling thoughts.

"I'm so sorry," he said, gripping her arm. "I know I promised I wouldn't, but…"

He looked from her to Theresa as Leila snapped, "What? What is it?"

"I told your uncle that Davis is FBI."

BECA WAS GOING DOWN.

Not all of the members, because the loosely connected organization had members across the country. But enough that Kane felt really good about today's arrest plan.

Except for one thing. No matter what argument he threw at her, Melinda refused to be shut out of the arrest.

Even now, she was babbling on in profiler mode, acting like she had any right to fish around in his mind.

He'd thought that when they'd last argued, when she'd revealed—intentionally or not—that she'd had some deep loss of her own, she'd back off. That she'd let him take the lead and she'd fade into the background, focus on the paperwork and the profiling. Let him dive into the danger. The way it should be, each of them focusing on their strengths.

But if nothing else, Melinda was persistent and stubborn. Even if she didn't want to work with him at all.

The idea stung. It was ironic, given how hard he'd tried to make her feel that way. Now that she did, he half wished he could take it back.

But not right now. Not with a dangerous large-scale arrest happening on a group known for its propensity for violence and a stockpile of ready weapons. The FBI had gotten a tip that a group was meeting that night. The arrest warrants had come in and the plan was to make a big arrest, grab a bunch of them before word could get out and anyone could run—or arm themselves and prepare for a standoff.

He didn't want Melinda anywhere near it.

"This is still about Pembrook's daughter," Melinda insisted, and Kane couldn't believe her audacity.

He ground his back teeth together, trying to hold in the anger that always rushed forward when anyone dared to bring up that incident.

"You're scared I'm going to get hurt like she did." Melinda kept pushing.

"Not *hurt*," Kane snapped. "*Dead.* She's dead."

"And I'm not her," Melinda stated, making him want to slap his hand over her mouth to shut her up.

Or maybe slam his lips against hers. Different method, same end result. She'd finally have to shut up.

"Let's go." Laura's voice preceded her. When their teammate finally appeared at the doorway, her expression as buttoned-up as the rest of her, she gave them a searching glance. Then she added, "Whatever you two are arguing about this time, maybe save it for after the big arrest."

Then she was gone and Melinda was staring back at him, with eyebrows raised.

"Fine," Kane said on a heavy exhale. If Melinda wanted to rush into danger, instead of staying in the office and doing her profiler work, so be it.

He strode past her, following the rest of the team out to the SUVs. On the way, he grabbed a submachine gun and slung it over his gear. Then, he climbed in.

This was going to be a dangerous batch of arrests, the kind the FBI would often hand off to one of their SWAT teams. But Pembrook had felt confident her team could handle it, and no one was about to suggest otherwise. In deference to the level of threat, every agent crammed into the SUV wore more gear than typical. They all had body armor—not from Petrov Armor, thank goodness—and even helmets.

The submachine guns weren't standard issue, either. They were usually reserved for tactical teams. But tonight, that was the agents of TCD.

Kane glanced at Melinda as she hopped on board. The SUV had been converted, so the backseats had two rows facing each other. She sat across from him, looking even smaller than usual weighed down with all the extra gear. She stared straight at him, her face an expressionless mask. But there was something in her gaze that looked like nerves.

His gut clenched. She didn't have the same level of experience on these kinds of arrests as the rest of the team.

Sure, she'd been a regular special agent once. Then she'd traded in the field for an office where she could analyze the mind-set of serial killers, terrorists and zealots. She didn't belong here.

But that wasn't his call.

He tried to hold in his anxiety, but it only got worse as the SUV started up, heading toward the site of the raid. With so much undercover work, he rarely felt anxious. But when he did, it always seemed to be a sign that something was going to go terribly wrong.

The last time he'd felt this much anxiety was the day Pembrook's daughter had died.

Chapter Nineteen

Uncle Joel *knew*.

Eric had told him days ago that Davis was an undercover FBI agent. He'd never said a word to her. Never chastised her for giving the FBI such unrestricted access to the company. Instead, he'd gotten chummy with Davis, spent more than an hour out of the office with him in the afternoon.

What had happened during that time? If Davis still suspected Uncle Joel, why hadn't he said anything to her? If Uncle Joel was really involved, what was his end goal with chumming around with Davis?

More than anything right now, she needed to know Davis's whereabouts. He'd left that evening with barely a word to her. Deep down, she'd known he wasn't coming back.

She'd called him three times in the last ten minutes, and each call had gone to voice mail. Maybe he was busy and she was overreacting. She didn't believe he was the kind of guy who'd ignore her out of spite, not after the closeness they'd shared.

Then again, could she really trust her own judgment? She glanced from Eric to Theresa and back again. In the space of a few days, she'd suspected them both of being the traitor. Maybe one of those suspicions was right and thinking it was Uncle Joel was way off base.

But the way her stomach was churning with fear, horror and betrayal right now, she couldn't risk that she was wrong yet again. She needed to find Davis.

If Uncle Joel had really murdered his own brother, what was one undercover FBI agent?

"I need your help." Leila's voice came out a frightened squeak.

"What do you need?" Eric asked as Theresa repeated for the third time since Eric had announced it, "Davis is FBI? Your assistant?"

"Yes, Davis is FBI," Leila responded, turning to fully face Theresa, studying her expression. By now, she'd had a good ten minutes to disguise whatever she was feeling. If Theresa was the traitor, she was cool under pressure.

"So, *that's* why he was asking about my access card," Theresa said, sounding horrified. "I should have known you were lying about the armor. It was ours, wasn't it?"

"Yes."

Theresa sank into the chair on the other side of Leila's desk. She shook her head, sounding lost. "I'm going to be ruined. This might be your company, but I'm in charge of development. How did this get past me? We have so many checks in place."

"Whoever did it knows every one of them and how to get around them," Leila replied, thinking it less and less likely that the traitor was in the room with her.

"And you honestly think it was your uncle?" Eric asked, the pain in his eyes mirroring her own feelings.

He'd never been close to her uncle, so Leila knew that pain was for her. She was grateful for it, knew it reflected how deeply he cared for her. But right now, with Davis potentially in trouble, Leila knew for sure the words she'd spoken to Eric earlier were true. Their time was over. She'd fallen in love with Davis.

As Eric stared at her, the expression in his eyes shifted. He'd known her too long.

She shook her head, wishing he hadn't realized it like this, wishing she could say something to stop the pain she was causing him.

Before she could say anything, Eric said softly, "It's okay, Leila. What do you need?"

"We have to find Davis," Leila said. "I know this is probably crazy, but I'm worried that he's in trouble. If my uncle really is behind this—"

"You think *Joel* made the faulty armor?" Theresa asked, her face going deathly pale. *"Why?"*

"Money," Leila answered simply. Part of her still couldn't believe her uncle would ever betray his own family to such a degree. Another part of her, the part that remembered how her uncle had been before he stepped up when her mom died, said it was possible.

A sob ripped its way up her throat and Leila swallowed it, her eyes tearing with the effort. Now wasn't the time to grieve all she was about to lose if she was right. She needed to focus on making sure Davis didn't get tricked like her father.

"Theresa, I need you to go to my uncle's house," Leila said, her voice strong and clear now that she was thinking only about next steps and not emotions. "See if he's there. If he is, make up whatever excuse you need, but text me right away." She turned to face Eric. "I need you to go to Davis's house and see if he's home. If not, I need you to call the FBI."

"What about you?" Eric asked.

"I'm going to the remote testing facility." They'd closed it down a year ago. Long-term, the plan had been to convert it into another armor testing location, but they didn't need it right now. The ones inside the main office were enough. It made no sense for her uncle to be at the remote location.

But he'd loved to go to there. She'd find him there randomly when she'd stop by to do checks, back when they still sold weapons. He'd be shooting one of their pistols or even just hanging around. In response to her surprise, he'd always joke, "We make guns, Leila. We should at least get a little shooting in."

"Maybe we should all stick together," Eric argued. "Check each place out in order and—"

"No," Leila cut him off. "Look, I'm probably overreacting here, but I need to be sure. And I need to know *now*. Can you do this?"

Theresa stood, her face still paler than usual, but with two deep red spots high on her cheeks. "Yes." Then she reached across the desk and squeezed Leila's hand. "Be careful. I know you love your uncle, but he's got a dark side. If you find him, don't let him realize what you suspect."

Theresa headed out of the office, and Eric gripped Leila's arms, turning her to face him. "Leila, this seems risky. I still think—"

She pulled free. "Eric, I don't care what Theresa says. My uncle loves me. He'd never hurt me. You're the one who needs to be careful. If my uncle is with Davis, just leave and call the FBI, okay?"

He nodded, his lips pursed in an expression she recognized. He didn't like it, but he knew he wasn't talking her out of this.

Then he was gone. Leila stayed in her office, trying to text Davis. She stared at the screen for another thirty seconds, hoping a response would pop up. When it didn't, she took off at a run.

The remote testing facility wasn't that far from the office by car, but while the area around their main building had continued to be built up year after year, the spot where they'd put this facility had stayed mostly deserted. *The perfect place to murder someone.*

The unbidden thought made Leila shiver and she punched on the gas, taking the back roads way too fast. As she pulled into the lot, her heart seemed to slam down toward her stomach.

Two cars were there—her uncle's and Davis's.

There had to be some innocent explanation. Maybe her uncle had offered to give Davis a tour of the place. She'd never mentioned it to him, so Davis had probably jumped at the chance. It hadn't even occurred to her, since they hadn't used it in almost a year. Frustration nipped at her because it was the perfect location to put together inferior armor.

Uncle Joel would never kill Davis. He'd never kill her father.

No matter how many times she repeated those things to herself, the fear remained.

Climbing out of her car, Leila glanced around. The place really was in the middle of nowhere, with woods on one side and a huge, overgrown field on the other. The fence around the lot was still intact, but the guard gate had been up when she'd arrived, some kind of malfunction. She had no idea how long it had been that way. It had been months since she'd made a personal check of this place.

Locking her car, Leila took her phone out of her purse as she ran for the door. With shaking hands, she pulled up the internet, looking for the number of the local FBI. But when she dialed, she got a recording with a list of options and hung up, not willing to wait.

Whatever her uncle was planning to do to Davis, whatever he might have done to her father, he'd never hurt her. If there was one thing she believed without question, it was that. As long as she could get there in time, she could stop him from hurting Davis.

She slid her access card into the reader and yanked open the door, stepping inside.

The lights were on, but the front area with its handful of desks and storage cabinets was empty. Beyond the entry was the testing area. Leila couldn't hear a thing, but if her uncle and Davis were back there, she wouldn't. Since they'd been used for shooting, they were all soundproofed.

Leila used her security card again to enter the shooting area, and her heart gave a painful thump. The testing space at the very back had a green light glowing over the door that meant it was in use.

With every step toward the active lane, Leila's breath became faster, more uneven. When she pulled open the heavy steel door, in front of her was the thing she'd feared most.

Davis was kneeling in the middle of the shooting lane, blood on his head and swaying. Her uncle stood at the front of the lane, a Petrov pistol centered on Davis like a target.

BECA HAD KNOWN they were coming.

One minute, the SUV was driving down the narrow lane toward the mansion where one of the wealthiest BECA members lived, toward a meeting supposedly in progress. Each member of the TCD team had been clutching their submachine guns, gazes steady, jaws tight. Kane's gaze had been on Melinda, cool and slightly angry, as she'd stared back at him.

Then, the world around him exploded in light and sound and the SUV tipped sideways, slamming to the ground on the side away from him.

Kane's head bounced off JC's. The agent had gotten stuck in the middle of their row. Pain filled his head and something dripped in his eye, and then the team around him was scrambling, most of them responding on instinct and training. Across from him, Melinda looked dazed, one hand to her head, blinking rapidly. JC, with his military background, was the first to move, despite the conk to the head.

"Move, move, move," JC ordered. "We're target practice here."

BECA must have had some kind of camera or alert system at the beginning of the long, winding entry to the mansion. They were the kind of group that was always armed, always prepared for a fight. They'd had the place booby-trapped. And Kane knew the BECA members would get here fast, to finish them off. He could already hear them coming, the growl of a large engine speeding toward them, then the screech of brakes.

He scrambled to both brace himself against the seat in front of him and the door and release his seat belt. It took longer than he would have liked. Then there was a face at the window, one that managed to be both snarling and smiling as he lifted his gun.

Forgetting the seat belt, Kane went for his pistol instead. He'd always been a quick draw, but as he saw his face reflected back at him superimposed on the guy intent on killing him, he wasn't sure he was fast enough. Even as he fired three shots and the window exploded, showering glass all over him and the teammates below him, Kane didn't know if he'd hit his mark until the guy dropped out of sight.

He waited for the pain of a bullet to his own body to register, but he only felt the needle-sting of what seemed like hundreds of tiny shards of glass. Not the searing intensity of a bullet. Then more shots boomed, way too many, and Kane cringed, knowing the SUV wasn't armored. A scream from inside the car emphasized the thought, and Kane's stomach clenched even as his mind cleared.

This was it. There was no good way out of this vehicle.

He'd always known he would die on the job. He'd accepted that years ago, in some ways longed for it, because it was no less than he deserved.

But he didn't want to go like this. Not surrounded by more teammates.

His gaze shifted to Melinda, still tethered to her seat, an easy target if someone else managed to clamber up to the side windows—now directly above them. He moved his gaze past her, to the front windshield, now on ground level. Past the two teammates in front, who were either hit or out cold, to the man bending down there, a furious intensity on his face as he lifted his weapon.

Kane shifted, aiming and firing at the same time as JC. Apparently Laura in the driver's seat wasn't as unconscious as she'd seemed, because her gun hand rose at the same time. The guy dropped in a shower of bullets. The front windshield shattered, too, and as shots started coming through the floorboards—now facing toward the zealots—JC yelled, "Ballistic shields!"

Then, someone was handing him a shield and Kane propped it between him and the bottom—now side—of the car, protecting him and the agents below him. Across from him, Melinda was being handed a shield, too. But she urged Evan Duran, in the seat next to her, to trade places.

Awkwardly he swapped with her. Melinda almost fell, but managed to slip between the agents, down to the other side of the SUV, pressed to the ground. But the vehicle wasn't entirely flat, Kane realized. The SUV had landed on something—maybe a boulder—putting the vehicle at a weird tilt. The front of the vehicle was actually slanted downward, too. And as Melinda shoved at the passenger door, it opened a crack.

"Time for BECA to get a surprise," Melinda muttered. Kane grabbed for her, realizing what she was going to do. Melinda was tiny—five foot four and no more than 115 pounds. She could fit through that crack. But no one else would be able to follow.

Kane's fingers closed around Melinda's shirt, gripped hard. But his angle was awkward, and the SUV was crowded, especially as Laura yanked the other agent who'd been sitting up front—Ana Sofia—into the back. More shields were pressed around them and JC lifted his arm over Kane's, firing through the space in the middle. A BECA member screamed outside the front of the vehicle.

Then, it was too late. The fabric slipped out of his grasp and Melinda was gone.

Out of the SUV, alone, facing an unknown number of armed BECA members.

Chapter Twenty

This was a very bad idea.

Melinda had been a regular special agent once, working a Civil Rights squad. With her background in psychology, her supervisor had figured she was a perfect fit for the myriad of human trafficking cases that came their way. That work had been dangerous at times, but it had been the people she'd run into—both victims and perpetrators—who'd made her go into profiling.

She'd been there so long, she'd started to forget what it was like in the field. Profiling sometimes sent her into the thick of a case, but often it left her buried in paperwork. Too many of her days had been spent fixated on the tiny details of a case file that gave her a behavioral analysis and helped her track down the criminal.

When she'd come to TCD, she'd needed a refresher in fieldwork. Right now, as the only agent not hunkered down in the SUV, it didn't feel like even close to enough.

She had no backup out here. Not unless one of the other agents could get clear long enough to rush through the shot-to-pieces windshield. And that was a death wish only one agent was likely to try.

Thinking of Kane made Melinda move faster. She sucked in her breath and turned her head sideways, shoving herself the rest of the way through the SUV's open door.

The helmet barely cleared, but she felt Kane's fingers peel away. Her shirt tore, but she kept going, worming her way toward the rear of the vehicle and praying the whole thing didn't crash down on top of her.

Her submachine gun wouldn't have been an easy fit through the door, so she'd left it in the SUV. Right now, she longed for the comforting feel of the big gun. Sucking in dirt and dust, Melinda angled her pistol awkwardly, praying no one saw her before she was ready. Body armor and a helmet wouldn't be enough if they saw her while she was still trying to squeeze out of here.

When she'd realized the SUV wasn't flat on the ground, that the back door would open just enough, she'd known what she had to do. Yes, the agents inside had covered themselves well with strong ballistic shields. But eventually, the BECA members would either get lucky or simply force their way inside. With no option of retreat, her teammates would be in serious trouble. Especially if the BECA members had other weapons, like grenades—which wouldn't surprise her.

The thought put a heavy weight on her chest, like the SUV really had sunk down on her. She was the agent least prepared for this. But failure meant they would probably all die here today.

She'd get one chance. One chance to take out as many of them as possible, provide a distraction that would give her team time to rush through the front windshield. If she did this right, together, they could eliminate the threat.

Boots came into view and Melinda froze, afraid to even breathe. Then, another pair joined them, and another.

She was trapped. No way to slip out from underneath the vehicle, dart behind the cover of trees like she'd planned. If she fired from here, they'd know exactly where she was, be able to hit her while she had limited visibility and few ways out.

"Climb up," one of them whispered. "You two hit them from the side, and we'll hit them from the back. Tell Don to stand near the front and pick off anyone who tries to escape that way."

Melinda's gut clenched, her breathing came faster, and her vision and hearing narrowed. Tunnel vision. Knowing it was happening—that her fear was overriding her senses—didn't make it easier to fix.

BECA had a good plan. The agents inside were still firing periodically, but only out the front windshield. A distraction, hoping to give her a chance. Not knowing what she'd planned to do, since she hadn't told them, since she hadn't fully known when she'd slipped out that door.

She was a pretty good shot. But there were at least four BECA members near the side and back of the vehicle, at least one up front. Even if she could hit the four closest to her, she had an angle only on their feet and calves. Enough to bring them to the ground, sure, but to take them out of the fight entirely? Unlikely.

All that mattered was taking them down long enough for the other agents to get out the front, not getting shot herself before she could yell a warning about Don's position.

If she was going to die today, she prayed she'd be able to do it giving the rest of her team a fighting chance.

Not daring to move her hand up to touch the ring dangling under her T-shirt, she focused on the feel of it. The simple gold band she'd picked out for her late husband. It always gave her strength. Thinking of it made her breathing even out, her senses sharpen.

Just as one of the BECA members started to clamber up the side of the SUV to get a shot through the window, Melinda lined up her first shot. Then, she said one more prayer, fired two shots in rapid succession. Someone—maybe two someones—dropped to the ground, screaming in pain, but moving around. Probably aiming their own weapons, a new target in sight now that they were lying in the dirt.

Melinda didn't waste time. She screamed a warning to her team as she pivoted toward the side of the SUV, toward the guy dropping off the vehicle, making it bounce up and down, too close to her. Then more shots joined her own and Melinda kept firing, wondering if the adrenaline was preventing her from feeling the bullets that had to be hitting her by now.

The two guys on the side of the SUV both dropped, and Melinda hit them again, not waiting to see if they were dead before she swiveled once more toward the two she'd hit first. The two who had to be recovered enough to shoot her fatally by now.

But as she turned, a new pair of boots slammed down to the ground and someone else fired, taking out those BECA members. One of them had his gun up, pointed directly at her head, and Melinda squeezed her eyes shut, expecting it to fire anyway. But instead of a bullet, she felt a hand on her leg.

She jerked, opened her eyes. And there was Kane, kneeling down, pulling her out from under the SUV.

"Nice job," Evan told her as he ran around from the front of the vehicle, Laura close at his heels. Both of them still swept the area with their weapons even though the shots had ceased.

Kane yanked her to her feet, took the pistol from hands she realized were shaking and holstered it for her. "You did good," he said, his voice deeper than usual.

Then he was pulling her against his chest, and she could have sworn his hand stroked the back of her hair before he let her go, started talking logistics.

Ana Sofia was hurt. Not shot, but knocked cold when the SUV crashed. Evan had taken a bullet to the arm, *Just a nick*, he'd said. Laura had a nasty bruise on her forehead and blood on the side of her face. But they were all alive, their suspects all dead. Not even remotely the plan, but better than the alternative.

Melinda sank to the ground, her heart rate—so calm in those important moments—now off and running again. She closed her eyes, tried to will away the nausea, as she let her teammates handle the logistics. Dead suspects still needed guns moved away from them, hands cuffed. It was procedure. Calls had to be made, to deal with the bodies, to report back to Pembrook.

Through her haze, Melinda felt Laura's hand on her arm, her calm, understanding words. "It happens to all of us. Just breathe through it. You'll be okay."

Then, from farther away, JC's voice, obviously on a phone call. "What do you mean we don't know where Davis is?"

She tried to focus, to contribute in some meaningful way. She was FBI, for crying out loud. She could handle this.

But the buzzing in her ears just got louder, the uneven cadence of her breathing got worse. Then, somehow, it was Pembrook forcing her head up, staring back at her. Her voice that finally snapped Melinda out of it.

"It's over, Melinda. We're getting help from the Knoxville field office to manage the scene. We'll need statements, but right now, we need your profiling brain. We need to figure out where Davis might have gone."

Melinda frowned, took a deep breath. "Last I heard, he'd left the Petrov Armor office. He'd gone home."

"We're going to send an agent there now. Davis's phone is off, so we can't track it, but Hendrick is doing his magic back at the office. In the meantime, maybe Davis went back to Petrov Armor headquarters or—"

"He said he was finished there." The brief text she'd gotten earlier from Davis said he strongly suspected Eric Ross, flat out announced his undercover time was over. She'd texted back, asking for more detail, but hadn't gotten a response. "Did you ask Kane?"

"Kane said he had nothing more to offer on this," Pembrook replied, and something about the way she was scowling made Melinda glance around.

JC was still on scene and Rowan was here now, too, looking a little queasy. But the rest of the agents had cleared out. Probably some of them had gone to get medically checked out, some had gone to the office to either fill out statements about tonight or help with the search for Davis. And yet...

"Where's Kane?"

Pembrook shook her head, her face scrunching up apologetically. "He's gone."

Dread made her press a hand against her chest. "Gone?"

"Back undercover."

"What?"

"It came up days ago, new movement on a major drug smuggling operation where Kane had a deep cover a few months back. We'd pulled him, but his cover was intact. It's not great timing, but—"

"He's really gone? Just like that?" After everything that had happened tonight? After all their hard work to bring down the members of BECA? And not even a goodbye?

Pembrook stood, dusted off the knees of her pants. "You're the profiler, Melinda. You should understand." As she turned away, she added, "Get moving. I need you."

Grimacing at the stiffness in her arms and legs and back, Melinda stood. Her mind whirled as she followed her boss.

Kane was gone.

She'd thought that the way she'd proven herself tonight, the way the entire team had banded together to survive, would have shown him that being part of a team could be a good thing. That being part of a partnership could be a good thing. Instead, it had just reinforced his desire to run.

Pain sliced through her chest, not at all connected to her sore limbs being forced to move again after she'd held them so stiffly while under the SUV and during her panic attack afterward. But she ignored it and hurried after Pembrook.

She couldn't worry about Kane now, couldn't think about losing him as a partner. Couldn't think about how much she wanted to keep working with him. How much she wanted to keep seeing him, talking to him, arguing with him.

Right now, she needed to focus on Davis. Right now, she needed to help *find* Davis.

JOEL PETROV HAD ambushed him.

The realization hurt more than whatever Joel had used to knock him out when Davis had arrived at the remote testing facility.

He'd come here full of excitement about a new lead on Eric Ross, but as he slowly sat up and discovered himself in the middle of a firing lane, Davis knew. Joel had planted all the records leading to Eric, the security card access times and the supply orders.

"When did you know?" Davis asked. His words didn't sound quite right, his tongue heavy in his mouth. He pushed himself up to a kneeling position, got ready to try to stand.

"Don't," Joel warned.

Davis looked up and his vision blurred, but when he blinked a few times, the two versions of Joel merged into one. And that Joel was holding a pistol, aiming it straight at Davis. Close enough not to miss, far enough that there was no way Davis could rush him.

Subtly, Davis used one hand to pat his pocket, searching for his phone. The other pressed against the back of his head, felt the sticky evidence of blood.

He wasn't sure how long he'd been out, but it was long enough for Joel to have dragged him into this firing lane. Between the heavy throbbing in his head and the blood now smearing his hand, he knew he had a concussion.

It wasn't the first time. He'd been too close to an IED on a ranger mission once, been knocked nearly twenty feet from the explosion. But back then, he'd had a team to drag him out of the line of fire, get him on a medevac helicopter. Now, he was alone, and he had no one to blame but himself and his desperation to close this case.

He'd told his team he suspected Eric. He hadn't told them he was meeting Leila's uncle.

"Looking for this?" Joel asked, holding up Davis's FBI phone and then setting it on the counter near the front of the shooting lane. "I've known you were FBI for days." An ironic smile lifted one side of his lips. "Eric told me. After I knocked you out, I turned the phone off."

His team couldn't track him. Davis swayed a little on his knees, felt nausea rise up his throat. How hard had Joel hit him?

"Sorry," the man said, seemingly reading his mind. "Couldn't take any chances you'd wake up before I was ready."

"And now what?" Davis croaked, his voice sounding as off as his head felt. "You shoot me? You honestly believe this won't come back to you? This isn't exactly a good site for a botched mugging."

Joel's lips twisted into an angry snarl. "You think I don't have a plan for you? You think this is going to be hard for me? After what I had to do to my own brother? I had no choice then. Neal figured it out. Believe me, if there'd been another way—"

"He wasn't in on it?"

"Neal? Not follow the rules when it came to his company, his baby?" Joel snorted, a nasty, jealous sound. "No way."

"It was you all along," Davis stated. "Did you step in after Leila's mother died to help your brother out, or did you just see an opportunity right from the start?"

He heard the anger in his own voice, knew it was for Leila. She'd been right about her father. He wished she hadn't been so wrong about her uncle.

"I took over the company for Neal," Joel bit out. "He needed me. It was the two of us again—mostly—like it had always been growing up. Back then, he tried to look out for me. Our parents were no picnic, you know. This was finally my chance to repay him."

As Davis remembered how Leila had mentioned the abuse her father and uncle had suffered from their parents, Joel continued. "We'd been so close once. But as we got older, we grew apart. Then he got married, something both of us swore we'd never do. I tried to be happy for him, but I never quite knew how. When they had Leila, Neal wanted me back in their lives and so I came." The bitterness turned wistful. "But when his wife died, I knew it could be the two of us against the world again."

Melinda would be fascinated by the psychology here. Davis's mind was drifting, probably the concussion. He shook his head, trying to focus on what mattered, but only managed to make it pound harder, putting zigzagging lines over his vision.

Focusing made his head hurt worse, made him feel like he might pass out again. But if he did, he wouldn't be able to talk Joel out of shooting him, and he'd never wake up again. So he pressed on. "Leila is just collateral in your quest for money? Isn't the millions you've already made illegally off that company enough? You needed to kill soldiers, destroy your niece, too?"

The anger turned to fury, enough that Davis imagined he could rush Joel, take him down. But it was wishful thinking. The man was too far away, and even when he wasn't moving—or didn't think he was moving—Davis felt like he was swaying back and forth.

"That armor wasn't supposed to kill anyone."

"Yeah, you sound all broken up over it," Davis snapped, unable to help himself as an image of Jessica—proud in her army uniform, showing him a picture of her three kids—filled his mind.

"Look, those parts were cheaper, sure, but they were going to be sold to someone. How was I supposed to know they'd fail so badly? You think I wanted that kind of scrutiny?"

Davis gritted his teeth, trying to hold in a nasty response. Eighteen soldiers and seven locals had died in Afghanistan, and Joel Petrov was still thinking about himself.

"As for Leila, she never should have found out anything was wrong," Joel said. "When her dad convinced the board to put her in the CEO role, I thought it was perfect. She was too young for the job, too trusting of the people she loves." He frowned, deep grooves forming between his eyebrows, then he shook his head and muttered, "She never should have stopped the gun production," as if what had happened was Leila's fault.

"You can't go back now," Davis said. "She let me into the company. She knows I'm FBI. If something happens to me—"

"She'll blame Eric, the way I intended," Joel said, finishing for him. He glanced at his watch. "And now, I'm sorry, but I'm finished talking." He centered the pistol more carefully, steadying it.

"This won't work," Davis insisted, putting a hand to his temple, the knock to his head or the blood loss making him way too woozy, making his brain feel like it was several steps behind.

"I'm sorry," Joel repeated, and Davis closed his eyes, knowing he was out of options.

Bullets traveled faster than sound, so Davis didn't expect to hear anything, but a noise made his eyes pop open.

"Uncle Joel, stop!"

Leila stood behind Joel, out of breath and looking horrified.

Joel shifted sideways, so she wasn't directly behind him, then took a few steps forward, toward Davis. But he turned his pistol on Leila.

"You shouldn't be here," he said, a note of finality in his voice.

"No!" Davis yelled, trying to lurch to his feet. He stumbled and fell back to his knees, his hands scraping against the hard floor, but Joel's gun whipped back in his direction.

"Uncle Joel," Leila said, her voice full of fear and disbelief. "Please don't do this."

"I'm sorry, Leila," Joel said, and he actually sounded it as he centered his gun on Davis once again.

"I love him," Leila burst out.

The gun wavered and Davis shook his head, as if there was water in his ears he needed to shake out in order to hear properly.

She loved him? Was she saying it just to stop her uncle from killing him? Or did she actually mean it?

Either way, his heart started pounding double-time, telling Davis two truths: he loved her, too, and he was probably going to die without ever getting the chance to tell her.

Chapter Twenty-One

The man she loved was about to die. And the man who'd helped raise her was going to kill him.

Leila took a deep breath, took a step closer. She kept her gaze centered on her uncle, not daring to look at Davis right now. She was too afraid of what she'd see. Not just because of the declaration of love she'd blurted, but also because he looked badly hurt. Blood saturated one side of his head, dripping down his neck and onto his T-shirt. He'd been swaying on his knees when she walked in, had almost face-planted when he tried to stand. Even if she could convince her uncle not to kill him—not to kill them both—he might not make it.

"You killed my father," she whispered, pain in her voice. "How could you do that? He was your only brother, your only real family besides me."

Her uncle's jaw quivered, but his gun hand didn't waver. "I didn't want to do it, Leila."

"Your greed was really worth more than my father's life?" Leila burst out, almost a yell.

"It wasn't about greed," her uncle Joel replied, his tone almost apologetic. Almost, but not quite.

"What was it about, then?" Leila demanded, still not daring to look at Davis. Maybe if she could slowly move closer to her uncle, get him to lower his gun—or try to take it from him—maybe she could save them both.

"Power," he said simply.

"Power? Is that supposed to be any better?"

"No." His gun lowered slightly, his attention on her instead of Davis.

From the corner of her eye, she saw Davis inch slowly forward on his knees. His chest heaved as he took in deep breaths, obviously in danger of passing out.

"I don't expect you to understand," her uncle said. "Your dad wanted to spare you the details of what happened to us as kids, but—"

"I know it was bad," Leila said softly. Her dad hadn't shared much of it, but he'd told her enough. Their childhood had been horrific. They'd only been able to rely on each other. Once when she was supposed to have been upstairs in bed, she'd heard her dad confiding to her mom that he was afraid Uncle Joel had locked up his emotions so tight that he'd never be able to feel anything.

But that couldn't really be true. He'd moved in with them for several years. He'd been there every morning, making her breakfast, walking her to the bus even when she insisted she was old enough to go by herself. Him telling her sternly that she didn't understand what dangers could be out there, how he'd never let her be hurt the way he'd been hurt.

He loved her. She knew he did.

That certainty bolstered her courage, made her take a big step closer. "Uncle Joel," she whispered, "I love you, too. Please, you can't do this."

"I can't go to jail," he whispered back. "Power. Control over my own life. It's all I ever wanted growing up. I know it sounds crazy, but no amount of money, no safety net, ever feels like enough. I know you don't approve, but I worked hard for this. I'm not letting him destroy it."

"You destroyed it," Leila snapped just as Uncle Joel started to focus on Davis again.

Davis, who was still inching forward, but so slowly he'd never get anywhere near close enough to rush her uncle. It would be a fatal mistake for him to try. He was way too disoriented from whatever her uncle had hit him over the head with.

"You destroyed my father's company," she continued, anger rushing back in. "You killed my father. You betrayed all of us. *How could you?*"

He shook his head, backed slightly away from her, his face shuttering, and Leila knew she was losing him.

"You love me," she insisted, stepping toward him again, even as she slid one hand inside her purse. "I know you do."

"Maybe I'm not truly capable of loving anyone," he said softly, sadly, as he aimed his gun at her again.

But it shook badly and he quickly re-aimed it at Davis. No matter what he said, she was pretty certain he wouldn't kill her. But she couldn't say the same about Davis.

"Yes, you are," she said, her fingers closing around the small pistol she'd carried since being attacked. Her own threat to counterbalance his, a last resort, since she wasn't sure she'd ever be able to actually fire on him. The man who'd help make her who she was, who'd taught her to be strong, made her feel like she mattered when her whole world had been crashing down. "You love me. You protected me. You always did."

As she said the words, her certainty grew. The fury she felt was still mixed with confusion, disbelief so strong that she knew it hadn't fully set in that he'd killed her father. It sounded so unreal, even in her own mind. The love she had for him, the man who'd put his whole life on hold for *years* to make sure she was okay? Even knowing what he'd done, she couldn't just erase it all.

Yes, he'd stumbled onto an opportunity to make money illegally in her father's company at the same time. But that hadn't been his original goal. If it had been the only thing that really mattered to him, he could have bailed on her at any time. He'd had enough control of the company at the time that a takeover would have been easy. Back then, he would have signed over his company without a word of protest. In his darkest moments, he'd tried to sell it to his brother, wanting to be rid of it. Uncle Joel had never accepted; he's just kept it going for his brother.

He'd never once, in all those years, let her down. As much as he'd betrayed her now, deep down she knew that her life could have taken a very different path without him. Children's Services had been on the verge of taking her away, placing her in foster care. She would have been alone in the world. Knowing how lost she'd been back then, there was no doubt it would have destroyed her.

In so many ways, she had her uncle Joel to thank for how she'd grown up. She'd never be able to forgive him for killing her father, destroying her company. Even now, hatred was blooming in her chest as she stared at him. But she couldn't completely turn her back on him, leave him alone in the world either.

"I still love you, Uncle Joel," she told him. She choked on the words, which felt like a betrayal to her father. But she reached a hand out to him, held it palm up, silently begging him to set the gun there. To be the man who'd raised her. To choose her over himself, to go to jail rather than kill another person she loved.

Because she did love Davis. She wasn't quite sure when it had happened, or how it had happened so quickly. She might doubt his intentions, doubt if what he felt for her was real, but she had no doubts about her feelings.

"Please," she begged her uncle, stretching her hand even farther.

His chin quivered, his gaze drifting to the weapon, then to her hand. If he noticed that Davis was a few feet closer than he'd been before, he didn't show it. Or maybe it didn't matter, since he still wasn't close enough.

"Please," she begged again, knowing he was wavering, knowing *him*.

His throat moved as he swallowed hard, and then his gaze went back to the weapon, his head giving a little shake, and she knew he'd made his choice.

She had a choice right now, too. The man who'd helped raise her, who'd without question saved her life when she was a child, the uncle she loved despite everything. Or the man she'd fallen for, the man who'd planned to leave in the end, but she loved anyway.

Leila let out a wail that sounded almost inhuman as she lifted the hand still hidden inside her purse, and fired her weapon.

And a man she loved fell to the floor.

Epilogue

Leila had killed her uncle.

One week ago, there'd been a single instant to make a choice—Uncle Joel or Davis. It had been half instinct when she'd fired that shot. But her aim had been true. Center mass, the way her dad had trained her so many years ago. A kill shot.

She'd never thought she'd need to use it on someone she loved. Never thought she'd do it to protect someone else she loved.

Davis had spent two days in the hospital. One of his teammates had updated her a few hours after she'd shot her uncle, telling her Davis had a pretty severe concussion. She'd been numb by then, having given her statement more than once to local police and then Davis's team, who'd rushed in a few moments after she called 911.

The woman who'd told her about his condition, a profiler with kind eyes, had called her a few days ago to let her know Davis had been released from the hospital, cleared to go back to work. Apparently he was already working on a new case.

She hadn't spoken to him since the paramedics had loaded him into that ambulance, clinging to consciousness through sheer will. In that moment she'd squeezed his hand, pressed a brief kiss to his lips despite all the FBI agents watching. Then she'd walked away.

Leila had killed her uncle for him. In that instant her entire life had changed.

Leaning back in the chair in her father's office, Leila glanced around at the familiar room, somehow made foreign without her dad in it. She hadn't officially moved into his office—and she didn't plan to—but being here made her feel closer to him. She hadn't been able to go into her uncle's office yet. She wasn't sure when that would happen, if it ever would. Every memory she had of him now was tainted by the knowledge that he'd killed her father, by the look in his eyes when she'd known he was willing to kill Davis, too. Yet, a part of her still loved him, the man who'd claimed he wasn't sure if he even knew *how* to love. But he'd loved her. She still believed that.

Pressing a hand to her chest—where her grief seemed to have taken up permanent lodging—Leila stood and walked around the office. It wasn't large, but with framed copies of some of her father's earliest deals, it reflected how hard he'd worked to build this company.

Petrov Armor might not survive. Once news broke about the armor, about her uncle, she'd received letters of resignation from more than a third of her employees. The rest had stayed, but each day they eyed her with uncertainty, looks that said she'd betrayed their trust by keeping the truth from them when news of the faulty armor first surfaced.

The military—their biggest client—had canceled all of their orders. Petrov Armor had taken a hit so big that Leila knew she might have to let go some of the employees who'd stayed loyal, stuck around to fight with her. But she'd made her decision and for now, the board was willing to let her try. She was going to rebuild, prove to everyone that she could go back to the company her father had once envisioned, that he'd worked so hard to build. A place where the mission was to help *save* lives.

Peering through the open doorway, Leila saw lights on in Eric's office. She knew Theresa was still here, too, hard at work creating plans for more transparency, more security in their build process. People who would stick by her, stick by the company. People who cared about her, too.

But they weren't her family. That was all gone now, no one left except her father's abusive parents, who she'd never contact, and her mother's family in Pakistan who she'd never met, except over a few brief video chats.

They weren't Davis. Davis, who'd somehow wormed his way into her heart while he was digging through her company's darkest secrets.

He hadn't called. Maybe he'd been too concussed to hear her declaration of love. Maybe it wouldn't have mattered even if he'd known how she felt.

Because he was an FBI agent. And she was just the CEO of a company he'd been investigating. His job was finished here. He was gone.

Even if he wasn't, could she be with someone who—intentionally or not—had put her in a position where she'd had to kill the only real family she had left?

A shiver racked her body, a sob lodging in her chest. But she blinked back the tears, forced the sob down. She'd already cried for her uncle. Knowing what he'd done, what he'd been willing to do, she refused to give him any more of her tears.

She couldn't cry for Davis, either. Couldn't cry for what might have been. Not yet, because that would mean admitting she'd truly lost him, too. And she wasn't sure she was ready to admit that yet.

"Leila."

The soft voice speaking her name made her jerk. Realizing her eyes had gone unfocused, she blinked and there was Davis. She blinked again, certain she'd imagined him, but he was still in front of her. Real.

Beyond him, in the dim lights of the space outside the office, Eric gave her a sad smile and a nod. Then, he slipped back into his office and she refocused on the man in front of her.

"What are you doing here?" she whispered.

"I couldn't stay away," he whispered back, stepping closer.

There was still a big Band-Aid on the side of his head. Underneath, she knew there were a dozen stitches. But his eyes looked clear, his gaze steady as he took one more step toward her, then reached out and took both her hands in his.

It was something Eric had done in her office not so long ago. But Eric's touch hadn't made her heart race, or made hope burst through the pain in her chest.

She gazed up at him, trying to read his intention in his eyes. And yet—did it matter? Had anything really changed in the past week? They'd lied to each other. And she'd killed one of the people closest to her in the world. For him. Could she ever get beyond that?

As he brought her hands up to his lips, closed his eyes almost reverently as he kissed her there softly, she knew: she desperately wanted to.

"I'm so sorry about your uncle," he said when he lowered her hands from his lips.

The pain he felt on her behalf was in the crinkling around his eyes, in the downturn of his lips, the way he gazed at her. But there was something else there, too, and even though it didn't seem possible, Leila's heart beat even faster.

"I never expected it to end like that, Leila. I never expected…" He gave a shaky—could it be nervous?—smile. "I never expected to fall in love with you."

The words that followed were a jumble she couldn't quite piece together, about being sorry he'd taken so long to come here, about wanting to start fresh. But all she could hear was the thundering of her own heartbeat in her ears, those most important words repeating over and over in her mind. *I never expected to fall in love with you.*

"What are you saying?" she finally interrupted him, unable to process too much about the past, needing to know more about the future.

Davis stepped even closer, as far inside her personal space as he could get without physically pulling her into his arms. "I'm saying I can't let go, Leila. Maybe it's what makes the most sense, given everything that's happened, but I can't do it. I love you. I want to give this thing between us a real shot. No more lies, no more half-truths. The same side." He turned one of her hands in his, stroking her palm enough to send shivers of awareness over her skin. "I think we've always been on the same side, even if it didn't always feel that way."

She nodded back at him. They'd always been searching for the same thing: the truth. And they'd found it, even if it wasn't what she'd wanted, wasn't the way she'd wanted.

"A new start," she said, feeling more certain as the words burst from her mouth without thought.

He smiled, tentative but genuine. He shifted his grip on her hand until it was more of a handshake. "Agreed," he said, an echo of the promise they'd made to each other weeks ago, when he'd first gone undercover in her company.

Then, he pulled her closer still, until she was pressed against him. She rose up on her tiptoes, the first smile she'd felt in a week shifting from a small, hopeful thing into a full-blown grin. "I love you, too, Davis."

"I know," he answered. "And I promise you this—whatever comes next, we're in it together."

Then, he sealed that promise with a kiss.

* * * * *

CONARD COUNTY JUSTICE.

RACHEL LEE

Chapter One

Cat Jansen was sitting at the front desk in the Conard County Sheriff's Office when trouble came through the door.

Rotation had brought her to this day of desk duty in the office. She wasn't expecting to be too busy, which was one of the reasons she had decided to stay in this county after her mother's death two years ago.

She had previously worked for a sheriff in Colorado but had left the job to come to Conard City to care for her ailing mother. Cancer was a brutal disease, and all Cat could say for the months she'd spent nursing her was that her mother hadn't been alone. Then she'd taken a job as a deputy to the sheriff here. Today she busied herself with a day of paperwork and a few relatively minor complaints.

Until the big guy in an Army uniform walked through the door. She took a rapid inventory as best she could. Major's oak leaves, a stack of colorful ribbons. He pulled off a tan beret as he entered.

His dark eyes reflected cold anger. More worrisome than rage, the coldness suggested a determination that wouldn't quit. *Oh heck*, she thought. What had made this guy look like this?

"Are you the desk officer?" he asked in a deep voice, suggesting a rumble of thunder in the distance.

"Yes, I am." An imposing man. And whatever had brought him so far out of his way was likely a serious problem.

"I'm Major Daniel Duke. My brother, Larry, was murdered a week ago."

Well, that explained the steel in his dark eyes. "I'm so sorry," she replied. "How can we help you?" But she had an idea. Definitely trouble. She could feel it brewing like a building storm.

"I want to know how the investigation is going."

"It's going." She wasn't permitted to give him confidential details of an ongoing investigation.

"Are you checking into the possibility of a hate crime? My brother was gay."

A bald accusation phrased as a question. If she hadn't felt so disturbed and chilled by the look in his eyes, she might have done more than sigh.

"Of course we are," she answered. "I knew Larry. We're not overlooking anything, believe me. But in all honesty, we've never had a crime of that type in this county."

"Not yet," he said flatly.

Which was a point she couldn't argue. This county evidently always seemed peaceful until something blew up. It wasn't as frequent as in heavily populated areas, but it still happened.

The major was framed against the front windows, the bright spring sunlight now casting him in silhouette. Not comfortable for her to look at.

She pointed to the metal chair beside her desk. "Sit, please. I'm having trouble seeing you."

He came around immediately and sat. Now she had a clear view of his face. It had the chiseled appearance of someone in prime physical condition, and sun had put some slight lines at the corners of his eyes. He looked as unyielding as the concrete she suddenly imagined him walking through. She suspected he wasn't going to hang around just to identify Larry's body, which hadn't yet come back from the medical examiner, and arrange a funeral. No, he had other things on his mind.

"I'm not going to leave this town until the murderer is caught."

"We'll find him," she said with more confidence than she felt. So far they hadn't uncovered any clues. At least none they could yet recognize. Maybe the ME would find something.

"You find him, or I will."

Whoa. She felt her first stirrings of sympathy sliding away into apprehension. "Let us do our job. You *do* realize that anything you find probably won't be usable in court, because you won't have a warrant. You certainly don't want to get in our way or get yourself in trouble with the law."

He didn't answer immediately. When at last he spoke, his voice was clear, flat, hard. "I don't care what happens to me. This is about my brother. He deserves justice. The dead should get that. Justice. That's one of the things Larry believed."

She saw pain pass over his face, quickly erased, and she sensed that this wasn't about his brother's death. Not exactly. Something else was going on here.

She also wondered what could be done about this man. He'd only said he wanted to find the murderer. He hadn't said he was going to do anything illegal in the process. What were they to do to prevent him? Jail him without a charge?

Never. So they were stuck with this cannon. Whether it was a loose one or not, she had no idea. She *did* suspect that a Ranger could probably cause more trouble than a typical man on the street.

"You need to talk to the sheriff," she said, ticking possibilities over in her mind. "If you coordinate your efforts with ours, there may be a way for you to satisfy yourself."

"Is he here?"

"He's at a county board meeting." To discuss funding for expanding the department by a couple more cops, hoping to get funding for a better dispatch situation. Sticking communications over in the corner with the coffee machines was becoming a problem. They needed better equipment, a place to put dispatch out of the line of fire and noise in the front office. She'd been kind of startled when she began working here to realize that the department had been so small for so long they were stacking most duties all in one room. Time to move into the twenty-first century.

But that didn't answer her immediate problem. She tried to lighten things a bit. "He said he'd be gone an hour nearly an hour ago. Given it's the supervisors and it's about money, it may become a longer wrangle."

His nod was short, sharp. The cold steel in his gaze hadn't lessened a bit. Okay, then…

"I'll wait."

She figured determination was bone-deep in this man. He had come here on a mission, one he considered righteous. Short of being given official orders, he wasn't going to be derailed. She hoped the sheriff would be able to find a way to steer him. From her position, there was little she could do or say without her boss's approval anyway.

"Larry," she said finally.

Those eyes became even sharper. "What about him?"

"I knew him. Only for the couple of months he was here, but we met in Mahoney's bar one night. He was enjoying a scotch, and I went in there to eat a ham sandwich, maybe have a beer. I sat at the bar near him, and we fell into conversation."

He waited.

"I liked him immediately. Nice man, but I probably

wouldn't want to be the target of one of his investigative pieces."

The faintest of frowns flickered over the major's face. "No one would."

"Anyway, we hit it off. He told me he was a journalist and that he was here on sabbatical to write a book. He even laughed, saying every reporter had a book in their bottom desk drawer. He never said what he was writing about. Did he tell you why he came to the back of beyond?"

"No." His expression shut down again.

"I saw him a lot while he was here. He liked Mahoney's—said it was his nod to Hemingway, whatever that meant. Do you know?"

He shook his head. "Probably a literary reference. A few years ago, he joked to me that you couldn't drink your way into a novel."

She felt a smile ease the tension in her face. "Well, he wasn't trying to drink his way into anything. He appeared to like the atmosphere, even played darts with some of the regulars. Never a heavy drinker. We talked whenever we ran into each other, sometimes meeting at the diner for lunch. I've known a few reporters, and they're never wallflowers. He'd started making friends around here."

"That's Larry, all right."

She suspected this man didn't find it easy to make friends. But maybe she was wrong. Too soon to know, except that while she wouldn't like being the subject of Larry's investigation, she would hate being the subject of this man's ire.

"He started having card games at his place once a week," she went on. "He invited me, but I'm not into cards, so I didn't go. Maybe six or seven guys attended. Never any problem from our perspective. Which I suppose means they were reasonably quiet and didn't get disorderly. Not much of an analysis on my part." She tried another smile. "We're looking into those friends."

"Good."

"You never know what kind of resentments might come out of a card game. Especially if they were gambling, but since Larry invited me, I doubt it."

"He was never a gambler that I know of. At least not that way. He gambled a whole lot in other ways."

Cat wondered if she'd just told him too much about the friends. About the card games. Dang, this man's mere presence was making her talk too much, maybe reveal too much. Everything about him demanded answers.

She had just decided to pick up some paperwork in order to truncate this conversation by comparing written reports to digital. Gage hated the duplicate work, both on computer and paper, but like it or not, the duplication was useful. Papers couldn't be manipulated as easily as a computer file, but a computer file was more readily accessible.

Just as she was probably about to mortally offend the major, the sheriff walked through the door.

"How'd it go, Sheriff?"

"High school wrestling match. Partial success." Gage Dalton was a tall man with a face scarred by burns. Long ago, when he was a DEA agent, he'd been the target of a car bomb. He still limped from his injuries, and even now some of his movements exhibited pain.

She spoke again before he could pass. Major Duke was already rising from his chair. Gage wasn't going to escape this, either.

"Sheriff, this is Major Daniel Duke, Larry Duke's brother. You need to speak with him."

Gage raised a brow on the unscarred side of his face. "Come with me, Major. My office is open."

The two men disappeared down the corridor, and Cat

expelled a long breath, only just then realizing she'd been holding it. Tense. Lots of tension surrounded the major.

The dispatch desk crackled to life with a call. "Burglary at 1095 Elm Street. Need backup and forensics."

Cat wished she were able to answer the call. She had a strong feeling she wouldn't escape the major.

A HALF HOUR LATER, as she finished up comparing reports, Gage called from the hallway.

"Cat, could you come in here, please?"

Oh God, she thought. She glanced at the dispatcher, an elderly crone who smoked like a chimney under the No Smoking sign. She had learned quickly that Velma was a fixture who must be respected. A couple of deputies had told her that the only way Velma was going to leave her job was toes first. Cat had learned that Velma mothered them all.

"Good luck," Velma said in her smoke-roughened voice.

Apparently, Velma had gotten the same kind of impression from their visitor.

Cat squared her shoulders and marched back to Gage's office. Maybe, just maybe, he'd found a way to contain this man. It wouldn't help anything to have the major interfering with the investigation. He could jeopardize the case.

"Hey, Cat," Gage said when she reached his office. "Come on in, close the door and grab a seat."

Close the door? Gage almost never did that. She followed his request, sitting only a foot away from Daniel Duke. Who, she had to admit, was attractive. He would have been more so if she hadn't seen the subzero chill in his gaze.

She turned her attention to Gage, hoping he had a solution.

"It seems," he said, "that Major Duke is determined to assist our investigation."

Oh boy. Gage describing it as assistance probably didn't bode well.

"I can understand the major's concerns," Gage continued. "If he wants to talk to people around the county, I can't prevent him. There's nothing illicit in that. But I've also made it clear that he's going to have to stay within the law so he doesn't destroy any case against a murderer. I've also made it clear that we *will* enforce the law, so he'd better not interfere in any way with our investigation. He won't be helping if we have to arrest him."

Cat nodded, glad Gage had made those points. Unfortunately, she sensed there was a big *but* on the way. Worse, her presence in this room probably pointed to involving her in some capacity.

She couldn't zip her lips any longer. "Is Major Duke suggesting we can't do our job?"

She knew that wasn't it. This was a man who needed to take up his lance for the sake of his brother. He *needed* to be involved. Still, she wanted to make her disapproval clear.

"I don't think that's it," Gage answered. "He's just not constitutionally capable of sitting on the sidelines, are you, Major?"

"No." A single syllable saying more than a page full of words.

"Anyway," Gage went on, "I can't prevent him from walking around asking questions or looking for some obvious clue that we need brought to our attention. Within the law, of course. So, we need to coordinate. You have a background in homicide investigations, Cat. You'll be our liaison, keeping me informed at all times. And, Major, if Deputy Jansen says we need a warrant for something, listen to her. We can get a warrant fast enough from Judge Carter if there's probable cause."

Oh man, Cat thought, feeling everything inside her become as taut as a guitar string. A brick wall and a concrete one had just met, and she couldn't tell which one of them had won. At least it appeared that Gage had gotten a few concessions.

But playing liaison on this? While she'd be glad of the change of pace, being more deeply involved with a murder investigation, she didn't want to do it this way. What was more, she'd known Larry, and that had been the primary reason she *wasn't* on the case. Why had Gage chosen her? Just because she had some experience?

She looked at Major Duke, fearing that trying to keep him in line would be like bull riding. Then she accepted the inevitable. This was her assignment, and even though it might put her on the wrong side of the investigation, in terms of her involvement, it was still important, and Gage thought it necessary. She had one burning question, however.

"How much information from our investigation should I share?"

"Whatever you deem necessary."

On her shoulders, then. Lovely.

GAGE HAD VELMA call another officer in to take over desk duty. "Seems like you two may need a bit of discussion. Get yourselves over to the diner for coffee, maybe lunch."

Cat smothered a sigh, figuring she was going to have to reinforce Gage's limits over coffee, and probably endure a brain picking by Major Duke.

They crossed the street together and walked halfway down the block to the City Diner, known to everyone as Maude's diner because of its cantankerous owner. Cantankerous or not, Maude was another of those people around here who was both a fixture and well loved. This kind of thing was also a part of the charm of living here.

For the first time, she faced the seated major across a table. She had a clear view in the light from the diner's front windows. Mavis, Maude's daughter, appeared in lieu of Maude but slammed down the coffee cups with similar disdain. She'd learned well.

They took their menus, and Cat remarked, "Everything is good, but everyone raves about the steak sandwich."

Cat ordered the chef salad. A light lunch seemed best when she didn't know how the conversation would go. Her stomach was already trying to knot. As she expected, Duke ordered the steak sandwich.

While they waited, he looked unflinchingly at her across the table. "You'd much rather volunteer to hike up and down Mount McKinley than be sitting here."

Actually, she would. She loved the mountains. "That obvious, huh?" Might as well be blunt, although she was bothered by being so readable. She'd tried for years to suppress that tendency in herself.

"I can't say I blame you."

Well, well. The admission surprised her. "Then you get it?"

"Yes." Their lunches arrived, and he sat back to allow the plates to be banged down in front of them. Coffee, dark and aromatic, filled their cups. She reached for one of the small creamers and dumped it in hers. Ordinarily she preferred her coffee black, but the way her stomach was feeling...

He glanced at his sandwich, then lifted half of it as though reluctant. He raised it partway to his mouth and looked at her over it. "I didn't ever not get it," he said before biting off a mouthful.

She paused with a container of blue cheese dressing hovering over her salad. "Then what was this all about?"

"Informing your office. Making a few things clear. Setting the boundaries I need to stay inside. Regardless, if you don't get the murderer, I *will*."

She believed him. She also feared what he might do if

driven by rage. This man was trained to kill. "Then why do you want to know the boundaries? Isn't this a pointless exercise if you just want to shoot someone?"

"I might like to prevent this bastard from ever breathing again, but I'd prefer to see him locked up for life." He looked down a moment. "In my opinion, life in prison is a far worse sentence than a quick death."

She nodded, stabbing her fork into a swirl of chef's roll and salad. "I'd agree with that."

"But I'm not leaving here without finding him. I have three weeks."

"Now we've got a time limit?" She arched a brow.

"It's good to know the boundaries," he said, echoing himself and Gage's earlier remarks. "For both you and me."

She supposed it was. And now her favorite salad and dressing had become flavorless. It was then she faced needing to get a handle on herself. Most of what was going on was in her imagination. Maybe he hadn't pressed as many buttons as she'd thought. Maybe he wasn't here to rip up half the county in his search for his brother's killer. Maybe he didn't want to barge through this place like a furious bull.

It was time to find the common ground where they could work together. Because that was basically what Gage had handed her. A job that required finding that ground. With the major. She wondered how much of an eye she'd need to keep on him and if it was going to be full-time. She supposed she'd find out, but it would be a heck of a lot easier if she didn't start out in complete opposition.

He amazed her by saying, "I guess I didn't create a very good first impression with you."

"No. You didn't. You had death in your eyes."

"Hardly surprising," he retorted. He was already finishing the first half of his sandwich.

Cat had hardly made a dent in her lunch. She forced herself to take another bite before speaking. "Look, we've got to work together now. We need to find some mutual understanding."

"I thought the sheriff had made that clear."

"He set the rules. Repeatedly, if I know Gage. But this is about more than rules. You're going to have to work with me on this. I can't have you doing things and telling me about them later."

"Understood."

Oh really? she wondered.

"Let me make something clear, Deputy. I'm a military officer. I follow rules all the time, some of them quite restrictive. My own judgment generally comes into play only in combat and tactical operations where the situation is constantly shifting. I have to stay within the Uniform Code of Military Justice. On the other hand, when my superior tells me something like *Go take that hill*, I have to figure out how. There's a lot in the balance, not the least the safety of my soldiers."

"Okay," she answered, willing to listen.

"There's not really a conflict here."

Time would tell, she thought. At least now she could taste her salad. "How do you want to set this up?"

Which was giving him a lot of leeway. Still, she wanted to know how he envisioned what they were going to do together, then decide how much of it was possible. She could still try to be the rein on him. *Try* probably being the operative word.

He glanced away, ruminating as he finished his sandwich. "I want to get to know people who knew Larry. Try to figure out if they know anything or sensed anything. Sometimes people find it easier to talk to a grieving relative than a cop. Or am I wrong?" His gaze snapped back to her.

"I've been a cop since I started dealing with cases like

this. I can't say for certain. One thing I *do* know is that friends and family try to avoid saying anything disparaging about the deceased." She almost winced as the word came out, knowing that it sounded cold. He was probably far from wanting to call his brother *deceased.*

"Never speak ill of the dead," he remarked. "Thing is, Larry wasn't perfect. Nobody is. Do I think it was impossible for him to have an enemy? Absolutely not. His job often made people furious at him. He could just as well have affected others around him the same way. I know he wasn't here long, but it doesn't always take long to make someone hate you. An ill-considered comment can be enough."

"Larry used words like a master."

"Exactly. And he could slice like a knife in very few words when he saw or heard something he didn't like. Anyway, people might find it easier to talk with me *because* I know Larry wasn't perfect. I hope."

That was a good point. Maybe. She ate another forkful of salad, getting a mouthful of delightful blue cheese, along with meat rolls. The knot in her stomach was easing, and her taste buds were evidently waking up.

He just wanted to speak to people who'd known his brother? Sounded innocuous enough. But there were other possibilities looming in the shadows. She stared down at her salad, suspecting that she'd let her tension leave too soon.

DANIEL DUKE STUDIED the woman with whom he'd been partnered. She clearly didn't like it any more than he did. He was a man used to going on missions and making his own decisions within the confines of what was legal. Things were different in a war, of course, but he knew where the bright lines were, and he kept himself within them.

He didn't like the idea of someone peering over his shoulder and trying to control him. She had been chosen to be his watchdog. He was already chafing at the idea. He could move more freely on his own.

The Ranger in him, he supposed. There had been a few times when he'd air-dropped into enemy territory with nothing to rely on but himself. He had always accomplished his mission.

He'd also seen enough of the expressions crossing Cat Jansen's face to guess that she didn't like this, either.

He'd managed to set her back up. In the long run, that wouldn't matter. He'd come here for two purposes only: to bury his brother and to find a killer. If the sheriff's people succeeded, he'd be content, although it wouldn't be as satisfying. But this wasn't about satisfying himself.

He glanced toward Cat as he finished his sandwich. It seemed she was eating without a whole lot of pleasure. Uncomfortable situation.

But he noticed again the arresting combination of black hair and brilliant blue eyes, a combination that would make anyone look twice. It had been the first thing he had noticed about her when he walked through the door of the office. And while uniforms seldom enhanced a woman's attractions, he still felt hers from across the table. When she moved, he could tell that she was fit, maybe even athletic.

But he wasn't here to notice a woman's beauty or anything else. They needed to forge a working relationship somehow, although he'd have been satisfied to tell her to continue her other duties and he'd keep her informed.

She didn't strike him as the type who was going to give him a leash that long.

Oh hell, he thought and reached for a potato wedge. He'd begun all wrong, but he didn't know how he could have begun better. He was furious beyond words over his brother's murder. He wanted the killer to face trial at the very least, and when he returned to his battalion, he wanted to know the guy was in jail. Caught. Going up the river as fast as possible.

Only when justice lay within reach would he be able to properly grieve for Larry. Because justice had indeed been important to Larry, something he'd been willing to risk his neck over. Then there was Duke's own guilt. He'd never be able to overcome that now, but he could deal with finding justice. Finding peace for Larry.

He spoke at last, trying to discover a way to meet this woman somewhere in the middle. Neither of them was happy to be here.

"Larry always used to say that the dead can't rest without justice."

Her head lifted from her salad, and he felt again the impact of her eyes. "You said he believed in it."

"The thing is, my brother was a realist, hardheaded and fact oriented. Then he'd say something like that. It was one of the things that drove his reporting."

"While I only knew him a short time, I didn't see anything remotely fanciful in him." She paused. "So you think Larry won't rest?"

"I don't know what comes after we die. It's all a mystery, and I tend to rely on facts, too. But since I don't know, I want Larry to get his justice. And frankly, I want justice, too."

She nodded. "I understand."

She sounded as if she did. Well, maybe that was a step in the right direction. He certainly needed to find one, since he'd started wrong, at least as far as Cat was concerned.

Parsing through the problem, trying to come up with a strategy, he slowly ate potato wedges and gave Cat space to enjoy her salad while he looked out the window. Spring sunshine drenched the street, and all the buildings appeared to have arisen early in the last century. He suspected renovations in this town tried to preserve the past, not erase it.

Maybe she needed to understand that he hadn't *had* to come to the police. He'd done so because he didn't want to get in a war with the cops here. That could mess everything up. And while he'd tried to make that clear, he wasn't sure he had.

There was Cat's reaction. He had to figure out how to persuade her before this became a bigger problem.

NEARLY TWENTY MILES AWAY, in a fold in the earth that cradled them in secrecy, three men sat around a small fire. The stream that trickled beside them, clearly runoff from the remaining snow high above in the mountains, made a pleasant sound as the afternoon began to wane.

It was far nicer than many of the places where they'd made a surreptitious camp. They all dressed casually, like campers or hikers, in jeans and long-sleeved shirts of varying plaids. Hiking boots finished off the unimpressive ensembles.

"You getting anywhere?" asked Man One.

"I hate these new phones," Man Two remarked. He held a smartphone in his hand. "The only contacts I can find are in recent text messages. The rest must be in the cloud somewhere, and we can't even get cell coverage here."

"What's a cloud?" Man Three asked. "And how can you be sure those aren't his only contacts?"

"Oh hell," said the first man. "He was a reporter. He probably had hundreds of contacts."

"No help to us," said the third man. "Hundreds of contacts? How do we weed through that?"

"We look at only the ones around here," said Man Two. "But I need his cloud access, and he's got it protected. When he said he'd put a copy in a place we'd never find, he might have meant that. And breaking into the house of one of his poker buddies last night turned up zilch."

"Clouds aren't that safe," the first man said. "Remember

when that motion picture company got hacked? He probably wanted a copy he could reach that would be safe. Maybe an external hard drive or flash drive."

"Or," said the second man, "he might have kept note-books and files. You know, old-fashioned paper. I dated a reporter a few years ago. She always kept her notes on paper. In those reporter notebooks, for one, and she had drawers full of files."

The first man looked at him. "Any reason?"

"She said it was the best way to protect her sources. She said that too many people could get into her computer."

If a breeze hadn't been wending its way down the nar-row gully, ruffling grasses and the just-grown leaves of spring, they might have heard a pin drop.

"Why didn't you mention this before?" the third man demanded. "We didn't know to look for that kind of stuff last night."

The second man shrugged. "Who thinks of paper files these days? I sure as hell don't. That just popped up from memory."

Their search had just gotten bigger.

"We can't break into that house again," said the sec-ond man.

"Nope," agreed the first man. "We may have screwed that up. But I'm still not sure about his poker buddies and other friends here. Did he know any of them well enough to turn over serious information to them? We don't know."

"There's no way to find out," said the second man. "Maybe the most important thing we can do is find out *where* he stashed the information."

"There's another team working on his contacts back in Baltimore," the first man reminded him. "Maybe they'll find out."

"I hope so," said Man Three. "Because I sure as hell don't want to go back without finding something."

The three exchanged looks.

"Why," asked the second man, "do I feel like we're Curly, Larry and Moe?"

"Because," said the first man, "we weren't given decent intel. We have to do that as well as find the stuff."

They all fell silent again. Each of them was thinking of events in Afghanistan.

Then Man Three stirred. "Hey, One? Did you know Larry Duke?"

"Why?"

"Because when you were…interrogating him, I got the feeling you did."

"Never met him," came the clipped response from the first man.

The other two exchanged glances. Neither was quite sure they believed it. They knew they'd come for the money. What if Man One had a different agenda?

Chapter Two

Daniel Duke made his way to the town's only motel, the La-Z-Rest. It didn't take him long to recognize the place had probably been here since long before he was born, but it was clean. Compared to a lot of places he'd slept, he wouldn't have complained regardless.

He doffed his uniform, putting it into a garment bag and hanging it in the closet. The shirt went into a laundry bag the motel provided. He'd chosen to wear the uniform for his arrival because it acted like a credential all on its own. Now he shed it so he wouldn't stand out.

Then he pulled on regular clothes, jeans and a chambray shirt, pretty much what he wore at home. Blending in with the locals was something he'd needed to do at times during his career, and sometimes that blending had required clothes he wasn't used to wearing. This was easy by comparison.

He felt he'd gotten a reasonable first concession from the sheriff. He hadn't expected to take part in the official case, but he hadn't wanted to be totally hampered, either. He might have a minder in Cat, and yet as annoyed as she was with the situation—he couldn't blame her for that—she'd shown signs of coming down off her high horse.

Looking back over their initial meeting, in retrospect he saw that he had probably come across as critical of her department. He was a naturally blunt man because he needed things to be clear when managing his own troops. On the other hand, he knew how to play political games when required. Until recently he'd been on an accelerated path up the command ladder, probably destined for a star on his shoulder one day.

Not anymore.

The simmering anger over *that* tried to surge, but he battled it down. There was one thing and one thing only he wanted to focus on right now—finding Larry's killer.

All right, he'd been impolitic. He needed to find a way to correct that so he and Cat Jansen could jolt along. He'd walked in and talked to her like one of his troops, making it perfectly clear what he expected, both of her office and of himself.

He'd looked down instead of up. The sheriff was like his superior officer in these circumstances. That meant Cat was, too.

Ah, hell. Talk about getting off on the wrong foot.

Her face swam before his eyes, and he felt the whisper of attraction once again. She was pretty, all right, with delicate features and those amazing blue eyes.

He brushed that feeling aside, too. Wrong time. Worse, he suspected Cat would be furious if she suspected she'd aroused his interest for that reason.

Judging by the few things Gage had indicated about her during their conversation, Cat must be very competent as a law officer, and that was how she'd want to be evaluated. The only way. She hadn't worked hard to get here only to be treated like she was a woman first.

He'd seen enough of that problem since women had started completing the arduous Ranger training. They were surrounded by a sea of men, all too many of whom believed the Rangers were a man-only territory. Considering what those women could have done to any guy who got out of line, that had always struck Duke as a stupid attitude to have.

Those women were Rangers first. Cat was a law officer first.

That settled, he paced the motel room. He was a man used to being physically active, to training every day for the next assignment. He'd spent too much time bottled inside a plane and then a car. He needed to work out some kinks.

He did some push-ups, some crunches, some squats. They weren't enough. What he needed was a ten-mile run. Some of it uphill.

He'd brought workout clothes with him, but they'd been used primarily on station. Not the kind of thing to wear around here if he wanted a low profile.

Damn. He'd seen what looked like a department store on the other side of town on the main drag. He decided to walk there to stretch his legs and get some new clothes. It would give him some time to get the lay of the land.

He always wanted to know where he was, if there were any obstructions to escape, what the shortest routes were between points. Recon. Basic, simple recon. It would be a good use of his time, if not all his energy.

He'd feel more comfortable, too. This might not be a very dangerous place, but that wouldn't change the habits of most of his adult life.

WHEN CAT RETURNED to the office, hoping Gage might put her on the burglary case, the sheriff called her back to his office.

"Door?" she asked, resigned to an inquisition.

"Please."

For the second time that day, she closed it, then sat across the desk from him. "And the winner is…"

Gage flashed one of his crooked smiles. "How'd it go?"

"I suppose you mean with Major Duke."

He shook his head a bit. "So, are you being difficult?"

"I suppose I am. I don't know if you saw it, but the man who came through that door earlier had death in his eye. Cold. Furious. And more than capable of carrying out any threat."

Gage sighed, leaning forward to rest his forearms on his desk. His chair squeaked, and she guessed from his faint grimace that some part of him was objecting to the simple movement.

"He's a Ranger," Gage said. "And from what I know of them, which admittedly isn't a whole lot, he's been to war more than once, he's gone undercover in enemy territory and he might even have gone on a few solo missions. You don't get to be a major at his age unless you're being fast-tracked, and you need that kind of experience to rise in the officers' ranks if you're in special ops."

"All of which is to say you saw the look, too."

"It didn't surprise me. Add to that the fact he'd probably love to get his hands around the throat of the guy who killed his brother, and you've got a man who's exercising some serious restraint. Yeah, he's a pressure cooker right now."

"How comforting," she said dryly.

"Anyway, I don't expect you to be able to stop him if he gets set on something. I just want to know what he's doing. It may sound like babysitting, but it's not. You know the stakes."

Cat did indeed. She'd tried to make them clear to Duke herself, and she'd heard enough of what Gage had said to know he had as well.

"I guess he set my back up," she admitted.

"Can't imagine why." A bit of sarcasm crept into his voice. "Just keep in mind that he's a military officer. He's used to commanding and to taking charge. Neither of which we can have him safely doing, but as long as he knows you're watching, he'll control himself."

"He said he's used to staying within the lines."

"Another thing he's had to do to achieve his rank. Do I think he will? Most likely, unless fury overtakes him. No guarantees about that. Cat, I can't emphasize enough that he's been to war. Basically left civilization behind. Some of that always stays with you."

"I know." Springing to memory were a number of vets she'd had to deal with when they lost themselves in depression, alcohol and drugs, or when memory or ungovernable rage had taken over. War inflicted indelible scars. "Okay, I'll keep all that in mind. But I guess it tells me why the military have their own special bases."

Gage cracked a laugh. "Caged up, you mean?"

Cat finally relaxed enough to laugh, too. "That was unkind. Okay, I'll do the best I can, but I make no promises. I was thinking earlier that this is going to be like riding a bull."

"You ever done that?" Gage asked as she stood up.

"Hell, no. Do I look crazy?"

His laugh followed her as she walked down the hall.

Guy Redwing had assumed her position at the front desk. He looked bored. "Need a little excitement?" she asked him.

"Depends on what kind." He grinned. "I'm starting to think about a beer at Mahoney's after work. Come with?"

She'd have liked to go with him, but before the words slipped out, she remembered she had a task with no punch-out time. And just then she saw Major Duke striding purposefully down the street. Hadn't he gone to the motel?

Wondering what he was up to, she said, "Sorry, Guy. Much as I'd like to, I just saw my current assignment walking down the street. Later."

She darted out the door and saw Major Duke looking across the street at Freitag's Mercantile. She quickened her pace, wanting to catch up. He must have heard her footfalls, because he turned swiftly. The speed of a striking cobra. Okay, this man was wired.

When he saw her, he relaxed and waited, so she adopted a more reasonable pace. She didn't want any passersby to think she was chasing the man. Even if she was.

She nodded and smiled at the greetings from other residents who appeared to be on errands. One woman in particular was trying to wrangle twin boys, who were just of an age to slip her grip and make her look harried.

"Hi, Joan," she said as she passed.

"Hi, Cat. Boys!" She dashed off after them.

Cat was grinning by the time she reached Duke. "That's a handful."

"Those boys? Plenty of energy."

Then she faced him. "Looking for something?"

"Workout clothes that aren't stamped with Army logos all over. This is the place, right?"

She nodded. "Old-timey, with creaky wooden floors that have probably been there for at least a century. However, now that we have an influx of students at the community college, you'll find all the latest and greatest in some items. You want superhero shorts? I think they have some."

He surprised her with a short chuckle. "I don't think I'm ready to go that far. So are you my armed escort now?"

To her horror, she felt her cheeks heat. How had he done that? It had been a long time since she'd blushed. "I'm kinda over-the-top, huh?"

"No, you're in uniform, is all. Are you planning to join me in the store? Or later after I change and go for a run around town? You might find it hard in that utility belt."

Her cheeks grew even warmer. "Point taken."

He shook his head slightly. "How were you supposed to know what I was doing? This is going to be impossible for both of us if you have to be the principal and me the student reporting my every activity. Tell you what. I'll let you know if I'm doing anything that approaches the case. Then you can relax and I can go running."

Her cheeks didn't cool any, but she *was* just trying to do this job. An unfamiliar job. New rules and groundwork were needed. On the other hand, he was lengthening his leash and asking her to trust him. Having known his brother, she was inclined to, but the simple fact was that Major Duke was a stranger to her. Plus, she'd seen the icy fury in his eyes. He wasn't going to make this easy for either of them.

"I understand your point, Major."

"Duke. Just call me Duke."

"Okay, Duke. You can call me Cat. But you were walking down the street a few hours after having expressed your intention to interview people who knew Larry while he was here." As she mentally reviewed what he'd said when she'd first reached him, she started to get seriously irritated. How dare he talk to her that way? He'd scolded her as if she were a thoughtless kid.

He nodded slowly, glanced across the street and said, "Give me your cell number. I promise to tell you before I talk to anyone, okay?"

"Or anything else to do with your brother's murder."

"On my honor."

She relaxed a bit. She suspected honor was very important to this man. "All right. I'll trust you. But if I find you've crossed the line, you're going to be in trouble. I won't stand for it, nor will the sheriff."

"We'll get it sorted. Your number?"

"I want yours, too."

"Of course."

"Keep in mind, though, the farther you get out of town, the spottier cell reception will be. Out there in the ranch land, there aren't a whole lot of cell towers. Not enough people to justify them. And the mountains are pretty much the same."

"I've operated in much tougher conditions."

Yeah, he had, she thought as she walked back to the office after they'd exchanged numbers. That was part of what worried her.

CAT WAS A FIREBRAND, Duke thought as he crossed to the mercantile. He had no doubt she'd try to call him to heel if she didn't like something. He'd only promised to let her know what he was up to, but she'd have to give him reasons if he objected.

While he was looking at shorts, a memory of Larry popped up. They'd often run together while they were growing up, but when Duke had returned from Ranger training, Larry had wanted to run with him again. The two of them had wound up laughing because Larry could no longer keep up the distances or the pace Duke used. He'd never forgotten his brother's grin as he asked, "What did they do? Replace you with bionics?"

God, he missed his brother, even though they'd been estranged for a while. Which made him ponder yet again how he—or anyone else, for that matter—allowed such rifts to grow when life was so short. You never knew...

He should have learned that after so much time in deadly environments. Life could often be too short, truncated by unexpected events.

Shaking himself out of impending gloom, he focused instead on rage. He'd have time to grieve later, once Larry had his justice.

He found a couple of pairs of shorts and some shirts and walked back to the motel. Man, he needed to run. A long, fast run.

Then he'd figure out what to do next.

WELL, THAT HAD gone well, Cat thought as she walked back to the office. *Not.* He'd managed to embarrass her, which wasn't easy in her line of work. Or maybe anger had heated her cheeks, not embarrassment. Regardless, after that she could easily dislike him.

It wouldn't help anything to dislike him, though. Not one thing. Besides, she could understand his thirst to find his brother's killer. She'd known more than one family who had been pursuing justice for a dead relative decades after the killing. Not unusual. Some called it closure, some referred to it as justice, but there was no escaping the fact that people needed a resolution. That need could consume them, and possibly their lives.

Cops understood that. They understood it so well that departments with sufficient resources ran a cold case unit. No one wanted to forget the dead.

A few cops even investigated cold cases after they retired, so haunted were they by some crimes.

So yeah, she got it. Totally. Which meant she needed to quell her reactions to Duke. They were too strong. Too reactive. She'd dealt with worse than a difficult relative before.

And that was what he was. However intimidating, however angry, he was still a grieving brother who needed his resolution.

Needing it in three weeks was the only unreasonable part. Larry hadn't been here long enough to create a big list of persons of interest. A poker group, eight people max? Not much to go on.

Nor were the regulars he'd met at Mahoney's, although they wouldn't be overlooked as the department worked to peel back the layers on this case. If there'd been an argument or altercation, Mahoney would know. If it had been bad enough, he'd have reported it. Nothing had seeped out of that bar.

When she returned to a desk she shared with other officers, she realized she was at loose ends. Her assignment to keep an eye on the major made it impractical to follow any kind of duty that she couldn't quit immediately.

Damn it. She *liked* to work. In fact, she liked it so much she averaged about sixty hours a week. That curtailed her social life, but that was okay. She was an introvert in an extrovert's job. Interacting with people all day made her crave solitude with a book or a movie. Recharging.

Or maybe she could work out in her tiny gym in her basement. The house her mother had left her on Poplar had made it possible, which was good because this town had one gym open to the public: at the college. Public hours were limited, of course, making its use more difficult.

The house was cozy, which suited her. Just two bedrooms and a dine-in kitchen, no dining room. One full bath. The extra bedroom served as her home office and contained the daybed she'd slept in while caring for her mother.

It was a newer house than many neighboring ones that had been built during the waning days of the Victorian era, but it displayed nice touches with dark woodwork and matching solid-core oak doors. Over the time since her mother's death, she'd started repainting the interior and had indulged her love of color, such as the Wedgwood blue in the living room and sunshine yellow in the kitchen.

When she walked through the door, she initially felt sorrow. Despite having many good memories here, she also had a lot of sad ones, and every time she entered the house, she missed hearing her mom call out, *Hi, honey.*

Sometimes she was almost sure she'd heard the greeting. Each time it happened, it arrested her. Even in midstep, she'd pause, listening.

She changed quickly into her workout clothes and headed down into the basement. There her weights, her exercise bike and her treadmill awaited her. This wasn't her favorite part of the house, but it was a necessary one, holding the washer and dryer, a utility sink and various boxes of stored items.

Items that she kept thinking she should give away. She had no use for her mother's clothes, for one thing. She'd already saved what she cared about.

An hour later, wishing for a TV so she'd have something other than her own rambling thoughts to keep her company while she exercised, she took her sweat-soaked body upstairs for a shower.

Then it was time to consider dinner. Dang, her life outside of her job had become a totally predictable routine. Exercise, dinner, book or DVD, or sometimes some browsing on the internet.

Occasionally she wondered if that was a reaction to all the many months she'd spent looking after her mother. A time to heal, maybe a time to hide from personal cares.

Whatever. She was in no mood to do anything about it just then. Major Daniel Duke was probably going to invade her entire life with his quest. He'd taken over the job part of it. Now she could live in expectation of getting a phone call even at night as he told her what harebrained thing he was planning to do.

She caught herself. "Not fair," she said aloud to the empty house. She had to stop ascribing things to him she couldn't yet know.

He'd really set her back up, right from the time he'd first walked into the office.

Why?

When it came, the answer annoyed her no end. He was attractive. Very attractive. A trickle of warmth passed through her as she visualized him. *Oh yeah.*

She needed that like a hole in her head.

Chapter Three

Duke decided to get breakfast at the truck stop diner across the highway from the motel. The rain outside was steady, and while it wasn't a downpour, there was more of it than a drizzle. The air felt a bit chilly as he stepped outside, making him glad of his lightweight jacket. Georgia had warmer weather, and he seemed to have lost the cold conditioning from Afghanistan. A few more days and he'd adapt.

If there was one thing he was confident of, it was his ability to adjust even to the worst conditions, and this was a long way from bad.

With a clearer head, he grew dubious about what he was doing here. As he ate a large breakfast, he wondered what he hoped to accomplish. Yes, he wanted justice for Larry. Yes, he wanted the killer behind bars on a murder charge. Yes, he'd been furious and aching with grief since he got the news.

But what was he going to do?

It wasn't as if he had a list of Larry's contacts here. As he'd been running the streets of this pleasant town late yesterday, he'd calmed down a bit and really looked around. No matter what he did, he was going to be a visible stranger in these parts.

Why should anyone talk to him? Maybe a few of Larry's acquaintances here might, but how was he to find them?

Larry was a meticulous note taker, so maybe he had some contacts at his home. Or maybe the cops had them.

Damn.

As he ate, gloom crept up again. He needed to fight for Larry, but he'd been stupid. His mission strategy had been essentially zip. Get out here and talk to people. Right. What people?

Maybe he could get Cat to give him some names, but considering the resistance he'd felt in her yesterday, he wasn't hopeful. Naturally she resented him thundering onto her turf. How would he have felt if she'd shown up at Fort Benning and made demands of him?

He'd have resisted, too.

He stared down at his plate, still holding eggs, bacon and home fries that he no longer wanted to eat. He forced himself to chew and swallow. A soldier learned to eat whenever the opportunity showed up, and he loathed wasting food anyway. He'd seen too many people who didn't have enough to fill their bellies.

So what now, genius? he asked himself.

Yesterday when he'd been running, he'd imagined Larry on these same streets. It had proved hard to do. Larry was a big-city guy, associated for much of his career with major daily newspapers. He thrived on the action both in his work and in his environment. He collected interesting stories from many he met, just because he was that kind of guy, truly interested in other people.

He remembered Larry saying once, "Everybody has a story, Dan. Most of them are fascinating."

Larry had lived as hard as he had worked, fearless and daring. This town just didn't seem like him at all. At least from what Duke had seen.

Which wasn't much. He faced it—he was going into this mission mostly blind. It couldn't be helped by learning a language, adopting local dress and eating local food so he wouldn't smell different to people.

It was vastly more complicated. He was out of place, and people around here would figure that out. They'd be rightfully suspicious about him hanging around, and not even the excuse of preparing a funeral or a burial would give him enough cover. Definitely not if he started asking questions.

Nor was three weeks necessarily long enough to solve a case.

Anger and frustration goaded him anew. He *had* to do more than that. Larry deserved more than being boxed and put in the ground.

And nothing, but nothing, could make up for their estrangement. They'd both had a part in it, but Duke had still been simmering when he got the news about Larry. Still unable to find his way back. Hell, they had been two brothers locked in separate notions of what had been right.

He pushed that away, too. It would do no good now.

Outside the rain continued to fall.

CAT STARTED TO get uneasy when the morning passed without Duke showing up or her phone ringing. Was he out attempting some kind of investigation without telling her? She hated to think she'd have to rely on people around here telling her what he was doing.

And tell her they would. Or tell any deputy. He was an unknown man from unknown parts, and they'd gossip. Or if he made anyone uneasy, they'd call or walk in the office door.

Whatever he was doing, nobody found it remarkable enough to pass it along to the office.

Thank goodness.

Twice she pulled out her cell to call him but changed her mind. After yesterday, she didn't want to seem ridiculous.

There had to be some trust on her part, or he might decide he was done with her and the whole department.

But she remained uneasy. Finally, she decided that if he didn't call her by noon, she would call him.

Satisfied, she made some busywork for herself at the office, all the while yearning to go back to regular duty. She couldn't even go complain to Gage about this impossible task, because he hadn't come in yet. Probably out talking to someone.

Not that she would complain. Nope, she prided herself on not being the type.

Shortly before noon, she could barely rein her impatience, but then Duke walked through the door. She summoned a smile, opening her mouth to speak.

He forestalled her. "I was over at the mortuary. They don't have any release date for Larry's body."

"The state has him," she answered. "We don't have the kind of forensics here that they have."

His eyes narrowed, but he didn't say more than "Can we get coffee?"

She grabbed her yellow uniform rain jacket. "We can go to Maude's if you don't mind a lunch crowd. Or we can go to Melinda's Bakery. She has a handful of tables for people who want to enjoy coffee and pastry, although at this time of day she's probably nearly sold out of baked goods."

Remarkably, he hesitated. While she'd known him less than a day and her experience of him was literally a couple of hours, he didn't strike her as indecisive.

"Or," she said reluctantly, "we can go to my place, where no one might overhear."

He raised an eyebrow. "Very generous."

"Well, I don't know what you want to discuss. You decide how much privacy you need."

"I don't want to impose."

Which was probably as good as saying he didn't want the diner or the bakery for this discussion.

"My place it is," she answered. "You got a car?"

"I walked here from the motel."

"Can't cage the beast, huh?"

A flicker of humor appeared then was gone. "Nope."

"Let's go."

The distance to her house wasn't that great, but given it was raining, she didn't feel like walking it as she often did. Plus, the sooner they got to her house, the sooner they could get this conversation underway and she could stop wondering if he was about to lob a bomb.

The drive was short enough but worth it just to watch him fold his way into her subcompact. She almost grinned, but he succeeded.

Once at her house, she started a pot of coffee and invited him to sit at her small kitchen table. There was room for a larger table, but it was the one her mother had used for many years, and it was enough for her.

He sat on one of the chairs that had a steel frame and a vinyl-covered seat. A relic of the '50s or '60s, she believed.

While the drip coffee maker hissed and gurgled, she sat facing him. "What's up?"

"Well, there's my brother. I get he was murdered, but what's taking so long?"

"All I can say is that it shouldn't be much longer. I don't know the timetable. I'm not sure anyone in the office does, but I'll ask."

"Thanks." He pushed the chair back so he could cross his legs, ankle on knee. "I have another question. I'd like to see where my brother was living. Have you people released it yet?"

"Hoping to find some information?"

"It's possible."

God, she didn't want to say this, but she was going to

have to because there'd be no other way. "It may have been. But... Duke? Are you sure you want to see it? Nothing's been cleaned up. You should hire someone..."

He shook his head. "I've seen worse."

She frowned. Her heart skipped unhappily. "You may have seen worse, Duke, but worse wasn't your brother."

THE WORDS HIT Duke hard. He felt his own head jerk a little in shock. He was getting warned about something far worse than he'd imagined. Shot? He'd seen plenty of gunshot victims. She had to know that, so what was she warning him about?

And she was right. Before this, it hadn't been his brother.

"What aren't you telling me?" he asked quietly. "What are you concealing?"

He watched her look away briefly. Then slowly her gaze returned to him. "It was ugly. I can't provide any details until we get the full report, but there's a reason we didn't give it to our local coroner. Can we just leave it at that for now?"

Black rage filled him, a rage so black that for a little while he didn't see Cat or the room around him. His hands clenched as if he could wrap them around someone's throat. God, he wanted to. Badly.

He closed his eyes, forcing the fury down into an internal box he'd had to use many times. It contained all the seething dark things inside him, the only place he could store them.

"I see."

"Do you?" she asked.

"Unfortunately, I do."

She compressed her lips, then opened them to speak. "Most people don't go back to where a tragedy like this happened. They stay away until cleaners come in to deal with it. There are some things people don't want seared into their minds."

"I get it." He certainly did. "But I've seen it all, I think."

"You probably have. But *not when it's your brother.*" She spoke emphatically.

The anger threatened to escape his control once again, but it wouldn't be fair to level it at this woman. She was doing her job as best she could. As for Larry...it was true, he didn't want to see it, but he didn't know how he could avoid it.

He drew a long breath, then said, "You don't want me to see it because you're afraid of what I might conclude. What I might see with experienced eyes."

A spark flared in her blue eyes. "Eyes experienced with a battlefield, not with a crime. You might draw the wrong notions about things. I've seen a lot, too, Duke, and I wouldn't reach conclusions until we get the forensics report."

As his anger settled back into the dark box, he admitted she had a point. He didn't have to like it, but she had one.

"What about Larry's contacts?" he asked. "I assume you know who they are. That you pulled every bit of information out of his place that you thought might be useful. You can tell me about that."

Her blue eyes sharpened as they studied him, making him feel almost like a bug under a microscope. Then she rose, pulled a couple of mugs out of the cupboard and poured coffee. "You like it black?"

"Yes."

He was still waiting, wondering if she was going to stonewall him. He watched her return with the mugs and sit down. He reached for his and cradled it in both hands. Hot. It was hot, and his fingers were not.

Eventually she spoke. "I'm going to give you one name. He'll tell you what he chooses. He's not a suspect, because he was out of town during the time frame of the murder."

He forgot everything else. "Who?"

"Ben Williams. Larry's boyfriend."

CAT WATCHED SHOCK hit him again. She leaned forward at once, a new conviction growing.

"You know him?"

"I don't know." He shook his head and put his mug down on the table. "I served with a Ben Williams. He left the Army a couple of months or so before…"

He stopped.

"Before what?"

"It's not relevant. Thing is, I introduced a Ben Williams to Larry one night about four years ago when we were all at a bar. They hit it off. Then Ben resigned his commission sometime later and I never saw him or heard about him again. It can't be the same man."

"Maybe not. I wouldn't know. I do know Ben moved here more than two years ago."

"That could be him. But why here?"

"I seem to remember he grew up here." She was trying to digest the possible ramifications if this was the same man. "Larry and Ben were quiet about their connection, though. I don't think many people even guessed they were an item. Ben never went to the card games, and I'm not aware of the two of them hanging out in public."

"Then how'd you find out?"

"Because Larry told me in passing, then asked me to sit on it. I'm not sure if it was one beer too many or if he just needed to tell someone. I had to share it when Larry died, obviously."

"Of course."

She could sense him thinking and she was doing the same. If Ben was the same guy Duke knew, and Ben and Larry had known each other long ago… Well, what did it mean?

She spoke again, sorting through what she knew. "Ben was in Gunnison visiting friends for a week at the time. When I called him, he dropped everything to get back here. We can go talk to him if he's willing."

Duke nodded. His gaze had grown distant, as if he were searching his own memory. "I don't know if my Ben Williams was gay. But if he was, military life must have been damn near unendurable. The changes in policy didn't change much on the ground. Some things can only become hidden, but never change."

She sat for a few minutes, sipping coffee, absorbing what he'd said. Eventually she asked, "Is it widespread?"

"The bigotry? I can't quantify it. One thing I know is that peer pressure is strong, and in a military unit more so. You live and die by the people you serve with, and sometimes it takes only one bad apple to affect everyone. It doesn't help when the command structure flips back and forth on gays in the military."

Duke sighed. "Anyway, a lot of those bad attitudes disappear under fire. Some people quickly realize that all that matters is whether you can trust the soldier beside you to have your back." He offered her a half smile. "Incoming fire can change your perspective on a lot of things. Or not."

Cat tried to imagine what it must be like for a commanding officer—at least she assumed Duke was at his rank—to have to deal with so many different problems. Not just how to fight and when to fight. Not just the stuff that sprang to mind when she thought about the Army.

"You have a lot on your plate."

"All I can do is be thankful for NCOs. They handle most of the nitty-gritty. Still, we're dealing with a lot of very young men. More hormones than brains, I sometimes think, but that's part of what makes them damn fine soldiers."

She laughed quietly. "You were that age once."

"Yeah, I was. I remember and shake my head at some of the crazy things I did." Then he zeroed in on his main concern. Not an easy man to divert. "Can we call Ben?"

She hadn't expected him to drop it, but she'd been hoping to avoid it for a while. She'd have liked to speak to Ben first and tell him Duke wanted to meet him. That would give Ben a chance to refuse, and he should have it. Ben had to be drowning in his own grief.

Allowing her a private conversation wasn't going to work with this man. On the other hand, she could see why. Was Duke supposed to trust *her* not to tell Ben to keep silent?

Cat twisted a little and pulled her cell phone out of her pocket. She kept related phone numbers on her contacts list while a case was ongoing and removed them later. Ben was there.

He answered on the third ring. Cat immediately identified herself.

Ben said almost eagerly, "What have you found out?"

"We're still looking for more evidence. I called because I need to ask you something."

"I told you I was out of town. Didn't you verify that?"

"That's not what I'm calling about, Ben, but yes, we verified your alibi."

A bitter laugh came over the phone. "Yeah. My alibi. That sounds so good, doesn't it?"

"It's a criminal investigation," she reminded him, trying to keep her tone kind. He was going through hell.

Ben's impatience came through. "Just find the killer. So what did you want?"

"Larry's brother would like to talk to you. Major Daniel Duke."

"I know who he is." Ben fell silent, the quiet conveying his reluctance. "Yeah. Okay. Why not?"

"You don't have to."

"Then you don't know Duke."

Cat was beginning to know him. She understood Ben perfectly.

Ben spoke after another hesitation. "Look, I don't know what I can tell him. I don't know what Larry was working on. He never, not once, talked about it. That was the toughest part about caring for him. He gave new meaning to the word *secrets*."

But Cat felt her heart thunder. "You think his murder had something to do with his work?" She wasn't sure anyone had considered that possibility. Larry had been here writing a book. Had his work followed him all the way from Baltimore?

"I don't know what else it could be. It sure as hell wasn't your ordinary burglary. But yeah, I'll talk to Duke. Where and when?"

"Privacy?" Cat asked.

Ben sighed. "That would be good, I guess. Bring him out here. I'll put the coffee on."

"Thanks, Ben. See you in a bit."

After she disconnected, she looked at Duke. "Let's mount up. He'll see you now."

Ten minutes later they drove through the rain toward Ben's house, an older structure on what could be called a mini ranch. In the past, a piece of a much larger ranch had been carved out for one two-story house surrounded by about forty acres. Cat suspected the subdivision had occurred for the benefit of one of a rancher's children. She couldn't imagine why else that could have happened.

Maybe one of these days she ought to go to the library and talk to the librarian. Miss Emma, as everyone called her, was reputed to be a truly great resource when it came to county history. Her family had been among the first to settle here in the late nineteenth century. Her father had also been a judge here.

Someday, she promised herself.

Beside her, Duke said nothing. Either he was lost in his own thoughts or he just didn't speak idly.

That might be difficult to get used to. No casual chit-chat? She wasn't accustomed to people who could remain silent for long. On the other hand, she admitted she wasn't much for it herself.

A half hour brought them to Ben's house, set back a few hundred yards from the county road. Tall evergreens towered along the property line, a useful windbreak.

Ben, a slender man wearing jeans and a gray sweatshirt, met them on the porch. His face, ordinarily attractive, now looked gaunt. To judge by the dark circles around his eyes, he hadn't been sleeping well.

Cat discovered that no introduction was needed. Ben was apparently the same guy Duke had known. Neither of them seemed especially warm in their brief greeting.

The old kitchen was a large room, big enough for a long table that could easily seat a big family or some ranch hands. It must have come with the house, since it was larger than a size most people would have purchased nowadays. Ben seemed awfully alone there.

He waved them to the table, grabbed three mugs in one hand and the coffeepot in the other.

He poured for all of them before sitting across the table. "What's this about, Duke?"

"Trying to get a picture. I want Larry's murderer."

"Don't we all?" Ben's laugh was bitter. "You care now?"

"I always cared."

Ben looked away briefly. "I suppose."

"I was wrong," Duke said flatly. "He wasn't exactly innocent, either. But you always think there'll be a tomorrow."

"Yeah. Only tomorrow disappeared."

Cat watched them both, wishing one or the other would fill in the blanks, but refusing to ask them. She had to let this roll between the two men, at least for now. The tension between them was almost palpable.

"Look," Duke said, "I'm sure I don't have to tell you about Larry's thirst for justice. I can't do anything else now except try to make sure he gets it."

Ben passed a hand over his face, and when he dropped it, there was a sheen in his eyes, as if he were fighting back tears.

"It made him a great investigative reporter," Ben said tautly. "You should know that."

"I *do* know," Duke replied. "I know it all the way to my gut."

"Then why did you freeze him out?"

Duke shook his head. "We froze each other out. I was angry because Larry didn't give me a heads-up on that story about the murders. I kept hoping that the repercussions would die down, but after my next performance report, I realized that story killed my career. If I'd known it was coming, I might have been able to distance myself."

Ben looked down. "He was right."

"About what? The crimes? Of course he was. But when his piece hit the papers, I couldn't begin to do damage control. I was suspected of being his source, when I hadn't known a thing about it until Larry's story was smeared all over the papers. Maybe you were suspected, too. I don't know."

"I wouldn't have cared!"

"Maybe you wouldn't, but you were already terminating. I wasn't. I was damned with faint praise, and there went any hope I had of promotion. I'm still getting damned."

Ben half smiled, but it contained no mirth. "No stars for you."

"Worse, no light colonel. I'm done at twenty."

It almost seemed they were speaking in code. Cat knew

she'd have to ask for some explanations later, but right now she let the men talk.

Ben retorted, "Larry wanted justice for those victims. He wanted to see the perpetrators punished. Your motivations were selfish."

"Maybe. Maybe not. All I know is I felt betrayed by my brother."

Ben swore quietly. "He couldn't tell anyone about that story before it hit the presses. Those higher up the food chain would have done everything they could to squash it."

Duke didn't answer. Cat wondered if it was because he agreed with what Ben had just said, or if there was another reason. She hoped her growing list of questions would stick with her. She wished she could write them down, but she didn't want to do anything that might halt this conversation.

Eventually it was Duke who broke the silence. "What was he working on while he was here?"

"I don't know. Larry was always secretive. I have no idea whether that was to protect the people who gave him information, or if it was for other reasons."

"Secrets caused us to split," Duke answered. "Given that story, I've got to wonder if he was working on something new that worried someone."

"I've wondered, too," Ben admitted. "I thought that once he arrived here, we'd be able to be more open about our relationship. No. Larry urged me to keep it quiet."

"Maybe he thought he was protecting you."

"And maybe he thought the same thing about you. Did you consider that? Why would he think you'd be connected to his reporting in any way?"

"He didn't know the Army," Duke answered. "I'll grant him that in retrospect."

Ben looked as if he might have eaten something sour. "I do know the military. I understand. God knows I faced enough of it."

Once again Duke shook his head. "I never heard a word about your sexual orientation."

"A lot of people had figured it out. Enough so that I wasn't surprised when my performance reports started going downhill."

"You, too? I was never in your chain of command, so I didn't see them."

For the first time these men shared a look of understanding.

After a minute, Ben spoke again. "It's a great way to hide prejudice, saying someone is excellent but not rating him or her higher."

Cat interjected a question, feeling it might be safe. "Better than excellent?"

"Oh yeah," Duke answered. "*Stands out above all peers* in the written comments is a good one."

"Oh man," she murmured.

"Lots of little, ugly secrets," Ben remarked. "You can make someone's life hell without ever revealing something that might be against regulation. You know, like discrimination that policy doesn't allow."

She was getting a much clearer idea of what Larry's story might have done to Duke, and why he might have stopped speaking to his brother. Other details she would ask about later, like the thrust of the story. It could be relevant.

Ben was relaxing a little. Duke seemed to be as well. Evidently they'd gotten past the problem between the brothers. At least for now.

"What are you looking for, Duke?" Ben asked. "My absolution?"

"No. Every single day I'm going to regret that I didn't try to close the gap between us. Too late for that. I'm hoping you might know something, anything, that could help to find his murderer."

Ben lifted his hands almost helplessly. "I told the sheriff

everything I could think of, and there's little enough. I'm sure he had enemies from his reporting. I *do* know that he received threats, some of them death threats. But that was all back East. I don't think he ever got one here. If he did, he never said a word."

The rain grew heavier. For the first time, Cat heard it rattling like pellets against the kitchen window. Ben looked around, noticing.

Duke spoke. The man could not be deterred. "Why did he come out here to write a book?"

Ben smiled sadly. "I thought he came for me."

"I wouldn't be surprised," Duke answered. For a few more minutes, he appeared to be looking at something far away. "Larry didn't ask for a lot. Just to tell a good story and to have his own family. I guess you gave him that, Ben. Thanks."

Ben nodded, his face sagging once again.

Duke rose then pulled out his cell. "Let me text you so you'll have my number. If you think of anything…"

"I doubt I will. But if I do, I'll call Cat."

Cat was surprised that Duke didn't bridle. He'd just been effectively dismissed by Ben.

But Duke did no such thing. "Let me know if you need anything. I'll help however I can."

THE RAIN WAS still coming down heavily, the distant sky and land meeting in an impenetrable gray. Driving them back to town, Cat tried not to drum her fingers impatiently on the steering wheel. She had so many questions.

But Duke remained mute beside her until she finally asked, "Are you going to run in this weather?"

"It wouldn't be the first time."

"I'm sure, but the question stands."

"The answer is probably."

"Well, I want to talk with you, so fit me in."

At that he turned his head. She glanced his way then returned her attention to the road. Too dangerous to get distracted.

"Pick a time," she continued. Getting pushy with this guy seemed like the best route.

"As soon as we get back. I'd like a drink."

An interesting non sequitur. She wondered if he felt a need after that conversation with Ben. "What do you want? I don't keep anything strong at my house, but I've got a few bottles of beer. Or we could go to Mahoney's bar. It probably isn't busy at this hour, and they do make a good sandwich. In fact, I'm getting very hungry."

"It's late afternoon already." He sounded surprised.

"Yup." Not much else she could say.

More silence. The rain fell heavily enough that water couldn't run off the road fast enough. She slowed even more and waited.

"Any place we can get takeout?"

"Of three places, two of them do it. Well, the market also sells subs. Depends on what your preference is."

"You're the one who's hungry. Me, I eat whenever I can, whatever I can."

Cat decided instantly. "Then it's a sub. I'm starved, and a loaded one just might do it for me."

The rain let up just as they reached the edge of town. The city looked sad in the gray light and rain. It suited her mood perfectly.

The market deli was quick, making the eight-inch subs in a relatively short time. Duke ordered an extra one and insisted on paying.

Cat greeted some of the other customers. Part of the job, although she didn't mind the casual hellos. People around here rarely ignored someone they knew, and much of the time when you passed somebody in a vehicle, fingers would lift while the palm remained on the steering wheel. A friendly gesture that had almost faded in a lot of places she'd been.

Back at her house, she didn't bother with plates. They could eat off the wrappers with the assistance of a couple of napkins. Her only effort was to get two bottles of beer out of her fridge and put them on the table.

Duke pulled the tops off both. My, she thought, wasn't this cozy? Hardly. He looked grim, and she braced herself.

"What was going on back there?" she asked, unable to bury her questions any longer. "It was like the two of you were speaking in code some of the time."

"It probably sounded that way. I don't know which part of it I want to discuss right now."

"You want me to ask questions? Or wait until after you've eaten."

By then he was chewing on a large bite of his sandwich. She joined him as her hunger won over her curiosity. Food first, she decided. She had him temporarily corralled, and everything else could wait. Why ruin good food with heavy emotion?

"You know," she said presently as food settled into her stomach and quieted the gnawing hunger, "I've got a treadmill in my basement. Some weights, too. If you'd rather do that than run in this rain, I'll share."

"Thanks. I might take you up on that."

"No barbells, though. It would be too dangerous when I'm alone. But I do have a curling bar."

He nodded, then gave her a faint smile. "Got any additional weights for those dumbbells?"

"Oh yeah, iron plates. Can't make it with those pretty little ones that come in different weights."

"Sounds good to me."

Given his career, he was probably an exercise demon. She almost looked forward to watching him wrestle those plates around.

When he finished his first sandwich, he offered her half of the second, but she shook her head. "I'm full, thanks."

The beer went down smoothly, icy cold and tangy. Then she was done eating, and he was close to it.

"What happened back there?" she asked. "At Ben's." As if he needed the elucidation.

"I think Ben and I came to an understanding. At least as far as Larry is concerned. Kind of feeling our way there."

"What happened between you and Larry?"

His face darkened, and she wasn't sure he was going to tell her anything. She was pretty sure it was a sore point for him.

He finished eating and wrapped up the other half of the sandwich. "He wrote an investigative piece about the Army. Heads rolled. I was collateral damage."

A succinct but unrevealing response. "Don't you think it might be germane to this investigation?"

"In what way? It happened over two years ago. The main thing that strikes me is that I shouldn't have remained angry for this long."

"What about Ben? I got the feeling from what you said that he was annoyed with you, too."

"*Annoyed* would be an understatement. I was furious that Larry hadn't let me know that article was coming. Maybe I could have found a way to distance myself, but he side-swiped me. He was really angry with me that I couldn't understand his position."

He sighed. "Ben was right, though. If anyone had found out what he was doing, there'd have been a lot of pressure on the paper and maybe on Larry to squash it. Not that I'd have told anyone in so many words. Hell, I didn't even have to know what it was about. Just mentioning in an ear or two that something was coming and that I didn't have any other clue might have been enough to stall this storm. At least the part that dumped on me."

"So it ruined your career?" She folded her sandwich wrapper and reminded herself not to make this sound like an interrogation. He probably wouldn't like it, and she didn't want to stem the flow of confidences now that they were coming. She couldn't help the feeling that they were teetering on the edge of something important. "How could it do that?"

"Easy. Don't rock the boat."

"But you didn't do the rocking."

"Doesn't matter. I wasn't involved in any way with what Larry did. Hell, I didn't even know until the article appeared that any of it had happened. It sure as hell didn't involve me or my troops, and it didn't happen anywhere in my chain of command. A few lower-ranking men in another regiment were arrested, but somebody way up must've been chapped. Or felt threatened. Anyway, I was an easy target. Nobody could have touched Larry after that article was published. Maybe they thought they could get back at him through me." He shrugged. "Whatever. It's done."

She hesitated, creasing the waxy paper in front of her until the edges were sharp. "How have they ruined your career? You arrived here in uniform."

"I'm still in uniform and will be until I hit twenty years. Then I'll be out."

She lifted her head, feeling seriously disturbed. "How can you know that?"

"Because my performance reports sank. I should be a lieutenant colonel in order to continue after twenty. I'm now considered 'low retention,' which means I'm definitely not going to be asked to stay on."

"But how can they do that?" Her feelings about this were starting to get tangled. She needed to understand.

"It's simple. There are a limited number of people who can get promoted. They don't find a slot for me, I'm on the way out."

"What did Ben mean by a star?"

His faint smile looked sour. "I was being fast-tracked and looking good to become a general eventually. I became a major early. Prospects were bright. Now they're very dim."

She let that sink in. As she thought it over, however, she could understand why he felt his career had been ruined. She didn't necessarily understand how all that worked, but he did. He was part of the machinery.

"I'm sorry," she said, feeling genuinely saddened.

"Me, too. And as the performance reports didn't improve, I got madder. Ben was right about one thing. I was being selfish."

The admission surprised her. "Why? Your career was wrecked. That had to be infuriating."

"Sure, but was that worth cutting off my brother? He'd done the right thing, but I didn't. I wish it weren't too late."

No way to answer that. No point in arguing against feelings. She sighed, then rose and gathered up the remains of their meal. "So now you want justice."

"I would have wanted it regardless. For Larry."

She believed him, felt a touch of his grief. "What a mess."

"Oh yeah."

She wiped up stray crumbs, then tried to smile at him. "Coffee?"

"I've intruded too much."

She put a hand on her hip. "I might have thought so earlier, but I'm not feeling that way now. This is important. I give a damn about Larry, and now I give a damn about you. You might not want it, but I care. So quiet down. Coffee? Or something else?"

"A beer if you have another."

As it happened, she did. "I buy this so rarely that you're in luck."

"Then why did you buy it?"

"Larry," she answered simply.

For the first time, they shared a look of real understanding. The sense of connection warmed her. She hadn't expected to feel this way, not when it came to Duke. Maybe it helped to realize he wasn't just a monolith of anger and unswaying determination.

As Cat returned to her seat, she said, "You put me off initially."

Another half smile from him. "I never would have guessed."

A laugh escaped her, brief but genuine. "I'm usually better at concealing my reactions to people. But there you were, looking like a battering ram. You sure looked hard and angry. Nothing about you made me want to get into a tussle."

He looked at the beer bottle he held. "Most people don't want to tangle with me. I can understand your reaction. I came through that door loaded for bear. Too much time to think on the way here, maybe."

"You looked like walking death," she told him frankly. "An icy-cold fury. Worse, in my opinion, than a heated rage. Scary."

"Comes with the territory," he said after a moment, then took a swig of his beer.

She could probably wonder until the cows came home exactly what he meant by that. Maybe it was better not to know. But she still had other questions.

"Duke? That article Larry wrote? Can you be sure it's not relevant?"

"It's been a while. Just over two years."

"That doesn't mean it can't fit into this."

He shook his head. "It was about a murder-for-hire scheme within the military."

Cat was taken aback. "Murder for hire? Someone wanted to get rid of someone else?"

"Not exactly." He put the bottle on the table and leaned back a bit. "There were apparently a few soldiers who were paid to eliminate certain Afghans. Contract killings. I don't know if it was ever discovered who paid them, but I do know they were all charged with murder. Larry uncovered the whole thing, and witnesses were willing to testify. At least the ones not in uniform any longer."

"My God," she murmured. "That's awful."

"Absolutely. A stain on the uniform."

"But why should that reflect on you? Did you know anything about it?"

"Not a thing until Larry's story broke." He leaned forward, and once again she caught a glimpse of the man who had walked into the office: hard as granite, angry. "If I had heard about it, I'd have done exactly what Larry did. Not in a newspaper, of course, but I wouldn't have let it go until I cut the rot from the tree. Ugly. Disgraceful. Cold-blooded murder."

Cat wasn't sure what Duke might have done to get himself out of the line of fire, but she could certainly understand why he had felt betrayed. To have the story hit the press and not even be prepared for it?

But at the same time, she had no difficulty understanding why Larry had chosen not to say anything.

"Do you suppose Larry might have thought he was protecting you by not including you in any way? Given what happened to you, maybe if you'd been able to send out a warning that the story was coming, people might have wanted to know why you didn't stop it."

His gaze grew distant again, as if he was reviewing the past. "It's possible," he said. "I didn't think of that at the time, but it's possible. On the other hand, when we had our argument, he never once said he was trying to protect me."

Well, cross that out, Cat thought. She needed to move, to mull this over.

"I need to change out of this uniform," she announced. "If you want, head down to the basement for a workout. I'm sure it's not what you're used to, but if you don't have to run in the rain, why do it?"

She heard a wind gust as she walked from the kitchen, rattling windows and flinging raindrops around. Not a great day to be outside unless you had to. Right now she didn't have to.

After a hot shower, she changed into some warmer clothes, including a blue flannel shirt. The weather had made the day colder, and her house as well. Drafts crept everywhere, and she thought about closing curtains to settle them down. Nah. Whatever was left of the day's light, she didn't want to shut it out.

In the kitchen, she discovered that Duke had washed the coffee mugs. Courteous guy.

As the borrowed heat from her shower wore off, she still felt a bit chilled. She went to the living room, turned on a few lamps, then curled up beneath a knit blanket on one end of the couch. Her book still rested on the end table, and she picked it up.

This case, she thought, was sprouting potential complications. Tomorrow she'd go to the office and catch up on what they'd learned. Right now, however, it was time to relax.

She heard a clang from below that told her Duke was working with her free weights.

Peace for a little while.

OUT IN THE RAIN, wearing camouflaged ponchos, three men sat in their gully and watched the creek rise even higher. It was too wet for a fire, which meant they couldn't even make coffee. Alcohol lamps could heat their rations a bit, but not make any decent coffee. Unless they wanted cups of instant.

They were used to the discomfort, but that didn't mean they liked it. At least with the cover of rain, they could walk a little, stretch out the kinks from being cramped so long.

On the other hand, the dropping temperature and the dampness reminded them of abuse their bodies had suffered over the years, of old wounds and battered joints.

"Ah, hell," said Man One. "We've got to figure out what we're going to do next. This rain won't last forever, and it'll wear out as an excuse pretty quickly."

"Who's gonna know?" asked Man Three. "Seriously. This takes as long as it takes, and if they don't get that, we need to refuse to go any further. It's not like this is an enforceable order."

The second guy spoke. "I like the money. Do you?"

"Hell, yeah," said the third man. "But we're operating under some pretty tight constraints here. And some pretty bad intel. We don't know exactly what we're looking for."

"Any information he might have wanted to use in that book he was writing."

The first man, who'd been listening, spoke. "But we don't even know what it was about. Someone has a suspicion, obviously, but without telling us, we can't know for sure if we've found it."

The second man jumped in. "I suspect," he said sarcastically, "that we'll know because it mentions the Army somewhere."

"Or some officers," suggested Man Three.

They all nodded, agreeing on that.

The second man spoke again. "Here we are, sitting in the damned rain again, freezing our cojones off—"

Man One interjected. "Don't exaggerate. We've been in worse."

Man Two answered him. "Yeah, man. We have. But my

point still stands. We're not *doing* anything. We're not even sure how to proceed. Staging a series of break-ins that look like some teenage fools did them is fine as far as it goes. But we wanted to do the jobs after dark when no one was home. We didn't want anyone to be able to say they saw big masked men. Hell, we don't want anyone to suspect these actions are anything except robbery."

"So here we sit," said Man Three. "I don't like it, either."

Man Two threw a pebble into the blackened firepit. "We already killed one man. Larry effing Duke. Do you really think they sent the body away because they didn't suspect torture? We can't leave a string of murders behind us."

The first man picked up a thin stick and flexed it, as if to test its springiness. Beneath his poncho hood, he didn't look any happier than the other two. But happiness wasn't a prerequisite. They had a job, and now it was time to figure out how to complete it. After a bit, he threw in his two cents.

"We'll leave murders behind us, but only if there's no other way. This was supposed to be a clean, quick op. It's not. Who would have guessed that Larry Duke would have refused to give us the info? I sure didn't. But we'd have had to kill him anyway."

"I'm not arguing against that. I'm just pointing out that the whole idea of waiting for these buddies of Larry's to leave town overnight isn't going to pay any dividends. How many of them do you see taking trips? How long are we going to wait?"

"I don't know," Man One said. "But I'm going to place a call soon and find out if our mission has changed, or if there are any better suggestions because of what we learned. We didn't come out here suspecting we'd need to pay a visit to anyone but Larry."

"Intel failure," said the second man. "A serious intel failure."

"We *know* that," said the third man.

The first man threw the stick he was holding. It fell into the rushing creek and vanished. "The thing is, nobody thought Larry would be able to withstand questioning like that. How many have you known who could?"

"His brother is a Ranger," said Man Two. "Maybe it's in the genes."

"That's ridiculous," snorted the third man.

The second man just shook his head. "Who would have expected such resistance from a reporter, for Pete's sake?"

Man One spoke. "It's irrelevant what was expected. We have to deal with what is. Now put your brains to it, men. It'll probably be sometime tomorrow before I can get someplace we can get a cell phone signal."

Which was kind of surprising to them all, considering they had a satellite phone. This was a communications dead zone for some reason. Or maybe the satellite phone was screwed up.

"Did anyone consider he might have left his research back in Baltimore?" asked the third man.

Man One answered, "I suspect I'll get that ball rolling when I call tomorrow. Just think, men. Try brainstorming ideas. If we're stuck with burglary, then we'll have to figure out how to do it without alerting the entire damn region to our presence."

With that they all fell silent, but irritation and gloom filled the air around them.

Not even a tent to cover them. Oh, it sucked.

Chapter Four

Duke refused Cat's offer to take him back to the motel. The rain had let up a bit, and despite his workout in her basement, he still felt a need to run.

He wasn't exactly dressed for a workout, but he didn't care if he got wet or sweaty. He didn't care about much except his brother.

Maybe his focus was getting too narrow. He wondered what he could learn from people who had played poker with Larry. Probably not much. If the cops had questioned Larry's poker mates, if one of them suspected anything of the others, they probably wouldn't remain mum.

He was pretty damp by the time he passed the sheriff's office and reached Mahoney's bar. Not so wet that he decided against going inside. Another beer was in order, and maybe some of the patrons would talk to him.

But the whole damn idea that he could just talk to people around here and learn something was beginning to look stupid to him.

Why in the world would anyone tell him something they hadn't told the cops? Because he was Larry's brother? Right now that didn't seem like much of a reason.

Feeling truly grumpy, he walked into the bar. He'd been out of his mind when he came here, swamped in grief and fury and the need to do *something*. Anything for Larry other than put him in a casket.

Inside, Mahoney's felt like an old-time pub. Dimly lit and bigger than he'd expected from the outside. A couple of dartboards and two pool tables could be seen through a wide door at the back of the bar portion. Wooden booths and tables filled the front end. Nice. It was filling up for the evening, mostly with men, and all of them talking to each other.

He took an empty stool at the bar and lifted his feet to the rail. A chubby man of about sixty came down the length of the bar and scanned him with sharp dark eyes before smiling and saying, "I'm Mahoney. What can I do you for?"

Duke took a chance. He extended his hand across the bar. "Daniel Duke."

Mahoney responded with a firm grip while saying, "Any relation to Larry Duke?"

"I'm his brother."

Mahoney's face sagged. "I'm sorry, Mr. Duke. Really sorry. I didn't know Larry for long, but he was a great guy. Made friends fast and made a lot of people laugh."

"That's how I remember him."

Mahoney nodded, seemed about to say something else, but finally chose the safest thing. Hard to talk to someone who was grieving, Duke thought. "What can I get you, Mr. Duke?"

"Everyone calls me Duke. And whatever you've got on tap."

"Be right back."

There was a big mirror over the bar, even in the dim light catching the glimmer from liquor bottles. The mirror was probably as old as the establishment, showing signs of losing its silvering in scattered spots. Mahoney returned a minute later with a big glass filled with beer and foam. Duke liked the foam, always had.

"On the house," Mahoney said. "I suppose you want to be left alone."

Duke shook his head. "I was hanging around thinking I'd like to meet some of the people Larry knew. A few stories might do me some good, and it would be nice to know that Larry had friends in the area. Cat Jansen told me he used to play darts here."

Mahoney smiled. "He was a mean dart player. He must have played it for years. It got so folks who watched him started placing dollar bets on whether Larry would lose." Mahoney chuckled. "Think about that. Not whether he'd win, but whether he'd lose."

Duke felt himself grinning. "Definitely Larry. I never could beat him in a game." Which wasn't strictly true, but it didn't matter. "And people still played against him?"

A twinkle came to Mahoney's eye. "You bet. After a beer or two, a challenge can become irresistible."

Duke laughed outright. He knew the mentality.

"Everybody liked Larry," Mahoney said. "That's why this came as such a shock." Then he looked around and called out, "Merritt? Can you come over here? I want you to meet someone."

Duke twisted his head and saw a big guy who looked like someone who worked outdoors a lot get up from a table he'd been sharing with two other men. He wended his way over with a loose gait.

Mahoney introduced them. "Merritt, this is Daniel Duke, Larry's brother. Duke, Merritt was one of them fools who was always trying to beat Larry at darts."

Merritt laughed and stuck out his hand. "I used to be the best darts player in this bar. Not after Larry came." He slid onto the stool to Duke's right. "I'm sorry about your brother, man. He seemed like a straight-up guy and funny, too. And the puns? He raised them to a new art form. Had

to be careful or prepared when you were talking to him."
Merritt's eyes creased with a smile.

"Larry was good people, although his knack for puns
sometimes nearly drove me up the wall."

Merritt nodded. "I get it. You'd be sailing along in a conversation, and he'd make a pun on some word or other. Then
everyone would crack up, and the conversation would get
derailed. But it was always fun." Then he shook his head.
"I don't get why anyone would want to kill him."

"Me, either." Which wasn't entirely true, because Larry
had gotten knee-deep into investigations that might have
made someone angry enough. But none of them were here.

He swallowed some beer, thinking. No, of course none
of them were here. Larry had come here to write a book,
and while that might be a useful cover, it wouldn't be about
this place. Hell, he couldn't imagine anything around here
that would draw the attention of a reporter of Larry's stat-
ure. Sure, there had to be crime and corruption, like everywhere else in the world, but nothing big enough to reach
Larry's radar.

Merritt spoke again. "So were you big brother or little
brother?"

Duke summoned a smile. "Little brother. Larry was two
years my senior. Didn't keep us from being tight, though."

Merritt paused long enough to raise a finger to Mahoney. "Let me buy you another beer. Then you come join
me and my friends. If you want, we can reminisce about
your brother. It was a short time, but it was a good time.
Would've liked it to be longer."

"Me, too." Truer words were never spoken. Mahoney
brought a fresh draft for Duke and a new bottle for Merritt. Then the two of them wound their way to the table near
the back where the two other men were looking curious.

"Larry Duke's brother," Merritt said to them, his thumb
pointing backward to Duke. "Just call him Duke, he says."

The two, introduced to him as Dave and Rich, were friendly enough, although maybe a bit cautious. Duke could understand. Maybe they feared an outpouring of grief.

But his grief was private, and he preferred to keep it that way. He'd nurse it in the quiet, dark hours and keep up whatever other appearance he deemed necessary.

Dave and Rich told him what a great guy Larry had been. Duke found himself remembering how he'd suggested to Cat that people might be franker with him because he knew Larry was imperfect. So much for that pipe dream.

Never had not speaking ill of the dead seemed like a heavy weight. How to get past it?

The other two men joined Merritt in talking about Larry's skill at darts. "He was pretty damn good at pool, too," Dave said.

"That's interesting," Duke said. "He never mentioned that he played."

"He sure did," Rich said. "Really good at it, so he must have done it a lot."

"Larry said it required being able to see vectors and forces, whatever he meant," Dave announced. "Never saw a guy make a ball curve around another the way he did, and right into the pocket. He should have played competitively."

But Larry wouldn't have enjoyed that. He had undoubtedly learned and used it as a tool. Duke nodded but remembered his brother's passion for investigating and writing. A very real passion. Just like Duke's passion for the Rangers. Duke wasn't as interested in getting a star as he was in being able to keep the job, which challenged him to his limit, mentally and physically.

Merritt spoke. "Larry was a reporter, right?"

"Yes," Duke answered. "One of the best. He did a lot of investigative pieces, some of which were pretty dangerous work."

The three other men exchanged looks. Then Dave said, "Wooee. He never mentioned that."

"He didn't like to brag." Duke sipped more beer, slowing down his consumption. Getting drunk wasn't on his menu for the night. "He was fearless, though."

Duke, who had a dangerous job himself, decided he might not have paid enough attention to Larry's courage. Not exactly something you thought of when it came to reporters.

But Larry had told him once the story of a female reporter in another state. The story had made Larry grin as he related it, but it wasn't truly funny.

The woman had uncovered some serious corruption in her sheriff's department. She'd been digging around for more information when the sheriff himself called her and said, "People disappear in the piney woods out here."

No, not funny, and the woman's editor had agreed. Larry's reaction should have revealed something to Duke, he now thought. Larry was used to threats. He'd said enough a few times for Duke to pick up on that. But to react that way to the woman reporter's story? Larry must have faced considerably worse.

And Larry treated it as if it was all part of the job. *Hats off to you, Larry.*

His three companions fell silent for a bit, drinking their beers, and Duke wondered if he should move on. He didn't want to become oppressive, or to make anyone uneasy. Strangers could do that if they hung around too long.

At last he rose and thanked them all. No one stopped him, but he caught the furtive glances of sympathy. They were feeling bad for him and didn't know how to act. The situation had to be uncomfortable. The dead man's brother, a guy they didn't even know, sitting here with them.

Well, that would put paid to a night of fun.

"Say, Duke?" Merritt stopped him. "Come on back when

you can. I'm here most evenings since the wife left me for a bull rider."

Duke looked at him. "Seriously?"

"Seriously." Merritt shook his head. "Anyway, no need to be a stranger."

"I won't." On the way out, he thanked Mahoney for the beer and received another invitation to return.

If they were hoping he'd be the life of the party the way Larry could, they'd be sadly disappointed.

Outside the rain had become heavier again, joining the deepening darkness to partially obscure the far side of the street. How apropos.

CAT WAS STANDING at her front window staring out into the renewed rainstorm as night blew in with it. A battered pickup pulled up in front. Then the driver climbed out and dashed toward her door. Under his rain hood, his face was concealed.

She heard the inevitable knock, and she went to answer it, positively in no mood to be disturbed. When she opened her door, she changed her mind. It was Ben Williams, and he wouldn't have driven all the way from his house through this rain for casual conversation.

"Hey, Ben," she said, trying to paste on a smile. Her mind was still half in the novel she'd been reading until a few minutes ago.

"Sorry to bother you, Cat, but I've been thinking about Duke's visit. The department told me you were here."

She gestured him inside with a movement of her head and led him to the kitchen table so she could offer him something. It only seemed neighborly. "Should I make coffee? Or I might have a beer left." She actually thought she had two, but she was beginning to wonder if she shouldn't drink another herself.

"I don't want to put you out."

Duke had said the same thing. She must be walking around with impatience written all over her. "You're not," she lied. "Have a seat. Beer or coffee?"

"Neither, thanks. If you want some, go ahead. I'm fine."

Given the hollow look in his eyes, Cat figured Ben was anything but fine. She ached for him, for his sorrow.

She sat across from him, wondering if she needed a bigger table. She'd never figured it would get this much use, but then, she'd never imagined working at home. Nope, that was what she had the department's office for.

"What's up, Ben?"

"I'm not sure. I used to know Duke."

"I kinda gathered that when he said he introduced Larry to you."

"Yeah." He nodded then sighed, a shaky sound. "We didn't tell him about us, though. It must have come as a shock to him."

"He wondered if you were the same Ben Williams. He was pretty sure you were. But I didn't get the feeling he had a problem with it."

"Maybe not. Larry and I had to be secretive when I was still in uniform. Things were bad enough for me, and Larry worried about it. We kind of crept around."

Cat frowned, her pain for this man growing. "That's horrible, Ben. Just horrible that you guys had to do that. I'll never understand it. Your personal relationship didn't affect anyone else."

"In theory. My parents sure didn't like it when I came out. Not a word for ten years now."

Cat shook her head and sighed heavily. "I don't know what to say except that's awful. I'm so sorry, Ben."

"I'm mostly used to it. I disappointed them, they kicked me to the curb, and after all this time…" He shrugged. "Their decision."

"Maybe they'll come around."

"I don't think I'd ever trust them again. Anyway, part of the reason I'm here is that I hope to get to know Duke even better because of Larry. If he still wants to talk to me. Plus, there's nobody I can talk to around here. Larry did a good job of keeping us private." He met her gaze almost as if he was making a plea. "I know I shouldn't lean on you this way, but…"

"You need someone who knows about you two. So you can talk freely."

He nodded. "Not fair to you, I know."

"Fairness is something we make. Besides, I really liked Larry, and he told me about you. Not much, but I knew. I guess he trusted me."

"I would say so." He sighed. "I honestly don't know what Larry was working on, but I think Duke wants to know. Did you guys find any hints at his house?"

"Afraid not, at least not yet. We're still evaluating evidence. But his computer was gone. I can't tell about much else."

Ben's head snapped up. "His computer? Who kills to steal a damn computer?"

"Good question." The more she thought about it, she felt that might be a pivotal question in all this. A bunch of kids who wanted to steal electronics would wait for the house to be empty. Wouldn't they? It was certainly a poor excuse for a bloody murder. She closed her eyes. It *had* been bloody. She really didn't want Duke or Ben to see the scene.

Then she looked at Ben again. "Why would he care what people around here thought of your relationship?"

"I don't know. I didn't expect it when he told me he was taking a sabbatical out here to write a book. Silly me, I was expecting picnics, hikes, dinners together…all that romantic stuff. Well, I got something quite different."

Cat's chest tightened. "That stinks."

"Yeah. But Larry was Larry, and I was used to his secrecy. I figured he had a good reason. Sometimes I even wondered what he thought he was protecting me from. If he was."

"That's also a good question." Ben had given her two points to put in the mental mill for processing. Hopefully some kernels would pop out of all the chaff.

"Anyway," Ben continued, "I was surprised by being kept out of sight. It left me wondering what he might be working on, though he wouldn't say, no matter how many times I asked. I quit asking. Anyhow, the year I was anticipating with the love of my life turned into two months, and they were…difficult. For me, at least."

Cat had no trouble imagining how that must have felt. "It would kind of make me wonder what kind of relationship we had."

"The thought crossed my mind."

Boy, did Cat feel bad for him. Relationships inevitably had their ups and downs, but to be kept out of the good things? To be relegated to a back room in Larry's life?

For the first time, she didn't think so well of Larry. "Did he spend *any* time with you?"

"He'd come over at night a lot. We'd share some beers or wine, cook together, spend hours just lolling around gabbing. It wasn't every night, though. Two months may not be enough time to judge long-term, but he *really* wanted me not to be connected to him."

Cat didn't have to say that was terrible. Ben already knew.

Still, the secrecy was another layer on this case. As outgoing as Ben was, she'd have expected him to squire his boyfriend around town. Instead Larry had shown up at least a couple of times a week to have a drink or play darts. Not fair at all to Ben to be left out. That must mean something. She made another mental note. She might have to question

Duke about it. Great. Most of the time that man did a great imitation of the Sphinx.

"I have some idea how it feels, Ben. I lost my mother about the time *you* moved here, but I'm sure it wasn't as bad as what you're going through." Useless words, but she needed to address this man's grief.

"I heard. You nursed her, right? Really tough."

"But I knew what was coming. I had time to say all those important things, and to show her. You didn't even get that."

He nodded slowly, then wiped under his eyes as if tears had overwhelmed him. "Damn," he said presently. "I keep crying."

"Anybody would. Let it flow." She rose and brought back a box of tissues to place in front of him.

He gave her a muffled thanks and wiped his eyes a few more times. "I didn't mean to dump on you. I just needed to talk to someone, especially about Duke. What does he want?"

"Justice for Larry. I think I'm supposed to keep him from wrecking the case. He was sure loaded for bear when he got here."

Ben wiped his nose, then reached for another tissue. "That would be Duke. He's a battering ram." Then Ben shrugged. "That's part of the job."

"Were you a Ranger, too?"

"I didn't try, honestly. Wasn't for me. I met Duke over in Afghanistan, though. I was on a patrol and we met one of his units, and there he was, striding along with his men. That night we all shared a camp, and Duke and I became friends. We met up a few times when we got back to the States. One of those times he introduced me to Larry, who was in town to visit him."

"I'd wondered, the way you two talked."

"We weren't best friends, but we could sure have a good time knocking back some beers."

Cat tried to imagine Duke having a good time and failed.

Of course, that wasn't a fair judgment under the circumstances. "And Larry?" she asked.

"We hit it off like a house on fire. A couple of weeks later, we were together. Secretly, of course."

Too many secrets, Cat thought. Entirely too many. First to protect Ben while he was still in the military, then hiding an investigation from Duke that had caused him serious problems, and now more secrets. To protect Ben again? No way to know now.

Given Larry's penchant for playing it close to his vest, she had to wonder what other kinds of secrets he might be hiding. A chill trickled through her. Not because she suspected Larry might be a baddie, but because now she had to wonder who else he might have crossed in his career. Especially recently.

Again, no way to know. Frustration began to build in her.

Ben spoke. "I don't know what Duke thinks he can do that the sheriff's department can't."

"I think he wanted to talk to people who'd met Larry. He thought people might be franker with him than with us."

"Not likely," Ben said sourly. "Larry didn't tell anybody anything. At least not about his work. At this point, I wouldn't be shocked if he had an ex-wife somewhere."

Ouch! Cat's sympathy rose another notch.

"Not that I think he did," Ben hastened to say. "But the last few days, I've been wondering what else he might not have told me. Pointless."

"I know. I'm sitting here wondering the same thing."

Ben sighed. "I'm sorry I'm taking up your evening. I'll go home now, but I want to talk to Duke some more. We may still have to iron out a few things."

"I'll tell him." Cat walked Ben to the door and watched him drive away over pavement that glistened beneath streetlights.

The weather had nothing on the storm she felt brewing.

THE RAIN WAS really beginning to annoy the three men in their gully. They'd had to move up the slope because the creek was so engorged, and now they sat with their boot heels dug in to keep them from sliding down into the rushing water.

"This wasn't a good idea," the second man said. "I know the gully conceals us, and we'd be able to move down it to cover if we needed to, but that damn mountain forest doesn't look quite as thick now. We could have maneuvered among the trees."

"Not as well," answered Man Three. "Come on. We've been through worse."

"I didn't retire to do this all over again."

The first man didn't say anything. If he sighed, it was lost in the pouring rain and the rushing of the creek. Bellyaching was part of a soldier's coping mechanism. He mostly ignored it.

The second man spoke again. "We can't do a damn thing tonight to finish this mission. That's bothering me more than the effing weather. I want this done and over with."

"Face it," said Man One, speaking for the first time in over an hour. "We've got a serious case of mission creep going on here. If you two would stop complaining and start thinking, we might get out of here sooner."

"Yeah?" asked Man Three. "What is your huge brain telling you?"

"That we need to be even more cautious. We need to be able to break in without the homeowners or kids waking up so we don't have to be on indefinite hold. Has anyone thought of halothane?"

"Like we can get any out here," snorted the second man. "And how are we supposed to aerosolize it to fill an entire house?"

"I wondered about that, too. Anyway, thinking ahead,

I brought a big canister, a tube and a mister that should do it. It's in my truck."

The other two fell silent, maybe stunned by the first man's prescience. Halothane, a surgical anesthetic, could put people to sleep for a little while. In theory it wouldn't kill them unless they got way too much.

"Why didn't you say so before?" asked the second man.

"Because I didn't want to use it. It'll leave traces in the blood. It's not easy to come by, so that would point in two directions—a hospital and the military. How many directions do we want these cops to be looking? Two isn't enough. And it sure doesn't point to a bunch of teenagers."

"Hell," muttered the third man.

"So try to think of something better," suggested the first. "I just threw it out there to stir your brains. Find a way around the halothane. Don't just sit here and moan."

"But you've really got it?" asked the third man.

"Absolutely. But it's the last resort, hear me?"

They heard. They understood. They didn't have to be happy about it, though.

Chapter Five

The morning brought sunshine and crisp air. The storm of the day before had caused the springtime temperatures to drop enough that Cat wondered if they might get more snow.

It wouldn't be unusual at this time of year. She loved the changeability, especially in the spring and autumn.

She considered wearing her uniform, then decided against it. Running after Duke mostly wouldn't call for it. And if she needed it later, she could put it on. One way or another, it wasn't going to be a day at the office.

She phoned him as she stood on her small front porch and waved to people driving to work. He answered immediately.

"Duke." Crisp, no nonsense.

"Hey, Duke. You ready to start the day?"

"Sure. I'll need a shower first. Just got back in from a run."

She couldn't resist asking, "So was it a run or a jog?"

She thought he snorted, but she couldn't be sure over the phone.

"It was a run. Where should we meet?"

"I'm hankering for a latte, so Maude's it is."

"That's the City Diner?"

"Yeah, but everyone around here calls it Maude's."

"I can see why," he replied dryly. "Give me twenty, please."

Presto, change-o, she thought as she tucked her phone away. Better take her car in case he got a wild hair. It would have been a great morning to enjoy a run of her own, except she had one problem Duke didn't: she was known to almost everyone. Privacy didn't exist for Cat on the street.

The morning breakfast crowd had begun to trail away by the time she arrived. There was one group of older men who had turned Maude's into their meeting place and always sat in the back. Generally they were too busy talking among themselves to pay much attention to anyone else.

Cat exchanged waves with them and took a table right in front of the window. A few minutes later, Maude appeared with a tall paper cup. "Latte, right?"

"You know me too well." At least Maude didn't slam it down the way she would have slammed a coffee cup. "Thanks."

"That new guy coming along? The one you're babysitting?"

Cat nearly froze in surprise. How had that gotten around? Loose lips in the department? "Where did you hear that?"

"Don't recall. You know how things float around here."

Amazing Maude said so much. A warning of some kind? She had the feeling that Maude, per usual, wouldn't say another word about it, so there was no point in asking. Maude had already turned away to stomp back behind the counter and wait for a customer who needed her to tromp back into the kitchen.

Given that Duke had already been out on a long run, she suspected that would be soon.

Sipping her latte, she waited and watched the street. More pedestrians were appearing, particularly women who seemed to be hurrying on errands. There was a small party store down the street, patronized by people who had a child's birthday coming up, and a very small organic food store that somehow was hanging on when there never seemed to be anyone walking in or out. At the far end of the street sat a meat-processing place where you could bring your deer in the fall or a steer you wanted to use to feed your family. They'd even age the meat to make it taste better.

On weekends, a small vacant lot turned into a farmers' market. As much good produce as could be raised around here. The environment for it had never struck her as the best, but people still managed.

Then she saw Duke striding down the street toward the diner. Of course—a long run followed by a walk. It was a wonder the man could ever hold still.

As soon as he came through the door, before they could do much more than exchange greetings, Maude appeared at the table to slap down a menu. "Coffee? Black?"

"Black, thanks."

After Maude brought it, she groused, "A big man like you needs to eat. Figure out what you want."

Duke stared after her, the corners of his mouth twitching. "She'd have made a good drill instructor."

"I wouldn't be surprised. *Have* you eaten?"

"Not yet." He sipped coffee then picked up the menu. "What about you?"

"Toast and peanut butter. My favorite since childhood."

"Sounds good. But I saw your basement gym. You could use a bit more than that toast. I think I see turnovers up there with the pies." Then he astonished her with a wink. "Maybe some doughnuts, too."

She laughed. It was an old joke, but most cops tried to enjoy it anyway.

He ordered a full-on breakfast plus a turnover. She suspected it was for her.

He spoke to her as he set aside the menu. "Are you incognito today?"

"Not really. Trying to draw less attention to you, but my badge is on my waist. Ben showed up at my house last night. He wants a chance to talk to you again."

Duke nodded. "Fine by me. Maybe we can share some good memories. But he didn't recall anything else?"

"Only how secretive Larry was, even after he arrived here. It seems he kept Ben under wraps, which was not what Ben expected at all."

Duke frowned. "I wouldn't have expected that of my brother."

"After what Ben told me, neither would I. I mean, I didn't think much about it when Larry told me Ben was his boyfriend, but I never really thought about not seeing the two of them together."

"I knew they flew under the radar before Ben resigned his commission, but that was the last I heard about it. Six months after Ben left, Larry and I had our...rupture. I guess the two of us really need to talk. Big blanks."

Shortly, Maude brought a heaping plate of scrambled eggs, breakfast sausage and home fries, with a side of ham and the turnover. "You want more, it's on the house."

"Thank you," Duke said. After Maude had walked away, he asked, "Where did that come from?"

"Her steadily softening heart, I guess. She probably heard you're Larry's brother."

"So much for a low profile." He pushed the apple turnover toward her. "Yours."

"Thank you." What else could she say? He'd done something nice for her, and she hadn't refused when he'd suggested it. Besides, as her mouth watered, she decided it was unlikely to add five pounds.

She pulled a napkin out of the dispenser and drew the small plate closer. Apple and cinnamon. The aroma was wonderful. The first mouthful was delicious.

"Anything else?" Duke asked after a bit, when his plate was half-empty and the ham was gone.

"Apart from the odd secrecy? One thing. When I told Ben that Larry's computer was gone, he remarked that seemed strange, to kill someone over a computer."

Duke's head lifted. "That was it? His computer?"

"There may be other things. I don't know yet. I was pulled off the case because I knew Larry. Obviously. But it got me thinking. That was an awful lot of violence for one laptop."

"Damn it, Larry," Duke growled quietly. "What the hell did you get yourself involved with this time?"

Cat couldn't answer. Nobody knew the motive for this murder, nobody evidently knew what Larry was working on and, given his natural secrecy, it was unlikely anyone in this area knew he was gay.

Duke went back to eating, but this time clearly without pleasure. He was eating for fuel, nothing more.

Cat eventually spoke, the turnover mostly gone. "We can't be sure it had anything to do with his work. Maybe he just ran into a bad actor. It can happen, Duke."

"Yeah." But he didn't sound as if he believed it.

Neither did she. There was an awful lot of violence. Someone had to be seriously angry with Larry to do that. But she didn't want Duke to get wound up again, not when he was being so cooperative with her. If he went out of here carrying a lance with blood in his eye, she didn't want to think about what might happen.

Gage had given her permission. She could share what she thought necessary. Given that, she needed to direct Duke.

"I'll call around, Duke. I'll see how many of the people who played poker with Larry are available to talk to you, and when."

"Okay. Thanks." He nodded and went back to eating like a kid whose mother had told him to clean his plate. He might have lost his appetite, but he wouldn't waste food. She liked that. She absolutely hated wasting food.

She was probably the only person around here who could have a meltdown when she discovered a rotting green pepper at the back of her fridge.

Okay, not a meltdown, but she always felt bad.

Maude swung by to refill his coffee and ask if she wanted another latte. Duke answered for her. "Sure she will. She may deny it, but she does. She can take it with her."

"Duke!" Cat felt a bit of annoyance. "I can make my own decisions."

"I know you can. I also know that you try to be polite. That's been obvious. If you can't drink it all, that's okay, too."

Man, he had her number, she thought when he insisted on paying the bill. She at least didn't feel uncomfortable about that. He'd ordered the turnover and coffee without listening to any objection and without getting her permission.

Served him right. It wasn't like Gage had suggested she use an expense account. Why should she? Duke was an uninvited complication.

She decided not to go back to the office, but to take Duke to her house once more. She would have peace to make phone calls, and she wasn't sure that any of the poker gang would be free before evening. If any of them even wanted to talk to him.

Back at her house, she paced as she made calls. First was to Gage.

"I'm going to take Duke around to talk to the poker group, unless you object."

"That seems harmless enough. We already got everything they could share or were willing to. Just pay attention in case he teases out something interesting."

"Will do." Cat hadn't expected a different answer, but this was one way to keep Gage up to date on Duke's activities. He *had* asked her to keep him informed.

"One other thing," she continued. "Nobody knows what Larry was working on. And Ben Williams commented how strange it was that someone would take only Larry's laptop. Did we find anything else missing?"

"His phone. These days everyone has a smartphone. We couldn't find one."

That sent a trickle of unease running down her spine. "Damn," she murmured.

"Yeah," Gage answered. "You didn't know that?"

"I got thrown out of there because I knew him, remember? I shouldn't even be on the case."

Gage snorted. "I use what I got. Anyway, we haven't released the scene yet. I sure as hell hope we can find if something else is gone. It might be a clue."

"How are we supposed to know?"

After she disconnected, she wondered if she should even tell Duke about the phone. Wait, she decided. Just wait. And there was that big question: How were they supposed to know if anything else was missing? Other items, such as cash, no one would know about. From what she'd read in the reports, they hadn't found Larry's wallet, either. But all those things could fit with a robbery.

Except Larry's horrific murder.

She felt Duke watching her from the kitchen. She turned to look his way. "The scene hasn't been released."

He stood. "You said it had been."

"I said it *might* have been. Gage said we're still not through."

Duke frowned. "It's taking a long time."

"We're a small department. Nobody wants to over-look something."

He nodded but clearly was disturbed. "And the poker group?"

"I'll start making calls."

It took most of the rest of the day to reach everyone on the list. She felt as if Duke would be happy to start with just one, but that would delay setting up the rest for meetings. She just kept plugging away until she had two appointments laid out.

"Was everyone agreeable?" Duke asked.

"Some of them even sounded eager. None sounded reluctant. Only two could schedule at this time."

"Good starting point. When's the first?"

"Matt Keller this evening. He owns the organic food store. He said he'd come over here tonight around seven. Next is Bud Wicke, tomorrow at lunchtime. We can meet him at the garage."

"And the rest?"

"They'll probably spread out over a few days. They'll call me."

Duke nodded.

"Mostly evenings. Most of them work, and only one is retired."

"Okay," Duke said.

"Why don't you get comfortable?" she asked. She was convinced he intended to remain planted here until Matt arrived. He must be worried that he might miss something.

He followed her into the living room, and at her suggestion, he sat at one end of the couch. She settled in the Boston rocker that her mother had loved so much.

After a few minutes, he spoke. "I'm wasting my time."

"How so?"

"You already questioned the poker group."

"You felt they might share more with you."

He shook his head impatiently. "They knew my brother for only a couple of months. What sounded like a good idea when I flew out here is beginning to sound less so."

Surprised, she studied him, wishing this man would be more open about his thoughts. "You want me to cancel the meetings?"

He shook his head again. "I've only got three weeks. I need to use them wisely, and I seem to be blowing them away. The problem is, I can't think of another line of attack. I *want* Larry's killer."

She ached for him. Her professional detachment insisted on draining away. She couldn't afford to let that happen. "We should go see Ben again. If you talk with him for a while, something new may emerge. Of all the people who knew Larry around here, he's the one with the most knowledge."

"Yeah. I want to see him again, anyway. But I can't keep spinning my wheels."

While she sympathized, she also knew something else. "Duke? This isn't my first murder investigation. I can tell you something you might not like to hear, but it's the truth."

"What's that?"

"Sometimes, however much evidence you think you've found, it's not enough to identify a killer. But then, seemingly out of nowhere, a new piece drops into the puzzle, and you're off and running. Patience is part of this job."

After a few beats, he nodded.

Cat also realized she wasn't going to be able to sit here like this and wait for Matt Keller to show up. She looked at her watch. Four thirty. There was time.

"Why don't we go to Mahoney's?" she said. "It's been a long time since my breakfast, and he makes great BLTs. Maybe have a beer, since I've been in that mood since Larry's murder."

He was agreeable. In deference to time, they drove in her car.

"I should drive my rental over here," he remarked. "At least my knees won't be ramming my chin."

She laughed. For the first time, it felt good.

THE GUY THEY were working for could only be contacted at night, so the first man had to wait. His call this morning had been dismissed with a brusque "I told you. After 4:00 a.m Zulu only." 9:00 p.m local time.

That hadn't made anyone happy, but they had to deal with it. The way they'd spent so much of their lives dealing with whatever happened, whether they liked it or not.

Then the second man let out a "Yesss!"

The other two looked at him. He was still obsessively holding Larry's cell phone. He waved it. "I found some names and numbers. They weren't on his contact list, but in his reminders list. They all have local area codes."

The third man nodded and smiled. "We'll get them now."

The first man wasn't as delighted. "We have to locate them. Then scope out where they live and figure out how to get in without being seen. And we still don't know what the hell to look for."

After a few minutes, the second guy spoke. "It has to be a flash drive."

"Why?" demanded the first man. "We were talking about reporters keeping notes on paper because they couldn't be hacked."

"I was thinking," the other man answered. Man Three chortled sarcastically, but the second man ignored him. "Thinking," he repeated. "If you're going to give someone a bunch of information to protect or hide, you're not going to give them the paper. You're going to copy a lot of the crucial stuff to a flash drive and encrypt it."

They regarded the idea almost glumly.

"A flash drive won't be easy to find," said the third man. "How will we know if we have the right one?"

"Take as many as we find. Bet they're near a computer, where they shouldn't stand out."

"Or between the mattresses, or in the cupboard, or…" The first man trailed off. "Better than where we were yesterday."

"Marginally," Man Three remarked. "Hell. But at least we've got a starting point."

Man One rubbed his face with his hands. "Let's get that fire up again. I want me some coffee." Then he zeroed in on the second man again. "Find anything on that computer?"

"Hardly. Didn't I tell you the battery is dead? I need a plug. Recharge it or run it on AC."

The third man spoke. "Just don't tell me you don't have the adapter or the recharger."

"I got them. But I gotta plug it in."

Man One leaned back while Man Three tossed some dry twigs on the fire. Soon it was crackling but not smoking.

"Okay," said Man One. "That's the easiest of our problems. We can charge it at Larry Duke's house tonight, depending on whether they've still got a cop watching it. And speaking of Duke? His brother's in town, I heard earlier."

"Daniel Duke?"

The first man nodded.

"Damn," said the third man. "It's like playing whack-a-mole. Start to solve one problem, and another springs up."

After that, no one spoke at all.

MAHONEY'S PROVED TO be just the pick-me-up that Cat needed. The country music wailing quietly in the background, the voices of people talking and Mahoney's warm greeting and his promise to give them the best BLTs.

Mahoney put a cold diet cola in front of her and a large glass of draft in front of Duke.

The place still hadn't heated up for the evening, so it was relatively quiet. Soon after five, the bar would be jammed.

Duke spoke. "This the only watering hole around here?"

"No. There are roadhouses around the county, serving scattered ranches. I imagine they did better in the days when every ranch employed a lot of cowboys. And there's one only a few miles outside town. Local bands play, it has a dance floor, that sort of thing."

"Popular?"

"Oh yeah. Can't beat the dancing, for one thing. A lot of the college students head out there for that, but they have a good mix of customers."

Mahoney brought the sandwiches, one for her and two for Duke, and conversation between them flagged. In the lull, Cat looked around and realized some of the patrons were staring at Duke.

Had they heard who he was and why he was here? Given the local grapevine, she thought that might be it, though she harbored a fleeting hope that maybe a few of them wanted to talk about Larry. If that was the case, she hoped she wasn't putting a damper on it.

While they ate, more patrons began to drift in. By the time they finished eating, the bar was at least half-full.

The hum of conversation had grown stronger, and occasionally laughter punctuated the background noises. A good night was on the way at Mahoney's.

Cat would have liked to kick back, enjoy a couple of beers, then go home to her basement gym and take a stab at working off her sins, but no. She was driving, first of all, and secondly, the man beside her seemed to be getting a bit restless. Probably impatient for the conversation he was awaiting with Matt.

"You in a hurry?" she asked as he finished his sandwiches.

"Sort of. Not really. Hell, we got time."

She glanced at her watch. "Yeah, but that's not necessarily a reminder that will make you less impatient. We can go if you need to move."

He turned his head, looking across his shoulder at her as he leaned into the bar. "I used to enjoy spending an evening like this."

"With friends. That's different."

"Probably. Or maybe I'm just feeling like I'm wasting time."

He might be, she thought. Even he had lowered his expectations for these meetings. Justifiably so, considering she truly believed that these poker buddies would know nothing they hadn't already shared in interviews with the police.

She spoke. "Your brother's secrecy didn't help."

"I think he meant it to protect. And not just his sources. But yeah, he's a blank slate in that regard."

"Tell me more about the story he did. The one that affected your career. It might have some clues in it."

He shook his head, and she thought he was going to shut her down. Then he said, "Not here."

"Okay, then. Time to go home." She was surprised how easily she used that word, including him in it. Not "my home" or "my place." Just *home*.

Dang, she thought as they walked out to her car. How had he gotten past her barricades? She'd hated this assignment, distrusted him, and now she was taking him *home* with her.

Egad.

THEY STOPPED AT the gas station and bought a six-pack at Duke's suggestion. When they got back to her place, she started coffee in case Matt didn't want a brew while he was there.

Then she sat facing Duke across the table again. He seemed to prefer the kitchen to the living room for some reason.

"That article?" she reminded him.

"I didn't forget." He rubbed his nose and sighed. "It'll give you some idea of the kind of reporter he is. Was." The past tense came with obvious difficulty to him.

Cat waited, giving him time to shift his thoughts around. Grief was doubtless weighing heavily on him since she'd brought up the matter that had caused him career problems. More important, it had caused a rupture between him and his brother. He probably didn't want to talk about it at all.

But she was hoping for something, anything, that might provide a clue to Larry's killing. She doubted Matt was going to be able to provide it while they talked this evening.

She'd known Larry herself, the whole time he'd lived here, and had learned very little about him. Maybe, just maybe, some of the poker players might have learned something over the cards and chips. The kind of free-ranging conversation that could happen with a few beers and having a good time.

But how would they know it was significant? The department had already questioned them, and nothing useful had come up.

Then another thought occurred to her. It wasn't that they might feel freer talking to Larry's brother. No, maybe Duke knew enough about Larry to elicit other kinds of information. Maybe he had some questions to ask that the cops hadn't thought about.

Maybe.

She was still waiting for Duke to speak when her front doorbell rang. Matt had arrived ten minutes early, jacket open despite the cold, still wearing the short-sleeved white shirt and jeans he wore at the organic food market he owned.

Cat introduced the two men and this time guided them into the living room. She asked Matt if he wanted coffee or beer, but he said he was fine as he settled on the edge of her recliner.

Duke took the couch and Cat sat on the Boston rocker again. During her mom's last month, Cat had added some cheerful pillows to it, to cushion her mom's shrinking bottom and back. Cat didn't want to remove them. There were few enough good memories left in this house.

"How's business?" she asked Matt, trying to ease past the initial moments of strangers meeting.

"Good enough." He flashed a smile. "Plenty of kitchen gardens around here, especially on the ranches. They provide a lot of our produce, and it sells as fast as they bring it in."

Cat arched her brow. "I have to admit I wouldn't have thought organic foods would be popular here."

"You need to keep up with the times. Now the grocery store is carrying them as well." His smile turned crooked. "I suspect they want to put me out of business."

"I hope not!"

"Me, too." Then he turned his attention to Duke. "I'm very sorry about your brother. He was a good guy, lots of fun. A shark at poker, though."

Duke managed a faint grin. "If he played it, he was good."

"Yeah, he had something of a reputation for darts, too. Anyway, it didn't matter that he was fantastic at Hold'em. We all just had a great time, and since it was only for chips, nobody went away annoyed."

"So no money?" Cat asked, although she had already guessed the answer.

"Not even penny stakes. No, it was just for fun."

"Did Ben Williams ever play?"

"Ben?" Matt looked pensive. "I know him, but I don't recall ever seeing him at the games."

Cat fell silent, hoping Duke would ask his all-important questions.

Duke spoke. "Larry ever tell you what he did?"

"Yeah," Matt answered. "Said he was a reporter, some paper back East. He said he was working on a book. But I don't remember him talking about it much. Just in passing."

"So you weren't curious?"

Matt shook his head. "Not my business. I don't pry, Duke. A person tells me what they want me to know. God, it feels funny calling you Duke. How'd you get the last name and not Larry?"

Another smile tried to be born on Duke's face. "My military career," he said. "Everyone started calling me Duke. It stuck. Before that I was Dan."

"Larry mentioned you once. He was awful proud of you."

That seemed to startle Duke a bit. But he said, "I was proud of Larry, too. Tough career."

"That's something, coming from an Army Ranger." Matt sighed, then leaned forward, resting his elbows on his knees. He looked down at his folded hands. "There must be a reason he was killed, but damned if I can figure it out. As far as I know, no one around here was mad at him. I guess that leaves kids who wanted something valuable and went too far."

"There was another break-in," Cat remarked. "Just the other day. No one was home."

Matt nodded slowly. "I heard about it. Burglaries have never been a common problem around here, but they happen every so often. Still, a group of kids wanting electronics or valuables… Why would they kill Larry?"

"I think we're all wondering that."

"Yeah."

For a half minute or so, they all remained quiet. Cat wanted to make sure Duke had a chance to ask any questions he needed to, so she let matters rest.

Duke spoke again. "My brother was an investigative reporter."

Matt sat upright. "Really? Hell, he must have had some

stories to tell. He never said. Was he good?" He caught himself. "That didn't sound the way I meant it."

"It's okay," Duke answered. "I was just wondering if he'd said anything about his job, more than just that he was a reporter."

"Not around me." Matt put his hand to his chin, then dropped it. "You think it had something to do with that?"

"I don't know," Duke replied. "I wish I did."

"But doing investigative stuff...he must have run afoul of people."

"It's possible."

Matt thought about it, then shook his head. "He didn't say anything to me about his work. Not even what he was writing a book about. Maybe it had something to do with his reporting?"

Duke gave a small shrug. "I wish I knew, but Larry never struck me as the type to try to write a novel."

Now, that was a bit of information they hadn't had before, Cat thought. It seemed Duke still thought the book might be an investigation. As far as she knew, no one else had thought that to be relevant. Writing a book sounded like an innocuous thing to do.

But considering how angry Duke had been about a story that hadn't even been about him, she could imagine a whole lot of reasons that others might have been even more furious. Or might think they had something to fear.

The fear idea nearly made her jump up, but she held on to her cool, not wanting to halt the growing conversational flow between the two men. After all, it had so far yielded one potentially useful nugget, maybe two, and nuggets were rare in this case thus far.

Matt spoke first. "I gotta admit, the idea of Larry being killed during a burglary bothers me. It has from the time I first heard. It's kind of random, you know? I'll be the first to admit I never really got close to Larry. I mean, it was only a couple of months, and we didn't get to the confessional stage, just the level of being friendly and having a good time. I never got the sense that anyone hated him. And I never got the sense that he was trying to get information from someone, like he was working on a story. If he was, it wasn't one from around here."

Cat caught herself. "Okay, that almost made me laugh."

Duke jerked around to look at her. "Why?"

"Imagine an investigative reporter from a big daily newspaper actually spending his time investigating anything around here. I mean, man. Our paltry scandals would probably bore him to tears."

One corner of Duke's mouth lifted, and Matt smiled widely.

"Yeah," Matt said. "And since there are hardly any secrets in this town, nobody'd want to read the story anyway. A city council member was inebriated and had to be assisted to his front door? Joe XYZ, a teacher, is having an affair? Great gossip."

"And not worth wasting ink on." Cat nodded.

"Definitely not the stuff of headlines," Matt agreed. Then he sighed, and his face drooped. "Larry became a headline." He shook his head. "I'm still having trouble grasping it. And for you, Duke, it has to be a whole lot harder."

Duke spoke slowly, as if dealing with his feelings was tough. "Larry and I hadn't lived in each other's pockets for a very long time. We'd get together once or twice a year. He wasn't part of my daily life, is what I'm saying, but he was always *there*. Now I can't even pick up a phone to call him."

Cat understood completely. She still ached from wanting to be able to talk with her mother about most everything.

Matt left shortly, having offered nothing more about Larry's murder, but Duke seemed satisfied with the conversation.

Then Duke left a few minutes later, explaining that he

needed to go for a run. He didn't look dressed for it, but Cat didn't argue. Maybe Matt had stirred up some of his memories and he needed to run off sorrow.

She had some other things to think about now, possibly useful things.

And she also needed more details on the second break-in. Was it related in any way to Larry's?

She was tired of being left in the dark.

Chapter Six

Duke hit the pavement, his booted feet pounding. No stealth there, but no reason to care about it. He'd get to the motel, change into his running gear and do his miles.

Maybe hit the truck stop diner for a late-night breakfast. He didn't figure Mahoney's BLTs were going to hold him all night. His calorie consumption had sometimes caused Larry's eyes to widen.

Well, hell, when you kept yourself in prime condition, worked out like a lunatic and had a lot of muscle mass to support, you ate a lot. More than average, anyway.

He'd also learned a long time ago that he lost weight while on a mission, so it didn't pay to start off too lean. Everyone lost weight in a war zone. Maybe it was the lousy food. Maybe it was the tension. Maybe it was as simple as troops not wanting to eat. He didn't know. He just saw the results.

Carrying a couple of extra pounds never hurt. But just a couple. If he ever stopped working out like a demon, he'd have to watch it.

Random thoughts, a meaningless diversion produced by his own brain. He was aware of it, the times his mind wanted to take a vacation from something. It could be dangerous under some circumstances, so he was usually good about stopping it.

But what did it really matter, right then? His grief over Larry was growing, not easing, and he felt like he had a crushing weight on his chest, as if his heart didn't want to beat again.

He jumped into his running clothes quickly: navy blue fleece workout pants—not shorts, because it was chilly out there. A long-sleeved white sweatshirt. Running shoes, which were at least a decent brand that fit.

The point of this was to heat up, not cool down.

The last thing he grabbed was a flashlight with an orange translucent cone on it. Because this time he was running toward the mountains, hoping to get some uphill work, and he needed to be sure cars could see him.

While he didn't much care about his own life right then, he *did* care about a motorist who might hit him. Why give someone nightmares for the rest of his life?

At first he jogged slowly to warm up his muscles, but, at the outskirts of town, with the mountains a dark silhouette against a sky dusted with stars, he hit his full pace, an all-out run.

He might have recalled nights spent in hostile mountains where he had to be alert for every little thing, nights when he'd slept sitting up with his rifle across his lap, nights when he'd been all alone and surrounded by threats or with comrades as uneasy as he was. Nights when terrible things had happened, things that he would never be able to expunge from memory.

He'd slipped down that path before, and sometimes he just let it happen, knowing he couldn't always stop it.

But not tonight. Tonight, Larry ran alongside him, residing in his memory, his easy laughter still audible in Duke's mind.

He'd never hear that laugh again. He'd never again listen to his brother's laboring breaths as he tried to keep up with Duke's pace. They'd never again share a few beers and shoot the breeze for hours.

Never.

He hit an upslope, and his calves reacted as if they were glad to meet it. Power surged through him, sweeping him upward. The flashlight he carried gave him just enough light to see the ground ahead of him, to avoid obstacles.

Cars were few and far between, however. He'd expected more traffic, but maybe he wasn't on the state highway. He had no idea and didn't care.

He heard Larry as clearly as if his brother were running beside him. "Think about it, Dan."

Think about what exactly? That Larry hadn't been working on a novel? As far as Duke was concerned, that was a given.

That maybe someone had been afraid of what Larry was writing, or afraid of something Larry knew?

Likely. Larry had never made a big deal out of it, but Duke was aware that his brother had received death threats. How many or over what, Duke didn't know. Larry had mentioned them a few times but had always laughed them off.

"They just show me that I'm doing it right," Larry had said.

Well, yeah. Duke's career had been shredded by Larry doing the right thing. He was sure Larry hadn't intended that, but his brother was like a bloodhound on a scent trail. He wouldn't be diverted.

"Maybe you shouldn't have laughed them off, Larry," Duke muttered, keeping his breathing as even as he could. Deep, deep breaths, but regular. No oxygen deprivation allowed.

Duke was thinking as he ran uphill. Okay. That thing that Matt had said about maybe someone had been afraid of Larry... That could put a different spin on all this.

He'd seen Cat stiffen when that came out and was sure

she'd had the same thought. Why would anyone here even consider the possibility? No one here, evidently, had the least idea of the kind of stories Larry had worked on.

Like all the time he'd spent on domestic terrorism, revealing links between some of the groups. Larry had mentioned he was still receiving threats a few years after the article was published.

What about other things? Duke tried to remember all the articles his brother had written, but the simple fact was he hadn't heard about any number of them because he'd been overseas for long periods. Impossible to really keep up, and Larry almost never mentioned his work on postcards or in the occasional telemeeting they had.

Not that Larry would reveal anything until his story was published, and even then he kept a lot close to his vest.

Duke was sure there were more kernels of information in Larry's brain than he could ever use in his published articles. Tips, clues, people, things he couldn't substantiate well enough to write about. But they'd all remain in the stew pot, because Larry never knew when one of his gleanings might prove useful at a later date.

Damn, Duke wished he had even a remote idea what Larry had been writing about. Maybe something had come together in a way that needed more than six or eight pages of newsprint. Something big enough to make it worth a few hundred pages.

It wouldn't surprise Duke to learn that.

He shouldn't be surprised if Larry's investigations had gotten him killed. The warnings had been there. But the idea was useless unless he could discover what his brother had been doing.

Crap.

Duke turned at the top of a long slope and began to run back down. Not as fast, because downhill was always tougher to negotiate without falling. But fast enough.

Larry. Damn it, Larry.

Duke had known his own job was dangerous, but he truthfully hadn't believed Larry's could be *this* danger-ous. If it was.

That was the next thing he needed to figure out. He'd go talk to this other guy at lunch tomorrow, but he expected to hear pretty much what he'd heard from Matt.

Stupid idea, questioning his poker buddies. Except for one thing: that someone might be afraid of Larry.

After his own experience, Duke figured that wasn't a far reach. Larry had exposed a terrible crime, murder for hire, but Larry had walked away alive, and for all that Duke's career had gone into free fall, he was still here. Still wear-ing the uniform.

Apparently no one had wanted to stir that hornet's nest up any more.

Unless maybe they had?

He was still wondering when he reached the truck stop diner.

CAT SAT ON her small front porch. A molded plastic chair cradled her, and she put her feet up on the porch railing. A jacket protected her, holding the cool night air at bay.

She was thinking about the conversation with Matt. About Duke, who couldn't wait to leave once Matt was gone. He'd even refused her offer to drive him to the motel.

The man was upset. Understandably so. Cat wondered if he'd yet felt the full impact of grief, or if he'd been so furious and determined to find Larry's killer that there'd been no room left in him for sorrow.

It might be that there was now.

Despite all her attempts to keep Duke at arm's length, partly because of her job and partly because she didn't trust that expression she'd initially seen in his eyes, she had begun to care.

"Oh, cool," she whispered. Yeah. Just what she needed: to become personally involved.

She was personally involved enough with Larry that Gage Dalton hadn't wanted her on the case. A murder investigation, something she'd done for her previous sheriff, and she was frozen out.

Maybe not totally. It was time to corner Gage and demand information. She needed to be kept in the loop, not only for herself, but so she could better assist Duke in ways that wouldn't cause trouble with the legal case they were building.

How was she to know what to keep him from plowing into if she didn't know the status?

If Gage had thought that herding Duke would be easier when she was wearing blinders, he was wrong. What was the chance that she would allow information to escape her? Zilch. She knew how to protect investigations.

She thought of Duke again, allowing herself a few moments to think about how attractive he was. She was a woman, she had normal impulses, and even in the midst of all this, she wasn't impervious.

Then she brushed such thoughts aside. Given the circumstances, Duke couldn't possibly entertain such thoughts, nor should *she*.

Then there was Larry. Whenever she thought of Larry, she pictured him smiling. A big grin, filled with the joy of life. A man who should never have been the target of a killer.

Maybe she needed to talk to Gage about the fact that she couldn't read any of Larry's articles. She'd tried once, searching his name online, but the articles were in the paper's archives, behind a paywall. It hadn't seemed worth the money when she'd just been curious.

But it might not be curiosity now. If Gage authorized it, she could call the paper and say she was investigating

Larry's death. Right now she didn't have the authority to
say any such thing, but it might be important to learn what
the man had been doing.

All she knew about Larry was that he was a friendly,
outgoing guy, and that she'd liked him a bunch. He'd been
a wide-ranging conversationalist, able to talk about many
things comfortably and always eager to learn something
he didn't know. Never afraid of admitting to gaps in his
knowledge.

When she thought about it, she realized he had gotten
her to talk more with him than she usually did with anyone. He'd brought her out of her introverted shell easily.

A great gift for a man who spent his professional life
digging information out of people, many of them reluctant to speak.

Determined to speak with Gage in the morning, she let
her thoughts drift more freely.

That Duke was like a puzzle box. She'd been seriously
worried about what he might do when he'd arrived here,
and now she was getting more worried about *him*.

So far he hadn't given her any major headaches, but if
he felt he was getting nowhere, if he was left to deal with
his grief without a resolution, how would he handle it?

Would Duke feel as if he'd failed his brother in this final,
monumental task? Would guilt overwhelm him because
this whole ugly mess was worsened by his rift with Larry?

She didn't understand how anyone could handle it well.
A double heaping. She'd seen other people hit with this double whammy, though. Mothers who'd fought with a kid before the kid disappeared, only to be found dead. That was
just one example. She'd seen plenty of others.

People dealt because they had to, but Duke was a man
of action. He'd already shown that he wasn't prepared to
wait for the police to do this job.

She sighed and rested her head in her hand. All she

wanted to do was help. That had been her motivation in becoming a cop. She hated it when she couldn't.

OUT IN THE COUNTRYSIDE, three men sat in a different gully. Moving was always wise in case someone had sighted them and started to wonder. New digs, no better than the old ones, but at least far enough away.

The chill didn't bother them much, and besides, they had the correct clothing. Dark jackets covered them; hoods covered their heads and shadowed their faces from the rising moon. After a brief debate, they'd decided to build a small fire and now were making coffee in a battered tin coffeepot.

They used water warmed on the fire to soften dried foods enough to eat and swallow. Not the best grub, obviously, but marginally better than rations. Evidently companies catered to hikers and campers who insisted their food be palatable. Sort of.

Anyway, there was no grousing that night. Just a lot of silence as they tried to think their way through their current conundrum.

"We could kill Dan Duke," said Man Three.

"Oh, for crap's sake!" growled the second man. "We're supposed to stay under the radar, and you want to kill the brother of the man we just murdered? You don't think that would send up a dozen flares?"

Man One, who hadn't said much for a while, spoke quietly. The other men sometimes resented the fact that the first man seemed to think he was smarter than they, never mind that he patently was. It was when his tone and pacing grew obviously patient that they resented him most. Right then he was sounding patient.

"We need to get a charge on that laptop. The cops are still watching Larry Duke's house."

"They've been there too long," groused Man Three.

"Maybe," said Man One, growing even more obviously

patient, "they're concerned about ghouls. Especially teenage ghouls. Word must be getting around that the guy was tortured. Or at least that the scene is gruesome."

"I wish we were plugged into the local gossip," said Man Three.

"Wishes and horses and all that," said Man Two.

Man One didn't disagree. "The real problem here is lack of intelligence. We didn't expect all these complications, and we sure as hell weren't prepared for them. But this isn't some backward country where we can operate freely."

"No kidding," said the second man. "A lot of places we've been, I'd just take out the guard, go into the house to charge this freaking laptop and do whatever else I want to. Not here. Kill a cop, and we're up to our necks. Kill Dan Duke, and we're in it big-time."

The third man spoke. "I know Duke is supposed to be some kind of big deal, but what kind of big deal?"

The first man answered tautly. "I'd give you his service jacket if I had it. Just know he was being fast-tracked for the top, and not only because he knew the right people. That was the least of it. When the military history books are written, his name will be in them."

The third man spoke again. "I take it you don't mean because he eventually gets a star?"

"No. His commendations would fill a book. He's reputed to be a tactical genius. He's faced everything that we have, and probably more. Some think he should get the Medal of Honor for one mission."

The second man blew air through pursed lips. "I hadn't heard about that." Then he turned toward the third man. "The point is, we've *all* heard about him. Even you. That should tell you everything you need to know."

The first man spoke again. "We're not talking about just going up against somebody's brother. If we have to, we will.

But I wouldn't advise it. The man could be capable of taking out all three of us."

Another long silence fell. The coffee started perking, and the second man leaned forward to move it to the side of the fire. Twigs and branches crackled as flames danced through them.

"And we can't do another break-in?" asked the third man.

The first man sighed. "We can. But first I want that damn laptop charged. We could conceivably save ourselves a whole lot of trouble."

"Except for what Larry Duke said about us never finding the info."

"He could have been lying."

They all hoped so.

It was so much clearer on an operation overseas. Here it was all muddied by lines they couldn't cross.

Nobody had considered these parameters.

CAT EVENTUALLY ROSE, deciding to go indoors. The evening had been peaceful, few people about, but the chill was beginning to penetrate by way of her hands and denim-covered legs.

A cup of instant cocoa sounded perfect.

Inside, she boiled some water in her kettle and pulled cream out of the fridge. She always liked a bit of cream in the instant cocoa. It tasted richer.

When the kettle began to whistle, she poured the hot water into a mug over the mix. An easy, relaxed evening would continue.

A twinge of guilt hit her as she remembered the exercise she was forgoing, an hour or so in her basement with weights and her bicycle. It was okay to skip a couple of nights, and it wasn't as if she needed to work out any tension.

Then her thoughts returned to Duke. Sitting at her

kitchen table, she wondered about him running along the roads of this county, dealing with his demons, missing his brother. Should he even be out there alone?

Remembering his palpable anger when he had arrived in town, she wondered if he should be alone with that, either.

Damn, that man wouldn't stay out of her head. She told herself he had to be her priority right now, but she suspected that was an excuse. Despite his initial anger, he'd steadily drawn her in. She cared about the hell he was dealing with, about how he was handling it.

Well, when she got additional information tomorrow at the office, she might have more she could safely share with Duke. One thing she *didn't* want him to know was that their initial assessment was that Larry had been tortured. God, she didn't want to be the person who had to tell Duke that.

Forgetting her relaxing evening, she put her forehead in her hand and stared down into her cup of cocoa. What happened to Larry had been awful, just awful, even without all the details. She couldn't imagine how much more awful it would be for Duke to know.

Finally she sipped her cocoa again, then thought about tossing it, because it had grown cool already.

The rap at her door startled her. The digital clock on her microwave said it was just before ten. An emergency? Heck, this town practically rolled up the streets by nine, if not earlier.

Concerned, she hurried to answer the door. When she opened it, she was astonished to see Duke. The breeze had picked up, and even though he stood a few feet away, she could smell soap and shampoo.

"Come in," she said, quickly stepping back.

"It's late…"

"You're here for a reason. Come in."

He passed her, heading straight for the kitchen. She

followed him, then asked, "What is it about you and kitchen tables?"

He shrugged. "In our family, this is where we always held conversations. Larry and I kept it up even sitting at tables when we went to a bar."

That made sense. She faced him at the table, pushing her mug aside. "What can I do for you?"

"I just had a question. When I saw your lights were on, I thought it might not be too late to knock."

"It wasn't. Another half hour might have been different."

He half smiled, reminding her of how attractive he was when he wasn't on the edge of fury. Something had changed since he'd talked to Matt.

"I'm beginning to realize I'm probably on a futile quest," he said after a minute or two.

Surprisingly, her heart squeezed. Not what she wanted to hear, despite all her initial objections. The fact was, she was now looking at a man who wasn't accustomed to being stymied. How much harder for him than the average person. Nor did she have any reply to reassure him.

He continued. "I was reacting to Larry's death. I needed to do something. My usual reaction to crisis. Useless under these circumstances."

"I understand it," she admitted.

"Still, there's reality, and I've been avoiding thinking about it. There are so many situations I've encountered where I've been able to do something. But to act, you need to know the parameters of the situation. You need intel. I don't know why I thought I could wring more out of people he knew here than you and the other cops could."

He shook his head. "But I was sitting there, talking with Matt, and it struck me that the folks Larry played poker with know the cops around here better than they know me. The idea that they'd say something to me that they wouldn't say to you all…well, I must have been out of my mind."

"Grief and shock will do that."

"Yeah. I should know that. I'm sure you do, too."

Cat shrugged one shoulder a little bit, then waited. She was convinced he hadn't come here to dump some uncomfortable feelings. She judged him to be a man who was largely buttoned up.

He seemed lost in thought, his gaze distant, and she wondered what had been so urgent that he'd come to see her this late. Maybe being alone was difficult for him right now? She began to think about offering him the single bed in her home office.

He suddenly zeroed in on her. "The reason I came over."

"Yes?" She couldn't help tensing.

"Is there any way I can get more information, about what you know? About that second robbery that Matt mentioned?"

She nodded. "I was planning to talk to the sheriff in the morning and ask. Whatever I can share, I'll tell you."

"Thanks." He looked down at his hands.

There was more; she could feel it. Then it struck her she hadn't offered him the most basic of courtesies. Dang, her mother would be disappointed in her. "Want something to drink? Obviously I've got beer, because you bought it earlier. Or instant hot chocolate. Or coffee, if you're one of those people who can drink it right before bed."

He made a snort that sounded like an almost laugh. "I learned to drink coffee round the clock. Strange how it doesn't seem to interfere with my sleep even when I'd like it to."

She had to smile. "So what'll it be?"

"A beer, please. Or I can get it. I've been here often enough to know the way to your refrigerator. Strange, I can see it right from here."

She laughed. "Okay, help yourself."

"What about you?"

"No, thanks. I prefer my head to be clear. My usual limit is one drink."

He rose and got his beer, returning to his seat as he twisted it open. No bottle opener for this guy.

"So that's what you wanted to know? If I can find out something else about Larry's case?"

"Not quite." He tipped the bottle back and drank before he spoke again. "What Matt said about fear. I sensed you noticed."

"Yeah, I did." No point in denying it.

"That would put a whole new spin on this. What's the point of looking for the killer around here if he might have been in and out? Sent by someone who had a grudge against Larry because of his reporting or was afraid of what he might write."

"I agree. So tomorrow I'm going to see if I can use my badge to get past his paper's paywall and read Larry's articles."

"Hell, I can get you past the paywall. Let me get out my credit card."

"You can't wait?"

He shook his head. "That's not what I meant. I just meant you don't have to use your badge or the department's resources. That's all. I was going to try to get into his archives anyway. I'd like to have copies of all those articles and exposés."

"I'm sure. Now I would, too. But I need to do it in official capacity. What if there's some kind of evidence in there? That article you two fought over? Do you think it could be that?"

"I don't know. I need more to go on. But it's possible. It's also possible he was working on something else and that story was over two years ago. On the other hand…"

She waited, then prompted, "Yes?"

"On the other hand, who knows how long that trail was? I told you about the guys who were charged as a result of that story, but who knows what information they might be willing to trade?"

She sorted through that. "But if some guy agreed to offer information in exchange for a lighter sentence, there'd be nothing for anyone to protect now."

"Maybe not. Or maybe someone is afraid of what else Larry might have known. But again, it could be any of his stories, or even a new one."

She thought about it. "But if he keeps everything secret, no one would know what he might be working on now."

"Not exactly. The people who gave him information might know. And maybe one of them got nervous and told someone else. Maybe we focused too much on his secrecy."

She became totally alert as he offered another new perspective. Maybe... But how to use this?

"We still have a lot of questions," she said. "And if we do find out something, how are we going to locate his sources? I'm sure Larry must have protected them." Even facing the difficulty of the task, her excitement continued to mount.

Duke answered. "Oh yeah. Protected better than classified information is my impression. I don't know if his editors even knew who most of his sources were. Never discussed that with him."

Cat changed her mind and got up to get herself a beer. "Want another?"

"Haven't finished this one. Thanks."

Cat brought her own beer to the table, glad she wasn't sleepy any longer. She'd needed this boost, a rush of adrenaline, the idea that they might have a direction to head.

She was driven hard by the desire to find answers, the need to catch the perp... Those were her fuel.

She stared down at the icy bottle in her hand. It wouldn't stay cold for long. "You can't pour beer over ice," she remarked.

The craziness of her words brought Duke's thoughts to a sharp stop and startled him into a laugh. "What?" he asked.

"Irrelevant," Cat answered. "Just one of those nutty thoughts that occur to me sometimes. I don't know why. Maybe it's a mental vacation."

She had a really sweet face. That was his own irrelevant thought, given the circumstances. But it *was* a sweet face, those blue eyes of hers bright, almost seeming to glow. He'd watched microexpressions pass over that face tonight, but they were slight and brief, and he had no read on what she was thinking right then.

"You can't pour beer over ice," he repeated. "That sounds strangely profound. Maybe you're trying to get at something."

She shook her head a little. "If I am, I suppose it will rise to the surface eventually. If it does, I might never make the connection." The barest of smiles appeared on her face. "Or maybe I'm just honestly thinking that this beer is icy right now, but it's not going to stay that way."

"Maybe."

He studied her, wondering at his own responses to her. Or maybe they were just normal *because* of the circumstances. Seeking a diversion, seeking an affirmation of life, wasn't exactly outside his experience.

Whatever. The fact that he found her sexy wasn't fair to her. He had a strong sense that she preferred to be judged on her other merits.

He turned his attention back to Larry, unable to dispel the feeling he'd been unwilling to acknowledge thus far: she knew something she wasn't sharing with him.

He understood that she couldn't tell him a lot of things. But the way she had reacted when he'd said he wanted to see Larry's house? That had been niggling at him, despite the reasons she'd stated. How could they still be treating the house as a crime scene after all this time?

Since he hadn't known Larry's address here, he couldn't even find the house. Conard County was a big, largely empty patch of earth. Look at how far out of the way Ben's house was. Without an address of some kind, he doubted he'd have been able to find it even with GPS.

So why wouldn't she let him see the place? When he'd argued that he'd seen a lot of horrific things during his career, her response had been to point out that those things hadn't involved his brother.

But they *had* involved people who had been his friends, people with whom he'd had the close bonds that could only come about from relying on one another in life-threatening situations.

Trust. Deep brotherhood, a kind different from what he had shared with Larry.

He sipped more beer, telling himself he'd achieved what he wanted, that he didn't need to take up more of her time. She'd promised to seek information and share what she could. However much she could share would be more than he had now.

As long as he wasn't beating down doors or threatening anyone, or going where the cops hadn't yet gone, he couldn't see a serious problem.

But it was still time to leave. He'd already busted up whatever had been left of her evening. Not much of an evening, but still hers.

He started to push his chair back.

"No," she said.

"No?"

"No," she repeated. "You can have my spare bedroom.

It's a little on the small side, and my office stuff is in there, but you're welcome to it."

The invitation surprised him. "Why?" he asked bluntly.

"Because." She shrugged and offered a fugitive smile. "Because," she said again. "You're a stranger in a strange land, and while I'm sure you're used to it, you still don't need to be alone with your grief. So stay. You're not an intruder anymore."

Not an intruder? An interesting way of phrasing it. Deciding to accept her kindness, he slid back to the table.

"Thanks," he said. "You must want to go to bed."

"Not any longer. I'm wide-awake now."

His fault, that. "I should have waited until morning."

"Nah. I was thinking about the similar things, too. Nice to hash it out a bit. Good to know you reacted the same way to Matt that I did. I'd been considering tons of motives, most of them pretty standard for murder, but I hadn't considered fear as a motivator. Seems like an oversight now."

It did, Duke thought. It certainly did, given Larry's reporting, but... "I didn't think of it, either. It should have been the first idea that occurred to me."

Cat frowned. "I usually think of fear when a wife kills her husband. I'm not always right, of course, but when there's been abuse, then I think of it. Maybe it's time to put that in my complete rucksack of reasons."

"You might never need it again unless, like you said, there's domestic abuse."

She rose from the table and started pacing the small space. "It should have occurred to me sooner, given..." She trailed off.

She was concealing something. His certainty grew. "Tell me how my brother was found again." He was sure she could tell him that much, because she had before. Maybe she would let more slip.

She stopped pacing. "Simple. Ben couldn't reach Larry,

so he called us, and we did a wellness check. And there needs to be a better term for that sometimes."

Her face darkened in a way that unsettled him even more. What wasn't she telling him? "And?"

"Larry had been dead approximately two days. I'm sure the medical examiner will have a more precise TOD. Time of death. Sorry. When I'm in cop mode, the abbreviations come naturally."

"That's okay. I've got plenty of my own."

"So yeah, we went over there thinking he might have taken a fall and couldn't get to the phone. Broken leg, cracked skull or something. I wish."

Duke waited, hoping she might continue to talk, hoping she might let another detail slip. After a bit, he asked, "Did *you* respond to the call?"

"Yes," she said tautly.

He prompted even though he could feel her rising tension. "It was bad. Finding a body after two days can be disturbing."

"I've seen it before."

"So there *was* more."

"Damn it, Duke! Quit trying to get me to say something I don't know for a fact."

That told him too much. Enough. He could see her jaw working, and now he gritted his own teeth. *Damn it, Larry. Damn it.*

His stomach plunged like he was on a roller coaster. He wanted to pick up his beer and smash the bottle against something. Smash his way back until the world righted itself somehow. Not that it had been right since he'd received word of Larry's death.

"Look," she said finally, leaning back against the counter and gripping it so tightly that her knuckles turned white. "You've probably seen a lot of things that never cross the desk in a sheriff's office in a smaller town, okay?"

Duke closed his eyes, feeling fury rising until his gorge rose with it. It pounded through his head, throbbed painfully in his chest, and he really, really needed to smash something.

He couldn't do that. Not now, not here. He drew several breaths, steadying himself. When he opened his eyes, he saw Cat still leaning against the counter, but now she looked stricken.

"I'm sorry," he said. "I shouldn't have reminded you."

She still didn't relax. He ought to get out of here now, before he made it worse for her. He remained glued to his seat anyway. The rage had subsided just enough for him to carry on. Maybe he needed to run another ten miles. The road called to him.

She spoke, her voice still tight. "I'm okay. But I just revealed too much, didn't I?"

"Only that his death was messy." But there was more to it than that. He was certain now. And he still needed to work out the fury. "Can I use your weights?"

"Of course." Her eyes looked dull.

The whole thing was ripping at her, he thought. All of it. Maybe in ways that didn't occur to him because she was a cop.

Then she straightened and poured the rest of her beer down the sink. "The office is down the hall, second door on the right. Look around, find what you need. I'm going to bed."

He'd been dismissed, and he was glad of it. Neither of them could take much more of this tonight.

Chapter Seven

In the morning, the sun burst from the east and painted the world in pink and gold light. High cirrus clouds turned into beautiful streamers of color against a sky turning deep blue.

It should have been a good morning to be alive, Cat thought as she drove to the sheriff's office. She had no idea what Duke planned to do that day. He hadn't emerged from bed yet, maybe because he'd pumped iron for a long time last night.

She didn't care. Except she did. This whole situation had begun to feel like her brain was on a hamster wheel, running around from one notion to the next.

Okay, so she didn't *want* to care. Fine. Too late.

Last night hadn't helped one thing that she could tell. She'd been cast back into the horrible hours after she and Guy Redwing had found Larry. She could tell that Duke had connected the dots, and that was her fault. She didn't feel good about it, either.

She had tossed and turned for a long time, hearing the occasional clank of iron plates from the basement. At least that had been a momentary diversion from her grim thoughts. She had eventually fallen asleep to the punctuation of that clanging.

She had no idea how much sleep she had gotten, but this

morning her eyes felt sandy, and even though she drank two glasses of water, her throat felt parched.

When she parked at the sheriff's office, she considered heading to the diner for a morning latte. Yeah, why not? Better than being tempted to drink Velma's acidic brew.

Ten minutes later, coffee in hand, she walked into the office. She'd worn her uniform this morning, and she was struck by how much more secure she felt inside it. Maybe that was a hang-up all its own.

Inside, her fellow officers greeted her, and when she asked Velma about Gage, Velma pointed down the hall. The sheriff's office must be open for business this morning.

Gage was, as usual, behind stacks of paper and the computer he sometimes cussed because it couldn't read his mind. A common problem with machines.

Gage looked up immediately and waved her to a seat. "How's it going?"

"I'm asking you," Cat replied. "And I think I slipped up last night and let Major Duke know that his brother's death had been messy."

"The understatement of the year." Gage leaned back, his chair creaking.

"You need some oil," she remarked.

"I need a better chair. Thing is, I know all the problems with this one and how to adjust myself. A new chair would be a whole new learning experience."

She laughed. "I hadn't thought of that."

"Or maybe I'm just resistant to change."

"Not that I've noticed, at least not when it comes to something important."

He nodded, his dark eyes still trained on her. "What's up?"

"I want to know about the Larry Duke case, and about the burglary two days after."

One of Gage's eyebrows lifted. "Why?"

"Because I need to know more than what I saw when I arrived on scene. Because I need to give Duke some additional information. Because I need to know where we're at, what I can share and if I need to keep him away from something. Right now I'm wearing blinders."

He nodded, then winced as he leaned forward to put his elbows on the desk. He picked up a pencil and tapped it lightly, one of his favorite thinking poses.

"I get it," he said after a moment. "But why the second burglary?"

"There's always the possibility of a connection of some kind. The homeowners were out of town, right?"

"True."

"So maybe they're still alive because they weren't there."

Gage sighed. "Yeah. It's crossed my mind. Maybe most everyone's."

"See why I need to be clued in? No point in me running over things the rest of you have already considered."

He tapped the pencil more rapidly. "I'm going to have to trust you when it comes to sharing with Duke." He wasn't asking.

"Yes, but you know me well enough by now. I've been a cop for over ten years. I get the point of keeping investigations close to the vest."

"I know. I know." He dropped the pencil and once again leaned back. This time he didn't grimace. "I was trying to make it easier on you, but I guess I didn't. How are the two of you getting along?"

"Well, I no longer think he's going to kick in a door and start shooting."

He laughed. "That's an improvement. When I first met him, all I could do was wonder how we were going to restrain this tornado. Short of throwing him in a cell without charge."

"I honestly think he could break out."

"Maybe. Okay, get the files. Read them. I'm not even sure I know all the details myself."

"Thanks. One other thing. I need to read Larry's news stories, and there's a paywall. Can I approach in official capacity?"

"Sure, or use the department's credit card."

She rose, then paused. "Any idea when we'll get the autopsy and forensics?"

He shook his head. "They keep promising that it'll be soon, but soon hasn't come yet. I can't nail them down to anything more specific."

"Probably the most interesting autopsy they've done in a decade."

"Maybe. Or maybe they just don't want to chance missing something when this case is so gruesome and we're short on clues."

It was as good an explanation as any, she thought as she headed out front to grab a computer. She could read the articles from home. The files? Not so much.

She paused just long enough to leave a message on Duke's cell. "I'm reading the files."

And probably unleashing a whole mountain of questions from him. This was going to be fun.

Not.

DUKE WAS OUT running again when he got Cat's message. The news quickened his pace without regard to endurance. He wanted to get back.

He'd stayed up late working with her weights. Then he'd added more repetitions. Trying to work through the maelstrom of emotions that wouldn't do a damn thing except cloud his mind.

Finally he had grown sleepy and had started looking for the bed and the bath. No clean clothes, so now he stopped at the motel on his way back from his run to shower and change.

Then he was off again. Remembering Cat had said something about a bakery, he detoured and found Melinda's Bakery facing the courthouse square.

"Hey," he said to the dark-haired young woman behind the counter. She had her head mostly covered by something like a shower cap.

"Hey," she answered with a smile. "Would you like lunch or pastries? At this point in the morning, the pastry levels have begun to shrink."

He looked in the case. "I bet you can hardly keep them full."

"For just as long as it takes me to fill the case and open the front door." She grinned. "I'm very popular."

He flashed her a smile. "Any idea what Cat Jansen likes?"

"Oh yeah. Turnovers and Danish."

"Then load me up with Danish, please."

She paused as she began to pull items out of the case and place them in a white bag. "I don't think I know you."

"I thought everybody within fifteen miles must know by now."

She laughed. "You've figured this county out. But no, I haven't heard about you."

He paused, then said, "I'm Larry Duke's brother."

Her hand froze as she started to fold the bag to close it. "Oh my gosh, I'm so sorry! He was such a nice man."

"He was." Duke hurried to pay, then left with his bag of delights. He wondered if he should take them to Cat at the office, then figured it would be uncivil of him to walk in those doors without enough to share.

He jogged back to her house and made coffee, then settled in for the wait.

CAT FINISHED UP by ten. It was disturbing to realize how little information they had about either case. Plenty of details, but little that was useful in finding a suspect. Were they going to have to wait until some item showed up in a pawnshop?

Hell, they didn't even know all that might be missing from Larry's house. Ben had supplied what he knew, but it was soon clear that he and Larry had mostly met at Ben's place. What was more, Ben was trying to cope with grief, they couldn't let him in the house and he had to guess about things that might have gone missing.

They definitely didn't want Ben inside that house. This was tough enough on him without adding nightmare images.

The Hodgeses' place was more informative, but hardly illuminating. However, that scene had been released. Maybe she should ask the homeowners if they'd mind if she brought Duke over. There was nothing there he could mess up in any way, and maybe he'd feel like he was doing something. Or that she wasn't trying to wrap him in a wall of silence.

Sighing, she finally gave up rereading for some nugget she had missed. She'd skipped breakfast this morning and just wanted to get home and eat.

She got one of the department's credit cards from the front desk, then headed out, hoping that Larry's articles might be more useful.

Maybe there'd be enough in one of them to kick-start an investigation at the other end of this trail.

Slim hope, because they'd have to offer some kind of link that wasn't as vague as "Larry wrote an article about…"

Crap.

She wasn't in the best of moods when she walked through her front door, but she saw Duke through the kitchen door, sitting at the table. Somehow that gave her a little lift.

She had a bigger lift when he held up the bakery bag, which always meant goodies.

He said, "Melinda packed it with your favorites. I made coffee. I know it's late for breakfast, but…" He shrugged.

"I haven't eaten yet. It's time for me." She felt a smile crease her face. "I hope you're hungry, too. This is fabulous."

Soon she had two dessert plates on the table, napkins and mugs of coffee. She was touched that he'd thought of such a thing, considering what he was dealing with.

"Did you go for a run?" she asked just before she bit into a raspberry Danish.

"Yeah. I needed it. I hope I didn't keep you awake last night. I tried not to bang around too much."

"You didn't." She'd had enough to keep her awake even if he'd never clanged a plate. "I'm sorry, but I didn't learn much this morning. Evidently there weren't a lot of clues in either house. Gage seemed to think both burglaries might be related. Anyway, the Hodges house, the second one, has been released, so I'm going to call them and ask if they'd be willing to meet you. They can tell you more about what was taken, and maybe their overall impressions."

"I'd like to look around." He settled on an apple turnover, eating with his fingers.

"I don't know if they'll give you carte blanche to wander around. Prepare to just talk."

"Yeah. But I want to ask if they knew Larry."

From the files she'd read, she wasn't sure anyone had asked that. In fact, the more she thought about it, it struck her as completely odd how little anyone had been able to discern from the crime scenes. Were they really down to forensics? No other clues?

Given how long it could take to get fingerprints through AFIS, it might take a week or more to get a complete check nationally.

Would anyone even want to do that at this point? They had no proof that someone from out of the area had committed the crime.

Duke spoke, his turnover gone. "You're thinking."

"Yeah. That could be dangerous."

His expression didn't leaven. "I doubt it. What's bothering you?"

"How very little evidence we have at this point. That may change with the completed forensics, but right now…"

When she left the thought incomplete, he spoke. "So both places were clean?"

"At the moment, that's how it seems. But more evidence will come to light. It always does." She wasn't exactly feeling hopeful, however. As she reached for another piece of her Danish, Duke caught her attention. He looked arrested, as if a thought had struck him.

"What are you thinking about?" Cat asked.

Slowly his eyes tracked back to her. "About how clean the scenes might be."

"And that tells you what?"

"Nothing yet."

God, now he was concealing things from *her*. If she didn't give such a huge damn about Larry and his murder, she'd run screaming from this whole situation.

Well, not really. She'd never been one to run screaming from anything. Still, the temptation was there.

"Damn it, Duke. If you've got an idea, share it."

"I can't. It's not exactly an idea. Not yet. I'll let you know once I've worked it through myself. About Larry's articles?"

"Yes. Gage told me to call the paper in my official capacity. If there's a problem with that, I've got one of the department's credit cards."

He nodded. "You'd think the paper would give me access, given I'm Larry's brother."

"Do they know Larry's gone?"

Duke grew grim. "Probably not. I guess I'll have to tell them."

"I'll handle that. And we'll get those articles today. I'm not going to be patient about it."

She just wished she knew what had caught his attention about the scenes appearing clean at this point. That didn't necessarily mean anything. People had grown savvier about forensics thanks to television and movies. Some of what they believed wasn't true, but, in her experience over a decade, more perps were leaving less of a trail behind.

She'd lost interest in her Danish but didn't want to offend Duke. He'd gone out of his way to bring her something she liked.

"As soon as I finish this, I'll call the paper," she said. "I'll have to wait until later to call the Hodgeses. Both of them are schoolteachers."

He nodded. "I'll survive." His smile was crooked. "Maybe I should try to extend my leave so I can drive you crazy a bit longer. Or maybe so I can relax a bit. I've set myself a tight deadline."

"It depends on the murder, Duke. Sometimes there just isn't enough information to point us in any direction. It will eventually turn up, however." She refused to remind him of how many stranger homicides that were never solved.

Then, hoping to get his mind going in another direction, she said, "*Can* you extend your leave?"

"I have enough time built up. My deputy can fill in for a while longer."

Amusement sparked in her. "You have deputies, too?"

That made his eyes dance. "Oh yeah. I could have said 'second in command,' I suppose."

"Then I would have missed my little joke."

"We wouldn't want that," he agreed.

She gave up on the Danish and rose to wash her hands. "I think I'll go dive into getting to Larry's articles."

"I'll be along in a minute."

Yeah, she fully expected him to be breathing down her neck and peering over her shoulder.

When she got to her office, she got a little start. She was looking at a twin bed made so neatly that she had to pause to admire it. He'd even squared the corners, something she never bothered with.

Duke had his advantages, she decided.

She knew the name of Larry's paper because he'd had a press card among his belongings. His wallet was gone, but a few things remained.

That could fit with a routine burglary: no cash, no credit cards remained. But the savagery of the murder made all that seem irrelevant. She closed her eyes a moment, unable to escape the memory of discovering Larry's body.

Stop! It wouldn't do a bit of good. *Work the problem.*

She reached for her landline, and when the paper's page popped up on the computer screen, she punched in the customer service number.

She hardly paid attention to the sounds from the kitchen, other than to recognize that Duke might be doing dishes. She had to work her way through three layers and finally landed at Larry's editor's desk. Lavinia Johnson. She scribbled the name down on her pad.

Evidently she was going to have to give the bad news first.

She identified herself, including her badge number, then

dropped the bombshell bluntly. There was never a gentle way to deliver this news.

"I'm sorry I have to tell you, but Larry Duke was murdered."

"Oh my God!" The exclamation reached Cat across the telephone line, filled with shock. "What…? How…?"

"At this time it appears to be a home invasion, a burglary. But we're trying to check everything out."

"Of course, of course."

Cat waited for Lavinia Johnson to speak again, giving her a little time to absorb the news. She heard Duke come into the office and pull a chair over closer.

Then Lavinia spoke. "Does his family know? I have his emergency contacts."

"The news has been shared," Cat answered.

"I didn't want to have to make calls," Lavinia admitted. "Is there anything I can do?"

"We'd like access to the archive of Larry's articles."

"Do you think…? No, I guess I shouldn't ask that. Ongoing investigation. Yes, certainly. If you have a pen ready, I'll give you the newsroom's log-in and password."

"I'm ready," Cat answered. She scribbled quickly and repeated the information to Lavinia.

"That's it," the editor agreed. "Damn, I still feel like the world's spinning. Larry was a fine reporter and a fine human being. We're very proud of him here."

"I've heard wonderful things about him."

"Every one of them is true," Lavinia answered. Her voice was growing tight, and Cat could almost hear the coming tears.

Cat finished up with, "I'm very sorry for your loss. I didn't know Larry for long, but it was definitely a pleasure."

When she hung up, she didn't waste any time logging in. "I figure we'll work back through time."

"I agree," Duke answered.

"Do you want me to print it out for your use?"

"You'll need a mountain of paper for that. No, I can get the articles myself when I get home."

She turned to look at Duke. "His editor said he was a fine reporter and a fine human being."

Duke's face darkened slightly. "That's nice to hear. From Larry's telling, it sounded as if the newsroom could be a powder keg. Deadlines, ugly stories, sources that didn't call back. High pressure leading to short tempers, I guess."

Well, that was another thing to keep in mind, Cat thought. It might not have been the subject of one of his articles who wanted him dead. Maybe he had some enemies in the newsroom. "Do reporters make much in big cities?"

"Not from what I understand. It isn't poverty level, but it's not generous."

"That's what I thought." So how could another reporter afford to mount any kind of trip to kill Larry? And really, how bad could a newsroom explosion be? Bad enough to want to murder?

She expected to find more fertile ground in his investigative pieces.

"Oh man," she said as Larry's articles began popping up in a list of titles.

"What?"

She felt Duke lean closer.

"It looks like he did a lot of articles. This list is huge."

"He wrote a bunch of shorter pieces, like every other reporter. Partly because the paper wasn't going to pay him for a couple of years while he wasn't writing anything. Partly because newsrooms were shrinking—probably still are— and the workload went up for everyone. I gather he might have written a story or two every week."

"That's going to help," she said sarcastically. "I don't know how well these stories are tagged. Give me that one that upset you. Maybe that'll get us into something. Or maybe we need to read them all."

"That's quite a body of work. How long do we want to spend reading?"

She looked at him again, wondering if he expected her to let him be a second pair of eyes. The problem with that wasn't him reading Larry's articles—he had every right to—but he wouldn't see them through a cop's eyes.

Plus, she only had one computer. They'd have to read over each other's shoulders or take turns.

He spoke. "Well, the murder-for-hire story was in September, just over two years ago."

"Okay, I'll start there. Then maybe we should come forward in time before we start going backward. In case it was a more recent story."

She looked at the screen again. There'd be some eyestrain before long.

AN HOUR LATER they headed for the truck stop to have lunch with Bud Wicke, the garage mechanic. The garage was conveniently located, in terms of his business. Bud sometimes had to run over to the truck stop to repair a long-haul truck, as well as performing routine repairs for locals.

As they drove toward the truck stop, Duke said, "Tell me a little about this guy, if you can. Just public knowledge."

Cat stifled a smile. "Like I could tell you much more than that."

"I know. Just the common knowledge."

"Well, Bud Wicke is one of our local garage mechanics. He started working for the place years ago and eventually bought it."

"Hard worker."

An insight. Cat hadn't really given it much thought. "I guess so. Anyway, I don't know much about him, because I've only been here a little over two years. Whether there's much more, I can't say. But I can still tell you he's a bit unexpected."

She felt Duke look at her. Amazing how you could tell when someone was watching you. "How so?" he asked.

"I hear he's got a college degree in math, as well as all his mechanic's certifications. Apparently, he just loves working on cars."

"He likes to learn."

"That would be my guess. Larry was interesting, too. He made friends with an eclectic group of people around here."

She turned into the truck stop parking lot and nosed toward a vacant parking space near the diner. On the far side of the lot there was parking for the big rigs, but that area was nearly full of idling trucks. Truckers preferred driving on nighttime roads if they had a choice, sleeping during the day to avoid heavy traffic. Hasty's diner stayed busy during much of the day.

Inside, the tables were busy. Hasty, a tall, lean man, flipped burgers on his grill and shuttled through breakfast orders and even veggies. He could do just about anything on that grill.

Bud Wicke sat at a corner table beside the wall of windows that surrounded the dining area on two sides. He smiled and waved them over.

Cat made the introductions, reminding Bud that Duke was Larry's brother in case he'd forgotten or she had neglected to mention that the day before when she'd phoned him.

The waitress zoomed over with some menus, and both Bud and Duke immediately ordered coffee. Cat chose a diet cola.

Bud spoke after the waitress charged off with their orders. Breakfast for Duke, burgers for Bud and Cat, who felt she needed some recovery from all that Danish earlier.

"I'm so sorry," Bud said to Duke. "I liked Larry. He

was a good man to play cards with and shoot the breeze over a few beers. He beat me at darts nearly every time I walked into Mahoney's. My ego was bruised." He said the last lightly, as if making fun of himself.

"I never wanted to face him in darts," Duke agreed. "Now, running—that was a whole different thing."

Cat spoke. "With you being a Ranger, I'm not surprised. Bet you could do more push-ups, too."

Duke laughed quietly. "I'm pretty sure."

"Larry mentioned you a couple of times," Bud offered. "He called you Duke."

"Everyone does."

Cat attempted a little humor. "Unless they call him *Major*."

That made a smile cross Bud's face. "Then I'll call you Duke. About Larry, I don't think I know anything useful. I was at the poker table and bar with him, but I sure as hell didn't see anything that would make me think he had enemies. Easy to get along with, always friendly. It must have been kids."

Although Bud didn't sound happy with that idea. He sounded like a man who would rather believe that than any alternative.

"So nothing about what he was here to work on?"

Bud shook his head. "I don't think I ever asked, either. He said once that he was here for the quiet to work on a book, but that was it. Oh yeah, he also said that he was a reporter."

Conversation lagged while they waited for lunch and started to eat. Cat's burger was perfectly cooked, juicy, the way she liked it.

She supposed that if she tried, she'd be able to ask a useful question, but she held back. It was important for Duke to ask the things he needed to know, certainly before she jumped in with any standard cop questions. Questions that Bud had probably answered right after the murder.

But suddenly she thought of something and asked anyway, mainly because Duke had fallen silent. "Did we interview you after the murder?"

Bud shook his head again. "Nobody came to me. Hardly matters, since after I heard about Larry, I tried to figure out if I knew anything, like him mentioning kids hanging around. If I'd thought of something, I'd have trotted over to your office. As it is…" He let it hang.

Then Bud straightened a bit, half a hamburger still in his hand. "I just remembered. Larry mentioned two days before he was killed that he felt watched sometimes. But he laughed it off, saying that anybody new around here would get watched. He was probably right."

Cat wasn't sure she agreed, and a glance at Duke suggested he wasn't buying it, either.

"Larry was good at laughing things off, including the threats he received as a reporter," Duke said.

"Threats? Seriously?" Bud looked appalled. "What was he reporting about? Major crime organizations? RICO violations?"

"In the past."

"Wow, I'm impressed. Every time I hear about something like that, I think the reporters must have a lot of guts." Then he shrugged. "Maybe it's in the family. You probably have a lot of guts, too, being a Ranger."

"I usually know where the threat is coming from. Larry would get these anonymous letters or emails. A few bothered him enough to turn over to the authorities, but most he just dismissed."

"Man. I liked the guy before, but now I'm feeling huge respect. I'd be looking over my damn shoulder every single minute."

"He wasn't, from what I saw of him. But his address? Under wraps."

"Understandable." Bud looked at the burger in his hand and put it down on the plate. "You think a threat might have followed him out here?"

"We don't know," Cat said swiftly, wanting to quash that rumor before it even got started. "But that's why we're asking if you heard anything about his work from Larry. To be sure."

"I get it." Bud's eyes darkened. "Makes more sense to me than some high school kids wanting his electronics."

Cat answered him. "Keep that under your hat, please. It's only a remote possibility."

At that, Bud's face relaxed. "I thought it was strange that Larry would come to the back of beyond just to write a book, but the idea that someone followed him out here? Even wilder."

Cat couldn't disagree. It *did* seem wild, and very unlikely. Chances were, Larry hadn't even told anyone where he was going. But no matter where he'd gone, he'd have received cell phone messages. Only law enforcement agencies could have tracked him, and there was no evidence for that.

Duke insisted on picking up the entire tab. Bud left, promising he'd think more about it, but Cat didn't expect anything.

"He played close to the vest, all right," she said to Duke as they walked back to the car.

"That's Larry. Damn it."

"The ultimate proof is that Ben didn't have any idea, either. Imagine not telling your significant other even the least little thing about what you were working on."

"Imagine not telling your brother you were about to wreck his career."

She looked at him over the roof of the car. "Do you think he could have known that?"

Once again, she watched him stare into the distance as he thought. It was as if he'd learned long ago that answers might not be right under his nose. A trained response?

He shook his head a bit, then folded himself into her car. She followed suit and turned over the ignition.

"He may not have known," Duke said as she steered them out of the lot. "But he might have ticked someone off farther up the chain of command."

"No way to know anything about this case," she remarked sourly. "God, I hate this. Usually there's a link to someone or to an event that gives us direction. We've got no direction here. We need someone to spill a few beans."

"Good luck with that."

It often proved to be exactly that kind of luck that nailed a criminal. For some reason she would never understand, people seemed to need to talk or brag about what they'd done.

Duke was disappointed, even though he'd admitted yesterday that his original plan had deflated. She wondered if she should set up meetings with the other five poker buddies anyway. Just to settle Duke's mind. Although at this point, if he thought it was a waste, he wouldn't want to pursue it any further.

Like Bud, she wasn't buying the teenage home-invasion theory. She'd had trouble with it since she'd discovered Larry's body. Too savage, too brutal to be kids who just wanted to steal. It would have been much easier for them to hightail it.

"You know," she said to Duke as they pulled into her driveway, "it would not be smart for us to start following a single theory about Larry's murder. It could blind us to something important."

"I agree." But that was all he said as he followed her into the house.

Now they were faced with reading more of his brother's

articles. Or at least the stories that seemed as if they could have lit a fire somewhere.

Like the one about murder for hire in the Army. That was the most recent investigative piece, and considering what had been happening to Duke, someone had been disturbed. Maybe more than disturbed.

Then she remembered Duke's reaction when he learned the crime scenes were too clean. "Did Larry ever write about corrupt cops?"

"I don't know. Like I said, I didn't read everything he wrote, even the big stories. He rarely mentioned them to me, so basically I never thought about it."

Thus, it appeared, they were going to wade through the work product of a very prolific man.

"I can't imagine being a reporter and having to write on such tight deadlines."

Duke followed her down the hall. "Larry seemed to thrive on them."

"He'd have to."

EVENING WAS SETTLING in with dim light, and once again the colder temperatures settled in with it. Spring around here could even mean snowstorms, but right now Cat thought she detected dry air with the cold.

Duke took himself out for a run. She watched him leave, loping easily. She wished she could find such a comfortable pace while running.

Then she headed for her refrigerator to see if she could rustle up something for dinner for the two of them. She didn't think Duke was going to want to stop reading after a meal. *Dog with a bone*, she thought, not for the first time.

He might even want to stay up all night. She wouldn't be able to blame him, but she groaned inwardly anyway. Lack of sleep never made any investigation easier. She'd had to do it plenty of times, but when the brain got tired, so did its thinking.

Of course, she hadn't been out to shop for two. Her fridge stared back at her with little that would stretch that far. She headed for the cupboard that served as her pantry and started scoping out the other foods.

All of which was a distraction from thinking about how dead in the water this case had grown.

Nothing in the fridge, nothing in the cupboard and nothing in the file.

Remembering the Hodgeses, she called. Mark Hodges was willing to meet with Duke. As an instructor at the junior college, he had a more convenient schedule for setting up an interview. His wife, Marjory, taught kindergarten, however.

"I don't think she could manage meeting Duke until tomorrow night," Mark said. "Will that do?"

"Absolutely. I appreciate this," Cat replied.

Mark Hodges sighed audibly. "Some of the questions from the cops who came to investigate made me uneasy."

Cat instantly grew alert. "How so?"

"Well…" He hesitated. "Frankly, I wondered if they were trying to connect it to the murder last week. It's not anything they said, but a feeling I got. It bothered me because of what happened to Larry Duke. Are Marjory and I alive only because we were out of town?"

Cat wanted to reassure him and sought a way to do so without denying what might be true, however remotely. "I don't think it's likely, Mark. I mean, the two crimes probably aren't related to begin with. Otherwise, from what I read in the file, they aren't at all similar in terms of the burglaries."

The last part wasn't exactly true. The fact that both scenes seemed to be clean of physical evidence seriously gnawed at her. But Mark sounded relieved, and that was what mattered.

After she hung up, she thought about dinner again, then just shrugged it away. She didn't have anything to cook other than eggs and toast, she didn't really feel like cooking, and if Duke was hungry, she could bring out the peanut butter, jam and bread.

She might be a woman, but that didn't make her responsible to cook for him. Heck, he wasn't even a guest so much as a necessary invitee.

Satisfied, she resisted the urge to go to the computer again because he'd just want to go over it all again. She doubted he'd be happy with *her* deciding what was important.

And my, wasn't she working herself into an absolute tear of a mood?

"Aagh," she said to the empty room, then settled in to wait for Duke. At this rate, she was going to want action as much as Duke. She wondered if he was exacerbating her impatience.

Go exercise, she told herself. She had the time.

WHILE DUKE WAS pounding the pavement and Cat was pounding her treadmill, the three men out in the gorge huddled around a fire.

"I'm not used to this cold anymore," the third man said. "I know it was worse in the 'Stan, but I'm feeling the freaking cold *now*." Grousing came with the territory.

"It's not the cold that's getting to me," said the second man. "I am so sick of being stuck. We've got to get this laptop charged. We've got to find a way to get Major His Mightiness Duke out of the way."

"Seriously?" The first man was past being patient. He was growing angry, maybe because of the way they were stuck. "Getting rid of Duke might be the stupidest thing we've done yet even if we want to. Scrub it from your brain cells."

"He's slowing us down."

"Bull!" said the first man. "We're stuck because we found out that Larry Duke might have passed data to someone for safekeeping. We've already made what may have been a wasted break-in, because we didn't know exactly what we were looking for. *I'll* decide about him."

The other two exchanged looks, wondering again if Man One might have a stake in this beyond money.

"Yeah, yeah," muttered the second man. "I gotta recharge this laptop and cell. How in the name of whatever am I supposed to do that?"

"You could just go into town and do it," said the third man.

"Oh, for…" said the second. "Haven't we been trying to avoid being seen? Place this small, someone would notice and remember."

"Yup," said the first man. "I'm getting tired of sitting on our butts stuck, just like y'all. But I've also been trying to figure out what kind of diversion would get that cop away from Larry's house, and what kind of surveillance we should do on another target around here."

"But we don't know what we're looking for," argued the third man, sounding just a bit whiny.

"Exactly," the first man agreed. "Exactly. I'm thinking about driving into town."

Silence greeted his words initially. Then the second man waved his hand.

"Hello?" he said. "We discussed this. No town."

A snicker escaped the third man. The first man let it pass.

Instead of responding directly, he said, "I've got to figure out a disguise. Then, after we get some intel, we can act."

"What intel?" the second man demanded.

"To find out more people that Larry Duke interacted with. More hiding places to look. I can probably do a recharge there. Enough waiting for the cop to disappear. It'd be better if no one broke into that house while we're still here."

He looked at each of them individually. "I'll figure this out, because you're not the only ones tired of spinning your wheels. Damn messed-up operation. I'm going to have to fix it somehow. And if I decide Major Duke has the info, I'm going to send him to the next world."

The other two didn't doubt he would.

Chapter Eight

Cat was waiting for Duke when he returned. He carried two large paper bags into the kitchen.

"I got us some dinner," he said. "And I hope it's okay that I parked my rental on the street."

She noticed his hair was still damp. "Thank you, the parking is okay, and how about we change the terms of this arrangement?"

He turned from putting the bags on the counter to look at her. "How so?"

"Just check out of the motel and bring your stuff over here. This is ridiculous. As near as I can tell, you're using the motel only for clothing storage and showers. Well, I've got the room for your clothes, and I've got a working shower."

He hesitated visibly. "I'm intruding too much on you."

"Really? This would be more convenient. Just get your damn stuff and move in. I can spare the room. I even have a washer and dryer that I hereby permit you to use."

At that, a twinkle appeared in his eyes. "You sure?"

"I sound sure, don't I? Or maybe I wasn't emphatic enough."

"You were," he allowed. "Okay, I'll move in. Now, dinner? Maude was making some fried chicken. I hope you like it."

"I think I'd like anything that came out of that woman's kitchen."

He smiled. "Good, because the deed is done."

HE GOT THE dishes for them, then spread the food out on the kitchen table.

"You know," she said, "you don't have to keep buying meals for us."

"Sure I do." He passed her a stack of napkins. "I don't want you cooking for me, and my cooking skills are limited. When you live a military life as a single guy, you get used to chow halls and restaurants. Or in the field you heat up rations. I have a kitchenette in my quarters, but it doesn't see much use."

"I didn't feel like cooking," she admitted.

"I don't blame you. And if you feel like you need to cook for me, stop. That's not your job. Hell, you don't have to be polite, either. I've moved in on you."

"At my invitation."

He sat across from her again. *His* chair now, she supposed. He spent enough time in it. Not that she had a problem.

While they ate Maude's fried chicken and her homemade potato salad, they chatted casually.

"You were lucky to get the potato salad," she remarked.

"Really? Why?"

"Maude only makes it once in a while, because it's time-consuming. When I complimented it one time, she groused, asking me if I had any idea how long it took to peel that many potatoes. Point taken."

He chuckled. "Never having made it, I don't know."

"I've made it, but once I imagined how many potatoes she'd have to peel and turn into cubes, and slices of celery she'd have to clean and chop…never mind the quantity of eggs and onions…" Cat shrugged. "I got it. Four servings is one thing. A ton for all her customers who want to eat it? A whole other game."

"I like Maude. She reminds me of more than a few drill instructors."

She had to grin. Having only seen them in movies, Cat could easily see Maude in that role.

Holding a piece of half-gnawed chicken leg, Cat was the first to dive into the interrupted conversation about the case. "I'm getting as impatient with all this as you are. I know better, but frustration is making me want to erupt."

Duke nodded. "I understand."

"I bet you do. In fact, I know you do."

"I'm that transparent, huh?"

"Maybe. It's not like you're trying to conceal it. Or are you?"

"Nah. It's an evident fact. I kind of announced it when I got here. You think of anything?"

Cat wondered how much she should wade into the morass in her mind right now. She didn't want her feelings to ratchet his up. On the other hand...

"Duke? What you said about the crime scenes being clean. I've been thinking about that, too. It bothers me. I mean..."

"Yes?"

Cat looked toward her kitchen windows over the sink. Dark outside now, she could see the reflection of the kitchen in them. Time to close the curtains, but she didn't move.

"What bothers you?" he asked.

She sighed. "Since I read the reports, I've been telling myself that people have learned a lot from TV and movies about evidence at crime scenes. Sometimes that doesn't mean a whole lot, but sometimes it could. If you start by wearing gloves and a hat over all your hair, then there's a whole lot less to worry about. Most people probably get that much. But what else is common knowledge? And if the knowledge isn't common, then you have to wonder who knows it."

"You're right. Eat, Cat. You didn't finish your burger earlier. So where is this leading you?"

"I wish I knew. But it certainly mitigates against teens, don't you think? Even knowing this stuff, they might not think of it in the rush of the moment. I'd actually expect them to be disorganized."

"I hear you."

Loud and clear, she thought. His tension had increased slightly since she brought it up. "I have some good news, though. The Hodgeses will see us tomorrow evening. I hope you can wait that long."

"I'll have to, won't I?"

"Uh, yeah. Anyway, I don't know what you expect to find that the techs didn't come across."

"I don't know. I want details, of course. I want to look around. I want their impressions, not a list of missing items."

"Okay. We'll see if it helps any."

She resumed eating her chicken and potato salad, deciding she should let him lead the conversation. At this point she was willing to look in any direction for a useful tidbit.

"Were you born here?"

The question surprised her, seeming to come out of left field. "No. My mom moved here to take a teaching job at the college. I visited a few times before I moved here to take care of her."

"She was sick?"

"Terminal cancer. At least I could help."

"That's a tall task. I hear it wears people out emotionally."

"I don't know. She was the only thing on my mind. I didn't have anything else to worry about. Anyway, I stayed on after her death because Gage offered me a job."

He nodded, then pushed his plate to one side. "You were in law enforcement before, right?"

"Yes. Which is why I'm hating this whole situation right now. I know from experience how frustrating cases like this can be, but that doesn't mean I like it."

Duke surprised her by reaching across the table to gently grip her forearm. It was a brief touch, but it sent her mind careening in a different direction. Right then, she'd have been happy to forget the case and focus instead on the warm honey he'd sent running through her veins. On the even more pleasant tingle she felt between her thighs.

God, bad timing. She wrestled herself back into line. "I understand that a lot of this job is sedentary. Paper trails, reading about evidence, making phone calls. Hoping that someone will spill the beans to someone else. Looking for bad relationships. An investigator needs to depend on a lot of other people, too. But no matter how many times I experience it, I will never like it when a trail goes cold."

"I can imagine."

She believed he did. Being stalled was never pleasant in any part of life. He was a person of action by trade. She was beginning to believe she was one, too.

"I'm impressed," he said, "that you dropped everything to come here and take care of your mother."

A diversion. Maybe she needed it. "It's what you do for someone you love."

A simple answer, straight to the point. It had never occurred to her to do anything else.

When they finished eating, she put the leftovers in her refrigerator while he put the dishes in her dishwasher. "There should be enough chicken and potato salad for lunch tomorrow."

"That was the plan."

Then they returned to her office and their reading. Sitting there, scanning articles without apparent end, didn't satisfy her. But no piece of evidence, no clue, was too small to consider. The downside of the job.

It was nearly midnight when they headed to their separate beds. For the very first time it occurred to her that she might prefer Duke beside her.

Oh, for Pete's sake, Cat. Straighten up and fly right.

Duke stood at the window in Cat's office. He'd opened the curtains to let the night in, having turned off all the lights.

He liked the night. While threats often worsened in the dark, he knew darkness also offered him protection. An opportunity to move surreptitiously. A way to conceal himself from the enemy or prying eyes.

Stealth was part of his job at times, and he knew its importance. He thought about the two crime scenes, about why no one had heard a break-in. Stealth. That was leading him down a path he didn't want to follow.

The three soldiers mentioned in Larry's extensive article had been charged. But someone must have paid them for those killings. Hired them. He'd assumed it might have been one of the warlords in Afghanistan, since no other charges had emerged.

Even if it had been a warlord, that could have caused ripples up the chain of command. It wouldn't be the first time commanding officers had gotten into trouble just for not being aware of what their soldiers were up to. For failing to control their men. For failing in their duty, which Duke sometimes thought required psychic talents or prescience.

But usually it didn't. Usually there was a whisper in the wind to alert officers that something below them was going seriously wrong.

The attack on Duke's career could have been as simple as that. Or it could have been based on the faulty assumption that Duke had been one of Larry's sources. Damned for breaking the code of silence.

Or to put it in the vernacular, *don't be a rat*.

Thinking Duke was a rat could have put some officers on a mission to ease him out of the officer corps.

But it could have been something far, far worse. As in someone in uniform had paid those soldiers to kill. Or someone in uniform had sold his soul to a faction. To a warlord or a politician.

He really needed to read Larry's article in detail, to look for a clue in his brother's writing that might tell him which it had been. But maybe Larry hadn't known how far up the tree this sludge went. And maybe someone thought he knew and was preparing to write a book about it. Or maybe that had been exactly what Larry was doing. Maybe he *had* known.

Too many maybes. Way too many.

He placed his hands on the window frame and leaned forward, feeling the muscles in his back and shoulders stretch. He needed that stretching. The tension there was building into a headache.

His thoughts drifted to Cat. He understood her impatience, even understood why she stuck with a job that often frustrated her. It was the challenge of the chase, the victory when a case was solved.

He was developing a serious admiration for her. She wasn't a quitter, not in any sense of the word. Imagine her caring for her mother that way. Determination and love, an awesome combination. Her job was difficult and frustrating, but she still did it. She believed in justice, too, just like Larry.

He was sure his presence was increasing the pressure on her. Sure, she wanted to solve the case for her own satisfaction, but now she had to deal with him wanting a solution for personal reasons.

Not that he thought she didn't care about the collateral victims in a crime of this nature. She'd said enough for him to know she wasn't a machine, that she did care about a victim's family and friends. But still, having him in her face every day must be uncomfortable.

He sighed and leaned away from the window a dozen times, stretching even more, modified push-ups.

She was an attractive woman, and this setup wasn't helping him to ignore it. The urge to explore her, to bury himself in her, was growing. He knew he just wanted to forget for a few hours, and that wasn't fair to her.

Or maybe the desire was more than that, but he didn't want to chance it as long as there was a question in his own mind about why he felt it.

Apart from his attraction to her, he liked her. Really liked her. He knew she was handling him, but except for that one minor confrontation in front of the department store, she'd managed him deftly.

Yup. She considered his feelings, fed him what she could to make him feel better about his part in this. She was measured when she could have exploded. She shared that she was frustrated, too, essentially telling him that he wasn't alone in this madness that had overtaken him.

And it was madness. He wasn't a man to go off half-cocked with a stupid plan. The fact that he had burst into her life making unreasonable demands, yet she'd treated him with such care…

A remarkable woman, a remarkable law officer. She, and her boss, could have kicked him to the curb and told him to stay in his own lane. He'd have been floundering, no matter how much he had initially tried to believe that he'd find *something*. Instead, between them, they'd thrown him a lifeline. Even though she clearly hadn't wanted to be his keeper, she'd shouldered the job.

He pushed away from the window one last time, then dropped to the narrow space between her desk and the bed and began to perform one-armed push-ups.

Exercise. It helped most things, most especially directionless tension. It wasn't as if he could jog out into the night and solve his brother's murder.

"Damn it, Larry," he said into the darkness. "Couldn't you have confided in just *one* person?"

But the person he might, just might, have confided in had already turned his back.

The guilt had become insurmountable. Larry couldn't forgive him now.

Justice. Larry cried out for it. It had been his guiding light.

It had become one for Duke as well.

Morning couldn't come soon enough.

Chapter Nine

In the morning, Cat found her sleepy way into the kitchen and started coffee. A quick scan of her fridge—which looked awfully familiar after her hunt last evening—revealed enough eggs to scramble for two. A reasonably fresh loaf of rye bread also sat on the counter.

Eggs, toast and jam this morning, she thought as she yawned. Or peanut butter on the toast. She always liked that, and it helped keep her full until lunch.

She was still yawning when Duke appeared. He had dark circles under his eyes, announcing the kind of night he'd had. He rounded the table to get himself some coffee then nearly sagged into his chair.

"Bad night?" she asked before yawning yet again.

"Yeah." He offered no additional information. Not that she really needed any.

"I was thinking," he said.

She felt there was more to that. "About what?"

"I'll talk once I have coherent thoughts."

Eventually she felt her stomach rumble and rose to make toast for them. "Raspberry jam?" she asked. "Or plain toast or…"

A small laugh escaped him. "Whatever you're having, if you don't mind."

She didn't mind. Facing another day of reading Larry's

articles didn't appeal to her. Necessary, but no fun. Larry had been a great writer, but news story after news story wasn't exactly gripping.

They took a couple of brisk walks during the day to work out the kinks. Running into Edith Jasper, who was walking her harlequin Great Dane, Cat and Duke stopped to talk to her for a few minutes.

Edith was upbeat as always. "Bailey keeps me in shape," she said when Duke admired him. "He's not going to settle for a trip around the backyard."

Duke flashed a smile. "He's a big guy."

"Folks tell me he's too big for me, but I've had him for four years, and he's never once been a problem. Doesn't tug hard, doesn't run into me when he's exuberant. Nope, he's a good boy. Aren't you, Bailey?"

Bailey's tail wagged happily.

Then Edith zeroed in on Duke. "You're Larry Duke's brother, right? I never met him but, on this town's endless grapevine, I heard he was a good guy. Friendly and fun. I'm sorry this happened."

"I guess my identity is running around on that grapevine," Duke said as he and Cat continued their walk.

"I'd be surprised if it wasn't. You're a stranger with an interesting backstory. Maybe I should have asked how much information was making the rounds."

He swiveled his head to look at her. "Worried about it?"

"Only where the information might have come from."

Back at her house, their legs comfortably stretched and unknotted from walking, they ate leftover fried chicken, then settled in once again at her computer.

Cat wished she had a second screen. So much more comfortable for them both if Duke didn't have to read over her shoulder.

Then she noticed something. "You've come back to that

military exposé several times. What's bugging you? Was that what you were thinking about this morning?"

"I keep trying to glean something more from it," Duke admitted.

"But you think it might be more of a problem than his older stories?" She swiveled her chair around so she could see him directly.

"I'm wondering."

"Because of what someone has done to your career?"

"Not entirely." He paused and rubbed his chin. "Sure, they could think I was a source for Larry's article. Even though I had nothing to do with those guys. Didn't even know they existed until Larry's story was published."

"They're not Rangers like you?"

"Nope. Regular troops, a few tours in Afghanistan."

"So what else do you think might be going on?" She had to keep from leaning forward in anticipation. She could feel the first little bursts of excitement that he might be providing a new angle.

"Well, somebody had to pay these guys enough to do the killing. Three that were evidently enticed into this operation. Now, people at their rank don't make a lot of money, but you'd still have to pay for their silence so they wouldn't brag about what they were doing."

He was probably right about that. "Go on," Cat said.

"Anyway, given that someone was paying them, the question becomes who. Officers receive decent pay, but enough to hire hit men? I don't think so, unless these guys were very cheap. Which could happen."

"You just don't think it's likely."

He shrugged. "I also wouldn't have thought that a person or persons would try to kill my career over something Larry wrote. Sure, rats are hated, but it also suggests that someone is seriously scared." He raised his arm and started drumming his fingers on the end of her desk.

"I don't have a link to anyone, obviously," he continued. "I may be all wet. But I started thinking about someone selling out to a warlord. There'd be a lot of money in that for whoever was directing this from above. Someone *had* to be. It's not as if these guys could just wander off for a night to kill someone. Wandering off gets you in trouble. So, it seems to me that someone was paying them, and someone ensured they weren't on duty at those times."

"Wait," Cat said. "Clarify, please. I take it you can't just call in sick and miss a day?"

"Nope. You have to go on sick call, seeking to get treatment of some kind. Get a duty excuse. If you're in a forward operating base or something like that, disappearing for even a few hours could get you charged for being absent without leave."

"Wow. That's a restrictive environment."

He shook his head. "For good reason. You see that in a lot of jobs in civilian life, too." Duke half laughed. "If you take time off without permission, you're stealing from the Army."

"Seriously?"

"Seriously. Uncle Sam owns you, the Army pays you. Hell, you can get in trouble for a bad sunburn, because you should have avoided it. Damaging government property, or something like it."

Cat remembered her own experience. "A long time ago, I worked with a guy who got fired for claiming jury duty for the second time in two weeks. The company found out when the police called wanting to know if he was on sick time or something. Well, the woman who answered the phones put two and two together. And as it happens, he didn't take sick time but put in the hours on his time sheet as being on jury duty, which meant he got paid his full wages for eight hours. Not once, but twice."

"I'm not surprised he got fired. Pretty much the same for a soldier. Although since you can't be fired, you get other consequences. Anyway, point remains, these guys had someone up the chain covering for them."

She rested her elbow on the arm of her chair and considered this new perspective. It was sure an interesting one. "But would some officer send someone this far to take out your brother? See, that's the part I'm having a little trouble with. Why would anyone at this late date want to take Larry out? He'd already done his worst."

"Maybe. That's part of what's bothering me, too. So many uncertainties. Fact is, however, if several people up the chain have reason to be concerned, yeah, they could send someone out here. For heaven's sake, they got three guys to engage in killing for hire. Why wouldn't they be able to hire some guy to put paid to Larry?"

"Do you think that's what he was writing a book about?"

"I don't know, obviously, and neither do they. Every way I look at it, I keep wondering who could do this and why. Yeah, years back he made some very public links between domestic terrorism groups, and heads rolled. He was involved in a RICO investigation that sent some people to jail. The question is, who would come after him because he was writing a book?"

"I wish we knew if it was even that." She glanced at her computer and was startled by the time. "I need to figure out dinner."

"No, you don't. I'll run out and get us something. Any preferences?"

"There's the supermarket subs. At least they have veggies on them."

His eyes crinkled at the corner. "And a whole lot less fat."

She didn't even hesitate. "I'll ride along, if that's okay. I need some stuff anyway."

"You're on."

And at least it was out of the house. At this rate she could get cabin fever.

THE THREE MEN gathered around their paltry fire again as twilight blanketed the land. The minute the sun went behind the mountains, the temperature dropped quickly.

The first man opened his rucksack and pulled out Larry Duke's computer and cell phone. "Charged," he announced.

Man Two looked delighted, but the third guy was still feeling annoyed. "You get seen?"

"Of course."

"What the hell? You weren't even disguised."

The first man just shrugged. "You ever been to a truck stop? The place is crawling with people who don't live around here. Even the locals wouldn't notice a new face in that crowd."

"Oh." Man Three grew subdued.

"I was wondering if I could gather much intelligence, though. I knew if I started asking questions, it'd be noticed. Especially questions about Larry Duke. So I just listened." He picked up a twig and snapped it, then threw it on the fire. One of the other guys had started the coffee.

"Did you at least get to eat real food?" the second man asked almost wistfully.

"I was in a truck stop diner." As if that answered the question. Which it did, however indirectly.

"So what now?" asked the third man.

The first man pointed at the second. "You spend tonight hacking your way into the computer and the phone. Hack as hard as you ever have." He indicated the third guy. "We're going for another break-in tonight."

"Is the house empty?"

"No. Plan on being silent. Completely silent. Guy is single, lives alone, owns a food store."

"How'd you find out about him?"

For once, Man One looked a little less angry. "Someone mentioned Major Duke. They were behind me while I ate, and he was curious about why Duke's talking to certain people. We start there. After that we've got a tougher problem. A guy who owns an auto repair in town. He was mentioned, too, and doesn't live alone."

It grew quiet for a while, the only noticeable sound the night wind blowing through surrounding growth. Spring was trying to emerge on this sparse land.

"Anything else?" the third man asked eventually.

"Only Duke."

"We're going to have to take him out," said the second man.

"We shouldn't, much as I'd like to," the first man said. "We're hardly covert if we do that. It's not enough that he's nosing around with the help of that damn deputy."

"He is?" The second man sat up straighter.

"That's what I'm gathering, little as it is. It's thin intel, but I'm going to assume my conclusions are true. Safest thing to do."

The gloom was deepening, both in the outside world and among the men. What had looked like a relatively easy mission had descended steadily into a chaotic mess. They'd seen that on the battlefield, but they hadn't expected it here.

"I hope," said the second man, "that this crap is as important as someone seems to think."

"I hope," said the third guy, "that you want the money enough to shut up and do whatever's necessary."

"Hell, yeah," said the second man. "But who's taking the risk out here?"

Good question. But it was always that way. The grunts

did the real work while too many of the candy-ass brass sat at computers and desks.

The first man poured himself coffee in the collapsible tin cup he carried nearly everywhere. It would cool down soon, but at least it was real coffee.

"Thing is," he said, "if I was sure the only person involved back there is the one who hired us, I might kill *him*. But I don't know that there aren't others."

"Too bad how much we don't know," muttered the second guy.

"I don't think whoever he is knew. I think he thought we'd get to Larry Duke and that would be the end of it. I got the impression he's not happy that we had to kill Duke. Not at all. It's a mess, all right."

But there was no point in beating that horse to death. They all agreed on that, so silence returned as they listened to the wind whisper.

THE HODGESES HAD been nice. They let Duke and Cat inside, showed them the scene and explained in detail everything that was missing. From a wide-screen TV to a computer, electronics appeared to have been the target.

What had interested Cat most was Duke's prowl outside the Hodges house. He'd studied the privacy-fenced backyard, the door that had been jimmied, the bottom edges of windows that had not. He'd been interested in looking through those windows, too.

"Did you learn anything?" she asked as they walked home.

"I may have. Can't be sure."

"Quit being inscrutable and share."

Mark Hodges's only connection with Larry had been playing darts with him a few times at Mahoney's. On the surface this robbery didn't appear to be related in any way to Larry's murder.

On the surface. She wondered if, during his inspection of the property, Duke had noticed something that other eyes might have missed.

"Let's go to Mahoney's," he said. "If you don't mind. When we went there together, I got the feeling a few of those guys wanted to talk to me."

"I got the same feeling. Let's go."

Mahoney's was in full swing for a weeknight. Not as packed as on a weekend but packed enough. Laughter had grown louder as the beer did its work. Two guys played darts; another four gathered around the pool table in the back room. Friendly enjoyment permeated the place.

This time Duke took a table. Cat noticed that he maneuvered himself in a way that kept his back against a wall. Interesting.

Duke went over to the bar and snagged a longneck for Cat and a draft for himself. It wasn't long after he sat again that a man came over to him and shook his hand before accepting an invitation to sit with them. Duke didn't move, his chair still positioned to keep his back to the wall.

"I'm Frank Ludlow," the guy said. "I enjoyed Larry's company. You never saw anyone get accepted around here as fast as he did. People barely met him before they liked him and decided he was okay."

Duke spoke. "A talent for a journalist, to be able to do that."

"Well, he seemed to do it naturally. You never got the feeling it was an act."

"It wasn't. That was just Larry."

Frank nodded. "That I can believe. He sure livened this place up. Not that it's ever dull, but when he'd play darts with some of us, he gathered a whole group to watch. He could always tell a good joke or a good story. Everyone was glad to see him walk in."

"Did he ever mention what he was working on?"

"A book. That seemed reasonable, given that he was a reporter. I don't think anyone asked more about it."

Cat spoke. "Did he ever seem to be questioning anyone?"

"If he was, no one mentioned it. Why? You think that could be a clue?"

"I don't know," Cat admitted. "I'm looking everywhere and anywhere that might help."

"I can help," Frank said. "I'll ask around, see if anyone noticed anything. I'll let you know."

That was a step in the right direction. It sometimes amazed her how much people knew that they didn't realize they knew. Little things, occasionally very useful.

"Mind if we stay for a second beer?" Duke asked her.

"Not at all. That may have been productive. If someone else wants to meet you, I'm up for it."

After a little while, he went to get more beer for them. He also came back with a bowl of nuts to share.

When he settled again, she noted the restless roving of his eyes, as if he were trying to take in every little detail. Or maybe to memorize faces. She could have asked him, but she didn't. It just didn't seem important enough.

"Did something grab you at the Hodges place?"

His gaze snapped back to her. "Only that it was an easy place to rob. Big privacy fence, windows low enough to peer into rooms, a door latch that could have been opened with a credit card. Not exactly much security."

"Not something you need a whole lot of around here. Is that important?"

"I'm not sure. I mean, it was easy enough to get in there unseen, so that argues for kids again. Or it just may have been easy."

She curved one corner of her mouth. "All that uncertainty you mentioned."

"It sure didn't clarify the matter. It wouldn't have required any real skill to carry that burglary off."

"Anything else?"

"Actually, yeah. The idea that Larry's story might have triggered someone in the Army? I could be targeted, too."

Shock rippled through her, icy and electric. "But no one could know you were coming out here."

"Really?" He arched a brow. "I took leave. Who wouldn't have guessed that I was going to show up here right after my brother was murdered? Only someone who didn't know we were brothers."

"But…"

"What if I'm the rat they suspect?"

Cat settled back in her chair, turning the cold bottle in her hands, feeling stupid for not having put that together herself. "Damn, Duke."

"Yeah."

She looked up from the bottle, noticed he had leaned forward, surrounding his draft glass with powerful forearms. "Is that why your back is against the wall?"

"You noticed."

"I'm not completely dumb. Yeah, I noticed."

"I don't think you're dumb at all. Why would you think so?"

Cat sighed. "Because I didn't make the connection you just did. It's not like you didn't give me all the pieces."

"Maybe I assembled them differently. I'm used to having to consider things in terms of threat. No reason you should be."

"It's my job, in a way."

"No, getting a solution is your job. Not planning for off-the-wall threats."

Duke had a point. She sipped more of her beer, seeing the bar in a different light. He hadn't just been taking mental snapshots. Maybe he was looking for something out of place.

She looked around, really looked, for the first time. "I know all these people. Regulars."

"Thanks for telling me."

She hoped he could relax a bit with that information. Not that she was sure she'd ever seen him truly relaxed. All she knew was that he sometimes seemed less tense.

A couple of other patrons came over to shake his hand and express their sympathy, but neither of them knew Larry, or even what he'd been working on.

"I hope Frank can find out something," Cat said later, while they walked home.

Agreement seemed to radiate from him.

That night, for the first time, she checked all the windows and doors to make sure they were locked. Remembering what he had said about looking into windows, she closed all the curtains. Then she considered upgrading her locks the next day.

She didn't like the feeling. She'd gotten used to the mostly bucolic life around here. Yeah, bad things happened, but usually on such a limited scale that folks around here didn't live in constant fear.

That might be changing for her, for a while.

ALONE ONCE AGAIN in his bedroom, Duke stared out at the night. It was possible that someone was watching him right now. Standing out there in the dark, out of sight, eyes on.

He didn't feel watched, however, and he had a deep trust for that instinct. It had served him well more times than he could remember.

He remembered Cat's reaction to him saying he might be a target. She shouldn't have felt stupid for not thinking of it. He hadn't exactly leaped to the conclusion himself. It sounded a little weird when he said it out loud. Over-the-top.

But given what had happened, and his suspicions, it really *wasn't* over-the-top. Not at all. He knew the kind of people he was dealing with, what they might consider doing to protect their careers and their reputations.

A few men went to war and came back killers. Even developed a taste for it. Most had a harder time with guilt and memory.

As a man had once said, "War is an atrocity-making situation."

Hell, yeah. Dealing with it afterward was rarely easy.

But then there were those who liked it. Psychopaths, or whatever they were called these days.

Regardless, if war unleashed psychopaths, then there were psychopaths inside the command structure. Someone who'd be willing to order Larry killed. Someone who'd be willing to order Duke's death. Someone who wouldn't care but felt he'd gain from it.

Hell. He pulled the curtains closed. He wanted to escape this obsession for a little while. He considered taking a long run, then decided against it. He needed distraction, not the rush of endorphins through his system.

Leaving the bedroom, he padded down the hall in his stocking feet, which felt exposed to him. *Boots on* was every infantryman's rule. Boots could help you run over dangerous ground and protect your feet.

But walking around in boots might disturb Cat, and he didn't want to do that.

In the kitchen, he started coffee. Checking the bakery bag on the counter, he found more Danish. Probably a little stale by now, but still edible. He placed one on a plate, then joined it with steaming coffee. Such luxuries.

Now that his initial shock was passing, memories of Larry were resurfacing. They were all good memories, and they could still make him smile. Even when his chest ached so bad he thought he might not be able to draw another breath. God, it hurt.

He knew he was trying to avoid it, but this grief was apt to kill him. Larry had been an essential part of his life even when distance and time had separated them.

He felt as if he was about to bury half of himself. The best part. And he knew he was going to miss Larry's voice and grin forever.

Sunny days playing baseball. Long, lazy summers during school breaks when Mom had always promised they were going to do exciting things. Inevitably, the planned day trips didn't last long, whether because she quickly wore out or the budget wouldn't support it. It didn't matter to either him or Larry.

Instead they'd had the hills near the house. Trees to climb in, forts to build, fish to catch and a river to swim in. In the winter, endless hours were spent skating on the frozen river and trying to master the art of building an igloo or playing hockey with friends.

Duke heard a sound and twisted to see Cat shuffling into the kitchen. She wore a bright blue terry-cloth robe over pajamas.

"Did I wake you?" he immediately asked.

"You might have if I'd been asleep."

"You, too?"

"Some nights are harder than others." She poured herself coffee, then peeked into the pastry bag. "You want this?"

"Help yourself. Just a little stale."

"A shame to let that happen to Melinda's baking."

Coffee and Danish in hand, she returned to the table. "What's keeping you up?"

"I was just thinking about Larry. Memories of good times."

Cat smiled at him, a soft expression. He liked it when she smiled, but this one was special somehow. Like a warm connection.

"Care to share?" she asked.

"Not sure what to tell you. I'm kind of having a collage of memories—golden moments, if you will. Snapshots. We were close, almost like twins."

"God, that must hurt."

"It does." No point minimizing it. Since she'd joined him, the steel band around his chest had loosened a bit, but it was still there, restricting his breathing.

He continued, thinking she might like to hear a little about Larry the kid. She'd known him, after all. "We were best buddies all the way up until we separated for college. Me to the military academy, him to another college."

"Wait," she interrupted. "You went to West Point?"

"Sure did."

Wow, she thought, impressed. Then, "I'm sorry I interrupted your memories of Larry."

"No problem. They're coming as they come. Like a river that's determined to flow, but not always rapidly. Tonight, like I said, it's random snapshots. A hazy recollection of golden days. I don't know about your childhood, but ours was mostly great. Having Larry there made it even better."

"A built-in playmate."

"You bet. Best friend. We liked to camp in the backyard when we were in elementary school. It was like a huge adventure to be out there alone in a tent with night all around. We loved the flashlights. I bet our parents got sick of buying batteries." He felt a smile crease his face. "Sometimes they really indulged us, allowing us to camp out for a couple of days. My dad even built a firepit, but we could only use it when he was there to keep an eye on us. We roasted marshmallows and hot dogs and felt so freaking special. Many times, neighborhood kids joined us."

"That sounds really delightful."

His smile widened a shade. "I'll never forget the smell of the smoke that somehow always came my way. Or the racket of the crickets chirping when it grew quiet. The sound of frogs in nearby water. Catching minnows with a net, then setting them free. Pollywogs fascinated us when they started to grow their frog legs. An amazing transformation even after we knew why it was happening."

"It does sound wonderful," she murmured, enjoying the way all the hard edges seemed to leave his face as he remembered.

"Maybe the memories have been enhanced by time. I don't care. I'll keep them the way they are now."

"I'll second that."

He regarded her as he finished his Danish. She'd barely picked at hers. He was sure, despite her denial, that hearing him stirring had dragged her out of sleep. He'd worried her by telling her he might be a target. He'd noticed how she'd checked all the windows and doors and closed all the curtains.

He asked, "What are you worried about? Me telling you that I might be a target?"

Her attention snapped to him. "I'm not sure I believe that."

"Neither am I."

"Okay." She stared down at her plate, at her barely touched pastry. "Belief is a dangerous thing sometimes. Best not to ignore the possibility, though."

He agreed, but he didn't want to press the issue. She had enough to concern her without worrying about him. He sought to give her a bit of reassurance. "I'm a hard guy to kill."

"That's patently obvious. You're sitting across from me and, given your job, being here is an achievement."

"It shouldn't be, but I guess it is." Unable to stop himself, he reached across the table to take her hand. His heart stuttered when her fingers wrapped around his and tightened.

There was such fatigue and sorrow on her face. He felt bad for bringing all this to her door. His brother's murder clearly concerned her, and she would have worked as long and hard as it took to solve it even without him. But he'd added to her concerns.

He spoke. "I'm sorry I've made this case harder on you."

She made a slight negative movement with her head. "It would have been hard anyway."

"But the sheriff was keeping you out of it until I arrived."

Her eyes grew fierce. "I *wanted* to be on this case. It wouldn't have been long before I'd have demanded it. Yeah, I knew Larry, but I didn't know him well enough to lose my objectivity. Don't blame yourself for that."

His brow creased as anger with himself began to grow. "Then I showed up, looking like trouble. You had to run around to try to prevent me from going ballistic all over the county."

At that, a small laugh escaped her. "It hasn't been that difficult."

"Because you were willing to work with me. But I'll be honest. Much as I hate to admit it, when I arrived here I did want to tear a few people apart. Obviously, I didn't know who."

She raised a brow. "Do you still want to?"

"Tear someone apart? Sometimes, but the urge isn't as strong as when I arrived here. I think you'd be safe not worrying about that."

She squeezed his hand again, then withdrew hers. He regretted the absence of her touch immediately. Damn, he was starting to get tangled up between grief, anger and the pull he felt toward Cat.

She nibbled some more at her Danish, then brought the coffeepot to the table, refilling both their mugs. "We might have made some real strides today," she remarked.

"Possibly. There's always some uncertainty in a combat situation. I'm used to it. But this feels like nothing *except* uncertainty."

"That's where it's at right now," she agreed. "Sometimes murders never get solved. I won't lie to you. But something different was going on with Larry. I'm convinced he was a target, not an accident."

He agreed. "Why hasn't his house been released? There has to be a reason."

He watched her chew her lower lip. Then she said, "The murder was brutal. We're preventing curiosity seekers from sneaking in there as long as we can."

That probably told him more than he wanted to know. He yanked himself away from images that immediately popped to mind. If anyone knew brutal, he did. Her choice of modifier certainly spoke volumes. Given what she did for a living, she'd probably seen multiple murder scenes.

He felt sick, facing a suspicion he'd avoided but now couldn't. What the hell had been done to Larry, and how much did he really want to know?

But Cat's consideration of the possibility that someone had tracked Larry from elsewhere also spoke volumes to him. She felt something much bigger than a burglary had occurred.

But she wouldn't talk in detail without evidence. She'd made that clear at the outset, and he had to respect her position. She might speculate about motives, but that kind of spitballing was part of her job. Turning things around and around until she saw her way to a solution.

"Let's go for a walk," she said.

He wasn't opposed, but he studied her. "Am I giving you cabin fever?"

"Right now this job is giving me cabin fever. The research must be done."

"But at the office, you'd have a lot more people to talk to than just me."

"That's true, but I'd still spend almost all the time reading. Plus, this new idea…well, I want to talk it over with Gage, if you don't mind."

"Sure."

Ten minutes later they stepped outside into the night wearing jackets. The temperatures were falling again, and Duke wondered if he smelled snow on the air.

It was easy, though, to bend into the night breeze, strolling alongside Cat.

He didn't need another run. What he needed was company.

TWO MEN, DRESSED completely in black, with ski masks over their faces and black camouflage cream around their eyes, came around the rear of Matt Keller's tiny little house. Concealed by the night and their clothing, they looked like darker shadows in the pale starlight. The moon was gone, concealing them even more.

They had scoped the house a couple of hours earlier after darkness had arrived, peeking into windows until they had a mental image of the interior. Mostly they knew which room they needed to get to.

Unfortunately, that room was a tiny ell, barely a jog in the hallway beside the bathroom and just in front of Matt's bedroom. Behind the ell, however, was a mud porch that might be useful. But they agreed they'd prefer their entry point to be as far as possible from the bedroom, which meant the front of the house, in case they made any noise while getting past the door.

They were prepared for creaking floors in such an old house. They had night-vision goggles to keep them from stumbling into things. They figured there wouldn't be any hidden obstacles on the floor, because this was a single guy—no dogs, no kids to spread toys around.

They didn't talk; they didn't need to. From here out hand signals would suffice.

They were also prepared to deal with Matt should he discover them. Not the way they had dealt with Larry Duke, but differently, so there'd be no resemblance.

Because spring was just beginning, despite the calendar, most plants offered little concealment. Aiding them, however, Keller had some evergreen shrubs along the front, back and sides of his house. They'd tested them earlier and found they weren't brittle.

The bushes provided a perfect hiding spot as they crouched down in the back, waiting for the entire world to go to sleep.

Except for one damn cop car that drove by every so often. A lot of protection in such a sleepy town. That cop also changed their plan. After a few hours, they realized he was random in his appearances. Back door it would be.

They waited, shifting position just often enough to keep from getting stiff.

Around two thirty, they began to move stealthily, freezing often in case some random person happened to glance out into the night and see some moving shadows. It made for a slower trip from the side of the house to the back door.

Several windows on nearby houses looked straight into Keller's yard, but the first man figured those windows didn't create as much of a threat as a sharp-eyed cop who was probably hoping for any kind of distraction, even investigating shadows.

The back door proved to be an easy open. A lousy screen-door type of lock, easily broken with little noise.

The floors creaked more than anticipated, slowing them down as they paused frequently to let the noise slip away. No other sounds disturbed the house.

At last they opened the interior door, which let into the hallway. It seemed odd to the first man that the mudroom didn't open to the kitchen, but it didn't really matter. It was close to the office in the ell.

Another few steps and they were inside their target room, through a door that had been left open. Searching everything took a while, too, because they were looking for tiny stuff, like a disc or flash drive, and even into files in a cabinet, hoping to spy a label that might come from a different source. And they were trying to be silent.

They found a bunch of those flash drives and were getting ready to leave with the laptop computer when a voice startled them.

"What the hell?"

They'd been ready for this. Man Three grabbed Matt Keller from behind, wrapping one arm around his chest and clamping a gloved hand over his mouth.

Man One stepped in to finish it.

As THEY WALKED, Cat was surprised to feel Duke touch her arm. She looked at him and saw him make the sign with two fingers to his eyes, then point toward one house.

Matt Keller's house. *Oh damn.* She peered into the night, trying to see what had alerted Duke. Then she noticed a couple of shadows that appeared out of place. Wrong size for a tree and shaped all wrong.

They weren't moving, however, so she was ready to dismiss them as a trick of light. But then she saw movement, and it wasn't the movement of a tree or large bush swaying.

Two people? Crouched down? She hadn't worn her gun, but now she wished she had.

She glanced at the house and thought she saw a light inside. Matt. Without hesitation, she ran toward the front door.

"Want me to chase them?" Duke's voice drew her up short.

He was off before she could say a word, although at that point she had a bigger concern: Matt Keller.

Without any more discussion, Duke took off into the night toward the alley.

Cat's attention centered fully on Matt. If someone had broken into Matt's house, was he still alive? Or had he been tortured like Larry Duke?

She couldn't waste time wondering about the perps until she made sure Matt was reasonably okay.

The front door was locked. She sped around to the back, running because Matt's life might depend on speed. They'd had to break in somehow, and a back door was concealed from the street.

Assuming those guys had gotten in at all.

Inside, she moved with reasonable caution while her heart hammered, aware that someone might be there other than Matt. After she'd checked the front rooms, she looked down the hallway. There was only one closed door, and light spilled from a little ell.

She checked that and the bathroom as quickly as she could, barely noting the mess in the ell, then called out, "Matt? Matt?"

No sound answered her. Cat's heart nearly stopped. *Oh my God.*

"Matt? Are you here?"

She thought she heard something from behind the closed door. Muffled. She couldn't wait any longer. She turned the knob and opened the door, prepared for just about anything.

When she flipped the light switch just inside, she found Matt lying on his bed, ankles and wrists wrapped in zip ties. His arms were above his head, his cuffed wrists tied to the headboard by rope. Duct tape covered his mouth.

Without another moment's hesitation, she hurried over to rip the tape from his mouth. "Are you hurt?"

"Mostly bruised, I think." His voice shook. "It was like being tackled by two linebackers. Damn, what happened?"

"I think you might have been robbed. And since I don't have my radio on me, can I use your phone?"

"Yes. Then get these damn ties off me. They're too tight."

She grabbed the phone beside the bed and called the emergency number.

Then she went on a hunt to find a tool to cut those ties. She already heard the sirens.

DUKE RETURNED TO a swirl of cops and EMTs. Matt Keller was being carried out on a gurney over his protests that he was just a little bruised. Some injuries might not be immediately apparent, one of the EMTs told Keller. Better safe than sorry.

Immense relief filled him, knowing that Matt was still able to argue.

He could tell that, inside, Cat had taken charge of the scene. He heard her telling two cops to tape off the ell. From what little he could see from the front, it looked as if a tornado had come through, but it was obvious even to his eyes that a computer had been stolen. And what else?

They'd probably have to wait on Matt's return to find out.

He stayed out of the way by the front door after his one attempt to get inside, hardly surprised when a cop informed him of the dangers in contaminating a crime scene.

Another twenty minutes passed until Cat was satisfied and had explained to at least two cops what she had found upon her entry. So the guy had been tackled, tied and gagged.

For Duke it was like a cherry on the cake. It confirmed his worst suspicions. What he'd seen—or failed to see—when he chased those men had been the first confirmation. He needed to tell Cat.

When she joined him, she said, "Let them work. We'll go to the sidewalk."

He nodded and followed. He figured she'd hardly notice the cold now. With doors open, the house was probably reaching the outside temperature, the change negligible.

"Did you get any identifying information?" she said the minute they reached the sidewalk.

"Not exactly. Tell me how Matt was bound."

She gave him an impatient look, probably resenting the way he tossed the question back to her instead of just telling her. She sketched what she had found. "Now you."

He nodded. "This was professional."

He watched her face stiffen, an instant of resistance followed by huge dismay. "Seriously? How can you know that?"

"By the way they melted into the night. No kids did this. It was someone who knew how to handle an op like this, how to get away."

"But why?" Then she paused. "Of course. We've been talking about it." She cussed, a word he'd never before heard her use. He felt the same way.

"Tomorrow," he told her, "we need to go see Ben, warn him."

"But Larry was keeping that relationship a secret!"

"He probably was, but that doesn't mean no one knows about it. Secrets have a way of getting out somehow."

She lowered her head. "Damn it, Duke."

"Yeah."

Cat visibly shook herself. "You might as well go home. Nothing you can do here. I'll follow as soon as I can."

He nodded, then walked off into the night.

Chapter Ten

When the sun rose in the morning, the three men sat in a different gully, one chosen because it was even more concealed, this one surrounded by whispering pines, buried in shadows. Yesterday had involved too much exposure around town for them not to be concerned.

The night's chill had lingered, possibly grown deeper, and the clouds overhead didn't help any.

"Yesterday was a screwup," said the second man. He'd drunk four cups of coffee already, and the two laptops sat beside him on rocks.

The first man's response was an indirect rebuke. "You get anywhere with Duke's computer?"

"Actually, I might have. I need to look a little more. But these batteries only last ten to twelve hours. I'm gonna need more juice before long."

"The other computer?"

"I haven't had it long enough," the second man replied sourly. "Hell, you just brought it in."

The third man agreed. "There's still no point getting in a fight. We're all nervous. Uneasy."

Man Two persisted. "I think we got a problem. *He*," he said, pointing at the first man, "went into public yesterday. Doesn't matter it was a truck stop. Someone still could have noticed him."

Man One shook his head. "The only time I opened my mouth was to order. Amazing what you can learn simply by *listening.*"

"Then there's last night. You nearly got caught during that stupid, stupid burglary. You even got chased from the scene."

"We *weren't* caught," Man Three argued defensively.

"I bet someone had an idea that you two were something more than juveniles."

"Who was that guy who chased us?" Man Three asked. "Do you have any idea?"

The first man remained silent, but the other two could tell he had a suspicion. Why didn't he tell them?

For a brief spell, it appeared that the second man was about to erupt. Unusual sounds emerged from the back of his throat. Finally he said, "I bet you didn't find anything, either."

Man One spoke sarcastically. "We won't know that until you look at those flash drives."

"I need some time. Larry Duke's laptop is getting low on power. That'll leave me with just the new one. Hell, I was on Larry's most of the night."

"You said you might have found something."

"Maybe. I need to look a little more, but there's this guy who turns up in some old emails. Repeatedly. And he seems to live out here. Ben Williams."

Man One leaned forward, his eyes still bruised by the long night. "How do you know he's around here?"

"I ran a search."

CAT DIDN'T GO home until after nine in the morning. She'd not only had to make sure the investigation teams were doing everything they needed to, but she had to fill out a report, detailing her entire involvement, from when she saw the two figures running away to finding Matt tied in his bed.

After that, she caught up with Gage and informed him about her and Duke's theory.

Gage sat forward so suddenly that she heard his chair thud. He must have been tipped backward far enough to lift some of the wheels off the floor. Dangerous, but she didn't think Gage was a man who worried about danger. If he had been, he'd never have gone undercover for the DEA.

"Someone from Duke's past?" he asked. "Not Larry's but his?"

"Both, actually. We'd begun to arrive there partly because of Larry's horrific murder—and by the way, I didn't give him details, but I probably said enough—and the fallout from Larry's investigation that involved the Army. Duke thinks someone who is still in danger from that investigation might be worried about whether Larry was writing a book about it."

"Was he?"

"I don't know, Gage. The man was a clam about his work. If his editor knew anything about what he was working on, she didn't say. And since he wasn't on the paper's time, she probably didn't know. Larry never shared anything until he put it in print."

"Great help." Gage leaned back, rubbing his chin. "What else?"

"Duke said the guys who ran away from Matt Keller's house last night were trained. Not some kids, but people who knew how to be covert. He went after them, but they slipped away like ghosts."

Gage's eyes narrowed. "I'd go with Duke's opinion on that. He's got enough experience to know. Hell."

"There's still nothing linking the burglaries," Cat pointed out scrupulously.

"There wouldn't be if they know what they're doing. Inexperienced juveniles might not be smart enough to conceal it. Why didn't Larry get tied up, too? And why was Matt tied up but not killed? Serious questions here."

"When was the last time there was a string of burglaries around here?"

Gage shook his head, then gave a mirthless half smile. "We've had a few. Kids. I remember one when they gave themselves up by their choices in clothing." His humorless smile turned back into a frown. "I don't like this."

"Me neither. And to frost the cake, Duke is wondering if he might be a target, too."

"Oh, for the love of— Why?"

"Because a person or several persons in the Army might think Duke was a source for his brother. Even though he wasn't and didn't know about the murder-for-hire thing until it broke in the paper. From what Duke has said, his career has gone by the wayside."

Gage just shook his head. This was a lot to take in, she thought, watching him absorb it. "Which story was this again?"

Cat started. "Oh man, I didn't tell you. Larry did an exposé about two years ago that uncovered three soldiers involved in a murder-for-hire operation. Duke thinks some officers had to have been involved some way. He could explain his thinking to you better than I can." She spread her hands. "I don't know the Army the way he does."

"Few of us do," Gage said absently. Then he snapped back again. "This settles better in my gut than our original random theories about Larry's murder. What are you planning to do next?"

"It's okay for me to get involved again?"

"You already are, from what I can tell. Do you see me objecting?"

Despite the night she'd just had, Cat had to smile. "I haven't heard it."

"And if you had, you'd become conveniently deaf. Sort of like the cat you're named after."

He leaned forward again and reached for a pencil, drumming it on his desk. "What's your next move?"

"Duke wants to go see Ben Williams. To warn him what might be happening. Is that okay?"

"At this point, I'm saying yes. Your case, your decision."

Cat walked out of there feeling a whole lot better. Well, in a few ways. The major part of this was going to be impossible to feel any better about.

WHEN SHE GOT HOME, Duke was waiting for her with coffee and a bag of buttery croissants. The man definitely knew how to spoil a woman.

Feeling almost as if the kitchen table had become the center of her life, she joined him, holding her mug in both hands, trying to warm up her fingers. He had placed a croissant on a plate in front of her, and the open butter dish with a knife.

"Aren't you going to eat?" she asked.

"I already did. I might have more later. How did it go?"

"It went."

"Any news about Matt Keller?"

She shook her head. "Not really. They're holding him for observation for a few hours, but no reports of serious damage. Apparently some good bruises, though. We'll have to go with him tomorrow for an inventory to find out what's missing, if anything."

"Did someone talk to him?"

"A deputy went to the hospital to interview him. Right now, I don't know any more." She raised weary eyes to look at him. "I don't think I'd want to go home today if I were Matt."

Duke sighed. "I wouldn't, either."

Cat felt a stab of anger. "No, but you'll waltz around this county acting like you don't believe you might be a target."

His expression grew flat. He spoke levelly. "I can leave if you're worried."

"Worried about what? Your safety? Of course I am. Worried about myself—no way!"

He frowned. "I'm the last person you should worry about. Anything these perps know, I know a thousand times better. Trust me, I may be infantry now, but I used to be Airborne. A long-range sniper rifle is the only thing I need to worry about, and snipers are few and far between."

She liked his confidence but wasn't as sure herself.

"I've got to get to bed," she announced. "I won't be good for anything without some sleep. I'll phone Ben when I get up."

But before she rose, she gave him another bit of information. "I'm in charge of these investigations now."

Then she marched off to bed, hoping her pillow would silence her racing thoughts and give her a break from all of this.

It had been bad enough when she found Larry. The weeds, though, seemed to just keep getting deeper. She needed some fuel for her tank.

"Anything yet?" the first man asked the second.

The second guy tossed another flash drive on the small but growing pile beside him. "No. Nothing seems to be hidden or locked. But this guy might have some trouble with the IRS."

"Why?" asked the third man.

"Because we may have all his business files and spreadsheets. He owns a store, and the litany of numbers is mind-numbing. I'm guessing he kept the information on both his laptop and backup flash drives, which he wouldn't need if he was using the cloud for storage."

The first man merely nodded, but the third snorted in disgust. "Cripes," Man Three said. "What the hell are we doing out here?"

"My guess," said the first man, "would be any information related in any way to the Army. So nothing personal? Nothing encrypted? Nothing out of place?"

"I'm not done yet. As for personal, I have his 1040-As for the last five years."

"That'd be great if he was a political candidate," offered the third guy. But he still sounded disgusted.

"If you don't find anything there," the first man said, "the three of us will scope out Ben Williams's place. He might be a better possibility because he's known Larry Duke for...how long?"

Man Two looked up. "Emails stretch back almost four years."

"Four years. Of all the people around here, he might have had Larry Duke's trust. Better than those poker buddies we've been trying to track down."

The two others nodded. "Then what?" asked Man Three.

"We plan. We might be able to go in tonight."

The second man looked between the other two. "What the hell happened last night?"

"Somebody chased us while we were leaving Keller's place."

"Daniel Duke," said the first man.

"Then you know him?" asked Man Two.

"Only ran into him once."

"So he won't recognize you."

"No reason he should. But if he gets in my way again, I'm going to take him out." The first man held out his hands and squeezed them into fists repeatedly.

"But you said..." The second guy trailed off. Then he changed course. "If we don't find anything at this Williams guy's house, what then?"

"Then I'm calling the jerk who sent us out here, and I'm telling him we quit. I've had enough of this, and I'm sick of the three of us being exposed on a mission that's poorly directed and conceived."

For once, nobody mentioned the money.

Then some snowflakes began to fall. Another complication.

CAT WOKE FROM some unexpectedly steamy dreams about Duke. *Oh man*, she thought as she scrubbed her eyes awake. She had believed she'd managed to put all that away in some locked box in her brain. It was a complication neither of them needed—not that he'd be in any kind of mood for it, considering why he'd come out here.

She shouldn't be in the mood for it, either, but it seemed she was. The man had leaped past too many of her defenses in such a short time. When she thought of him now, she no longer felt the spark of irritation. Instead it was as if a kitten had curled up with her.

Dang, he was no kitten. A lion for sure.

She forced her feelings back into the mental safe, then remembered a couple of times when she had thought Duke's gaze reflected desire. She must have been mistaken. He couldn't possibly want *her*, and not under these circumstances.

She indulged a few minutes remembering how broad his shoulders were, how narrow his hips were. The way he smelled after a run and a shower. His comfortable lope when he ran, and his equally comfortable walking stride.

Quite the figure of a man. But more than that, she'd watched him deal with horrific things, watched him face emotions that must have him knotted inside. She was impressed.

She showered and donned some civvies, her favorite

jeans and a sweatshirt against the cold that seemed to fill the house.

She paused at the thermostat and turned the heat up a couple of degrees. Reassuringly, the furnace started.

She'd half expected to find Duke in the kitchen, and there he was, phone pressed to his ear, a mug of coffee in front of him, along with some croissants.

At least she didn't have to think about food yet. She grabbed a croissant for herself, along with a mug of coffee, and sat down with him. She buttered her pastry while he talked.

"I'm just wondering if there's any scuttlebutt about who is pushing back at me. I know my CO is involved in some way because he signs the reports, but there's got to be someone higher, and I can't ask Jeffries. He'd deny it."

He paused then said, "Thanks, Crash. Whatever's in the wind."

"Crash?" Cat asked as Duke put down his phone.

"Nickname. He and I became buddies back at the academy. Good man."

"You trust him not to tell anyone you're asking?"

"Absolutely. I phoned a handful of others I feel the same way about. Maybe we'll get some intel. I don't expect it right away, though."

"Nope," she agreed and bit into her croissant. She was glad he had people he could trust with this. One of the things she liked about living here was that the people she spent the most time with were people who seemed totally trustworthy. Duke's friends probably went back a lot further.

"Is there some kind of code?" she asked.

"I'm getting skewered on it right now. The code not to talk. But that's no guarantee that lips are always zipped. Obviously. And things can be said within the Army that should never be shared with nonsoldiers."

She'd pretty much gathered that from an earlier conversation, but she felt edgy now that he'd made the calls. Word might get back to the wrong ears.

Nothing she could say or do now, however. Not that she could have argued him out of the calls. He probably would have turned into a brick wall again. "So you think your CO is involved?"

He shrugged. "It's possible. He is, after all, writing my performance reports. On the other hand, he may be getting some pressure and not even know why. He's got a career to consider, too."

That sounded ugly. She tried to shift to something less disturbing. They already had plenty of reasons to be disturbed. "Did you sleep?"

"I snagged a few z's."

Her landline rang, and she went to answer it. A short time later, her stomach plummeted to the ground. She hung up and faced Duke, braced for his reaction. Her mouth turned so dry she wasn't sure she could speak. "Larry's body is on the way back."

His entire face tightened. "Good." The word came out sharply, edged in darkness.

"They'll take him to the funeral home, the only one here. Do you want him shipped back with you?"

It took him a few minutes as he seemed to stare into some bleak place inside him. "I think Ben should decide."

She did, too.

He raised his head, suddenly looking gaunt. "Cat… Cat…"

Not knowing what else to do, she moved to wrap her arms around him from behind. Her heart was breaking for him, yet she still enjoyed his scent, the hard strength of his shoulders.

Damn, she was losing it. So inappropriate right now.

But he surprised her, reaching around and tugging her until she could sit on his lap.

"Cat," he whispered roughly, "this doesn't make sense, but I…"

She got it. Totally. She didn't care if it didn't make sense, didn't care if this didn't fit with the concerns that swirled around them. She felt it, too. Needed it.

His arms snaked around her, tightening until he held her close to his heat, until her face rested between his shoulder and neck. She closed her eyes, reveling in his hug, and rested her hand on his chest. The man was nearly as hard as rock, and his embrace made her feel so soft…

Then she felt a shudder rip through him. Oh God, it was hitting him—hitting him hard. Whatever form of denial he'd been using had just been torn away by the news that Larry's body would arrive soon.

Another shudder took him, but when she tried to move, he just held her closer. She didn't want to get away; she wanted to be in a better position to comfort him.

But maybe this was what he needed? She couldn't decide that for him. So she relaxed and remained silent while grief gripped him. Aching for him and feeling utterly foolish for thinking this might ever have been anything else.

She was sure he'd lost others in his life, given the nature of his career, but this had to be different, even worse. As close as he must become with his fellow soldiers in unimaginable circumstances, there must be an even deeper connection with the brother you'd grown up with. Families of different kinds.

As carefully as he held her, as much as his arms supported her, she began to feel restless. This wasn't exactly a natural position, not for long.

His shuddering had passed, and maybe this was a time she could move. His arms hadn't loosened any, and she didn't want to make him feel any worse, but still…

Carefully, slowly, she pulled away a little.

"I'm sorry," he said, his voice low and quiet. "You've got to be uncomfortable."

"A little," she admitted, "but don't apologize."

Slipping off his lap, she bent a little side to side while keeping her attention on him. His eyes were closed, but there was no sign of tears on his cheeks. He'd gone through the storm without a tear. She'd have been blubbering her head off, as she knew from when her mother had died. Tears were a release, an expression of feelings for which there were no adequate words.

"Duke?" She spoke quietly.

His eyes opened, and he looked hollow. "Yeah?"

"Can I get you something? Coffee? Beer? Milk?" Useless questions, answering only her own need to do something for him. "Do you want anything?"

"You," he said.

Her heart slammed, and her knees turned to water.

CAT BARELY REMEMBERED getting to the bedroom. Like a scene from a movie, the world turned into a blur as they pulled clothes away and stumbled into her bedroom, kissing wildly all the while. She'd never believed those scenes. Now she did, with the haziest of memories to support it.

All that mattered was how quickly they'd come to be lying naked on her bed. The curtains were still drawn, and little light seeped into the room, leaving a twilight that felt right for the unreality that had seized her. Bright light would have interfered, made everything stand out starkly. Would have kept her from slipping away into a place where nothing existed except Duke and the desire that poured through her like lava.

Heavy breathing. Palms stroking skin as if trying to create fire from friction and unleashing a very different kind of fire. Damn, his skin felt good, and his touch felt

even better. She skimmed over what felt like scars, stories
yet to be told.

She gasped as he caressed her, a merciless reconnais-
sance of her every curve and hollow. His hands and fingers
took liberties that left her moaning as he teased her breasts,
then slipped his hand between her legs, pressing until she
arched, needing ever so much more. She grabbed his shoulders like a life preserver in dangerous waters, feeling as if
she would drown in him and never return.

Then his mouth followed his hands. She nearly went
mad, writhing under his every touch, trying to reach him
and reciprocate, but he wouldn't let her. He was in command this time, and she finally let it be. His need for control was hardly surprising, and she was willing to grant it
to him. Another time...

Coherent thoughts were few and far between and becoming rarer by the second. Swept away by his demand-
ing desire, she let him carry her to wherever he wanted.

Like the eternal current carrying them both. She felt
herself rising as if on a rogue wave, higher and higher until
she felt a fear of tipping into the trough below. Then a fear
of not tipping over at all.

He slipped inside her, filling her until she ached from
it. When he started moving, she followed helplessly, needing it, needing him.

She fell over the edge, feeling him fall with her, jerking
suddenly against her, giving her one last trip to the top before she tumbled into peace.

THEY LAY TOGETHER in a tangled mess of bodies and bed-
covers. At some point Duke rose up to grab a pillow and
place it under both their heads, but then she disappeared
once again into his embrace.

Cat had never had such an experience. Never. Delicious,

fraught with a maelstrom of sensation and feelings that kept her on a scary edge until the moment when release set her free.

Wild.

Never before had she felt quite as satisfied, either. As if no part of her had escaped the experience.

He stirred a little, his hand running along her back. "Magic," he murmured.

"Yeah," she breathed. Oh yeah.

Then, bringing the beautiful moments to an abrupt end, he stiffened. "Ben."

"Oh God." She wiggled, breaking free, and sat up. "You're sure he might be in danger?"

"I don't want to risk it."

"Neither do I. You grab a shower while I call him. We'll go over there, if you want."

"I want. But…"

Cat paused as she pulled on her robe over her cooling body. "What?"

"This isn't romantic."

She leaned over him, resting her hands on the bed. "If the past hour wasn't romantic, I don't know what is. I'm a grown-up, Duke. I don't need flowers, or lingering in bed, or taking showers together. Another time. Now get your butt in gear."

"Yes, ma'am."

She thought she heard a tremor of amusement in his voice as she hurried to the phone.

Before she could pick it up, it began ringing. Her heart slammed with the fear. What now? She had a sudden memory of the old sheriff, Nate Tate, remarking once on another case since she'd moved here, "This county's going to hell in a handbasket." Apparently, it had been his signature complaint, but never in her time here had it seemed more true.

"Jansen," she said into the phone.

"Gage," said the familiar voice. "I got the forensics report."

She swallowed hard, sensing what was coming. "It's bad."

"As bad as our worst fears. You don't need the details, but Larry was definitely tortured. Maybe for an hour."

"Oh my God," she whispered, closing her eyes. "I suspected, but…"

"We all did. Being human, we hoped it wasn't true. Larry's remains should be arriving at the funeral home tomorrow afternoon. Unless there's another plan."

"Duke wants to talk it over with Ben first. I think we're going out to see him tonight."

Gage sighed. "Damn it. I never wanted to see anything like this ever again. We've got to find this bastard so I can nail his hide to a wall. And Duke gets to use the nail gun first."

"I think he's going to want a hammer."

CAT WAS SHAKING so hard that she sat at the table before calling Ben. A whole bucket of horror was about to drop into the laps of these two men, Ben and Duke, and she wished she didn't have to be part of informing them.

She glanced at the phone in her hand. She had to call Ben and try to do it without giving him reason to guess that the case had just leapfrogged past gruesome to horrific. She drew a few steadying breaths, centering herself in professional reactions, then made the call.

"Hey, Ben. Duke and I want to come to see you. Okay by you?"

"Absolutely. I took some time off, and sitting out here by myself is driving me nuts. Too much empty space to fill with sorrow and anger."

"I hear you. Duke will share that, I think."

"I'm sure. That's part of the reason it'll be good to see him. Plus, way back when, we were acquainted."

But Duke had been too busy trying to avoid his own grief by chasing a killer to be thinking about Ben. "Thanks," she said. "Want us to pick up some dinner?"

"If you go by Maude's, a steak sandwich is always welcome."

"Done."

WHILE DUKE WENT to Maude's to pick up dinner, Cat visited the sheriff's office. "I'm taking two shotguns and a rifle, and some body armor," she said to Sarah Ironheart, who was sitting at the duty desk.

Gage must have the hearing of a cat, she thought, as his head poked out his door. "Cat?"

"Coming."

She hurried back, aware that heads were pivoting to look at her. She was past caring that she'd caused the room to seethe with curiosity. She couldn't just take the guns without checking them out.

"You expecting trouble?" Gage asked, motioning her to close the door.

"Maybe. I don't know. Duke is worried that Ben could be a target in this mess, too. If this guy is looking for information of some kind, eventually he'd light on Ben, wouldn't he?"

Gage rubbed his chin and nodded. "Maybe so. You want some backup?"

"For what? A feeling? No. I want to make sure we're armed. Just in case. That's all. The same as going out on patrol or answering a call. Because you never know."

"All right." He paused. "About this report…"

"The forensics?" she interrupted. "I don't want to hear any more today. Maybe tomorrow. Right now I've got to be with two grieving men, and the less I know, the better."

"Can't argue with that. Take the guns. Goggles, too, if you want. And plenty of ammo. Hell, just take one of the patrol vehicles."

She thought about that. "Advertising."

He just shook his head. "Do it your way, Cat. Your case, your decision."

The guns would fit well enough in the back of Duke's truck under the tonneau. Two Mossberg riot guns and a long rifle. Boxes of ammo. Clips. Three sets of night-vision goggles. Three sets of chest armor. Ready for war.

Part of her wanted to find this ridiculous, but the rest of her just couldn't do it. Larry's murderer was still out there, a man who would torture someone for an hour or more. Two men, she corrected herself. Duke had seen two men running from Matt's house.

No, she wanted Ben protected even if she had to demand he come stay with her along with Duke. And if Duke decided he needed to stay with Ben, then the two of them were sure as hell going to be adequately armed.

But taking a patrol vehicle? No. Why draw attention? What if someone had Ben's house under observation? Sure, tell 'em a cop was inside.

And Duke was right. Larry and Ben might have tried to keep their relationship on the q.t., but people still found things out. Still made connections and assumptions. Then there was the fact that Larry had shared it with her. He had just dropped it, asking her to keep it to herself. What if he'd told someone else and they'd shared it further?

God, Duke was right. Too many maybes.

Hope for the best, prepare for the worst.

SHORTLY SHE AND Duke were driving along county roads toward Ben's house. Bags from Maude's were tucked behind the seats. The back end was loaded, literally and figuratively.

As they started to reach quiet roads, snow began to fall, thicker than the few flakes that had fluttered down earlier.

"Great," she said. "Weren't there enough complications already?"

He glanced her way as he drove. "You're loaded for bear."

"Believe it. *Fed up* would be a good description. I want this case solved. I always do, but this is one that's eating me alive."

He didn't answer.

What could he say? she wondered. He didn't know what Gage had told her, which was more than enough to light her fuse. He might suspect, but he didn't know, and she wanted to keep it that way. For now, at least. She couldn't just drop this on Ben, either.

He spoke. "So is Cat short for something?"

She shook her head and glanced at him. "Nope. Just Cat. I asked my mom about it once, and she couldn't explain it except that it had caught her fancy."

"Dad?"

"He never had any input. Gone before I was born. Anyway, once I got past the teasing, I decided I like it."

"You should. It's unique. Like you."

Here she was talking about her name. She kept giving herself mental kicks, trying to calm down. She shouldn't have let the news put her into hyperdrive. But, like Gage had said, they were human and had hoped they were wrong, but she'd known. They'd known. Maybe they just hadn't wanted to accept it.

"Listen," he said after another mile or so, "about earlier…"

"You don't have to say anything," she interjected swiftly. An apology right now would kill her. There was still a glow to be had from their sex, and she wanted to hang on to it. Tightly.

"I *do* have to say something. You weren't just a distraction. Not an escape. I wanted you. I've been wanting you ever since you confronted me in front of the department store."

She snorted quietly. "So you like women who stand up to you?"

"I sure don't like doormats. I don't wilt."

"I noticed."

It was his turn to yield a short laugh. "Seriously, Cat, it was wonderful, and I hope we can do it again when all kinds of ugly things aren't whipping around us. When we can just take our time and savor it."

She liked the sound of that. She turned a little in her seat. "I'd like that, too."

"I just wanted you to know I wasn't using you. Every other time I wanted to have sex with you, I've stopped myself because I couldn't say that with certainty. Now I can."

She had to admit to herself that it felt better to know that. She'd told herself it didn't matter, but it seemed it did.

"Still," she couldn't prevent herself from saying, "there's no real future in it." That was one she had to face squarely.

"Future?" He shook his head. "Lady, you're talking to a soldier. Long-distance relationships aren't an obstacle. Just saying."

She hadn't thought about that before, either. *Hmm.*

But as they drew closer to Ben's house, she felt her stomach trying to knot. There was danger ahead, although she didn't know of what kind. Emotional explosions? Ben having a breakdown? Like she could blame him if he did.

When they pulled up beside Ben's house, he came out to greet them. Before he and Duke could do more than shake hands, Cat opened the tailgate, ready to pass out the armament.

"Don't say I don't come prepared. I've got two riot guns,

a rifle and a heavy bag of ammo. Oh, and night-vision goggles and armor. Who's carrying what?"

Cat saw Ben stiffen. "What the hell?" he asked.

Duke spoke first. "Let's get this gear inside. Then we'll talk. C'mon."

Ben didn't argue, maybe because he heard an order as an order. Something to be said in favor of military experience, Cat thought sourly as she grabbed the two cases holding the riot guns. Ben took the rifle and the heavy ammo carrier.

"I'll get the food and armor," Duke said. With a gesture, he motioned Ben toward the door. "Step lively, soldier."

That drew a half smile from Ben, who otherwise looked as if he'd been walking through the hallways of hell.

Cat followed Ben inside, hearing the sounds as Duke slammed the tailgate closed, then got the bags of food from the cab. She'd barely had time to lean the riot guns against the wall in a corner before Duke joined them, his hands full, his shoulders burdened by the heavy body armor.

Cold had entered the house through the open door, and it took several minutes before the air heated up again. Nobody shed a jacket while they put Maude's bags in the kitchen.

Then Duke sat down to unzip carrying cases and examine the guns. "Good selection," he said to Cat as she sat across from him on a flowery upright chair. Ben took another chair nearby.

Ben cleared his throat. "Guns?"

Duke didn't exactly answer. "I'd prefer the rifle myself, if you two are okay with the shotguns."

"I'm okay with anything that can cause trouble to anyone on the other end," Cat said. "Ben?"

"Shotgun is fine with me, too." He cleared his throat. "Why?"

Cat indicated Duke with an open hand. Let him explain

this maze. She wasn't at all sure they weren't overreacting, and this might not be a good time to inject any doubt.

"First things," Duke said. "Larry will be back in town tomorrow."

Ben leaned forward, resting his elbows on his knees, burying his face in his hands. "Oh God," he whispered.

The pain in this room was palpable. Two men dealing with heart-crushing grief for which there'd never be a cure. Cat felt tears well in her own eyes and blinked them back.

A few minutes passed. Then Ben lifted his head. His face was marked by two tear streaks running from his eyes. "They didn't let me know. Of course not. I don't matter. It's not like we were married."

Duke spoke, his voice gruff. "You matter to *me*. And I haven't been officially notified yet, either. Cat got the call as the lead investigator, and she told me. Now we're telling you."

Ben leaned back, closing his eyes. "Yeah," he murmured. "It's just…"

Too much, Cat thought. How many avenues were closed to Larry and Ben unless they married? She could only begin to guess at it. A million rights were defined by blood relationships and marital contracts.

Ben spoke again, his tone leaden. "Let me know what you decide about the funeral, Duke. Are you taking him back East?"

Duke cussed and rose. He looked overwhelming in the small space. "Ben, I'm not planning anything without your blessing. I may have the right, but I'm giving you the right to decide everything. I'm not taking him back East unless you want it. If you want him here, he stays here. Got it?"

Ben nodded.

Cat stared up at Duke, admiring him more in that moment than she ever had. He might be tough, even hard as nails at times, but apparently his heart was as big as every-thing else about him.

Ben took a few more minutes, steadying himself against the pain. Then he stirred. "Okay," he said quietly. "What's up other than dinner from Maude's? As in the arsenal."

"I could have brought more," Cat said, trying a lighter moment. "I wasn't sure how useful pistols would be, but I threw a few in the truck if we want them."

"Pistols." Ben's eyes widened. "Are you expecting an invasion? Where are the flash-bangs? The grenades? The fifty-cal machine gun?"

She was grateful to see him rise to attempted humor. Some things you couldn't just deal with at one time. Ben needed to shake it off for a little while. To give himself an emotional break. Well, this was certainly going to be dif-ferent.

Duke leaned forward. "We can talk over dinner before it gets too cold, or we can do one or the other first. Up to you."

"I'm curious as hell what the two of you are worried about, but let's eat. I don't remember…" Ben shrugged. "I think I haven't eaten since yesterday."

Cat felt good about being able to slip into gear. "Then let's go, gentlemen."

Ben had a large trestle table in his farm kitchen, and they laid out their food, along with plates, utensils and napkins. Three foam boxes yielded the steak sandwiches, another a large salad, and the final one was dessert: Maude's peach cobbler. A feast.

It amused her a bit, too. She'd never been big on dessert, but Duke seemed to favor it.

Ben broke out some beers, and soon they were seated at one end of the table, Ben at the head, Cat and Duke on ei-ther side. They draped jackets over the backs of their chairs.

The crusty sandwich bread was still fresh, not soaked

through yet from the steak juices. It smelled so good she could have slipped into a gourmet heaven.

Reality wouldn't allow that.

Duke spoke, answering Ben's questions that seemed to be hanging urgently. "Okay, here's the deal."

Ben nodded, his mouth full.

"We think Larry's murder may be related to that story Larry wrote about the murder-for-hire scheme."

Ben swallowed, then choked a little. He drained some beer to wash the food down, then looked at both of them. "Tell me you're joking." But as soon as the words tumbled out, more of them followed. Ben's face reflected an element of shock. "Damn it, Larry."

Duke responded. "I've been saying a lot of that."

"Damn it," Ben said again. "Damn it, Duke, that was one of the first things I thought of when I learned Larry was murdered. Damn it."

Ben jumped up from the table, paced the length of the kitchen, then disappeared. Cat could hear his footfalls in the next rooms.

She looked at Duke. "He thought of it, too."

Duke nodded. "Nobody wants to, but we both know certain types in uniform. We know the code."

Ben returned with reddened eyes after a couple of minutes and sat down, starting to eat again. Cat followed suit. If this night turned long for some reason, she'd regret failing to eat even though her appetite had died.

Ben had been thinking as he absorbed the news. "I wondered. Then I wondered if any of them thought I might be a source. Like you, Duke. Then, the last day or so, I've been wondering if they might come after me, too. If that's the reason. But that cat was already out of the bag!"

"I would have thought so." Duke finished his sandwich, allowing Ben time to adjust to this.

There was more, Cat knew, but she'd let Duke explain it

to Ben. He might even be able to use some shorthand that she couldn't because she didn't know their shared culture.

"What changed your mind?" Ben asked. He pushed his plate to one side.

"There was a break-in in town. Cat and I happened to be on the street when it occurred. The break-in involved a guy I'd already talked to about Larry. And I saw two men flee."

Ben nodded. "And?"

"They weren't kids, Ben. I went after them. They were trained. They were ghosts."

Ben closed his eyes briefly, then swore. "What else?"

"The fact that he was here working on a book but hadn't told a soul what it was about. He might have been developing that story or building a case against some others involved in that crap. And given the men I saw running, I'm not prepared to dismiss a military connection."

Ben clearly didn't want to be eating, but he plugged away at it. Sometimes even the best food became a mere fuel.

After a couple more mouthfuls, Ben spoke again. "That would make sense. Awful, ugly sense. Damn it, Larry."

Duke just shook his head. "That was Larry. We both know it. I wouldn't be surprised if there were things he couldn't mention in his original story because he didn't have enough corroborating evidence or testimony. It also wouldn't surprise me if he couldn't let those loose ends go."

"He never would," Ben agreed. "Never. They'd have been driving him nuts until he found answers."

"Much as he could be a clam," Duke replied, "he was talking to people. Maybe some dangerous people."

"Didn't he always do that? Way of life for him." Ben compressed his lips, his entire face tightening. Then, "You think they might be after me."

Cat spoke. "We can't ignore the possibility, Ben. They might be coming for Duke, too. Whoever they are, they probably aren't familiar with Larry's secrecy about his work. They might think that anyone who knew him might have information."

"But Larry kept us secret."

"There are always people who know," Duke said. "Always. Unless you were living in an isolated cave, someone would know you were close."

After they put the leftovers away, they repaired to the living room with coffee. No beer. Not now, as night began to fall in slow stages. Cat looked outside and saw the snow was still falling slowly but not yet sticking. She hadn't heard any other vehicles on the road out front, and from where she stood at the front window, she could see no signs of life.

But night approached, and the cover of darkness could bring threat.

If the break-ins were related to Larry's murder, the perps had spaced them out a bit. It should be too soon for another attempt.

By the same token, since Duke had chased those two guys, their timetable may have sped up. Or maybe the two intervening burglaries had merely been diversionary. Maybe they had their sights on bigger targets, like Duke and Ben.

Duke interrupted the heavy, tense silence. "I'm going to take a walk around the perimeter before it gets dark, maybe move the truck farther away so it doesn't provide concealment. You two button up the house. Curtains closed. Later we can turn out all the lights and keep watch."

"Great evening," Cat said, winking at Ben.

He smiled faintly. "Oh yeah. Standing post. Love it."

During the passing hours, she had grown considerably more convinced that Duke had been right about what was coming down. She hoped not, but her stance was shifting. Maybe it helped that Ben had no problem believing the theory. She sure hoped she'd brought what they'd need.

THE GROUND HADN'T yet become muddy from the snow-flakes that melted as soon as they fell on it. It had, how-ever, softened just a bit, silencing Duke's footsteps as he slipped around to the back and began his patrol of a wide perimeter. He didn't wear the goggles because he wanted his full field of vision. Peripheral vision was great at de-tecting movement.

Much as the early twilight messed with depth and shad-ows, he could still see enough. The falling snowflakes amplified the remaining light. What he sought was any evidence of someone having been out here creeping around. This wasn't the kind of place a person might take a casual walk. Too far away from anything else, including other dwellings.

He also needed to scout the terrain. From a tactical and strategic perspective, knowing the ground was essential. Where could a team hide when approaching the house? How many significant ditches and dips lay out here? Any formations large enough to hide behind? Easy approaches?

The tall evergreens that lined the property about three hundred feet from the house didn't worry him. They'd be temporary cover at best. But a gully deep enough to pro-vide concealment for someone to approach the house? Big problem.

Each time he paused to view the ground, he looked back to the house, considering angles of attack, soft points to approach.

Because the first thing he'd done was move his rental truck down the driveway, so it was near the road, he didn't have to take care of that. Insofar as possible, it didn't an-nounce that Ben had visitors. But mostly he didn't want to give them a place to hide.

Duke didn't want to scare them off. He wanted these creeps to come after Ben. He wanted to take them down.

For Ben, because he deserved to live without fear, especially fear that his relationship with Larry had brought hell raining down on him. Larry wouldn't have wanted that, nor did Duke.

And of course he wanted justice for Larry. Assuming these guys were out here trying to bury something to protect brass or others back home, he might never get to the root cause of it. Not ever. Duke was resigned to that. What he wasn't resigned to was letting his brother's murderers get away with it, with letting them get away with all the other people they'd frightened.

Nope, time for justice.

Chapter Eleven

"We go tonight," Man One said.

The three of them huddled beneath the tall evergreens, more shadows among already deep shadows. The steadily falling snow magnified a little bit of light despite the darkness above. Enough to see by. Maybe too much. Man One was past caring.

"Are you serious?" asked the second man. "Damn it, I haven't even finished searching for the information on the computer or the flash drives. We might already have it."

"Yeah," agreed the third man. He'd seen plenty of action during his years in uniform and wasn't afraid of it. The only thing that truly scared him was stupidity. He didn't want to be stupid or to be led by it.

"The guy's there. He's sleeping. We can handle him and take our time to search."

Man Two bumped his head as he moved. A quiet curse escaped him. "What about that truck down by the end of the driveway? Somebody else is in that house. Just maybe."

"I don't freaking care," said the first man. "You two wanna spend the rest of our lives out here hunting for something we can't find? You want to bring huge numbers of staties down on this place because we commit so many burglaries? At this point it's hardly likely that we'll have this gig much longer. They'll call us failures, refuse to pay what they owe us and send someone else out here."

"Sure," said the second man.

"It's a wild-goose chase," the third man agreed morosely. "I mean, damn! What if all the information was in Larry Duke's head? We're going on a lot of supposition here. Like, if he dumped a disc or a drive or a file on someone else that they'd even know what to make of it. They'd probably just trash it."

"Word," said the second man reluctantly.

"Exactly," said the first man. "The longer we're out here, the more I start wondering if someone isn't trying to get rid of the three of us."

Shocked silence greeted the words.

After a minute or so, Man Two asked, "Why would they want to do that?"

"Damned if I know. This whole op is so fishy I'm wondering how I ever got talked into it. Well, money, I guess. Retirement ain't so easy. But apart from that, it didn't sound so damn difficult. It *wasn't* difficult until Larry Duke said we'd never find the info. That's when it all blew up."

"True," the third man agreed. "I thought it would be simple, too."

"In and out," said the second man. "It should have been." Instead...

Man Two stirred again. "But they have no reason to get rid of us."

"Now they do," the first man said grimly. "From the minute we interrogated Duke, we screwed up. Made a mess. Even if we get out of here, we're in trouble. Somebody might worry that we'll be found out and can spill the beans."

"What beans?" demanded the third man. "We don't have any beans!"

"I do," said the first man. "I talk to the boss. Why would anyone think I haven't told you who that is?"

"Aw, hell."

"Exactly," said the first man. "We're in it now. Whichever way we go. So tonight we go into that house, search it, then get the hell out of this state."

"But what if there's another man in there?"

"Then I hope it's Daniel Duke," said the first man.

"You got a grudge?"

"Now I do."

The other two had no idea what that meant, but they weren't going to ask. They were stuck and figured the first guy would shoot them both in the back if they refused to follow him.

Things sure changed when you were up to no good.

THE THREE INSIDE the house had agreed to spell each other on lookout duty, allowing the others to take naps. They'd opened the curtains at one window on each side of the house. The idea was to give themselves a full view of outside approaches without allowing anyone to scope the entire indoors from out there. The night seemed to devour the inside of the house, little light to break up the darkness. The only glimmer they had at all was reflected by the falling snow through the uncovered windows.

Each of them took turns walking window to window to keep an eye on the land surrounding the house. The night-vision goggles that Cat had brought helped. Reasonably clear, green-tinged images made the house safely passable indoors and gave a clear view of the world outside the windows.

And it was boring, Cat thought as she wandered window to window, riot gun in hand, peering out into the night. Those guys probably had goggles, too, if they were what Duke suspected.

Well, if they showed up, at least they wouldn't have an advantage.

There'd been little time for it yet, but her mind kept trying to wander back to her lovemaking with Duke. She wanted to replay every detail repeatedly on an infinite loop. Except she couldn't remember a lot of it.

She almost giggled at herself. She'd been so swept away at the time, she'd hardly been aware of anything besides the stormy sea of emotions.

Now this. Life had been rushing by. Too many things to think about, to worry about. No time for wandering through dreams.

Nor could she afford to indulge now. The lives of others depended on her being alert, not dopey.

She heard a creak on the stairs in the hallway behind her and turned to see Duke descending. "Cat," he said quietly.

"You're supposed to be sleeping."

"I rarely sleep well on a night op. Doesn't matter. Morning will come, and I'll feel like a fool for putting everyone through this."

She pushed her goggles up, then realized that could be a mistake. Without their light amplification, total darkness surrounded her. "You're not a fool. And you know they might not come tonight. What matters is that we're here to look after Ben if he needs us."

"And tomorrow night?"

She shook her head. "I already told you. I'm going to insist he come into town and stay at my place. Out here he's hanging in the wind."

He caught her chin with his fingers. "You're a great person, Cat."

"Right now I'm not being a very good sentry."

He laughed quietly. "I can see over your shoulder, Deputy. But you go cadge some sleep. I'll take over."

"No." She turned from him reluctantly and looked out

the window. "We're getting to the witching hour. Two sets of eyes would be better."

"Witching hour?" he asked. "I thought that was midnight."

"For this, I'd bet it's more like 2:00 a.m. As the world falls into its deepest sleep."

"Those were the hours we preferred for operations," he agreed. "I just thought 'the witching hour' referred to something else."

"It might. I don't know." She pulled her goggles down, treating herself to a few seconds of looking at him, then started her patrol again.

"Stay back from the windows," he reminded her.

Yeah. Stay back because the guys out there might have night vision, too, and could catch sight of movement in here. And why had she started to grow so tense? A tightening through her muscles, the back of her neck prickling. Well, she *was* edgy.

A level playing field? She didn't think so. Those guys could move freely out there. Here inside, she and the two men were practically caged.

"I'll do the far side of the house," Duke said quietly. "More eyes on. We can start switching off every half hour."

"Yeah." She paused. "When you did your recon, did you find any features that concerned you?"

"Actually, yeah. From the kitchen side of the house. There's a gully that could be deep enough to conceal crawling men. Assuming the snow doesn't start to stick. Then it all becomes different out there."

Considering how much light was being reflected by the snowflakes that fell almost lazily, she couldn't imagine what it would all look like under a white blanket out there. They might not even need the goggles from in here.

Unless someone managed to get inside.

"We need to get Ben," she said before Duke could disappear to the other side of the house. "I don't know why, but my skin is crawling."

"He's already watching from upstairs."

"Oh." So much for them taking turns.

Duke faced her. "Your skin is crawling? Like somebody's watching?"

"Imagination, maybe. I'm wound up. It only just started, though."

His reply was quick. "Don't ignore it. I never do."

He headed for the kitchen side of the house, and she resumed her patrol, easing to each window, minimizing any quickness of movement that might draw attention if someone was out there watching.

She looked out that same window again, wondering. Was someone looking in? She hadn't noticed any movement, but she'd been distracted for a minute or two with Duke. Bad. Thank goodness Ben had decided to forgo sleep.

Sentry duty had to be the worst assignment in the world. Things creeping in the dark, a threat possibly looming and weariness making it even harder to stay alert.

TWENTY MINUTES LATER, Duke thought he caught sight of movement in the direction of that ditch that had snagged his attention. These guys, whoever they were, didn't think anyone was watching for them. Reasonable stealth, but not the best.

He peered more intently, waiting for a second movement before he sounded an alert. No point ramping everyone up if all he'd seen was a small animal.

Five minutes later, he was sure. More than one thing moved out there, and they were spreading out slowly. Three.

He couldn't leave the window, needing to keep an eye on the three moving lumps, waiting for the image to clear up, and tried to judge how loudly to warn the others.

He didn't need to. Ben came clattering down the stairs.

"Something's moving," Ben said tautly. "Kitchen side."

"Eyes on," Duke answered. "It may not all be on this side of the house. Cat? You hear?"

"I heard."

Duke looked at Ben. "Are they just planning a break-in? Or an assault?"

Ben shook his head a bit. "I don't have an assessment. I keep thinking of Larry. That was no simple break-in."

"No. We'll keep watching, but get ready for an assault. We need to know how many are out there."

Cat joined them briefly. "I don't see anything from my side, but I'll go back to watching." She hurried away.

"Why would there be so many?" Ben wondered. "Three? More than three? What are they doing, raiding Fort Knox?"

"Maybe," Duke said heavily, "they don't figure you're alone."

FOR THE THREE men crawling across the ground to the house, the situation had become clearer. There was more than one person in there, and they were moving around. Not much, but they were still moving. A glimpse here and there spelled it out.

They were prepared to take out everyone if they needed to. Even if they never found the information, they'd have eliminated the one person who might know anything at all about what Larry was doing: his partner.

That thought made the first man's gorge rise, but he was a realist. The first person a guy was likely to spill classified info to was his wife. In fact, the military wives' grapevine was legendary.

Had to be the same for two guys, reasoned Man One.

And if Daniel Duke was in there, so much the better. He hated Duke. Had hated him since the man had shown up armed to the teeth to rescue the first man's squad. Single-handedly. Risking life and limb to do it.

Duke hadn't needed to come. Man One still believed he could have handled it, but no. Man One had come out of it feeling like he'd been punched, and people had talked about Duke getting the Medal of Honor for saving a pinned-down squad like some kind of screaming avenger. In the face of extremely heavy fire. Duke had been wounded, but he'd still managed to drag two of the wounded soldiers to safety and take out most of the insurgent nest.

Sounded real good for Duke. Man One didn't quite remember it that way. His squad could have handled it. Would have handled it.

His bitterness had been slightly assuaged by the fact that Duke and he had both received the same commendation for that action. But not completely assuaged, because Man One should have received all the kudos. All of them. ·

Being told to come after Larry Duke had been one of Man One's deciding factors when he accepted this assignment. It might also have given him an additional reason to torture Larry.

He wouldn't think about that now.

He had a mission to accomplish.

DUKE WOULD HAVE liked to get outside for an improved view of what was happening. He knew better, however. He'd alert those men and probably become their first target.

Given that they were creeping up so slowly, he was doubting more and more that they'd come merely to rob the place. No, they were staging an action, they knew Ben wasn't alone and they didn't intend to leave anyone behind.

He could feel his scalp prickle and his shoulders tighten. The battle was about to begin. He just hoped they could stop those guys before things grew truly ugly.

Another movement caught his eye, and he stared at it, for the first time seeing a silhouette that looked like an assault rifle. They were arriving with heavy firepower. Bad news.

He called to the other two, "Getting closer. Armed. Watch it. They may spread out more to encircle the house." He checked his clip. The shotguns were ready.

Another minute or two crept by. Then one man rose up, leveled his rifle and fired.

The bullet zinged through the window Duke faced. War had been declared.

"Here we go," he called out. "Stay low, stay alert." As if they wouldn't. They had to have heard the shot.

And those men had just given up any hope of surprise. Which meant they knew someone was aware of them. Which meant they didn't care but were prepared to take extreme action.

The question was, were they expecting the kind of greeting they were about to get?

CAT JOINED DUKE at the kitchen window. "Have they divided?" she asked quietly.

"They're starting to. You take the front window, unless you want me to."

"I'm thinking about firing right now. A warning shot. No reason they have to get any closer."

He looked at her quickly before looking back out. Were they trying to set a trap or put an end to this?

He reconsidered. Yeah, a trap would be nice, as it would separate them, but a whole lot more dangerous.

"Okay," he said. "When you catch sight of one near the front, fire away, identify yourself and tell them to stop. Ben and I will deal with what happens then."

"Fair enough."

Outside, apparently emboldened when their shot didn't receive return fire, the men rose up, crouching, but much more visible. Two headed toward the front, which meant they intended to enter. Why was that one staying on the side?

But his question was quickly answered. The last of them

started to move toward the front. He watched, then joined Cat and Ben in the foyer.

"They're here," Cat announced. "I'm going ahead."

Ben reached out swiftly. "Be careful."

"I'm not going out there," she said reassuringly. She then opened the door a crack and put her mouth to the opening.

"Conard County Sheriff. Freeze right there!"

But they didn't even hesitate. *Cripes*, she thought, raising the shotgun and edging it through the door. She fired a warning blast.

"I said halt!" She fired again.

She felt one of the guys push some more shells into her hand and she quickly loaded them, for the first time wishing she'd brought magazines. Who would have guessed? She'd honestly believed that a few warning shots would stop them. If not, a couple more well-placed shots should have done it.

But nothing was stopping these men.

Then the rain of fire began.

The three of them swore and fell to the floor. Automatics, Cat thought. No three-round bursts to preserve ammo, so they must have plenty.

The bullets came through the entire front of the house, as if they wanted to saw it down, and ricocheted off metal or punctured the walls and staircase. Glass shattered.

"Let me," Duke said, edging her to one side.

"Careful," she couldn't help saying, although he didn't need the reminder. He was far more experienced at this than she'd ever be.

Ben cried out as more bullets pierced the house.

"Ben?" she called.

"A graze. Damn it. I can't lift my arm…"

Just then, Duke rose on his knees, pushed the door open wider and fired into the night. A single crack.

Almost simultaneously a man's cry could be heard.

"One down," Duke said. "Hang on."

Cat rose up. Without asking, she hurried over to the broken front window and used the butt of her shotgun to get more glass out of the way. Then she aimed for one of the attackers.

Enough, she thought. *Enough. This one's for Larry.* Her heart pounded in her ears, and rage filled her.

Another swath of bullets cut through, and she had to duck, but then she rose up and fired another round. A riot gun wasn't particular. Nor was she, at this point.

All the while fear tapped along her spine. Fear that Ben had been downplaying his injury. Fear that Duke would get shot.

Her own safety was the last thing that worried her. Strange. Must have been the fury.

TEN MINUTES AFTER the firefight began, it ended in total silence. Eerie silence.

Cat felt almost dazed as she tried to look around.

"I need to go out there and check," Duke said. "You help Ben."

"No," said Ben. "I'll be fine. I managed to put on a tourniquet."

Cat looked at Duke. "You're not going out there alone. They're still armed, and if any of them can shoot…"

"It's common tactical sense, Duke," Ben argued. "Don't go alone."

Duke was having none of it. "Cat, you stay here with Ben. He can't defend himself. I'll deal with those three. Quite effectively."

Then he slipped out the door.

Ben spoke as if in answer to Cat's instant anxiety. "If anyone can do it, he can."

CAT WISHED SHE could see more. The night-vision goggles were displaying all kinds of static as the snowfall grew heavier.

She thought she saw Duke moving slowly toward the three men. Then a volley of shots rang out. Her heart stopped.

One man must be capable of shooting. At least one.

While the subsequent silence seemed to last forever, it didn't. She knew it didn't.

Ben spoke, his voice weaker. "Cat? What's going on?"

"Damned if I know."

The anxiety was going to kill her. One dark figure began to move toward the house. She lifted her shotgun, ready to fire, then recognized Duke's familiar stride.

She could have collapsed with relief. With her radio, now certain no one else would get hurt, she called for help and relief.

Not too long after, the two medevac choppers arrived. The first one took Ben. The second took two of the wounded men. The other was dead.

The medics had flex ties and used them on the two shooters. They'd survive, but no one was taking a chance that they could cause more trouble.

Cat, knowing Ben would receive the best care, joined Duke, who was looking at the man who lay dead on the ground, the snow starting to collect on his clothing. The dead man was on his back, his eyes open and fixed on night he could no longer see.

"He shot at you?" she asked. "You shot him?"

"Yeah." Duke's voice was heavy. Then he said, "I know him."

A shiver of shock ran through Cat. "You do?"

"Yeah. Years back, we were both in the 'Stan. I was on a solo mission when I heard a firefight. I had my own mission, and maybe I should have ignored it, but…" He shook his head. "I couldn't," he said simply.

Cat waited, still trying to deal with the hurricane that buffeted her. "And?" she asked after a minute.

"Oh, I found a squad under attack. Some wounded guys, and it didn't look good for them. I got involved." He indicated the corpse with his hand. "He was leading them. I thought at the time that he wasn't happy I showed up, but that wasn't the point. Those wounded men were. I helped. Dragged the wounded guys to safer ground and joined the fight."

"You did that under fire?"

"Hell, yeah. Bad situation. No reason the wounded should become target practice."

"But why would he be here now?"

Duke just shook his head.

It seemed like a weird confluence, Cat thought, but stranger coincidences happened. Random, unexpected things.

The patrol cars had begun arriving, and soon Gage limped toward them, his shearling jacket hanging open, a tan cowboy hat on his head. He looked down at the corpse then at Cat. "Explain quickly, then get home. You can fill out reports tomorrow."

"Three armed men approached the house and started to make Swiss cheese out of it. We returned fire. Ben was wounded. Two of the intruders were as well. This one wasn't that lucky."

Gage turned his head. "The house doesn't look very good."

Understatement of the year, Cat thought. "I should go back inside, get anything Ben might want."

"Make it quick," Gage said.

She hurried back inside, looking around. She doubted Ben would want any clothes before tomorrow, but then she spied a photo of Ben and Larry together. Framed, it had been protected behind glass that was now shattered. She took it. Broken glass or not, she could put it beside his hospital bed.

"Now go," Gage said. "Both of you. We'll talk tomorrow. Leave the weapons behind and let us get to work. This is one thing I don't need you for, Cat."

She didn't even want to argue. As the adrenaline began to wear off, she began to feel wrung out, limp. Exhausted.

She and Duke didn't say much on the drive back. Too soon for an after-action report, she thought. Both of them needed time to absorb it all.

But that bit about knowing one of the guys, a man he'd assisted in Afghanistan, must have rocked him. He was probably sitting behind the wheel chewing that over. He hadn't struck her as a man who easily accepted coincidence as a reason.

Maybe he was right. She just hoped he wasn't blaming himself for Larry.

DUKE DROVE STRAIGHT to the truck stop. Cat, now dozing, hardly stirred as he went inside to order up two loaded breakfasts and a half gallon of coffee. If she could go to bed when they got to her house, that was fine by him. He doubted he'd be able to.

Not until he pulled up in front of her house did she actually wake. Then she yawned and stretched, and he watched with mild amusement as she staggered toward her front door. Yeah, it was still the middle of the night, but he suspected she was having a physical letdown. Just wait until that passed. She was going to be all over the night, the entire case, when she had the brainpower.

She made it inside. When he followed with the take-out bags and the tray full of coffee cups, he was astonished to find her sitting at the kitchen table. She rested her chin in her hand, her eyelids at half-staff.

"Go to bed," he suggested. "You're beat."

She shook her head slowly. "It's hitting."

"Thought it would. Then join me for breakfast."

"Sorry I fell asleep."

Duke paused as he pulled out the containers and offered her one of the coffees. "I'm not. I wouldn't have been much company. Besides, you were coming off adrenaline. I know what that's like."

"But not tonight?" she asked groggily as he opened boxes and put one in front of her, along with a fork. She blinked. "Did you get everything?"

"On the breakfast menu. We need the calories."

She nodded and speared a home fry, carrying it to her mouth. "Probably."

They ate quietly for a while, but Duke knew the questions were going to come, probably the same ones he had. As the fuel hit their systems, they would both reenergize.

When they were finally sated, he pushed the nearly empty containers aside and handed out two more cups of coffee.

"Is it still snowing?" Cat asked.

"It stopped while we were driving home."

She nodded and let out a big sigh. She began to turn the foam cup in front of her. "I need to get an espresso maker."

That comment came from so far out of left field that Duke felt taken aback. Was she still half-asleep? Or was she not ready to deal with the night's events yet?

Either way, he didn't blame her and just let her sit and settle. He knew her too well already to believe stasis would last long. He'd also been through enough situations like this to understand that some people needed longer to crawl back inside their own skins.

Besides, he was trying not to deal with a larger picture that kept occurring to him.

"We need to go see Ben," she announced.

"Rest a little. Ben's probably pretty busy about now."

"Did you see his wound?"

"Upper arm, tourniquet. Bad enough, I suspect. But he'll be fine. He just needs some stitches and maybe a shot of morphine."

Cat nodded.

Duke waited, his mind buzzing like a hive of bees. Not a coincidence. Couldn't be.

Cat sighed again and drank quite a bit of coffee before speaking. "You knew that guy?"

"Not really. We only ran into each other that once. But the minute I saw him, I knew who he was."

And every time he remembered that, his gut twisted in a knot. Had that man turned Larry into a proxy target? God, he hoped not. That was the only thing that could make this worse.

Cat stirred. "I hate to say this, but I can't deal with this right now. Maybe in the morning."

Which was how they came to be snuggled together under the covers. Just hugging. Duke had never found such comfort after any action. Wasn't supposed to need it.

Right then, he discovered that he *did* need it.

ALL TOO SOON, the day began. Cat awoke shortly after Duke, and the two of them headed straight to Community Memorial Hospital, Cat carrying the shattered photo of Larry and Ben.

Cat wore her uniform, and that got them past any gatekeepers.

"Ben needs some family here," Cat said under her breath.

"Yeah," Duke agreed. "I think they all disowned him, though."

"Damn."

"Larry used to laugh it off, without mentioning Ben by

name, saying he'd never have an in-law problem. Honestly, I don't think either of them was able to really laugh it off."

"I couldn't."

Ben sat up in bed, eating from a tray of food that looked more appetizing than it probably was. He offered a weary smile. "Cooked prunes, anyone? Oatmeal? I've always hated oatmeal."

"Me, too," Cat answered. "Sticks in my mouth." She held out the photo. "I thought you might want this. Careful of the broken glass."

Ben took it and looked down at it. "That shattered glass feels like my heart."

She was sure it did.

"How are you doing?" Duke asked him.

"Nicked the brachial artery. Tourniquet saved me." He gave a snort. "Military training can be good for something."

"It appears," Duke agreed.

Ben continued to stare down at the photo. Then he ran his hand over the backing, as if stroking it. He'd probably have stroked the photo if it had been safe to do so.

Then his hand froze. "I've held this a million times in the past," he said slowly.

Duke leaned forward. "What's wrong?"

"There's something behind the backing. Something that wasn't there when I first put it in the house." He looked up, his eyes wide. "Duke?"

Duke looked at Cat. "Maybe you should take it."

She nodded. Evidence of some kind? Or just damage from the firefight last night? Only one way to find out.

She placed the photo facedown on the table, then felt the backing carefully. It rocked slightly. Picture backing, no matter how thick, didn't usually do that.

Carefully, she bent back the tabs that held it in place. "I'll remove the glass once I can get the photo out."

"Sure," Ben said.

She could feel both men watching intently. Her heart was climbing into her throat. At last she was able to lift the backing off—and what she saw caused her breath to catch.

"What?" both men asked.

She slowly lifted out three discs in their paper sleeves and held them up. "Could these be it? Larry's secret?"

Chapter Twelve

Four days later they stood in Good Shepherd Church for Larry's memorial. Cat hadn't expected much of a turnout, given that Larry had barely arrived in town and Ben was still only slightly known.

But the church was packed.

She smiled faintly, glad to see it. Ben needed to feel community support right now. Support even from relative strangers.

The last few days had been tough for both Ben and Duke. Enough details of the autopsy had been shared to give both men a crystal clear awareness of what had been done to Larry. The minimum, but still too much. At least neither of them had pressed for more information, although they could have.

Rocked by that, Duke had nonetheless forged ahead, working with Ben on a service for his brother while keeping his finger on the pulse of the interrogation of the two men who had survived their assault on Ben's house.

It seemed someone had hired the men to come out here to remove any evidence Larry might have of misdeeds among higher-ups in the Army relating to the murder-for-hire plot. The information was on those discs—lots of it. Names, dates, places, witnesses. It would indeed have filled a book.

Duke planned to turn it over to military authorities for

investigation, but not before he asked the sheriff to make copies for safekeeping. A chain of evidence.

In addition, they'd found out that the dead man, Jason Lewis, had a burr under his saddle about Duke.

"When he heard you were in town," one of the killers said, "he started to go kinda nuts. I don't know why."

The other man did. "Just before we began that attack, he told me that Major Duke had interfered with an operation of his in Afghanistan."

Questions answered, Cat thought as she waited for Reverend Carson to make her appearance. It wasn't often that *all* the questions got answered.

Ben had decided he wanted Larry buried nearby. He also wanted to give the eulogy. Duke seemed content to be guided.

When Ben rose, his arm in a sling, his eyes were visibly wet. "I planned to say a whole lot, but somehow I can't. Larry was one of the good guys, always a warrior for justice, unafraid in the teeth of death threats. A hard-driving reporter who always wanted the truth and wouldn't settle for less."

Ben's voice broke, and he dashed at his eyes, wiping away tears.

Cat's throat tightened, and she had to blink herself.

"Anyway, maybe Larry's brother can do a better job of this than I can. But I just wanted to say, I love Larry. I loved him since the first time we met. And I was hoping when he came out here, we'd start a real life together. We weren't granted the time, but…"

His voice broke again as he stuffed his hand into his pocket. When he drew it out, he held a gold ring.

"I was going to ask Larry to marry me." He laid the ring atop Larry's casket and walked down the steps toward the aisle.

Then the most beautiful thing happened. People rose from the pews and surrounded him, offering hugs and kind words. Offering him a sense of belonging, a sense that his grief was shared.

Cat couldn't hold back the tears any longer.

MUCH LATER, CAT, Ben and Duke gathered in her living room. It had been a wrenching day for all of them, especially the men. First the service, then the trip to the cemetery. Then a funeral supper back at the church, where a whole lot of friendly people delivered a potluck.

Now they kicked back with beers and let all the grief and fatigue wash over them.

"Larry loved what he did," Ben said. "I would never have asked him to stop. He was made for that job."

"I agree," said Duke. "Definitely. A remarkable guy, and I don't just say that because he's my brother."

"He said that about you, too." Ben smiled faintly.

After a few minutes of reflection, Duke looked at Cat. "I know this is quick, but it's driving me crazy. Would you consider marrying me eventually? I love you."

Cat caught her breath. *Seriously?*

Then Duke turned to Ben. "If she says yes, will you be my best man?"

For the first time since the murder, Ben smiled broadly. "I wouldn't miss it."

Then the two men looked at Cat, who was bouncing between amazement and joy. "Are both of you asking?"

"Seems like," said Duke. "One big family now. If you want."

Oh, truth rushed through her. No deliberation or time needed. "I want," she breathed. "Yes, definitely yes."

A bright ray of sunshine filled her, warming her.

So much joy out of so much sorrow. Life could still be beautiful.

And justice could still be served.

* * * * *

COMING SOON!

We really hope you enjoyed reading this book.
If you're looking for more romance, be sure to
head to the shops when new books are
available on

Thursday 14th May

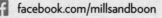

MILLS & BOON

THE HEART OF ROMANCE

A ROMANCE FOR EVERY KIND OF READER

MODERN

Prepare to be swept off your feet by sophisticated, sexy and seductive heroes, in some of the world's most glamourous and romantic locations, where power and passion collide.
8 stories per month.

HISTORICAL

Escape with historical heroes from time gone by. Whether your passion is for wicked Regency Rakes, muscled Vikings or rugged Highlanders, awaken the romance of the past.
6 stories per month.

MEDICAL

Set your pulse racing with dedicated, delectable doctors in the high-pressure world of medicine, where emotions run high and passion, comfort and love are the best medicine.
6 stories per month.

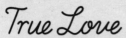

Celebrate true love with tender stories of heartfelt romance, from the rush of falling in love to the joy a new baby can bring, and a focus on the emotional heart of a relationship.
8 stories per month.

Indulge in secrets and scandal, intense drama and plenty of sizzl hot action with powerful and passionate heroes who have it all: wealth, status, good looks…everything but the right woman.
6 stories per month.

HEROES

Experience all the excitement of a gripping thriller, with an inter romance at its heart. Resourceful, true-to-life women and strong, fearless men face danger and desire - a killer combination!
8 stories per month.

DARE

Sensual love stories featuring smart, sassy heroines you'd want as best friend, and compelling intense heroes who are worthy of the
4 stories per month.

To see which titles are coming soon, please visit

millsandboon.co.uk/nextmonth

JOIN US ON SOCIAL MEDIA!

Stay up to date with our latest releases, author news and gossip, special offers and discounts, and all the behind-the-scenes action from Mills & Boon...

 millsandboon

 millsandboonuk

millsandboon

It might just be true love...

MILLS & BOON

HISTORICAL

Awaken the romance of the past

Escape with historical heroes from time gone by. Whether your passion is for wicked Regency Rakes, muscled Viking warriors or rugged Highlanders, indulge your fantasies and awaken the romance of the past.